THE WAITING TIME

'Seymour is writing at the peak of his powers . . . in a class of his own' – *The Times*

'Stunning . . . Seymour is on top form' – *Mail on Sunday*

'One of the best plotters in the business' – *Time Out*

'One of Britain's foremost pacy thriller writers' – *Sunday Express*

HAVE YOU READ . . . ?

CONDITION BLACK

In the final months before Saddam Hussein's Invasion of Ku
in 1991, the only man who stands in the way of the total collap
of the Middle Eastern situation is a young FBI agent hot on th
heels of a deadly assassin working for the Iraqi government.

HARRY'S GAME

A British cabinet minister is gunned down by an IRA assassin.
The police trail goes cold, and undercover agent Harry Brown
is sent to infiltrate the terrorist organisation and uncover the
killer. It's a race against the clock, and one false move will be
enough to leave him dead before he reaches his target.

THE FIGHTING MAN

Gord Brown, a former SAS soldier and Gulf War veteran,
comes to the aid of Guatemalan resistance fighters caught up
in a hopeless war against a brutal military dictatorship. Also
pitted against them is another veteran, an American helicopter
pilot who owes Gord his life, but, in the depths of the South
American jungle, the past is forgotten.

THE UNKNOWN SOLDIER

In the depths of the Arabian Desert, American and British
counter-terrorism experts are desperately searching for one
man. If they fail to find him, he will re-emerge in a teeming
western city, carrying only a suitcase that will wreak havoc and
devastation when detonated.

ABOUT THE AUTHOR

Gerald Seymour spent fifteen years as an international television news reporter with ITN, covering Vietnam and the Middle East, and specialising in the subject of terrorism across the world. Seymour was on the streets of Londonderry on the afternoon of Bloody Sunday, and was a witness to the massacre of Israeli athletes at the Munich Olympics.

Gerald Seymour is now a full-time writer, and six of his novels have been filmed for television in the UK and US. THE WAITING TIME is his seventeenth novel.

For more information about Gerald Seymour and his books, visit his Facebook page at
www.facebook.com/GeraldSeymourAuthor

GERALD SEYMOUR

The Waiting Time

Hodder & Stoughton policy is to use papers that are natural, renewable and recyclable products and made from wood grown in sustainable forests. The logging and manufacturing processes are expected to conform to the environmental regulations of the country of origin.

HODDER

First published in Great Britain in 1998 by Bantam
Press, a division of Transworld Publishers

This paperback edition first published in 2013

2

A CIP catalogue record for this title is available from the British Library.

Book ISBN 978 1 444 76033 0
eBook ISBN 978 1 444 76034 7

Printed and bound by Clays Ltd, St Ives plc

Hodder & Stoughton policy is to use papers that are natural, renewable
and recyclable products and made from wood grown in sustainable
forests. The logging and manufacturing processes are expected to
conform to the environmental regulations of the country of origin.

Hodder & Stoughton Ltd
338 Euston Road
London NW1 3BH

www.hodder.co.uk

To Gillian, Nicholas and James

THE WAITING TIME

Introduction by Frederick Forsyth

Habitually, I refrain from endorsing the work of another writer of thriller fiction (and absolutely of criticising it). But all good rules deserve an exception and for me this must be Gerald Seymour.

We both began by treading similar paths. We were working journalists who moved from print to television. We both covered 'hard' stories abroad, I in Europe and Africa, Gerald in Northern Ireland. Then we both had a venture at a first novel.

I believe I was first in 1971, being a little older. He later indicated *The Day of the Jackal* might have given him the hint. I suspect he thought: 'If that fool can do it, so can I.' And he did, with the incomparable *Harry's Game*, the best thriller novel to come out of the maelstrom of the Ulster 'Troubles'.

Years later, in 1998 came *The Waiting Time*, now on re-release.

We both strive for a taut beginning, full of menace and hidden questions, bidding the reader to turn further to find out what happens next. With *The Waiting Time* Gerald starts on the utterly bleak and freezing Baltic coast of the old East Germany with the brutal execution of a young man dragged from the sea.

It has been years since I read it first, on its release, but the same passages came back to me in a rush. So also did the memories, for Reuters once posted me for a year into the heart of East Germany and I spent some time – not long but quite enough – in the hands of the rather unpleasant Stasis.

Then (in the book) some years pass. The Cold War is over at last, and all is forgiven. Or perhaps not . . .

On second reading, I was again quickly hooked and, reader, so I suspect will you be also.

Frederick Forsyth
Beaconsfield, 11 April 2013

PROLOGUE

He opened the door and carried the thin plastic rubbish bag to the front gate. The cat followed him and he heard, carried by the wind from the north, the first shot.

The aircraft had been over a minute or so earlier and he had seen its navigation lights and flamed exhausts through the window – the house had shaken below the flight path.

He dumped the plastic bag on the far side of the gate, on the paving. The cat howled because it could not scratch a hole in the frozen ground, and he heard the burst of automatic firing, sharp but distant in the night air.

The pastor shivered. He should have put on a coat because the bitter wind brought a chill to his shoulders and the small of his back. He heard more shots from behind the house, and the singing of the wind in the wires, against the roof of the house and around the squat brick tower of the church across the road. She called to him from inside. Why had he left the door open? Why did he let the cold into the house? The cat bolted for the open door. He heard more shots and saw, above the sharp-angled roof of the house, a flare merge with the low cloud. He went inside, pushed the door shut and banged his hands across his arms and chest to warm himself. Far away, in the long distance, a siren shrieked. He went into the living room, off the hallway. The cat was already on her lap, and he told her that there was shooting at the base, there must be a night exercise. She did not look up from her knitting: she was making a small cardigan for the newest grandchild and her forehead was furrowed with concentration. She murmured with concern that it was a bad night for the young soldiers to be out.

The pastor sat at the table in the living room and worked at his address for the coming Sunday. He wrote his notes, turned the pages of his Bible. She put her knitting under the chair, and said she was going to bed. The cat lay on the threadbare carpet in front of the low, open fire. The radio played Beethoven softly, a concert performed by an orchestra from Prague. He heard her go up the creaking stairs. Where he came from, south of Leipzig and east of Erfurt, a bishop had said that it was more important to obey God than human beings. Simple for a man of his status to make such a statement, hard for a humble pastor. The quiet was around him. He had been thirty-six years a pastor in the Evangelist Church and censorship came easy to him: he had nothing bold to say, he lived within the walls of the system, and it was his delight every November to come with his wife from the small industrial town between Leipzig and Erfurt to the wild winds and storms of the Baltic coast. He came for three weeks to free the resident pastor for conferences and seminars, and he intended to move here when he reached the retirement age, to live his last years beside the seashore, if permission was given. He made the notes for his Sunday address. He would do nothing, in his preaching and in his conduct, to threaten the granting of that permission. He knew exactly when his retirement was due: in three days he would have twenty more months to serve.

That night of the week, whatever the weather conditions, the aircraft came low and thundering over the base and then over the pastor's house, but he had never before heard shots at night. He listened for more shooting and heard nothing. He switched off the radio, crouched in front of the fire and stroked the cat fondly. He drained the last of the coffee from the cup and took it to the kitchen at the back of the house. He stood at the sink and rinsed the cup, the water icy on his hands. He heard the clatter of a machine gun, then the siren again, and more single shots.

Slowly the pastor climbed the stairs. His wife grunted in her sleep. The bedroom was in darkness. He went to the bathroom to wash his face and under his armpits, and to brush his teeth. The tap water ran and he undid the buttons of his shirt.

No curtains hung over the bathroom window at the back of the house, and in daylight there was a fine view from here, the best view from the house. From the bathroom window he could see the dull-lit and empty square, around which were built two-storey concrete apartments. He could see the narrow road that sloped down to the shoreline and the older homes that fronted onto the road. He could see the wind-stripped trees that formed a wall between the community and the beach, and the old piers. The water beyond was white-flecked and the foam of a boat's wake cut at the water. The local people called the water the Salzhaff, and he gazed across it to the dark shape of the penin-sula. He had never been there: it was closed to the local people. The peninsula was a military camp.

A wavering light climbed. It was engulfed by the cloud. A flare burst, was muffled by the cloud, then fell in brilliance over the water. Before it splashed down, another had soared, burst, and another. No longer the darkness over the Salzhaff. It was a panorama laid out for his entertainment. The tap water gurgled down the drain, ignored.

He saw the small fishing boat bucking across the water. He saw the cascade of the flares. He saw the ripple lines of the tracer bullets as they swept out from the shoreline, red tracks dying in the water, seeming to hunt and probe for a target.

Then he should have turned off the tap, forgotten about washing his face and his armpits and about brushing his teeth. He should have gone out of the bathroom, crossed the landing and closed the door of the bedroom behind him. He should have turned his back on the brilliance of the flares over the water of the Salzhaff, and the lines of the tracers, and the wake of the fishing boat closing on that place in the water where the bullets died. He should have gone to the bedroom where his wife slept and buried his eyes and his ears in the hardness of the pillows.

The water ran into the basin. He leaned over it and opened the window that he might see better. The cold of the night was as nothing to him. He understood. It was no exercise. It was not training for the young soldiers of the base. He watched.

3

The tracer lines lazily converged from four, five points on the peninsula. They locked together where they died. The fishing boat veered towards that point. An amplified shout, tin-toned through a microphone, was brought to him on the wind gust from the peninsula. The tracer lines were cut, as if in response, their life gone. A small spotlight beamed from the fishing boat onto the Salzhaff.

His eyes were old and wearied. He dragged his spectacles from his nose and wiped them hard on his shirt-tail. Now he could see more clearly. The cone from the searchlight caught, held, lost, caught again and held again at a bobbing shape in the water. He saw the fishing boat circle the shape and then stop, riding idly in the water. He saw the shape pulled on board. The boat swung and headed back towards the piers. They were on the edge of the town, distanced by the water of the Salzhaff from the peninsula and the military base . . . It was another moment at which the pastor could have closed the window, turned off the tap, gone to the bedroom and settled beside his wife. He would have seen nothing and known nothing . . . The fishing boat came fast towards the shore, streaming a wake behind it, its engine churning.

He saw a man jump from the boat onto the planking of the central pier, take a rope that was thrown to him and make it secure against the pier's piles. Five men were standing forward of the wheelhouse and they looked down from their circle, fish-ermen who had made a trophy catch, and he heard a faint ripple, when the wind surged, as if they laughed. They stood in front of the white light of the wheelhouse lamp and their shadows were thrown across the pier and the beach.

The pastor watched.

They bent, all together. They lifted up their trophy catch. They gripped a young man by his clothes and by his hair. His body was slight, and he seemed to shudder as if a great pain ran in him. They dragged him over the pier towards the shoreline where the beach was piled with dried-out seaweed left behind by the last storm. The clock on the church tower struck the hour.

4

There were two cars on the road at the end of the pier. Their interior lights were on and their doors sagged open. The clock on the church tower chimed shrill in the night. The four men pulled the young man towards the cars, and a fifth, who was tall and walked with authority, came behind and gestured instructions. The young man seemed hurt, or maybe it was exhaustion from the time he had spent in the water, but his feet flapped on the planks, and if they had not held him it seemed that he would have fallen. The clock on the church tower was silent, past ten. They were at the end of the pier, they were near to the cars.

The pastor saw it clearly . . . So much better if he had seen nothing, known nothing . . .

I

They trailed behind.

The Colonel led, and congratulated and complimented the star attraction. The minders walked alongside their man, smug with satisfaction.

Perry Johnson let them go ahead, Ben Christie stayed with his major. The evening rain blustered against them. He knew the old boy was about to launch, felt sort of sorry for him, stayed with him to offer a shoulder and an ear. It had gone well, standing ovation. Only a taster, though, and the Americans were bigger players – they'd get more when the man went to Washington. But, for all that, it was a taster, Ben could recognize quality material, the like of which seldom came their way, and it was German. The three warrant officers and the two sergeants, who had attended the briefing, held umbrellas over the guest and the Colonel, the Brigadier and the civil servants who were down from London. It was ritual to take an honoured visitor to the officers' mess at the end of the day.

They weren't twenty-five paces from B block, not even within two hundred yards of the mess, before poor old Perry, the dinosaur, began to flush it out of his system.

'Look at him, so damn full of himself. Forget the past, all cuddle up together . . . I'd trust him as far as I could kick him . . . They were insidious, they were revolting. I used to lie awake at night when I was in Berlin, couldn't damn sleep because of them. Pushing, probing, testing us, every day, every week, every month. Had their creatures down at the gate at Brigade to photograph us going in and out, take our number-plates. Used to pay the refuse people to drop off camp rubbish

6

then cart it to Left Luggage at the S-Bahn, and they'd take it back through the Wall, sift every last scrap of paper we threw out, notepaper headings, telephone numbers, signatures and rank. Had to employ West Berliners, German nationals, some very decent people, but imperative that we regarded them all as potential corrupted traitors, good women in Library or just cleaning your quarters, had to treat each of them as filth. Throwing "defectors" at us, dropping "refugees" into our laps, hoping to twist us up, bugger us about. Met some fine and courageous people but had to treat them like lying shit. Used to go across, guaranteed access under the Four Power Agreement, they'd watch you. You were alone, out of your car, dark, four thugs on you and a beating you'd remember a month . . . Cold bastards. I tell you, I like moral people, I can cope with immoral people if I have to. What I find evil is "amorality", no standards and no principles, that was them. You work up against the Stasi and you get to suspect the man, German or British, who sits next to you in the mess, in the canteen. Perpetually on guard . . . but it doesn't matter now because we're all bloody chums . . . You didn't get to Germany in the good old days – Belfast, wasn't it? Nothing wrong with Belfast, but the heartbeat of the Corps was Germany. Straightforward enough life, whether in the Zone or Berlin – us confronting an enemy. The threat, of course, was the Soviet military, but the real enemy was the Ministerium für Staatssicherheit, shorthand was Stasi. Stasi were the secret police of the former DDR. They came out of the heritage of the Gestapo and out of the training camps of the KGB. In intelligence-gathering, in counter-espionage, they were brilliant and ruthless. They ran the Bonn government ragged, they gave us a hell of a headache. They were the cream . . . Don't think I'm sentimental. They didn't play by our rules, nothing Queensberry. Their rules were intimidation, corruption, fear, the manipulation of the individual, the destruction of the human personality. Turn a man against his friend, a woman against her husband, a child against parents, no scruples. They bred psychological terror, their speciality, and if that failed they fell back on the familiar thuggery of basement torture, isolation cells and killings. That the clapped-out, no-hope East Germany survived for more than two summers was because of the Stasi. They kept that regime of geriatrics on its feet for forty-five years . . .'

'Led you a bit of a dance, did they, Perry?'

'Don't short-change me, young man . . . It sticks in my throat, a bone in the gullet, socializing with "new" friends. There's a generation in Germany that's been scarred by the Stasi. There's blood on their hands. What do I sound like? An emotional old fart? Probably am . . . So, the Wall came tumbling down and a hundred thousand full-time Stasi just disappeared off the face of the earth, bar a very few. A few had something to offer the arisen greater German empire. Counter-espionage in Rostock, in bed with the Soviet military. Of course this bastard has something to offer.'

They followed the group into the mess. The warrant officers and sergeants peeled away from forbidden territory. From the end of the wide corridor, came the baying of laughter and voices spilling from the bar. They shook their coats. Not like the mess of the cavalry or artillery or the engineers, no battle paintings, no hanging portraits of men decorated for bravery, nothing to identify past success. The Colonel, the guest and the guest's minders had gone towards the window, with the Brigadier from London and the civil servants.

A big voice: 'Perry, be a good chap, tunnel through that lot. I know what we want.'

Perry Johnson, poor bugger, pleased that ridiculous name was used, went to his colonel, took the drinks order, looked helplessly at the crowd competing for the single bar steward. He copped out, came to Ben Christie. 'It's like a bloody bingo night. Why's there only one chap on? Get Barnes down here.'

Christie turned and hurried for the door. He heard Perry call out that reinforcements were on the way, stupid bugger.

He ran in the rain past F and H blocks, past the dreary little Portakabins. He ran down the corridor to G/3/29.

8

She was at her desk. It was cleared. There was a neat pile of letters to be signed, there was a note of telephone calls incoming and outgoing. His dog was sitting beside her knee with the wrapping paper of a biscuit packet under its paws.

'All right, Corporal? No crises? Went on a bit . . .'

She shrugged, not her business if it went on all night. Why should there be crises?

'Please, they're short of bodies in the mess. Major Johnson would be very grateful . . .'

She was expressionless. 'Been waiting for you, thought you might.'

'Nelson been good? Sorry . . .'

She was standing, gathering her coat off the hook, then smoothing her hair. 'Stay there, big boy. Course he's been good.'

She locked the outer door, went after him.

'Sorry . . . How did you know that we'd want you?'

They were out into the evening rain.

She said flatly, 'Administration's got the audit team in, they're mob-handed. There's Major Walsh's leaving bash – free drinks bring them out of their holes. The mess corporal, the spotty one, he's got flu. Penny's on holiday . . .'

He grinned. 'Be a black day, the darkest, Corporal, if promotion ever claimed you.'

'Just try to do my job. How did it go?'

The beginning of her day had followed the same precise routine as every working morning. It was sixteen minutes past seven when Corporal Tracy Barnes had unlocked the outer door to building G/3, gone down the empty corridor and used a second key to let herself into Room 29. She was always in G/3/29 before twenty past seven. The rest of them, Major Johnson, Captain Christie, the warrant officers, sergeants and clerks, would drift into G/3 before nine. She valued that time to herself: she always said it gave her the chance to get on top of each day.

She had put the kettle on. With her third key, and her knowledge of the combination, she'd opened the safe. She kept the coffee in it, the tea, biscuits and apples. The rooms of G/3 were the home of the unit of the Intelligence Corps at Templer Barracks, Ashford in Kent, dealing solely with the subject matter of RUSSIAN FEDERATION/MILITARY/ANALYSIS, and they were the kingdom of Corporal Tracy Barnes. The kettle had boiled. She had crunched the biscuits and bitten at an apple. It was her place. She could put her hand on any sheet of paper, any map, any photograph in the wall of steel-plate filing cabinets, padlocked in the Major's office, the Captain's office and in the cubbyhole space between them where she worked. She could flit her way through the banks of information held in the G/3 computers that linked Templer Barracks with the London offices of the Chief of Defence Intelligence and the new Bedfordshire base at Chicksands. She knew every code that must be dialled in for the secure fax transmissions. They told her, Major Johnson and Captain Christie, that she was indispensable . . .

A drip of water had gathered on the ceiling beside the fluorescent strip light, fallen and spattered on the linoleum floor.

'Fucking hell,' she'd said. 'That's the fucking limit.'

The roof always leaked when the rain came from the east. She'd seen another drip forming and the rain hammered harder on the windows. She'd been locking the safe – the safe must always be locked when the section was unattended – she had been about to go down the corridor to the wash-house for the mop and bucket, when the telephone had rung. The start of her day.

Outside the office, in the rain and the gloom, walking, it was so good to talk to her. Sensible, rational – just a conversation without officers' pips and corporals' stripes. The rain was on the gold of Tracy Barnes's hair and the highlights made jewels there.

'Slow to start, thanks to the Colonel. We had to sit through his lecture on the Russian military threat, chaos and anarchy there, massive conventional and nuclear strength but with no political

leadership to control the trigger finger. Seemed a bit remote –
am I supposed to tell you?'

'Please yourself.'

'It's a profile of a Russian who's the Rasputin of the defence
minister – he was chummy with a Stasi chap back in the good
old Cold War days. Seems that today the minister doesn't blow
his nose or wipe his backside without the say-so of his staff
officer – he's Rykov, Pyotr Rykov, ex-para in Afghanistan and
ex-CO of a missile base in former East Germany, and you could
write on a postcard what we have on him. Our larder's bare, and
the Germans come over with Rykov's chum, parade him as
quality bloodstock – Rykov's motivation, Rykov's ambition. If
the military were to take over in Russia then this Rykov would
be half a pace behind his minister and whispering in his little
ear. The truth – may hurt to say it – the German chum was a
high grade HumInt source, the best I've ever heard . . . Perry's
suffering, thinks we're supping with Lucifer. You'd know about
the Stasi – you were in Berlin, yes?'

'As a kid, first posting, just clerking . . . Jolly news for you,
Captain. They've put you on a crash Serbo-Croat course, means
you're booked for Bosnia. Mrs Christie'll be well excited, eh? I
mean, she'll have to look after the dog.'

'Bloody hell.'

'It's on your desk.'

They reached the mess block outer door. He forgot himself.
He opened the heavy door for her to go through first.

She stayed put. He flushed. Bloody officer and bloody
noncommissioned junior rank. He went through and she followed. Coats dumped on a chair in the corridor. They hit the
noise.

Perry Johnson boomed, 'Thanks, Ben. They're dying of thirst
and restless – Corporal, the order is three Glenlivets, ice and
lemonade for our guests, seven gin tonics, two orange juice, one
with ice, five beers. You'll need a tray.'

A wry smile on her face, at the edge of impertinence. 'Whose
tab, Major? On yours?'

She was gone. Ben watched her. He thought she kicked Captain Wilson's shin. Definite, she elbowed Captain Dawson. He saw her reach past Major Donoghue's back and rap his right shoulder and when he turned right she'd wriggled past his left hip. She was at the front, arms on the bar and stretching. She caught the steward's arm, held it. Ben could have clapped her. No mucking, she was brilliant. He blinked. An officer and a corporal, a married officer and a single corporal, it would ruin him and ruin her . . . Yugoslavia. The guys who went there said it was seriously awful, said Belfast was a cake-run compared to a year in Sarajevo, Vitez, Tuzla . . . Shit. He'd ring Trish that night . . . Shit . . . She was tiny behind the bulk of the tray. He thought that if he tried to help her he'd just get in the way . . . There'd be all the usual tears with Trish . . . Must have been her shoe, but Major Donoghue was backing off, and the shoe again because Captain Wilson was giving her space . . . and Trish would be screaming when he started up about her having to look after the bloody dog . . . She headed for Perry.

The Colonel and a civil servant flanked the German. The German had his back to them. Hands groped to snatch the glasses off her tray. She was only a corporal so she wasn't thanked, and they wouldn't need her again. Major Walsh's 'happy hour' would be finished in ten minutes, and his bar tab closed, be space then. He saw the two minders take their drinks, and then the Colonel. Only one drink on the tray, the last Glenlivet, ice and lemon. The Colonel touched the German's arm. Tracy was dwarfed behind the German's back. He turned, mid-conversation, smiling.

Ben saw them both, the German and Corporal Tracy Barnes.

Her face frozen, her eyes narrowed.

The German reached for the glass, smiling with graciousness.

And the ice of her face cracked, hatred. Her eyes blazed, loathing.

The glass came up into his face and the tray with it.

The German reeled.

The Colonel, the minders and the civil servants were statue still.

Corporal Tracy Barnes launched herself at the German, and he went down onto the mess-bar carpet.

Her body, on top of his, was a blur of kicking and kneeing, elbowing, punching and scratching.

Hissed, a she-cat's venom, 'You bloody bastard murderer!'

Ben Christie watched. Her skirt had ridden up as she swung her knee, again and again, into his privates. She had the hair of his beard in her fingers and smashed his head, again and again, down onto the carpet floor.

Shrieked, a woman's cry for retribution, 'Bloody killed him, you bastard!'

Blood on her hands, blood in her nails, and the German screamed and was defenceless. Her thumb and forefinger stabbed at his closed eyes.

Howled, the triumph of revenge, 'How'd you like it? Bloody bastard murderer! What's it like?'

Only her voice, her voice alone in the silence. The minders reacted first.

A chopping blow to the back of her neck, a kick in her ribs. The minders dragged her clear, threw her aside.

The German was bleeding, gasping, cringing in shock.

He heard Johnson's shout, hoarse: 'Get her out, Christie. Get the bitch under lock and key.'

Their fists clenched, standing over their man, coiled, were the minders.

. . . He had started his day shitty cold and shitty tired.

Julius Goldstein knew of nowhere more miserable than a commercial airport in winter as the passengers arrived for the first flights of the day. They had flowed past him, business people and civil servants, either half asleep or half dressed, either with shaving cuts on their throats or with their lipstick smeared, and they brought with them the shitty cold and shook the snow patterns off their legs and shoulders.

He had gazed out into the orange-illuminated darkness, and each car and taxi showed up the fierceness of the

cavorting snow shower. Of course the bastard was late. It was
the style of the bastard always to be late. He had managed to
be punctual, and Raub had reached Tempelhof on time, but
the bastard was late. He was tired because the alarm had gone
in the small room at the back of his parents' home at four. No
need for his mother – and him aged twenty-nine – to have
risen and put on a thick housecoat and made him hot coffee,
but she had. And his father had come downstairs into the cold
of the kitchen and sat slumped at the table without conversation, but had been there. His mother had made the coffee and
his father had sat close to him because they continually needed
to demonstrate, he believed, their pride in their son's achievement. The source of their pride, acknowledged with coffee
and with a silent presence at the kitchen table, was that their
son was a junior official in the Office for the Protection of the
Constitution. Not bad for a little Jew boy – maybe just a token
to beef up the statistics of government employment for Jews,
but he had made it there and they oozed pride. One night only
in Helmstedt with his parents, giving them pleasure, and the
cost to Julius Goldstein was that he had been on the autobahn
at four thirty, hammering on the gritted roadway to Berlin
and Tempelhof, driving at stupid speed to be certain that he
was not late. His mother had said that he would be cold, and
had fussed around him, had tried to press on him his father's
scarf from the hook on the kitchen door. He did not wear a
scarf, or a tie, and his shirt of midnight blue was unbuttoned
at the neck so that the gold Star of David hanging from a
slight gold chain was clearly visible. He did not go to the syn-
agogue. He had been only once to Israel, seven years before,
and had loathed it. He wore the chain and the Star of David
as his own personal small gesture towards the past. It made
them squirm in the offices in Cologne.

Raub had stood beside him and whistled his annoyance
through his teeth, so Goldstein had smiled as if there was no
problem with the bastard being late. Raub wore an overcoat of
mahogany brown, a silk scarf, a striped suit and a white shirt,

and Goldstein had known what Raub would wear so he had dressed in casual outdoor shoes, designer jeans, an anorak and an open shirt. Raub had worn a tie, Goldstein had worn the Star of David. Raub had carried a polished leather attaché case, Goldstein had a canvas bag hooked over his shoulder. They were calling the flight, the last call. Raub had the tickets and the boarding passes.

The taxi had come to a halt in front of the glass doors, where it was forbidden to stop, the driver reaching back for his fare, his face lit with pleasure. It would be a good tip because it wouldn't be the bastard's own money, because it would go down on the expenses and for this bastard, high priority, expenses were a deep black hole. The bastard was out of the car, striding the few paces to the glass doors, which had swept open for him, and Goldstein had shuddered again as the cold caught him and the snow flurry settled on his face and his arms.

Goldstein and Raub were the minders from the BfV: they were the escort from the counter-espionage organization.

He was a big man, as tall as Raub and taller than Goldstein, with broad shoulders. He kept his back straight, as if he had stood on a parade-ground and commanded lesser men, and held his head high. His fair hair was neatly combed, his beard carefully trimmed. He had moved between his minders with the effortless step of arrogance, and Goldstein thought it a class act. They had gone straight to the head of the queue, paused long enough at the desk for Raub and Goldstein to flash their passports and identification cards at the girl. Hadn't waited for her permission, had gone on through. He never hurried. They had followed the lights and the indicator boards. They had taken the first flight of the day from Berlin Tempelhof to London Heathrow . . .

. . . Ernst Raub would have liked to say, 'It's not Interflug, Doktor Krause. It's not Aeroflot. There are two knives . . .' He had said, 'For an airline breakfast, the egg is very good.'

It was the nature of his job to be polite to the man, but he despised him. He thought the man ate like a pig.

15

He would have liked to say, 'With two knives you can use one for the scrambled egg and one for the roll and the marmalade . . .' He had said, 'Personally, I would prefer jam, summer fruits, to marmalade, but the marmalade is acceptable.'

They sat in business class. Goldstein, appallingly dressed, was by the window, then Krause. Ernst Raub was across the aisle, but after the stewardess had passed, he leaned towards the man.

He would have liked to say, 'There are always two knives on Lufthansa, standard or business. Were they short of knives on Interflug and Aeroflot?' He had said, 'Always so much better when you have breakfast inside you. Then you can face the world.'

They were so ignorant, these people, so lacking in sophistication. Ernst Raub had a friend in Cologne, Army but on attachment to BfV, who told him that when people like Krause had been inducted to the Bundeswehr Inner Leadership Academy they were so naïve that they did not know how to use a bank, how to buy insurance, did not know how to choose a bottle of wine for dinner. In Cologne, over a beer and a barbecue with his family and his friend's family, he used to shake with laughter when he was told how pathetic were these people.

He had leaned back in his seat, the aircraft was steady and cruising above the storm turbulence, closed his eyes. He had scratched at the sunburn on his face, but the peeling skin on his shoulders was worse, aggravated by the new shirt he wore. Two good weeks with his wife, the boys looked after by her parents, in the Seychelles . . . but fewer Germans there than when they had holidayed on the islands six years before, because too much money was leaking out of western Germany and into the swamp pit of eastern Germany, too much money going to these people who did not know how to work, and did not know how to use a different knife for their egg and for their roll and marmalade . . . Ernst Raub could not criticize the man, must only sweeten him. Ernst Raub, sixteen years with the Office for the

16

Protection of the State, had gone too many times into the buildings of the Bonn ministries to seal offices and desks, filing cabinets, computers and bank accounts, to lead away junior officials to the interrogation rooms, to recite the charge of espionage to a grey-faced, trembling wretch. He had heard, too many times, the sobbed and stuttered confessions and the names, too many times, of those who had compromised and ruined those junior officials, the wretches. It demeaned him to escort and mind Doktor Krause, but the man must be sweet-talked, the man was a nugget of gold.

There were no formalities at London Heathrow. They were taken off the flight before the other passengers and down an open staircase onto the apron area where two unmarked cars had waited for them . . . .

In abject misery, Major Perry Johnson walked in the rain, desolate, to the guardhouse.

Each image, sharp in his mind, was worse than the one gone before.

The Colonel had been on his knees beside Doktor Dieter Krause. 'I really cannot apologize sufficiently. I'm quite devastated by what has happened to a guest of the Corps. I can only say how sincerely sorry I am, and all my colleagues, for this quite shameful and unwarranted assault. I promise, you have my word, Doktor Krause, that I will get to the bottom of this matter and that the culprit will be severely punished.'

The Colonel had attempted to touch the German's shoulder, but the younger minder, the sallow Jewish boy, the one who had kicked the corporal, had blocked his hand.

The Colonel had stood and the minders had stayed close to their man, a snarl of contempt on the face of the older one. 'Immediately, Captain Dawson, get Doktor Krause and his people down to Sick Bay. I want him treated, looked after. I want the best for him. Well, come on, stir yourself, man.' And Captain Dawson had drifted, dream-like, forward, had offered a hand to get the German to his feet and had been pushed aside. There

17

was blood on the German's face and he walked bent because of the blows into his privates.

The Colonel had turned to the men and women in the mess. They stood, sat, in the silence of shock. 'I don't have to tell you how shamed I am that such an incident should happen in our mess, to our guest. If anyone should think this a suitable subject for gossip inside or outside our barracks, then that person should know I will flay the living skin off their back.' He had challenged them all, the Brigadier from London, the civil servants, the officers holding the last free drinks of Major Walsh's 'happy hour', and the bar steward.

The Colonel, deliberately, had picked the tray, the broken glass, the cubes of ice, the two garish slices of lemon from the carpet, and carried them towards Johnson. There was only a small stain left behind on the burgundy and white patterns of the carpet, like the aftermath of a street stabbing, so little to say what had happened. He gave the tray to Johnson, who held it, hands shaking. 'Your responsibility, I fancy, Perry, to clear up this shambles. I want your report to me within two hours. Your corporal, your responsibility. You'll not spare the rod, Perry. An honoured guest has been grievously abused while taking the hospitality of the Corps, so you should consider the need to provide a goddamn good answer. What the hell was that about?'

The Colonel had allowed him to carry the tray to the bar, then boomed behind him, 'You might feel it necessary, Perry, after you have reported to me, to seek out Major Walsh and offer him your personal apology – because she is your corporal and your responsibility – for having ruined what should have been a memorable evening to mark the completion of twenty-nine years' service in the Corps. You should do that before he leaves Templer in the morning. Beneath your damn dignity, was it, to queue and carry a tray of drinks?'

He'd never liked Harry Walsh – Harry Walsh was brimful of Ireland, claimed Ireland was the core work of Intelligence, and that Germany, Russia, was merely academic self-gratification,

18

called it a bloody wank from his corner at the bar. Perry Johnson had put only a fifty-pence piece in the collection bucket for the purchase of the crystal sherry decanter and glasses set.

He had gone out into the night. There was rain on his face, and there were tears.

He walked fast.

He had been later than usual that morning, running behind his self-imposed schedule. Been talking on the telephone in his small room above the mess to his sister and the woman, dear soul, had little sense of time and less idea of creating an agenda for a conversation. She'd rambled and he'd not been rude, had allowed her to talk, and now he was later than usual coming to his office in the G/3 building. But, then, Major Perry Johnson could hardly afford to be rude to his sister because in thirteen months he would be moving from bachelor quarters at Ashford to her cottage. Ambleside, the Lake District, would become his retirement home. Nowhere else to go but his sister's cottage and seasonal work with the National Trust if he was lucky ... What a goddamn waste.

'Morning, Barnes.'

'Morning, Major.'

She hadn't looked up at him, looked instead at the big clock on the wall across her cubbyhole space, above the filing cabinets.

'Well, you know, running a bit late ... Telephone call just when I was about to leave ... Rotten morning.'

He'd barked his excuse. He was fifty-three years old, a primary expert on the old Soviet Army and now on the new Russian Federation Army. He briefed the chief of staff on one to one, and the chief of defence intelligence, and the secretary of state. He as fluent in German, Russian, the Pushtu language of the Afghan tribesmen, and he always felt the need to make an excuse to Corporal Tracy Barnes when he was late to work.

Her eyes had been on her screen. 'Careful where you stand, Major, ceiling's leaking again. I've been on to Maintenance and bollocked them. They're sending someone over – won't make any difference unless he comes with a bulldozer . . .'

'Of course, excellent – what's my day?'

'On your desk, waiting for you. Oh, the Captain rang on his mobile, took the dog walking off camp, lost it – his story . . .'

He'd unlocked his door.

'Don't take your coat in there, Major, get wet all over your carpet. I'll take it outside and shake it.'

'Would you? Thank you.'

'Dogs are as bright as their masters, if you ask me – give us the coat.'

She'd been beside him, reaching up and helping him off with it, tutting criticism because it dripped a stain on the carpet, and she was gone . . . Other than his sister, Corporal Barnes was the only woman he knew. Only went to his sister, the cottage near the water at Ambleside, for his three weeks' leave a year, but he was with Corporal Barnes for the other forty-nine. Four years she'd been with him – didn't know where she went for her leave, never asked, assumed she went back to her mother. No-one could say it was against her wishes, but he'd quietly put the cap on any question of her promotion to sergeant and he'd blocked any proposal for her transfer. He gazed around his room. Not much that was personal to him, other than the pictures. Leave charts for the section, night-duty rosters, photographs of their new armoured personnel carriers and new mortars and their new minister of defence. The pictures were his own. He was not a happy man, and less happy now that the certain days of the Cold War were consigned to the rubbish bin, and certainly not happy that a working lifetime of deep knowledge was about to be ditched into the same bin.

The pictures represented the happiest time of his life. *The Last Stand of the 44th Regiment at Gundamuck* was his favourite, the little knot of men gathered round their officer who had tied the colours around his chest, their ammunition exhausted and bayonets their only defence, the tribesmen circling them in the winter snow of the Khyber Pass – good stuff – and *The Remnants of an Army*, Lady Butler's portrayal of the surgeon's arrival at Jalalabad a couple of days after the Gundamuck massacre, only chap to get through. The happiest time in his life had been in Peshawar, debriefing tribesmen, training them to kill Soviet helicopters with the Blowpipe air-to-ground system. Living in Peshawar, just across the Afghan/Pakistan border, watching from a safe distance the Soviets catch a packet, just as the 44th Regiment had 141 years earlier, at the heart of real intelligence gathering. Happy times, useful times . . . She had been hanging his coat on the hook.

'You haven't read your day, Major.'

She nagged at him. It was almost domestic. His sister nagged at him, not unpleasantly but just nagged away until he'd done his chores. Not a great deal of difference between his sister and Corporal Barnes.

'It's the German thing, isn't it?'

'On your desk – it's all day, buffet lunch. Colonel's hosting. There's a load coming down from London. In lecture room B/19. Guests is the German with two spooks to hold his hand. Coffee at ten, kick-off half an hour after that. The background brief's on your desk as well.'

'Have you enough to amuse yourself?'

She had snorted. There were those in the mess who told him that he permitted her to walk to the bounds of insolence, but he wouldn't have that talk, not in the mess or anywhere else. He had picked up the brief, two sheets, scanned it, and she was gazing at him, rolling her eyes.

'Don't know about amusement . . . There's the expenses from your Catterick trip. There's your leave application. I've got your paper for Infantry Training School to type up. Have to confirm your dentist. Got to get your car over to Motor Pool for valeting. The stuff you wanted from Library . . .'

He had seen the two cars go by, black and unmarked, glistening from the rain, heading towards the B-block complex.

'Morning, Perry . . . Morning, Corporal.'

He quite liked to be called Perry. It gave him a sort of warmth. The use of his name made him feel wanted. In the mess he always introduced himself with that name, encouraged visitors to use it. He had a need for friends that was seldom gratified. He'd turned towards the door.

'Morning, Ben, bit off schedule, aren't we?'

'Morning, Captain,' she'd intoned, as if he was out of order.

He was young. His hair was a mess. He was red-flushed in the face. The Labrador, black, was soaked wet, on a tight lead and choke chain, close to his heels, the tail curled under the stomach and mourning eyes.

'Went after the rabbits – took a bloody age to catch him. Christ, we're up against it, aren't we? Should be moving, should we? Corporal, be an angel, Nelson's food's in the car. Half a tin, three handfuls of meal, warm water not boiling to mix in, lunchtime, OK? Oh, those biographies, 49th Mechanized Infantry at . . . God, where is it?'

'At Voronezh, Captain Christie. The 49th Mechanized Infantry is currently at garrison camp at Voronezh.'

'It's updated, in the safe. Needs retyping – hope you can read the writing. Look, I'm short of petrol vouchers. You'll give Nelson a walk. No titbits for him, nothing extra, supposed to be dieting . . . Be an angel.'

'Time we made a move,' the Major had said.

He walked under the lights, and away ahead of him were the high lamps over the wire. There was no-one within the wall of wire around Templer Barracks in whom he could confide, so damned unfair, no-one to comfort him.

It would be across the barracks within an hour. The whispering, giggling, gossiping and tittering would be sieved through the officers' mess, the officers' married quarters, the sergeants' mess, their married quarters, junior ranks' canteen, junior ranks' quarters. The Colonel had said that it was Perry Johnson's responsibility, and every bastard out there would have a little story, grist fed to the mill, about the liberties taken by Corporal Tracy Barnes towards her commanding officer. He had not the

22

merest idea why she had attacked the German with such animal savagery.

The guardhouse sergeant snapped from his chair, stood to attention, but he was sure the damn man had smirked. On the table was a plastic bag holding a tie, a belt and a pair of shoelaces.

'Where is she?'

'Cell block, number four, sir.'

He went to the steel-barred door, and the dull-lit corridor stretched into shadows in front of him.

'Well, hurry up, Sergeant.'

'Yes, sir. Captain Christie's with her, sir, but I've kept an eye out just in case she thumps him.' The sergeant's face was impassive.

He smeared his eyes with his coat sleeve. Should have done it before entering the guardhouse. The wet would have been noted. He was admitted to the corridor of the cell block. Good material for the mill of gossip and more bloody tittering.

He went into the cell. Christie was standing inside the open door, white in the face. A central light shone down, protected by a close-mesh wire. The walls, tiled to waist height and whitewashed above, were covered in graffiti scrawls and line drawings of genitalia that were quite disgusting. He had only ever been in the cells once before, to escort a civilian solicitor when one of his corporals, Russian-language translator, had confessed to selling off hire-purchase video-recorders. A foul smell, urine and vomit. There was a window above her, reinforced opaque glass set into concrete.

'What's she said?'

'She hasn't said anything. I haven't asked her anything.'

'Asked her anything, "Major" . . .'

'I haven't asked her anything, Major.'

A thin mattress was on the bed. The bed was a slab block of concrete. A blanket of serge grey was folded on the mattress. He felt raw anger towards her. She had destroyed him.

'Well, Barnes, what the hell is this about?'

23

She sat on the mattress. Her arms were around her knees, which were pulled up against her chest.

'Waiting, Barnes. Why, in God's name, did you do that?'

She was pale, except for the red welt at the side of her neck where the chop of the minder's hand had caught her.

'Don't play the bloody madam. You're in a pit of trouble. Bugger me about and you'll be sorry. Why did you do it?'

She gazed back at him. Just once she breathed deeply, grimaced, and he remembered the kick she had taken in the ribs. Her body shook, her shoulders and her knees, but her face was expressionless. No insolence, no defiance, no fear.

'Assault, actual bodily harm, grievous bodily harm, could even be Official Secrets Act. Barnes, understand me, you're for the jump, so don't fuck with me.'

Ben Christie glanced at him, contempt. 'Tracy, you know us and we know you, you work with us and you trust us. Please, Tracy . . .'

She said nothing. She gazed at them, through them. She seemed so small, hunched on the mattress, so vulnerable.

'We'll squeeze it out of you, damn sure we will. Last time, what was it about?'

Ben Christie said gently, like he was talking with that damn dog, 'All we want to do is help, Tracy, but we have to know why.'

There was the shake in her shoulders and knees. It could have been the shock, but he'd have sworn that she was quite in control, so calm. The silence hung around them. The way she sat, the way she held her knees, he could see up her thighs. He turned away. The blood was in the veins of his cheeks.

'Don't damn well come back to me tomorrow, next week, with your story and expect sympathy from me. Made your own bed, Barnes, and you can bloody well lie on it.'

Captain Christie reached out his hand to her, as if to touch her. 'Please, Tracy, I meant it. I meant it absolutely when I said we wanted to help you . . .'

She flinched away. She rejected him, said nothing. Johnson looked at his watch. The Colonel had given him two hours and he'd eaten into that time. He turned on his heel and the Captain, no bloody spine, followed him out into the corridor. He called the sergeant and told him to secure the cell, no access, no visitors, without his express permission. Out again into the night ... Maybe he should have belted her ... He led. No small-talk between them, Captain Christie stayed a pace behind.

They were on a gravel path, and Walsh came past them. He was carrying the big cardboard box that held his leaving present, flanked by his chums from Irish postings. He'd heard they were going on to dinner in Ashford. The clique stepped off the gravel, made way for him and Christie, stood silent like an honour guard. They walked on and heard belly laughs behind them. Into G/3. Past the small rooms where the warrant officers and the sergeants worked, doors all closed and locked, no light from underneath. They'd all know by now, in their mess, in their canteen, in their quarters, and damn good fun they'd be having with their knowledge. They'd all know that, in public, he'd been whipped like a clumsy recruit was whipped on the parade-ground by a drill instructor ... So bloody unfair.

There was a scraping sound, and a whimpering. He unlocked the door. Christie's bloody dog bounded at him and he raised his knee to ward it off. Christie was muttering that he'd better take the dog to the grass. He flapped his hand, past caring where the dog peed. He went inside. He was alone. He thought the rooms of G/3/29 were like his mother's house, after she'd died. She'd used frail strength to clean her house the day before she had gone to the hospital. His room, Christie's, and the area between them were as ordered as his mother's house had been. He rocked. On her desk were the neat piles of paper – his typed speech for the Infantry Training School, his expenses-claim form with the stapled receipts of his Catterick trip, her note in copperplate handwriting of the time, date of his dentist appointment, what time in the morning his car would be collected for valeting. Beside his pile was Christie's – the revised appraisal of the 49th Mechanized Infantry Division at Voronezh, the petrol vouchers held together with a paper clip . . . The dog came from behind him, settled under her desk.

He said, grimly, 'Search her area, your desk drawers, I'll do mine . . .'

'What are we looking for, Perry?'

He exploded, 'How the hell do *I* know? How should *I* know why the best corporal in this whole bloody camp makes an unprovoked attack? I don't know, except that it's about the past.'

'He leaves when I say so. Don't care who he is, when he's in my care he leaves when I'm satisfied that he's fit to go.'

The sick bay was the territory of Mavis Fogarty. It was many years since she had left the farm near Balinrobe and enlisted as a nurse in the British Army. She seldom went home because it would embarrass her family, but she retained the big hands suited to work on the Co. Mayo bog fields. She had his trousers off him and his underpants at his knees, and with surprising gentleness examined the bruised testicles of Dieter Krause. She'd done time in the military hospitals at Dortmund and Soest, spoke passable German, and told him there was no lasting damage. She didn't ask how it was, during a social drink in the officers' mess, that he'd managed to get so thoroughly battered – she'd learn later, in the canteen. She pulled up his pants, covered him. She started with sterile hot water and cotton wool to clean the raked nail slashes on his face. He wore a wedding ring. If her husband ever came home with scratches like that on his face then he'd be put to sleep in the garage. She'd earmarked a salve for the grazes at the back of his head where the bruising showed through his hair. The minders, sullen and watching her every move, were across the room from her. One nursed his ankle as if he'd kicked something heavy, and the other rubbed the heel of his hand as if he'd hit something solid. She wiped the scratch wounds and established her absolute authority over them.

26

'Funny thing, shock. Soldiers here get into Saturday-night fights, get back to camp and think they're fine, then collapse. He stays here, right here, till I'm ready to let him go.'

The accommodation block for junior ranks (female) knew, each last one of them, that Corporal Barnes was locked in a guard-house cell. They also knew that she had done heavy damage in the officers' mess and had put a German guest into Sick Bay for repairs. Her major and the captain with wife trouble were in the block and searching her room. The traffic down the first-floor corridor was brisk, but the fourth door on the right was closed and there was a provost sergeant outside. Those who did pass could only feed to the rumour factory that the room was being ripped apart.

They ransacked the privacy of the sleeping area, but Ben Christie backed off when it came to the chest of drawers, left it to the Major. Perry Johnson, frantic, didn't hesitate, dragged the drawers clear, shook and examined each item of under-wear, knickers, bras, tights and slips – all so neatly folded away before Perry's hands were on them . . . and Trish just dumped her smalls into a drawer, out of sight and out of mind . . . So neat, so small, what she wore against her skin. Christie caught the Major's eye, hadn't intended to, but Perry had flushed red. The clothes were out of the drawers, the drawers were out of the chest and on the bed. The bed was already stripped. The sheets and blankets, with her pyjamas, were heaped on the floor. The curtains were off the window. The rug was rolled away . . . He had taken each coat, skirt and blouse, civilian and uniform, from the wardrobe, checked the pockets, felt the col-lars and the waists where the material was double thickness, and hung them on the door. He would take the wardrobe to pieces because there was a double ceiling in it and a double floor. Out in the corridor a telephone was ringing. For Christ's sake, the bloody man Johnson was holding up a bra against the light. What was she bloody well going to hide in there? In summer she didn't wear a tie, or a tunic or a pullover, and

27

she'd the top buttons of the blouse unfastened, and she'd have called him over to check her work on the screen before she printed it up, teasing, and he'd see the bra and what the bra held . . . There was a photograph of a cat, and of an elderly woman, taken from their frames, checked. There was a book, woman's saga, shaken and then the spine pulled off. Johnson looked at him, and Ben shook his head. Johnson knelt, grunted, and began to rip back the vinyl flooring. A knock.

'Please, sir, what do I do. It's Tracy's – Corporal Barnes's – mum on the phone for her.'

Ben opened the door. 'I'll take it.'

'She always rings this night, this time, clockwork.'

The girl, lance-corporal, Karen something, fat ankles, pointed down the corridor to the pay phone. The receiver was dangling. Just what he bloody needed . . . He went over and picked it up. He waved the hovering lance-corporal away.

'Hello, Captain Christie here. Good evening . . . I'm sorry, Mrs Barnes, very sorry, but she's not available . . . What? Could you speak up? . . . No, I can't say why. I can only say that Corporal Barnes is unable to come to the telephone . . . Afraid I don't know when she'll be available. Goodnight, Mrs Barnes . . .' At every door on the corridor a face was watching him. He said, loudly, that if there were more calls from Corporal Barnes's mother, she was to be given the camp number and extension number of the Adjutant's office, manned through the night . . . The lie hurt him, hurt him as deeply as seeing bloody Johnson handling the underwear she wore against her skin.

Christie smiled, spoke gently. 'It's Karen, isn't it? Come here, please. I'm not going to bite you. Actually, I need a bit of help.'

The girl soldier with the fat ankles came, hesitating, forward.

'Corporal Barnes is in, I have to say it, a packet of trouble. Yes, you've heard, everybody's heard. I want to help her, but for me to help her then you have to help me. Please . . . did something happen this morning, anything, anything unusual? I need your help.'

The blurted answer. 'Nothing was different, it was all just usual. There was all the din in here at get-up time . . . You know how it is. Downes was bawling she was late with her period, Geraghty was giving out she'd got no clean knickers, Smythe's got a new CD player that's a right blaster. All bloody noise in the corridor. I went to her room, lost my tie. She gave me her spare. She was just sitting on the floor, hadn't got her skirt on, quiet as a mouse, in front of the fire. She was humming that bloody song, so old, what she always sings. She was all gruff, about the tie, but it's only an act. She comes over all heavy, but that's not real. She lent me the tie, she didn't give out that I was late on paying her what I owe her, what I borrowed last week. Under the gruff she's all soft. I owe her, half the girls in the block owe her, but she doesn't chase it. But for all that she won't be friends with us. I asked her to come with us to the pub tonight, no chance. Just sits in her room. She's done nothing in that room to make it her own like the rest of us have. No mess, no muck in there, everything tidied. She's older than the rest of us, right? Keeps herself to herself. We don't know nothing about her. Just her work, all she seems to live for, no boys, no fun. She pushes you away, but you get underneath and she's really kind . . . I brought her over a message from Admin this afternoon, for you. She was down on the floor with your dog, she was feeding him the biscuits she keeps in the safe. She was singing to the dog, same song . . . Some old Irish thing . . . She's sort of sad, really. She makes out she doesn't need us, doesn't need anyone. That's sad, isn't it? I can't help you, Captain, honest. Your question, there was nothing different about her . . . I'm sorry.'

She fled down the corridor, past the watching faces.

He let himself into the room. He stepped over the bent-back vinyl. The sweat ran on Johnson's forehead. Johnson pointed to a board, lifted it and a section came away cleanly, as if the work of loosening it had been done long before. He reached into the hole and lifted out the black and white photograph protected in Cellophane wrapping. Greyed buildings, a greyed street, greyed and broken pavings, a greyed road sign. The light was in Tracy's face and on her cheeks and at her eyes, the love light. A boy held her, grinning as if proud to have her close to him. They were the brilliance in the greyness of a street, buildings and a pavement.

'Sorry,' Perry Johnson said. Seemed so damn tired. 'Old eyes aren't what they were, can't read that street sign.'

Ben Christie held the photograph close to his face, squinted at it. 'The sign is for the junction of Prenzlauer and Saar-brucker . . .'

'Thought so. Give it me back, please.'

'Where's that?'

Up from his knees, Johnson brushed his uniform trousers. 'Berlin. Prenzlauer Allee runs east from Alexanderplatz. A bit further up than Karl Marx Allee, on the other side, is Saar-brucker Strasse. She looks rather young – I'd say it's ten years old. The junction of Saarbrucker Strasse and Prenzlauer Allee, ten years ago, was in East Berlin. That's the wrong side of the Wall, that's enemy ground . . . Oh, God . . .'

'Do we hear skeletons rattling?'

'Shit, man, do we need imbecile banalities?'

The room was to be sealed.

She had not moved, knees tucked against her chest and arms around her knees.

The drip of Johnson's questions: 'You were posted to Berlin, start of 'eighty-six to end of 'eighty-nine? . . . This photograph was taken between the start of 'eighty-six and end of 'eighty-nine? . . . Who are you with in the photograph? . . . How did you know of former Stasi official Dieter Krause? . . . You accused Krause of murder, the murder of whom?'

No word from her, staring back at them, no muscle moving on her face.

Christie wanted only to give her comfort. 'Tracy, you have to see that you're not helping yourself. If something happened in Germany, involving Krause, tell us, please.'

Away down the corridor the radio played quietly on the ser-geant's desk.

'You're a bloody fool, young woman, because the matter will now pass out of our hands, out of the hands of the family of the Corps.' Johnson walked out of the cell.

Christie looked back at her. He looked for her anger, or for her bloody-minded obstinacy, or for fear, or for the cheek in her eye. She stared through him, as if he were not there.

2

He was in the bathroom, standing at the basin in warm flannel pyjamas with his mouth full of toothpaste when the telephone rang downstairs in the hall. It was Albert Perkins's night as standby duty officer (home). He spat out the toothpaste, rinsed his mouth and hurried downstairs.

'Perkins here . . . Good evening, Mr Fleming . . . No, not inconvenient . . . Hadn't gone to bed . . . How can I help? Secure? Just hold a moment, please . . .'

There was a switch at the side of the base of the telephone and he nudged it forward. All section heads, like Mr Fleming, and all stand-by duty officers (home), like Albert Perkins, had the equipment at home to make and receive secure calls.

'On secure now, Mr Fleming. How can I help? . . . Yes, I've paper and a pen . . .'

He listened. He scrawled on a pad: 'TEMPLER BARRACKS, ASHFORD – INTELLIGENCE CORPS. KRAUSE, DIETER, exMfS – RYKOV, PYOTR, col, DefMin staff – WUSTROW base, w. of ROSTOCK.'

The grin formed on his face. 'She did what?'

He wrote the name, 'BARNES, TRACY, cpl.'

'In the officers' mess? That's choice . . . There's a fair few I know who wish they'd the bottle, kick the Hun where it hurts – sorry, Mr Fleming. What it's all about? Is that it? No problem . . . I'll come in and get some files and then get down there . . . I have authority, I take the reins, yes? . . . No, I haven't been celebrating, I can drive. I'll be there about three, I'll call you in the morning . . . No problem at all, Mr Fleming, goodnight . . .' He pushed back the Secure switch.

He climbed the stairs. He dressed. Work suit, that day's shirt and tie, clean socks. He hadn't had a drink that evening at home, just a Coca-Cola with the take-away pizza, and a coffee. In the kitchen, on the sideboard, were the four birthday cards, from his wife, Mr Fleming, his friend in the Supporters' Club and Violet in the typing pool. He had not been out to celebrate his fiftieth birthday because Helen was still at the art class she taught that night of the week and she usually stayed for a drink with her class, and he wouldn't have had alcohol, anyway, if he was standby duty officer (home). He tore the note from the pad beside the telephone and pocketed it. Then he ripped out the four sheets of blank paper underneath, as was his habit, took them into the living room and tossed them on the low fire behind the guard. He wrote a brief note of explanation on the pad to his wife and offered his love. He double-locked his front door.

It was a damn awful night, and he thought the roads might have gone icy by the time he reached Ashford. His car was an eight-year-old Sierra, parked on the street so that Helen could use the drive when she returned home. Three things mattered in the life of Albert Perkins, aged fifty that day. His wife Helen, Fulham Football Club, the job. He ignored Helen's indifference to his work. He coped with the catastrophic results of Fulham FC, as he would with a disability that must be lived with. He adored his work, dedicated himself to the Service. It had never crossed his mind that he might have told Mr Fleming that he was already undressed for bed and asked whether it could wait till the morning.

He left the 1930s mock-Tudor semi-detached house, his and Helen's home in the Hampton Wick suburb south-west of the capital, and headed for central London. He would be at Vauxhall Bridge Cross, in Library, by midnight; an hour later he would be at Defence Intelligence and digging in their archive. He hoped to be out of London by two in the morning, and at Ashford by three.

He drove the emptied streets, and he wondered where the

choice story would lead him. It would lead him somewhere, and he'd be there, at the end of that road. Mr Fleming would have called him out because he'd have known that Albert Perkins would follow a scent to the end of any road.

There wasn't an officer at Templer who would have described Perry Johnson as imaginative. He didn't read fiction, he didn't listen to music and he didn't look at pictures.

He was called to the gate. Under the arc lights, the far side of the heavy iron barrier, was a green Sierra. Ten past three in the morning. The man behind the wheel had a pinched weasel face, a small brush of a moustache, combed and slicked hair in a perfect parting, and his skin had the paleness of one who avoided sunlight and weather. He got out of the car, carrying a filled briefcase, and threw his keys to the sentry. He didn't ask where he should park, merely assumed that the sentry would do the business for him.

Perry Johnson thought that the man came to the barracks just as a hangman would have come to a gaol at dead of night. He shivered and his imagination rioted. The briefcase could have held a rope, a hood and the pinion thongs of leather.

'Who are you?'

The man spoke with what Johnson thought was a common voice and the accent held the grate of West London.

'Johnson, Major Perry Johnson.'

'What's your involvement?'

'I'm Corporal Barnes's commanding officer. She does my typing.'

'Thought you people did your own typing, these days, or are some too idle to learn how to use a keyboard?'

'There's no call . . .'

The man smiled, without humour. 'There were a few old contemptibles in my place who tried to hang on to their typists so they wouldn't have to learn the new skills. They were booted out. Where's Krause?'

34

'I didn't catch your name.'

'Hadn't given it you. Take me to Krause. I gather you found a photograph, please. I'll have it. I'm Albert Perkins.'

Johnson took the picture from his tunic pocket, offered it. They were under a light. It was examined. Perkins took a buff file from his briefcase and opened it. He read from the file and looked again at the photograph, put both back into the brief-case, and walked on. Johnson felt the fear a prison governor would have experienced when meeting for the first time a hang-man coming in the emptiness of the night. He led. The rainclouds had gone.

He babbled, 'I'm wondering if our tracks haven't crossed. Face seems to register from way back. There was a Perkins, a Six man, working out of the Naafihaus, Helmstedt, would have been mid-seventies. Up and down to Berlin on our military train, debriefing autobahn people. Was it . . . ?'

'I find that really boring – "Weren't you? By Jove, so was I. God, small world. Remember?" Tedious.'

They reached Sick Bay and went into the dim light of the waiting area.

Perkins said, 'My advice, Major, don't go playing all uptight because I've been sent here, because your people are whining that they're out of their depth, don't. I'll tell you why I'm here, words of one syllable. They're the power and the glory. We bend the knee to them. We grovel rather than offend "greater" Ger-many. We slobber at the ankles of their Chancellor, their Central Bank, their foreign ministry, their industrialists. They are pre-mier and we are division three. They deign, kind of them, to throw us crumbs, to send us a prime intelligence asset, who gets the warmest of welcomes. She called him a murderer, cor-rect? They're hardly going to enthuse when we name that prime asset as a killer who should be before their judges. Not on a junket, not bathing in the limelight, but in handcuffs and in court. They won't be happy people. So, we're all smiles and apologies. Got me?'

There was a sentry on the inner door. Perkins went past him, didn't acknowledge him. The bright light of the room lit the paleness of his face.

Krause sat on a hard chair. The wounds were cleaner than when Johnson had last seen him, but the scratches were deep. As if drilled, the minders each took a step forward from the wall to stand either side of their man.

The smile beamed on Perkins's face. 'The name is Perkins, I've come from London – try and sort this dreadfully embarrassing business out. I want to express our most sincere apologies.'

'I am Doktor Raub. We wish to go. We are being kept here. We wish to leave.'

'What I heard, it was thought advisable, on medical grounds, to suggest you waited.'

A mocking voice. 'I am Herr Goldstein. On medical grounds, was it necessary to have a sentry at the door?'

'So sorry, put it down to tangled wires, no intention to delay you. A hotel in London, yes? And you are . . . ?'

His voice tailed away. Perkins stood in front of Krause.

'I am Doktor Dieter Krause. I wish to go.'

A voice of silken sweetness. 'Then go you shall. Just one point, excuse me . . .'

They were standing, waiting on him. Perkins took his time and the younger minder flicked his fingers in impatience. Perkins rummaged in his briefcase and took out the photograph. He held it carefully so that his thumb was across the face of Corporal Tracy Barnes. He showed the photograph, the face of the young man.

'So good of you to wait. A young man, we'll call him Hans. Hauptman Krause, did you kill that young man? In cold blood, did you murder him, Hauptman Krause?'

In raw fury: 'What is your evidence?'

And Perkins laughed lightly. 'Please accept our apologies for what happened this evening – safe back to your hotel, Hauptman.'

He stood aside. He allowed them past. The sentry would take them to the cars.

'Where is she?'

'In the cells, the guardhouse,' Johnson said.

'Take me.'

It was easy for Albert Perkins to make an image in his mind. This was among the skills that his employers in the Service valued.

He saw a briefing room, modern, carpeted, good chairs, a big screen behind a stage. An audience of officers and senior NCOs, civil servants bussed down from London, talking hushed over their coffee and nibbling biscuits before the Colonel's finger rapped the live microphone.

Probably . . . 'Whether we like it or not, whether our political masters would acknowledge it or not, the Russian Federation remains in pole position as our potential enemy. While that country, with such awesome conventional and nuclear military power, remains in a state of convulsed confusion we would be failing in our duty if we did not examine most rigorously the prime and influential power players in Moscow . . .'

Photographs on a screen of Rykov, Pyotr, whoever he might be, on a wet November morning, and a background brief on previous appointments. Had to be Afghanistan, had to be a military district in Mother Russia under the patronage of a general weighted down with medals, and command of a base camp up on the Baltic coast. Photographs and voice tapes, but all adding to sweet fuck-all of nothing.

Lights up, the Colonel on his arse, and stilted applause for the honoured guest, for the friend of Rykov, Pyotr, for the former enemy, for the old Stasi creature . . . Albert Perkins made the image, saw it and heard it.

Krause at the podium, no scars on his face, no cuts in his head and no bruising at his balls.

Probably . . . 'I was Pyotr Rykov's friend. We were close, we were as brothers are. We fished together, we camped together. There were no microphones, no surveillance. He talked to me with trust. I tell you, should the state collapse, should the

Russian Army assume control, then the most powerful man in Moscow would be the minister of defence and a step behind the minister is my friend, my best friend. I wish to share my knowledge with you of this man . . .'

Drooling they'd have been in the briefing room, slavering over the anecdotes, and all the stuff about former enemies and former Stasi bastards flushed down the can. The red carpet rolled out for the walk in the rain to the mess, best crystal for drinks, silver on the table for dinner afterwards. Except . . . except that some little corporal, little bit of fluff, had gate-crashed the party, fucked up the evening. Wasn't a bad story, not the way that Albert Perkins saw it and heard it. Must have been like a satchel of Semtex detonating in the hallowed territory of the mess.

The manufacturing of images had always been among the talents of Albert Perkins.

They walked on the main road through the camp, towards the gate and the guardhouse. When the headlights came, powering behind them, Johnson hopped awkwardly off the tarmacadam for the grass but Perkins did not. Perkins made them swerve. The two cars flashed their lights at the gate sentry and the bar lifted for them. It was a rare cocktail that the man, the hangman, had served them, Johnson reflected. Apologies and insults, sweetness and rudeness. In three hours it would be dawn. Then the barracks would stir to life, and the gossip and innuendo would begin again. The target would be himself. By mid-morning coffee break, the barracks would know that Perry Johnson had been a messenger boy through the night for a civilian from London. They went into the guardhouse. The corridor was unlocked for them. He frowned, confused, because the cell door was ajar. They went in.

'Who are you?'

Christie was pushing himself up from the floor beside the door.

'Ben Christie, Captain Christie.'

'What are you doing here?'

'I thought it best . . . with the prisoner . . . I was with the corporal in case she said—'

'Is this a holding cell or is it a kennel?'

The dog was on its side, its tail beating a slow drumroll on the tiles. It lay under her feet with its back against the concrete slab of the bed.

'Nowhere else for him to go. Sorry.'

Perkins shook his head, slow, side to side. Johnson recognized the treatment. The tack was to demean, then to dominate. She sat on the bed. She did not seem to have moved, knees drawn up and arms around her knees. She was awake, she watched. Perkins didn't look at her. He rapped the questions.

'When she attacked Krause, how was the attack stopped?'

Christie said, 'One of his escort hit her, one kicked her.'

'Has she been seen by qualified medical staff?'

Christie shook his head.

'She's been interrogated – once, twice?'

Christie nodded.

'You did, of course, caution her first?'

Christie shook his head.

'She was told her rights, was offered a solicitor?'

Christie grimaced.

'Before her room was searched, did you have her permission? Did you have the written authorization of the camp commander?'

Christie's chin hung on his chest.

'During the interrogations did you use profanities, blasphemies, obscenities? Was she threatened?'

Christie lifted his hands, the gesture of failure.

Perkins savaged him. 'If she had said anything to you, fuck all use it would have been. Oppressive interrogation, denial of rights, refusal to permit medical help. This isn't Germany, you know. It isn't Stasi country. Get out.'

They went. Christie called his dog. Perkins kicked the door with his heel. It slammed. Christie and Johnson stood in the corridor.

Johnson understood the tactic: Officers rubbished by a civilian in front of a junior rank so junior rank would bond with civilian. Basic stuff. The hatch in the cell door was open. They could hear him. He was brusque.

'Right, Miss Barnes . . . Tracy, isn't it? I'll call you Tracy, if you've no objection. I'm rather tired. I had a long day, was about to go to bed, and I was called out. I don't expect you've slept, so let's do this quickly. I deal in facts, right? Fact, 'eighty-six to 'eighty-nine, you had lance-corporal rank. Fact, 'eighty-six to 'eighty-nine, you were a stenographer with Intelligence Corps working out of Berlin Brigade, room thirty-four in block nine. Fact, in November 'eighty-eight, Hans Becker from East Berlin was being run as an agent by room thirty-four. Fact, on the twenty-first of November 'eighty-eight, the agent was lost while carrying out electronic surveillance on the Soviet base at Wustrow, near to Rostock. I'm sure you're listening carefully to me, Tracy, and you'll have noted that I emphasized "lost". Fact, on that date, Hauptman Krause ran the counter-espionage unit at the Bezirksverwaltung des MfS in Rostock. All facts, Tracy. The facts say an agent was "lost", the facts say that Hauptman Krause was responsible for counter-espionage in that area. The facts don't say murder and they don't say killing. Do you have more facts, Tracy? Not rumours running up the walls of room thirty-four. Got the facts or not got the facts? Got the evidence of murder and killing or not got the evidence?'

From the corridor they strained to hear her voice, a whisper or a sobbed outpouring, and they heard nothing.

'I'm tired, Tracy. Can we, please, do this the easy way?'

Johnson thought it was what a hangman would have said: 'Right then, sir. Let's get this over with, no fuss, nice and simple, then you can go off, sir, and get nailed down in the box and I can go for my breakfast.'

He thought she would be looking back at him, distant, small. He realized she was like family to him. Who spoke for her? Not him, not Ben Christie, no damn man, not anywhere.

'Tell you what, Tracy. You try and get some sleep. Soon as you're asleep I'll be told. I'll come and wake you, and we'll start again. There's an easy way, Tracy, and a hard way. What I want to hear about is facts and evidence.'

The lorry driver spat. The target of his fury was Joshua Frederick Mantle. The spittle ran on the back window of the taxi and masked his face, which was contorted in rage.

The prison officer tugged sharply on the handcuffs they shared, jerked the lorry driver from the window.

The lorry driver was driven away, the taxi lost in the traffic.

He watched it go. He wasn't wearing a raincoat and the drizzle flecked his shoulders. It wasn't necessary for him to have stood ten minutes at the side gates of the court. He had gained little from having waited, from having seen the last defiance of the lorry driver, except a small sense of satisfaction. A detective constable wandered over to him, might have been about to cross the road but had seen him and come to him. His eyes followed the taxi until a bus came past it.

'You going over the pub?'

'Wouldn't have thought so. Got a deskful to be getting on with.' He had a soft voice for a tall man.

'Come on – don't know whether I'll be welcome, but she'll want to see you.'

He hesitated. 'I suppose so.'

The detective constable took his arm and led him into the road. They waited a moment at the bollard half-way across.

'Mind if I say something, Mr Mantle? Whether you mind it or not, I'm going to say it. Times in this job I feel proud and times when I feel pig sick. I feel good when I'm responsible for a real scumbag going down, and I feel pig sick when it's my lot or Crown Prosecution Service that's chickened out. First time I've watched a private prosecution . . . Come on, through the gap.'

They hurried across the road, and again the detective constable had a hand on his arm. 'Why I'm pig sick, Mr Mantle, it was

41

your witness statements that nailed him. I worked eight months on that case and what I came up with was judged by CPS as sufficient only for "without due care and attention". What you got was "death by dangerous driving" . . . Fox and Hounds they were going, wasn't it?'

They walked on the pavement. The women with their shopping and their raised umbrellas flowed around them.

'I was wondering, Mr Mantle, were you ever in the police?'

'I wasn't, no.'

'Didn't think so. If you had been, at your age all you'd be interested in was growing bloody tomatoes in a greenhouse – wouldn't have put the work in.'

He said quietly, 'It wasn't that complicated. If there was an industrial estate then it stood to reason that someone was coming or going, or looking through the window, or had gone outside for a smoke. Someone must have seen the lorry hit him.'

'We'd had posters up, all the usual appeals, nothing. Nobody wants to get involved. How many did you go and see? A hundred?'

'Might have been more.'

'You found the star witness, Mr Mantle, and I didn't. You put that scumbag away, and I didn't. You should feel quite proud for having done the graft, stood up for her when we failed her.'

'Decent of you to say it,' he said.

'Gives you a good feeling, doesn't it, if you've given your hand to someone when nobody else will? Fox and Hounds, yes? Wish I had. You're only a legal executive, aren't you?'

'Afraid I'm not quite that, not qualified yet. Just a glorified clerk.'

They went inside. The pub had opened only minutes earlier. The bar smelt of yesterday's beer and the polish on the tables. The barrister was clapping his hands, the beam of success on his face, for the attention of the woman behind the bar, who stubbornly polished glasses. The senior partner, Bill Greatorex, was talking with the widow. She wasn't listening – she caught Mantle's eye. She was a pretty young woman. She'd dressed in black for the court, skirt and jacket, and deep tiredness showed round her eyes. He'd thought of her, and her small children, all the hours that he'd tramped round the industrial estate in search of a witness. He'd kept her in his mind through all the disappointments and all the shaken heads and all the dismissals from those who hadn't the time to stretch their minds back to the moment of the death of her husband. The barrister bellowed, 'God, there's a serious risk in here of death from thirst.'

She walked away from Bill Greatorex, left him in mid-sentence and came to Mantle. The detective constable backed off. 'What they tell me, Mr Mantle, is that that bastard who killed my Bob, if it had been left to the police, would have been fined five hundred pounds and banned for twelve months. Because of you, he's been put away for three years where he can't drink, drive, kill. Me and the children, all the family, we're very grateful.'

'Thank you,' he said.

She reached up, rather too quickly for him, took his face in her hands and kissed his cheek. 'Very grateful.'

She was gone, back to Greatorex. The barrister had the barmaid's attention and was reciting the order.

The detective constable was beside him again. 'Don't think I'm out of order, Mr Mantle, but what age are you? Fifty-three, fifty-four? I'll bet you're on the money a twenty-year-old would get, a kid with spots all over his face. What that tells me, and I'm no Sherlock, you've a bit of a history.'

'A bit,' he said. 'You'll excuse me.'

He went towards the door. He heard the shout of the barrister behind him, what was 'his poison', pint or a short? He went out onto the street. He did grubby little case-work in a grubby little town, and across the road was a grubby little court-house. He walked back in the drizzle to the offices of Greatorex, Wilkins & Protheroe. He touched the place on his cheek where she had kissed him, then took out his handkerchief and wiped the skin hard.

*　*　*

43

The sleep was in her eyes and her head rocked. She sat on the bed. The food on the tray beside her was untouched.

Perkins yawned, grinned. 'Yes, Tracy, we know there was a man-hunt on the base, across the peninsula where the base was – actually most of it's a wildlife park now, we know that from radio traffic. Yes, we can assume that Hauptman Krause would have been called out from Rostock when the Soviets started howling. The radio traffic ended, and we didn't have a monitor on their landlines. We have a lost agent, we have the assumption that Krause arrived in that area at some time that evening. That is not evidence of murder. You should try and get some sleep. As soon as you're asleep, I'll wake you and I'll ask you again about evidence . . .'

'Bloody movement, at last.'

'You going to do a note?'

They were old friends, good friends, and had to be. For twelve-hour shifts they shared sandwiches and body odours and a plastic piss bucket.

'What Mr Fleming said – doesn't want to wait for the tape to be transcribed . . . They're waking him.'

'You got good German?'

'Good enough, and Italian and French. If my water's right I've good Lebanese Arabic . . . His two minders are in . . .'

'Arabic's a right bastard.'

'Here we go.'

The parking meters where the van was parked were covered over – they always carried the hoods so they could stop where it was best for the reception.

(CONVERSATION STARTED, ROOM 369, 12.11 HOURS.)

KRAUSE: They come to Rostock, they come pushing their noses – (Indistinct) – I deal with it. I and my friends, I take what action . . .

MINDER 1: But, Dieter, there is nothing to find, you gave your word to the Committee . . . (Indistinct.)

44

The van was in front of the hotel, in a side street. On the roof was a small antenna, inconspicuous, but sufficient for quality reception from the microphone in the third-floor room.

> MINDER 2: You told us that all compromising files were cleaned. If there was evidence of crimes against human rights, a problem—
>
> KRAUSE: There is no evidence because there was no crime.
>
> MINDER 2: We have an investment in you, we have the right to your honesty. If there was a problem . . . ? (Indistinct.)

The two men were in the closed rear of the van. A different team had put the microphone in position so it was not their concern whether it was in the room telephone, the bedside radio, the television zapper or behind a wall socket. They were concerned with the reception from it and immediate translation of the conversation.

> KRAUSE: There is no problem. Now, I want to shit and wash – I tell you, if anyone comes to Rostock and tries to make a problem – (indistinct) – I don't ask your help. My friends and I remove the problem, if anyone comes to Rostock. Can I, please, shit . . .
>
> MINDER 1: We cannot accept illegality.
>
> KRAUSE: Do not be afraid, you will not hear of illegality, or of problems. You want to come with me and see me shit?
>
> (CONVERSATION ENDED 12.14 HOURS.)

'You may, Tracy, be under the misapprehension that I am some sort of policeman. Not true, couldn't care less about prosecuting you. What I care about is that you called Hauptman Krause a murderer. Let me backtrack, Tracy. The last days of the regime and the Stasi were frantic, burning, shredding and ripping the key files. Everything was on file, you know that. The fires couldn't handle the weight of paper they tried to destroy, the shredders failed, and they were reduced to tearing paper with their hands – what we'd call the removal of evidence. OK, the very heavy stuff went by air to Moscow, but it was left to the lowlife guilty men to do the slog for themselves, burn and shred and tear. Hauptman Krause would have reckoned to have sanitized his past . . . That's December 'eighty-nine. Let's jump to March 'ninety-seven and yesterday. Krause is the star billing now. He's important to his new friends, and they are not, I assure you, going to chase after evidence that knocks him down. If there is evidence, if you have evidence, then we can demand that he is charged with murder, prosecuted. I can't go digging for evidence, Tracy – that'd be a hostile act against a beloved and respected ally. I have got to be given it, have to be handed it. Tracy, what is the evidence?'

Mrs Adelaide Barnes, Adie to her friends at bingo on Fridays and in the snug lounge of the Groom and Horses on Saturday nights, had two jobs through each working day of the week. She trudged home in the last light of the afternoon, and her feet were hurting. Buses cost money, and there wasn't much money in cleaning. The chiropodist cost a fortune. She walked in pain at the end of each day back to Victoria Road. Her street, little terraced homes, was off Ragstone Road, almost underneath the railway embankment. Two things were worrying Adie Barnes as she turned off by the halal butcher's on the corner, went past Memsahibs, the dress shop, the Tandoori take-away and into Victoria Road. At the afternoon house she hadn't left a note for the lady to say she'd finished the window cleaning fluid, and that bothered her. Her second worry was that she hadn't been able to speak to her Tracy last evening, and she must try again tonight. That nice Captain Christie, that her Tracy spoke of so well, had been short with her.

She saw the big police wagon half-way down Victoria Road, and the police car. She saw her neighbours, the Patels, the Ahmeds, the Devs and the Huqs, standing in the street with their children.

As fast as her bruised and swollen feet could take her, she hurried forward. The door of her house was broken and wide open, the wood panel beside the mortice lock splintered. She stopped, breathing hard, and a policeman carried two bin-liners out of her front door and put them in the wagon. She pushed past her neighbours, and through the little open gate. The policeman with the bags shouted after her.

Her hall was filled with policemen and men in suits, and there was a young woman in jeans and a sweater with a yapping spaniel on a leash. One of them in a suit came to her. It was like she'd been burgled – not that the thieves had ever been in her house, but they'd been in the Patels' next door, and she'd seen the mess when she'd gone to make Mrs Patel a good cup of tea. Adie could see into her living room: the carpets were up and some of the boards, and there were books off the shelf, and the drawers were tipped out.

'You are Mrs Barnes, Mrs Adelaide Barnes? We have a warrant issued by Slough magistrates to search this property because we have reason to believe that a possible offence under the Official Secrets Act may have been committed by your daughter. I apologize for the mess we've left you. I can provide you with a list of items taken from your daughter's room for further examination. If you find that anything not listed is missing, if you find any of your possessions to be broken, then you should put that down in writing and send it to Slough police station. I regret that I cannot offer you a fuller explanation, and I wouldn't go bothering the police because they are not authorized to make any statement on this matter.'

She stood in front of him in shock.

He shouted past her, 'Get that door fixed, made secure.'

The yapping of the spaniel filled the hall. In the kitchen, down the end of the hall, was the fridge-freezer her Tracy had bought her. On top of it, crouched, arched, was Fluff. She wished that the young woman in jeans would let go the bloody leash so that the spaniel could jump at Fluff and have its bloody eyes scratched out. Behind her she could hear the hammering of nails through plyboard and into the old wood of her front door. She started up the stairs.

A young constable was on the landing. He looked at his feet. He whispered, 'We're really sorry about this, love, all of us locals are. It's a London crowd in charge, not us. I shouldn't tell you . . . We weren't told what they were looking for – whatever, they didn't find it.' He went down the stairs heavily, noisily.

Tears welled in Adie Barnes's eyes. She was in her Tracy's room. Her Tracy's clothes were on the floor, carpet up, boards up. She heard the quiet, then the noise of the wagon engine starting. Her Tracy's music centre was in pieces, back off, gutted. Her Tracy's bookcase had been pulled apart. The books were gone. Her name was called. Her Tracy's bear – she'd had it since she was eight – was on the stripped bed and it was cut open. Mr Patel was at the door of her Tracy's room.

Mr Patel was a good neighbour. Some of the old people at bingo on a Friday, those who had been in Victoria Road for ever, said there were too many Asians, that they'd brought the road down. She'd never have that talk. She thought Mr Patel as well mannered and caring as any man she knew, and Mr Ahmed and Mr Dev and Mr Huq.

'It is disgraceful what has happened to you, and you a senior-citizen lady. You should have the representation of a solicitor, Mrs Barnes. A very good firm acted for us when we bought the shop. I think it is too late for tonight . . .'

In ten minutes, with her coat on and her best hat, ignoring the pain of her feet, Mrs Barnes set off for the offices of Greatorex, Wilkins & Protheroe in the centre of Slough. The offices might be closed, but it was for her Tracy, and she did not know what else she could do.

'Only a stenographer in Berlin, weren't you, Tracy? So you wouldn't have understood much about the intelligence business. I doubt you were alone, doubt that the people running

48

Hans Becker knew much more than you. Did they tell you, Tracy, that running him was in breach of orders? Doubt they did. The running of agents was supposed to be given to us, the professionals. You made, Tracy, the oldest mistake in the book. You went soft on an agent. You couriered to him, didn't you? Slap and tickle, was there? A tremble in the shadows? So, it was personal when you beat three shades of shit out of Hauptman Krause. Why him, Tracy? Where's the evidence? You want to talk about the murder of your lover boy, then there has to be evidence . . .'

When he heard the banging down below, he was bent over his desk, studying the papers of another grubby little case off the streets of another grubby little town that would end up in the grubby little court on Park Road. Two youths fighting over first use of a petrol pump. The client was the one who had hit straighter and harder.

It was not a loud banging, just as if someone was knocking on the high street door.

The partners were long gone, and the typists. The receptionist would have been gone an hour. He worked in the open plan area among the typists' empty desks, word processors shut down and covered up. The partners' offices were off the open area, doors locked, darkness behind the glass screens. He worked late so that Mr Wilkins could have all the papers in the morning for the pump rage and the affray, then the indecent assault, a remand job, and the possession with intent to supply.

The knocking continued, harder, more insistent. He pulled up his tie, hitched his jacket off the back of the chair and went out of the office down the stairs into reception.

She was outside the door. He let her in.

She had been crying. Her eyes were red, magnified by the lenses of her spectacles.

She asked him, straight out, was he a solicitor, and he said that he was 'nearly' a solicitor. He took her upstairs, made her a pot of tea, and she told him about her Tracy, and what the officer had said about the search and the warrant.

'Mrs Barnes, what unit is your daughter with?'

'She's a corporal. She's with the Intelligence Corps.'

And that was a bit of his history – quite a large part of Josh Mantle's history.

3

He dialled the number that Mrs Adie Barnes had given him. 'Hello.'

'Could I speak, please, to Corporal Barnes, Tracy Barnes?'

A hesitation as if, so early in the morning, her brain was grinding. 'Who is it?'

'A friend, a solicitor.'

He knew that block, knew where the call had been answered. He could hear the radios screaming behind her and the shouting, bawling, hollering.

Softly, and with a hand cupped over the mouthpiece, the voice said, 'Needs friends, locked up, in the cells, 'cos she bashed that German.' A voice change, loud and disinterested. 'Any calls for the corporal are to go to the main camp number, and you should ask for the Adjutant's office.'

He rang off.

He had showered early. He lived in a small part of a large house, the roof space converted into two rooms. There was a kitchenette area in one and a wash-basin in the other. The lavatory and shower, no bath, were down the stairs. If he used them early he didn't have to queue. He shaved carefully. It seemed important that day that he should look his best. When he had shaved, checked in the mirror that he had not cut himself, he went to his wardrobe.

There were only two suits to choose from. There was the one he wore five days a week at Greatorex, Wilkins & Protheroe and there was the darker one, which carried the story of Joshua Frederick Mantle's recent life. Worn for the job interview eighteen months before – a formality because Mr Greatorex had already offered him office-boy employment. Worn for her funeral twenty months before, a bright May day with daffodils still out in the graveyard. Worn for the appointment with the specialist and for the wedding thirty-three months before, autumn leaves scrambling against the steps of the register office and only enough witnesses behind them to make it decent. Bought and worn for the leaving party in the mess a very long time before, and he had been a washed-up casualty of the 'peace dividend'. From the wardrobe he took the dark suit and the white shirt hanging beside it. He laid them on his bed, which he had already made – it was the routine of his life, from far back, to make his bed as soon as he was out of it. Back at the wardrobe, he glanced over his ties. Two of silk, both from Libby, both for his birthday, but they remained hanging on the bar. His fingers touched two of polyester, Army Intelligence Corps and Royal Military Police, then left them. Two from the high street in Slough, neutral ties that gave away nothing of him, of his past, green and navy. He took the green one, and placed it on the shirt, beside the suit, on the bed. In a cardboard box on the floor of the wardrobe was the shoe polish, the brushes and the duster. He took the better black pair of shoes, the pair from the interview, the funeral and the wedding, the pair he didn't wear in court or at the offices of Greatorex, Wilkins & Protheroe. The routine was to clean his shoes each morning, to spit on the polish and to buff the shoes to brilliance. It did not matter to him that it was raining, that the shoes would be quickly dulled. He dressed.

He had the radio on, not for music or the weather forecast or the early news bulletins of the day but for the traffic information. It was important to him to know how long a journey would take him – another of the discipline routines that governed him. He took little comfort from the radio in the evenings, seldom used it, which was peculiar for a man who lived alone and who had reached the statistical age at which he had entered the last quarter of his life. It was as if he had rejected the outside living world that the radio would have brought him. He switched it off, then the bedside light.

He stood for a moment in the gloom.

Downstairs the lavatory flushed – perhaps the seed company's representative or the computer programmer. Both the other tenants on the floor below had offered friendship, been deflected, and the family on the ground floor. They had all tried to build a relationship, drinks at Christmas, small-talk on the stairs, and had not been rewarded. Joshua Frederick Mantle distrusted the hold of a friendship, the tie of a relationship. He had adored his mother, shot dead in Malaya. He had respected his father, Military Medal pinned on his chest by the King. He had made his commitment to the Intelligence Corps, had been transferred out compulsorily after the matter in Belize. He had buried himself in the work of Special Investigation Branch, had been made redundant in the 'downsizing' after the collapse of the Soviet Union. He had loved Libby, sick, then dead and buried. He had no desire to be hurt again.

There were few books in the sitting room, none recreational. He had hardly touched the fat volume in his hand for seven years. It was *The Manual of Military Law, Part 1*, and he scanned the section relevant to assault. Then it was *Stone's Justices' Manual*, then *Criminal Procedures and Sentencing in Magistrates' Courts*. He had a tight memory, no need for note-taking. The books went back on the shelf. He locked the door of the flat behind him.

All that he owned, all of his life, was left in the two small rooms behind the locked door. Mrs Adie Barnes, red-eyed, had told him that her Tracy was in trouble.

He went to his car, humble and old, parked on the street, and wiped the windows with a cloth. A bit of his history stirred in him.

The cell was cold. The central heating did not function. She had refused the blanket. The tray he had brought, cereal and milk, three slices of bread, jam and a mug of tea, was untouched. There was an electric fire in the cell that he used, but he had not demanded heating for her. He sat in front of her on a hard chair

53

with his overcoat across his shoulders. The ceiling light beamed down on her, as it had all night.

'I think you reckon you're being a clever little girl, Tracy. I think you reckon you can see me off. Did my arithmetic just now. It's forty-nine hours since you last slept, it's forty-something hours since you last ate. You're exhausted, famished, but you're conceited enough to believe you can see me off. Don't you believe it. I'm here for as long as it takes . . . Only me, Tracy, nobody else. The Colonel isn't going to chuck me out, nor the old fart, nor the limp dick with the dog, because I have control of you. Inside the wire they all hate you because they've had to bluster their apologies to their honoured guest, washed their hands of you. Outside the wire doesn't count. Nobody's in your corner, Tracy. You're alone. Do you hear me? Alone. So shall we stop being clever and start to be sensible? I want to know if you have evidence of murder. What is the evidence of the murder in cold blood of Hans Becker at the hand of Hauptman Dieter Krause? Is there evidence?'

Goldstein watched him. For an hour they had sat in the outer room. Raub had the ranking and it was for him to make the report to the senior official.

They waited. They were brought coffee and biscuits.

Goldstein thought he looked better, as if he had slept well in the house where the BfV always accommodated him when he came to Cologne, as if the anger at the scratch scars had slackened. They had been up since dawn and were the first appointment of the senior official's day.

There was movement, at last, at the door. It was half opened, as if a final word was exchanged.

Goldstein marvelled at the calmness of the man. He regarded Krause as predictable and boring, but the calm was incredible because his future would have been thrashed out by Raub and the senior official. If they had decided, over the last hour, that Krause was to go forward then it was Washington in two weeks and his position was confirmed. If they had decided to cut the link then he was back to Rostock, removed from the 'safe' house, the money dried up, the account closed and he was on the streets, grafting with the rest of the Stasi scum for his food and shelter.

Raub called them in.

The inner room was filled with the senior official's smoke. Goldstein coughed hard. A junior man had to go through all the exit security from the building and huddle in the winter cold in the back yard where the vehicles were parked to smoke his cigarette, then return to the building through the entry security. The official flapped his hand to clear the smoke cloud in front of his face and waved Krause to a chair. Krause settled . . . and Goldstein wondered whether he would have found old Gestapo men merely boring.

The senior official stared down at his notes, then eased the spectacles from his face. 'I am happy to hear, Doktor Krause, that your injuries are not severe. Notwithstanding, the attack raises important questions, and those questions must be answered.'

'Ask me the questions and I will answer them.'

'Is it accepted, Doktor Krause, that the BfV has invested heavily in you, money, time and resources, and in prestige?'

'As I am often told.'

'The basis of that investment was your guarantee to us that there were no matters in your past work that could be uncovered that would show criminal violation of human rights. Correct?'

'Correct.'

'I asked you at the beginning of our association for a most detailed brief on your work with the Ministerium für Staatssicherheit. I asked whether there were acts in criminal violation of human rights that might in the future be uncovered. You understand?'

'I understand.'

'Is there, in your past, an act in criminal violation of human rights that might in the future be uncovered?'

Where he stood by the door Goldstein could see little of Krause's face. He could recall what the girl had said, the

55

accusation she had made. In the last, long hour, Raub would have given the exact words to the senior official.

'There is nothing in my past that could be uncovered.'

'The woman in England made an allegation of murder. Yes?'

Goldstein fancied a smile came to Krause's face.

'The same accusation was made by a security man when I was in the medical area. They had detained us there until he arrived. I asked him, "Where is your evidence?"'

'If I order a further search of the archive material of the MfS-Zentrale at Normannen Strasse . . . ?'

'You would find nothing.'

'If you lied to me, Doktor Krause, if evidence were ever produced, there could be no protection.'

Goldstein craned forward and saw the grin play on Krause's face. Goldstein thought the man lied, and spoke the truth: the lie, that no criminal act in violation of human rights had been committed; the truth, that no evidence would be uncovered.

'There is no evidence.'

The senior official stubbed out his cigarette and came round his desk. He shook Krause's hand with warmth. 'Thank you, Doktor Krause. You have now a few days at home to prepare for Washington? We place great importance on that opportunity.'

Krause said, without emotion, 'I tell you very frankly, if people come to Rostock and make a difficulty, come to make a problem, then I do not wish to involve you. If they come to Rostock and try to make a difficulty then they will find pain, but they will not uncover evidence.'

'Good day, Doktor Krause.'

He pulled up at the gate. The fence either side of it was higher than he remembered, embellished with more shiny wire coils on the top and where the grass grew at the base. The rain had stopped and low sunshine blistered on the razor points of the wire. He left the engine running and sauntered towards the sentry. He knew what was important, knew how to behave. Josh Mantle had come through that gate for the first time as a fledgling recruit thirty-three years before, when there had been no coils of wire, when the sentries hadn't carried sidearms, hadn't draped automatic rifles across their chests, and hadn't worn bullet-proof vests. The Intelligence Corps and the Royal Military Police had been his life for twenty-seven years. He knew how sentries reacted at a gate, which was why he had worn the dark suit, the new shirt and the better shoes.

'Yes, sir?'

The sentry drifted towards him, relaxed.

'My name is Josh Mantle. I represent the legal firm of Greatorex, Wilkins & Protheroe. Corporal Tracy Barnes is being held here under close arrest, and I am instructed by her family to act on her behalf. I need . . .'

The smile of welcome had fled the sentry's face. 'Who is your appointment with, sir?'

'You are required under the terms laid out in *The Manual of Military Law, Part 1* – I can quote you the page – to give me immediate access to my client. That's what I need.'

'I asked, who's your appointment with, sir?'

'When I come to see a client, I don't need an appointment with anyone. I'm not a dentist's patient.'

'You can't just drive in here without an appointment. I am not authorized to let anyone—'

A bread-delivery van had stopped behind his car, and another car behind that. Two cars and a Land Rover were waiting to leave.

'What you are authorized or not authorized to do, soldier, is quite irrelevant to me. Just get on with the process of providing the access to which I am entitled.'

The sentry backed away. Josh Mantle had known he would. The sentry would pass it to his sergeant in the brick fortress block-house beside the gate. The sergeant would see a man in a dark suit, a new shirt and good shoes, and he would pass responsibility up the chain. Five cars now waited behind the delivery van, and three more behind the Land Rover. There was a beep. Mantle walked casually back to his car and rested his buttocks

57

on the bonnet. Through the window of the block-house he saw the sentry speaking to his sergeant, and gesturing towards him. A little symphony of horns came from two more cars and from the Land Rover. Faces jutted out of vehicle windows, annoyed, impatient. The sergeant spoke on a telephone, as Mantle had known he would. The symphony soon reached its crescendo. The sentry ran back from the block-house.

'You've got to wait, and move your car, sir.'

Josh knew the game. Into his car, into reverse, swerving past the delivery van. Across the main road. Onto the grass verge opposite the camp gate. The barrier came up and the cars surged in and out.

He sat again on the bonnet in the sunshine. A hundred yards past the barrier, down the road inside the camp, was the guard-house, graced with a clean lick of paint, which was usual for late winter, where Mrs Adie Barnes's daughter would be. The barrier was down.

The sentry shouted across the main road, 'You can't park there, sir.'

'I require immediate access to my client.'

'That's a restricted area. No parking there.'

'Immediate access. If you haven't the authority get someone who has. Move it, soldier. Oh, what's your name? So I can report you for obstruction.'

It was not pretty, not right for a civilian to take on officer status, but he had given his promise to Mrs Adie Barnes. The sentry doubled back to the block-house, to report, to have his sergeant telephone again. It was a few minutes after nine o'clock: the Adjutant would be concentrating on his coffee, and the Colonel would be out on an inspection round. None of the fat cats would know where to find *The Manual of Military Law, Part 1*. They would be like disturbed ants.

'Tell you what I'm thinking now, Tracy, I'm thinking you do not have evidence. I'm a logical man, Tracy, and I've given you every opportunity to provide me with that evidence. You've refused, so logic says to me that the evidence does not exist. My opinion, when you were in Berlin, when the agent was lost, it was discussed in front of you – you don't make waves, do you? Nobody notices you – it was talked about, and some loudmouth used the name of Krause, counter-espionage in Rostock. You joined the circle. The agent was missing, therefore he had been caught, no word was heard of him, therefore he had been killed. Who killed him? Try counter-espionage. Who was responsible? Try the man in charge of counter-espionage at the nearest regional centre. Krause. Do you think I don't have better things to do? For fuck's sake, Tracy Barnes, let's get this bloody waste of time over.'

'Where is it, Major?'

Johnson snapped, 'It's in RUSSIAN MILITARY/ARMOUR/STA-TISTICS. It's where it always is.'

'Yes, Major, but where's that?'

She stood in his doorway. He couldn't even remember her name. He shouted past her, 'Ben, I need RUSSIAN MILITARY/ ARMOUR/STATISTICS – show the corporal where it is.'

The call came back, through two open doors, across the cubbyhole space. 'Sorry, Perry. Wouldn't know where to start. I've been looking half an hour for my Voronezh notes. Sorry.'

Johnson said, spiteful, 'You'll just have to look for them, Corporal. Look a bit harder.'

The telephone was ringing . . . Barnes could have found RUS-SIAN MILITARY/ARMOUR/STATISTICS, she would have laid her hands on the Voronezh notes, and made his coffee and known how much milk she should add, and picked up the bloody telephone and not let it ring.

Johnson said, bitter, 'If you cannot find the files we need then would you, please, Corporal, answer the telephone?'

They did not know the filing system she used. God, they were blind without her. The corporal was back at the door, the call was for him. She should transfer it to his extension. What was his extension number? But there wasn't an extension number written on his telephone, new security measures. What was his bloody number? Too flustered to remember it. He pushed past the corporal and into the cubbyhole space. He thought, he was nearly certain, that Christie's bloody dog snarled at him and showed its bloody teeth. The dog had its jaws close to the door of the wall safe. She should have been there, should have been handing him the telephone and rolling her eyes to the edge of impertinence. The corporal said it was the Colonel who wanted him. She'd have pulled a damn cheeky face.

'Yes, sir, good morning, sir . . . At the gate? . . . A solicitor? Christ . . . Quoting what? . . . *Manual of Military Law*? I wouldn't have the faintest idea where there's one. Yes, liaise with Mr Perkins . . . Straight away, sir . . .'

There had been 97,000 full-time officers working for the Staatssicherheitsdienst at the Zentrale on Normannen Strasse in Berlin and at the fifteen Bezirksverwaltungen across the former German Democratic Republic. What they learned from their informers, their surveillance, their telephone taps, the confessions made in their special cells, they wrote down. What they wrote down, they filed. What they filed was sent to the Archive at the Zentrale.

He had flown from Cologne. Julius Goldstein had been driven east through Berlin to Normannen Strasse. He was met at the heavy barred doors of the Archive, his visit cleared ahead by telephone from the senior official of the BfV. He had priority status.

It was said that, over the forty-five-year life-span of the old regime, the files collected, if put spine to spine, would stretch over a distance of 180 kilometres. The betrayal of family, friend and work colleague by the 175,000 informers listed the names, habits, thoughts and actions of six million of the GDR's population. There were card-index cross-references by the million, photographs by the million, recordings from microphones and telephone intercepts on magnetic tape measured in metres by the million. The several levels of the Archive floors in the subterranean chambers were shored up with coal-pit timbers to take the weight of the files. The Minister for State Security had not trusted the modern invention of the computer, had believed it possible for power cuts to wipe an electronic archive. Yellowed low-quality paper filled the files, tired and thin, and on the paper were the reports, typed through tired, thin, low-quality ribbons.

He gave the name of Hauptman Dieter Krause, the service number, and date of entry into the MfS. He was offered the help of three assistants. When Krause had first come to them, had first arrived in Cologne, the files had been searched. He thought his answer, when he telephoned Raub that evening, would be the same answer as it had been then.

The Chancellor of reunified Germany had said the files gave off a 'nauseous smell from which nothing good can be gained'. There were, more often now, cries for them to be closed and destroyed. More frequently now, they were accused of 'destroying reputations, wrecking marriages, breaking friendships, ruining careers'. Former President von Weizsacker accused the German media of 'smearing' politicians with the rumour that they figured in the files. The files were about guilt. Guilt was history. Guilt ran with the history of the state. Guilt could not co-exist with the rebuilding of 'greater' Germany. The little people who figured in the files, the betrayers and the deceivers, who had sold out to the regime's police, shouted, more raucously now, for the files to be closed. Only the little people were named on the tired, thin, low-quality sheets of paper. The files on the big people were long gone or destroyed. The big people's files had been crated and shipped by air to Moscow in the last days, or they had been burned, shredded and pulped in the last hours.

'The loss of the agent is the past, Tracy. The attack on Hauptman Krause is the present, Tracy. Marry the past and the present, and the offspring of the union will be the future, Tracy. I am only concerned with the future. But, to make a future that interests me, I must have evidence . . .'

He heard the light knock. The cell door opened.

'What do you want?'

'We need to speak,' Johnson said.

Perkins stood, rocking with exhaustion, and left her hunched on the bed, her knees against her chest, her arms around her knees.

'What I'm telling you, you shift that motor.' The sergeant had come from the block-house and shouted across the road.

'What I am telling you, Sergeant, I can be an impatient man.'

'It's a secure area. Shift that motor – and now.'

'I am happy for you to inspect my driving licence, which will show you that I am not from the Falls Road, and for you to inspect my car, which will show you it is not loaded with mortar tubes or explosives. You weren't listening, Sergeant, I was speaking about my impatience.'

'I'll have you done for trespass.'

Josh Mantle gave him a sweet smile. 'Know the law, Sergeant? You establish legal ownership of this road verge, have a meeting with the council's highways committee, get a judge in chambers, win an eviction order, employ bailiffs . . . How long will that take, Sergeant? Ten minutes or two months? Get back on the phone.'

The sergeant hesitated. The sentry watched his sergeant. Face was at stake, and dignity.

Josh sat on the bonnet, took his mobile from his pocket and held it up. 'When you telephone tell them I'm an impatient man. Tell them that in twenty minutes from now, unless I am granted access to my client as the law demands, I will start to ring the yellowest of the tabloids, some real shit-stirring MPs and the civil-liberties crowd. Tell them it'll be a proper old circus down here.'

He held up the mobile and pointed to his watch.

He watched the sergeant trudge back to the blockhouse.

Perkins yawned.

He walked out of the guardhouse and into the sunshine. He blinked. He stepped over the sign that forbade walking on the grass, and went to the middle of the road leading to the gate. Cars went by him both ways. He gazed through the gate at the man who sat easily on the bonnet of a car.

'That's him,' Johnson said. 'That's the cause of the headache. The Colonel wants to know what you—'

'He's worn quite well, considering everything.'

'—what you suggest should be done. The popular press, to the Colonel, is a definition of a nightmare. Throw in maverick MPs and the civil liberties rent-a-mob and he could have a coronary . . . Do you know him?'

He stood beside Johnson and held his hand over his eyes as if to shade them from the sun.

'That's Mantle, Joshua Frederick. Yes, I once took a look at him. Started here as a clerk, as I remember – I've a good recall on files – went to Aden in the "gollie"-bashing days, then here again, then Osnabruck. Keen, his file said, anxious to please. He was a staff sergeant in 'eighty-two, when it all went wrong for him. Were the Guatemalans going to invade Belize? was the burning question of the hour. I Corps sent a captain and Mantle. It was a pressure situation. There was a difficulty, people were squeamish . . . Did they want the Guat Army turning up unannounced for breakfast in Belize City, or did they want advance notice, the artillery sited and the Harriers armed up? The squeamish people won the day and shouted for a court-martial. If Mantle had testified against his superior then the officer was for the high jump, but he was leaned on, held his tongue. The deal was that the officer retired, doing rather well now and running a charity, and Mantle was transferred, well balanced with an equally weighted chip on each shoulder, to the Military Police. The Service was involved because of the political implications, but I was in the shadows, knowing him when he didn't know me, the way I like it. I saw him again, a few years later, Tidworth Camp. He'd been given a commission. He was a cuckoo in the mess, twenty years older than the others of his rank. There'd been a dirty little business in the camp, some missing funds but a minimal sum, and the consensus opinion

63

was that it should have been papered over, but he went after a rather popular officer, and the officer had to resign. He was ostracized after that, just ignored. When the cuts started I fancy half of the mess would have written in suggesting he was top target for the heave. I meet that sort of man from time to time, obsessed with legality, a hatred of anything that smacks of privilege, looking to champion the disadvantaged, bleeding the creed of principle on his sleeve. A couple of years back I was talking with a chap from the police who knew of him, said he'd been married and was working with delinquents, that his wife had died, that he'd dropped out, gone derelict. Obviously someone's given him another chance, a last chance. I'd say he's obstinate, awkward, bloody-minded . . .'

'What are you going to do about him?'

Perkins turned away and began to walk back to the guardhouse. 'I'm going to send him home, and when he goes he can give little Tracy a lift.'

Perry Johnson did not understand. He hurried to catch Perkins. 'Are you quite sure, Mr Perkins, you have the authority?'

'Try me.'

Perkins had the barred door unlocked, then the cell door. He told her to come with him, even asked her if she needed his arm to lean on. He took from the table the plastic bag with her watch, belt, tie and shoelaces. He instructed the sergeant to lace her shoes.

She walked shakily beside him along the path towards the block for junior ranks (female), but she never took his arm.

It was Perkins who stopped half-way up the stairs, a wry little smile on his face, and leaned against the wall, drew breath. She gave him her glance, the roll of her eyebrows, as she would have done, Johnson thought, to himself or Christie in her cubbyhole.

The door of her room was sealed with adhesive tape. Perkins ripped it off.

The room was as they had left it, wrecked. In the panic moments after the attack, in the heat of an investigation, it had seemed quite acceptable for Perry Johnson and Ben Christie to do this. She glanced at Johnson, who died under her eyes. Perkins had reached up to lift down her bag from the top of the wardrobe.

She knelt on the floor and moved among her clothes. Each of her own garments that she picked up she folded carefully before placing it in the bag. Her blouses, her skirts, her jeans, her underwear, the bra that Johnson had held up to the light went into her bag, and the photographs of the cat and the elderly lady and the broken pieces of the frames.

She zipped the bag shut.

She started on her uniform items, tunic, blouses and heavy brown shoes. Perry Johnson bent to pick up a skirt to help her, and she snatched it from him. He recoiled as if in fear of a cornered cat.

She put the uniform items back into the drawers, and the drawers back into the chest.

Perkins carried her bag out of the block.

It was midday, the start of the lunch break at Templer, and too many bastards, with not enough to do, watched Perkins carry her bag to the gate.

Perkins gestured for the sentry to raise the barrier.

Perkins called across the road, 'You wanted access to your client. She's all yours.'

Mantle came off the bonnet of his vehicle, pocketed his mobile. Johnson saw the rank dislike on his face and the wide smile at Perkins's mouth.

Perkins turned to her. 'Please listen, Tracy, carefully. Pursue this matter and you will very quickly be out of your depth. If you're out of your depth, you will sink. Remember that the German BfV regard Hauptman Krause as a jewel, and that he would see you as a threat. A great deal is at stake for both the BfV and Krause. There is always a serious risk that a person who represents a threat, when high stakes are played for, will meet with an "accident". Accidents, Tracy, hurt. My warning is meant kindly. You should forget the past, you should be sensible. It would all have been different if you'd had evidence . . .'

*   *   *

He kept to the speed limit, cruised in the middle lane of the motorway.

He'd thought she might have just flaked out, slept, babbled her story, or just thanked him. But she sat beside him with her eyes open and murmured a song. He could not make out the words – too much noise from the cars, vans and lorries they passed and which went by them – but the tune was vaguely familiar.

That she hadn't spoken annoyed him like grit in a walking boot, a growing pain.

'I make it forty-seven minutes we've been going, forty-one miles. A word out of you would be pleasant.'

'What sort of word?' she challenged.

'Well, for a start, you could express a little bit of gratitude.'

She thought he was silly, pompous. She turned her head to him, quite slowly, a sharp light in her eyes. 'Don't think it was you who got me out. You were just convenient. You saved them a train fare.'

'That's not called for.'

Against the tiredness there was a crack of mischief at her mouth. She reached out. He thought it was going to be her gesture of gratitude, that she was going to rest her hand on his where he gripped the wheel. The tips of her fingers, small, brushed the hair at the back of his hand. She had hold of the wheel with a grin on her face. She didn't look into the mirror in front of her, or the mirror beside her.

She wrenched the wheel, swerving the car from the middle lane into the slow lane, from the slow lane into the slip road. There was a scream of brakes behind him, then the blast of a horn . . .

'For God's sake!'

'I'm hungry,' she said.

They were off the motorway. His hands shook on the wheel. 'That was idiotic!'

'I'm half starved,' she said.

They found the café where lorries were parked up outside.

She told him what she wanted to eat, took her bag from the car boot and carried it into the lavatories. She was so small, so slight, and the uniform she wore was crumpled, creased. He ordered at the counter.

He carried the tray to an empty table.

A bread roll, a small piece of curled cheese and a plastic beaker of thin orange juice, squeezed onto the tray, for himself. For her there was a plate of chips, double portion, a king-size hamburger with oozing dressing and a large Pepsi – which was what she'd demanded.

She came out of the lavatory. She had changed into jeans and a sweater. Her uniform blouse, skirt and battle green pullover were stuffed into the top of the bag.

She gulped at the food.

'Are you going to tell me?'

She had the hamburger in both hands, and the ketchup ran red on her fingers. 'Where were you in 'eighty-eight?'

He thought she ate quite disgustingly. 'That year I was a captain in the Special Investigation Branch of the RMP – I'd transferred, six years before, out of I Corps.'

'Thought you were a solicitor.'

He said, 'I'm a solicitor's clerk, qualifying to be a legal executive. While your mouth's full, I might just tell you that your mother asked me to come. She's had her home turned over by Special Branch . . . because of you.'

He felt old, boring, and he hoped he had wounded her. She snatched again at the hamburger.

'Then you know about I Corps?'

'I was in I Corps for nearly twenty years, before the transfer.'

She seemed to ponder for a moment, mouth moving and throat heaving as she swallowed, as if she needed to decide whether he was worth talking to. Then . . .

'In 'eighty-eight, I was the junior stenographer, tea-maker, errand-runner in the I Corps section in Berlin. They were all analysts and debriefers, not couriers. They weren't supposed to run agents. They all looked like soldiers, like police look like police. One of the staff sergeants was over the other side of the Wall, had lost his tail for once, and there was a contact, approached on the street, no warning. He had time to fix the next meeting, then he had to bug out because the tail had found him again. It was kicked round all day. Then some genius came up with the idea of me going over and doing the meeting. Said that I wouldn't be noticed, didn't look like a soldier. They were all crapping themselves the first time, but it went fine. It got to be normal, me going over and taking stuff and bringing stuff back. Our "Sunray" couldn't believe his luck – he'd got the best agent going that any commanding officer of I Corps in Berlin had had in years, used to get his head patted. He was supposed to have handed the running of any agent over to the spooks. Sunray said we were keeping him for us, not for any other bugger to get the credit . . . Come on.'

She smeared up the last of the sauce with the last of the chips, hitched up her bag and he followed her back to the car.

He drove.

'He was in East Berlin – I went over once a month with cameras, equipment, whatever the agent needed for what he was tasked at. I brought back the films, the reports, in my knickers, in my bra. The risks were worse each time because Sunray pushed him harder each time. Each job was jammier than the last, and that was the way Sunray kept getting his head patted. They'd set me up with a cover as a student and got me permission to use the Library at the university over there, the Humboldt . . . Seemed to go like clockwork . . . I just did the easy bit. I went over and dumped the stuff and picked up the stuff and came back through the checkpoint. He was the one that took the risks, and he just used to laugh about it, more worried about me than himself. He was super, he was really brilliant . . .'

Mantle drove steadily. There were times when she stopped, when she stared ahead and held her arms tight around her chest, and when she stopped he did not prompt her. It had been a bit of his history, a long time back, seeing the grey concrete of the prefabricated Wall, and the watch-towers and the dogs and the guards who carried the automatic rifles. He had been to West Berlin but never across to the old East. He had stood on the viewing platforms and looked over the Wall and across the death strip. Talking quietly, she summoned up for him that part of his history.

'Hans Becker . . . twenty-one years old, I was a year older. He didn't do it for money, or out of politics. He did it because it was a buzz, and he used to laugh about it . . . Christ, and he used to make me laugh. He was just wonderful to be with . . . We would be over there in that dump country, full of bloody police and bloody Soviets – I'm not good with words – and we used to laugh. He knew what would happen to him if he was caught, and each time Sunray stacked the odds a bit higher against him and he never backed off. I used to see the sort of guys that the other girls in Brigade went with, fat guts and ignorant and boozy, and I thought I was so bloody lucky to be with Hansie . . . I loved him.'

They were off the motorway. He had caught the first sign for Slough. She had not had to tell him that she had loved Hansie Becker. When she had used the word, she had looked into his face and grinned, as if she reckoned he was too old to know about love. Love was the part of Josh's history that hurt the worst.

'It was a rubbish little thing they sent him on the last time . . . You know what? Twenty months later, when the Wall had come down, they'd have had it for bloody free. But, they didn't know, did they? Didn't know the Wall was coming down . . . All those brains at work, all the clever little bastards, didn't know. There was a Soviet missile base at Wustrow, west of Rostock. Hansie had always been given jobs before that were close to Berlin, where he knew. He hadn't been to Rostock, didn't even know where this place was. It was the first time he was anxious and he tried to hide it, but I could see that it worried him. The MiG-29s used to fly from Ribnitz-Damgarten at night for exercises with the missile, radar, crews at Wustrow.

Sunray said that if Hansie could get close into the base he could monitor the telemetry of their radar systems. I took him the gear to do it with. It was rubbish and Hansie was caught for nothing. He was killed for nothing . . .'

She waved and he took a left. He saw the Asian shops and businesses that lined the streets and the small homes of old brick. He remembered the photographs he had pored over, with the magnifying glass, of Soviet bases, missiles, aircraft, radar dishes. Because of his history, because he understood, he could imagine the pressure exercised on the agent, the youngster, driving him towards hazard.

'The Wustrow base was almost an island – a sort of cause-way linked it with the mainland. North was the Baltic, south was a big bit of sea separating it from the land. For the equip-ment to register the detail he had to be on the peninsula where the base was. I don't know, I suppose a sentry saw him. There was all hell, flares, shooting. He'd got this dinghy, sort of thing kids use on our beaches, but he was cut off from it. He must have crossed the peninsula, right through the base. He tried to swim for it, to the mainland. He was shot in the water, wounded. He was brought to this village on the mainland, Rerik, where they killed him.'

He wondered if she had told anyone before. They turned again, and she pointed up the street.

'The man who killed my Hansie was the counter-espionage officer from the Stasi in Rostock, Dieter Krause.'

He stopped the car. A panel of plyboard was nailed to the front door.

'Two days ago they brought Dieter Krause to Templer, paraded him. Our lot were on their bloody knees to him, treated him like he was a friend. He was all swank and arrogant and laughing until I thumped him. I kicked him in the balls for Hansie.'

Josh said, 'You should let it go, let time bury it.'

The scorn played across her face. 'It was murder. Murder is murder. Or do you compromise?'

Josh dropped his head. 'I try to be sensible. You were there, weren't you? Of course you were there. Your boy was stressed up and you'd gone along for the ride to hold his hand. Not authorized, was it? Certainly a disciplinary offence, maybe court-martial, but you were there.'

She had reached into the back of his car and lifted the bag onto her lap.

'Did you actually see the killing?'

'No.'

'You saw a part of it, not the end of it?'

'Yes.'

Josh said, 'You didn't see the killing. What you know is second hand, conjecture. Christ, I admire your guts. Without eye-witnesses, affidavits, evidence you can't touch him. Forget it.'

She spat, 'You're pitiful.'

'Understand power? Power runs like a big river. Go into that river and you drown. My best advice, let the dead sleep. If he was brought to Templer then he's an asset. If he's an asset then he's protected. God, don't you understand?'

The scorn on her face was like a blow. She was out of the car.

She unlocked the front door. He heard her call for her mother. He was drawn after her.

He stood in the doorway. She hugged her mother and the cat was against her legs. She had humiliated him. Compromise was another part of Josh Mantle's history.

She went up the stairs and he saw where the carpet had been prised up and tacked back badly onto the steps. Adie Barnes shook his hand, grasping it in her small calloused fist. She let go to take a purse from her handbag.

'There's no charge,' Josh said. 'Let's say I enjoyed a ride out in the country. She's a lovely girl, Mrs Barnes.'

Adie Barnes busied herself in the kitchen.

He stood, awkward, and feeling like an intruder in the small front room. He thought she must have skipped work that day and laboured to remake her home. Someone must have been in to help her refit the units and shelves to the walls. The room was a shrine in photographs of her daughter.

'It's everything to her. They'll take her back? It'll be all right?'

He took the cup and saucer, and the plate with the cake. He wanted to be gentle. 'She'll need your patience and a long rest. Most of all she's going to need love.'

He drank the tea and ate the cake. He heard the footsteps fast on the stairs, the opening and closing of the door and the clatter of the little front gate. The photographs were of Tracy Barnes as a recruit, sitting with the team at Brigade in Berlin, at Templer, in uniform, smiling, and crouched with a black dog. Josh hadn't the courage for honesty.

He let himself out.

He drove away. He felt no achievement, no pleasure.

It was only a few minutes' drive from the street to the car park close to the offices of Greatorex, Wilkins & Protheroe.

She was in a telephone box. There was a car down the road, two men in the car, one smoking and one talking into a mobile telephone. He saw the lustre of her hair, caught by a street lamp. He didn't stop and shout at her, 'Go home, stay there, he's an asset and protected. Go home or you can be hurt. Forget it ever happened.' He was used to marching into people's lives and then walking away from them.

A bad taste of failure in his mouth, Julius Goldstein telephoned Raub. The file of Hauptman Dieter Krause showed no evidence of criminal activity in human rights. He reported, also, that pages of the file concerned with Hauptman Krause's relationship with the Soviet officer, Major Pyotr Rykov, were not present, and a part of the separate file dealing with the military base at Wustrow. He told Raub that it was not possible from the files to find evidence of murder. He was authorized to return to Cologne on the late flight.

The most senior of the researchers escorted him from the basements. 'You should not take it personally. If you wanted to know which teacher in a school in Saxony-Anhalt informed on

72

his colleagues, then I could find you the answer. Which environment activist was beaten up because his wife betrayed him, which student reported on his colleagues, which poet infiltrated an arts group. I can tell you, names and dates and contact officers. Here, there is only the chaff of human misery, and that does not reach to the level of murder. They were busy in those last days, sanitizing the files, sterilizing the past. That is why, today, they swagger on the streets, certain of their safety. From what you looked for, from what is missing, I can tell you that the link between Hauptman Krause and Major Pyotr Rykov was sensitive in this matter of murder. If there was not guilt then the files would not have been cleansed. Is it important to you, this question of guilt?'

He stepped into the chilly floodlit yard. Julius Goldstein said, 'The possibility of guilt is important because it can obstruct an advantage that we seek. My thanks to you, goodnight. The advantage is in the man, Rykov.'

'Is that him?'

'That's our boy.'

The Briton and the American stood against the wall, a little apart from the guests in the salon where the Americans always entertained.

'In the shadow of his man.'

'I get the impression that the big shot doesn't go to the toilet without the say-so of Rykov.' The eyes of the Briton watered from the foul-smelling cigarettes around them. His diplomatic accreditation was for a second secretary (consular).

'Use the soft tissue, imported, or the local ass scratcher – need a man with a sharp clear mind for the big decisions.' The American, on the list submitted to the foreign ministry, was a cultural attaché.

From where they stood, with soft drinks, they could see the line of guests filtering into the salon, past the handshakes of the ambassador and the deputy chief of mission. The minister, whose chest flashed ribbons, was in conversation with the deputy chief. The ambassador welcomed the short stocky Russian with the colonel's insignia on his shoulders and the chest free of decoration colours. A heavy-built woman stepped forward hesitantly to meet the ambassador.

'And brought his lovely wife with him.'

'Our Irina – not what you'd call an ocean racer.'

'More of a bulk carrier, Brad.'

'Heh, look at that, David. Enjoy that.'

The minister had moved on to the centre of the salon, couldn't have seen where he was headed. The Colonel had left his wife and was powering to him. The minister had blundered, stormy night and no navigation, into what Brad called the 'recons'. They'd had eight different names in seven years, so Brad always won a laugh out of David with his name for the reconstructed KGB people. Eyes sparking, a stand-off, mutual hostility – military facing up to the 'recons'. The Colonel had seen the opportunity of confrontation and come fast to his man.

'You think they might actually fight, bare fist?'

'I'm out of Montana, they used to have a betting game there. Put colours, for identification, on the back of a couple of rats which hadn't been fed in several days, drop the rats in a sack and knot the top, tight. Bet on the winner.'

'The loser's dead?'

'One rat lives. Where'd you put your money?'

Without finesse, Rykov had taken the arm of his minister and propelled him round like it was a parade-ground.

'My paint's going on Rykov's back.'

'Be a hard fight in the sack, he has to be clever and lucky. You rate him lucky enough – clever enough?'

'I'm told he is. He wears a good face, a strong face.'

'But you can't see into the face. The way of this damn place, you never see behind the face of the man who matters . . .'

In the crowded room, the Briton and the American had eyes only for Colonel Pyotr Rykov. For the last four months, each, in his own way, through his own unshared channels, had sought to explain the man, unmask the character and analyse

74

the influence. Both had failed. They were two veterans, middle-aged, heavy with experience; both had exploited the resources available to them to satisfy the hunger at Langley and Vauxhall Bridge Cross for hard information on the mind of Colonel Pyotr Rykov; both acknowledged that failure.

'This guy the Germans are hawking . . .'

Droll. 'Don't, Brad, intrude on private grief.'

Chuckling. 'Heh, is it right that a feisty little cat scratched his face? That's pretty un-British manners.'

'When's he going across to your lot?'

'A couple of weeks. The guest list's the best and the brightest. They're screaming for a profile on Rykov. He has undivided attention.'

They watched the Colonel. He was always a pace behind his minister, and they saw his lips move as if murmuring guidance. He was there for thirty-five minutes, the barest decency, before he was gone, slipping away with his minister and his wife, back into the frozen darkness of Moscow's night.

4

It had been a late rail connection to the last ferry boat of the evening.

A squall had whipped off the harbour waters. The wind, even behind the high sea walls of packed rocks, had the strength to shake the pleasure boats, the tugs and the few fishing boats on their moorings, and to roll the ferry before the hawser ropes had been cast off.

Under scudding cloud, it ploughed through the waves, made a direct course across the Channel and towards the coast of Europe. It was the territory of the long-haul lorry drivers and the few passengers prepared to sacrifice comfort and time in the interest of economy.

She stood alone at the forward rail of the ferry boat, as far forward as passengers were permitted to be.

She did not seek the company of the lorry drivers in their lounge or other passengers, who clustered round the gaming table, the fruit machines and the cafeteria's counter. She was unnoticed and unwatched. The night ferry was, for her, the most suitable way to travel from Britain to the Continent, the passport check would be the briefest. The spray, as the prow of the ferry ducked into the waves, spattered her hair and her face, her shoulders and her body. The tang smell of it was on her. She shouted her anthem to the night wind. It was a song of parting, waiting and death.

And she did not think of them, the men who had intruded into that aloneness and privacy in the last hours, days and weeks. If she had . . . Major Perry Johnson sat solitary in a corner of the mess, isolated, near to that place on the carpet where the drink

76

stain had dried out. He was the man whose corporal had soured an excellent occasion. He was shunned. He was not called to the bar by Captain Dawson, or by Major Donoghue, and in the morning he would try again to attempt the impossible and discover the pattern of Tracy Barnes's filing system. That afternoon, aggressive spite, he had told Ben Christie to keep the bloody dog out of G/9, and Christie had called him a 'vindictive old bastard' and applied for a transfer, immediate. He nursed his drink, he reflected that his world had fallen . . . but she had not thought of him.

The salt of the sea spray was on her lips and in her mouth . . . Albert Perkins fought his tiredness. He sat at a plain table in the archive of Defence Intelligence. The material, too old to have been transferred to computer disk, was paper, bulging from a cardboard box, old sheets of typed and handwritten notes that were the bones, not the flesh, of an incident in the past that had a resonance of the present and might affect the future. He was brought coffee, a fresh mug every fifteen minutes. Without it, he would have slumped over the table.

The wind and the spray slicked the hair on her scalp. She did not feel the cold, did not shiver . . . Josh Mantle was by himself in the open area on the first floor. There had been a sharp note waiting for him from the partner, Mr Wilkins. Where had he been? Who was his client? Why had he not cleared his absence with Mr Greatorex? He worked on the cases that Mr Protheroe would be handling before the magistrates the next morning. He had returned to the grind of his daily life. He would be late away from his desk – it would be the small hours before he returned to his high flat near to the London road.

She did not try to wipe the water from her face or to keep the gale wind from her hair. The lights were ahead of her, winking and rolling with the motion of the ferry.

She came off the boat. She bought, from the one shop open in the middle of the night at the harbour terminal, a big gift box of Belgian chocolates and asked for them to be wrapped in fancy paper. She had her rucksack on her back and carried her gift to the waiting train. She huddled in the corner of an empty carriage and before the train pulled out she was asleep, at peace.

'Another hundred and ten pounds in the kitty, but earned with blood and sweat, eh, Josh?'

'I was surprised, Mr Protheroe, that he was given bail.'

'Sick mother. I expect I laid it on rather heavily, as if the ambulance siren had already started up and she was on her way to intensive care. I tell you, Josh, if my Miriam ever makes the bench then a yob like that will need more than a sick mother to keep him out of the cells. Well, I look upon that revolting little creature as an investment for the future, lorryloads of legal aid at fifty-five pounds an hour where that one's going.'

Josh Mantle, back in the familiar suit, the old shirt and the poorer shoes, walked across the hallway of the court with the partner.

'And getting those louts bound over to keep the peace – some hope – was a second triumph for humanity, eh, Josh?'

'There are serious tensions in the Sikh and Muslim communities. The youths are bound to reflect those tensions in their homes.'

'You have a sympathetic eye, Josh. You know, Mr Greatorex did a run-through, last week, of the firm's legal-aid earnings, criminal cases. Bit over a year you've been with us? Legal aid's up for the firm more than twenty per cent. You've a good way in the police cells, drumming up business. Heh, God, you must need a damn good scrub when you get home at night, some of the scum you meet. I'm not complaining . . . but very sympathetic.'

'As long as you're not complaining, Mr Protheroe.' Most nights he was on call, or down at the police station at Slough beside the court, to argue for bail, to sit in on the interviews, to take statements from inarticulate and hostile youths. 'What about this afternoon?'

'There's a problem, Josh. The bottle-slashing, yes? It's a remand in custody, no question of letting him out. I'd rather

78

thought it was for this morning, up and down. The problem is, I'm on the golf course this afternoon, a charity job, good cause. Look after it, will you, Josh? We're not arguing with a remand. I'm going to dash.' He was away, hurrying up the street.

She must have seen him with Mr Protheroe, and she must have waited, diffident.

'Afternoon, Mrs Barnes.'

'They told me you'd be here – at your work they said you would.'

'How can I help, Mrs Barnes?'

'It's my Tracy . . .'

She was breathing hard. He wondered how far she had walked to come to the court. There were bag lines at her eyes, as if she had been crying. She seemed to him so tired and so frail.

'Hold it there, Mrs Barnes. Let's go and find somewhere we can sit down.'

He took her arm, led her into a deserted court-room and sat her on the polished bench where the public could sit when the court was in session. He saw the fear on her face. He touched her hand. 'Now, Mrs Barnes, what about Tracy?'

'She's gone.'

'I'm sorry, Mrs Barnes, where has she gone?' He was trying to concentrate, trying to focus, and she was difficult to hear even in the hush of the empty courtroom. 'Where has she gone?'

From her handbag she took a small piece of paper. It had been crumpled, squashed in a fist and discarded as rubbish, then carefully smoothed out. 'God forbid, I'd ever spy on her. I went to bed early. I'd got her back – you'd brought her back. I suppose it was the relief. Slept solid. I woke this morning, to go to work. I made my usual cup of tea and one for her. She wasn't there, her bed wasn't slept in. It was on the floor, like it'd been dropped.'

She passed him the slip of paper. He did not have to be a solicitor's clerk, or a former staff sergeant in I Corps, or a one-time captain in the Royal Military Police to register what was on the paper. There were columns of figures, written precisely. He

79

read them as arrival and departure times. Above the figures was the single word 'Victoria' and below them 'Bahnhof Zoo'.

'What's it mean, Mr Mantle?'

It meant that she had kicked him in the teeth. It meant that she had taken the boat train from Victoria to Folkestone or Dover, then a ferry, then a train across Europe to the station in Berlin for trans-European trains.

'She's gone to Berlin.'

'Why?'

'It's about what's happened to her.'

'Please, Mr Mantle, because I'm frightened for her.'

'I really don't see what I can do.'

'I don't suppose there is anything.'

'You want me to find her, bring her home . . . I've a very busy workload at the moment, Mrs Barnes.'

She was into her handbag. The purse of worn leather was out of it. Her fingers, thin, dried out, took the roll of banknotes from the purse and unfolded them. She held them out for him to take. There would have been a biscuit tin under the bed, or at the back of a drawer, or under the spare blankets in a cupboard. The money would have been her savings. A few coins and the odd banknote would have been put by each week and each month . . . Her voice shouted in scorn at him, 'It was murder. Murder is murder. Or do you compromise' . . . She would have saved the money over many years. He put his hand over hers, pushed it back towards the purse.

She said, accusingly, 'What's wrong with my money? Good enough, isn't it?'

'It won't be necessary.'

Tracy Barnes walked out of the Bahnhof Zoo. It was seven years since she had been in Berlin. There were men doing the hard stuff outside the station, small swarthy men against the wall of the station, protected by their dogs. Seven years ago there had been men here doing hard drugs. She heard the music against the traffic hum. She had always liked the music on the plaza by the ruined Nikolaikirche. She carried the wrapped gift and idled towards the church, which had been firebombed more than half a century before and was kept as a monument to war's ravage. She watched the band. They might have been from Peru, or perhaps from Costa Rica.

She was another youngster come to the city of history. She was unnoticed. She was small and over-whelmed by her rucksack and unremarkable, just another kid who had travelled to the heartbeat, the core, the junction point of Europe.

She walked boldly towards the east, a fine strong stride, as if she were not intimidated by the city, as if she were not cowed by the history of Berlin. Past the funfair, where she remembered it. Through the Tiergarten, the trees bared by winter and snow powdered on the ground. She came to the Brandenburger Tor. At the great gate of grey-brown stone old history had been renovated and new history had been destroyed. She paused on the pavement corner and faced it: the cars swarmed between the columns over which was the victory chariot.

Either side of the gate was emptiness, where the Wall had been seven years before. The Wall had been her life. Through it she had carried the equipment, the unexposed films and the instructions for Hansie, and she had brought back the equipment, the exposed films and the reports he had made. The Wall had gone. In place of the Wall were cranes. She had never seen so many in one place. Huge, lofty, caterpillar-driven cranes replaced the Wall . . . She was about to cross the wide road, green light showing, when she saw the crosses. Fifteen white plastic crosses were tied to a fence between the pavement and the Tiergarten. They had been there seven years before, but prominent and confronting the Wall. Now, they were tied to a fence. Behind them was an advertisement board for a museum and they were ignored. The young men and women who had died on the Wall were forgotten, their memory consigned to plastic crosses pinned in obscurity against a fence, hard to see.

She crossed the road. She walked past the emptiness where the cranes gathered, where the Wall had been.

She went by the stalls where the Romanians or Poles or Turks sold military souvenirs of the Soviet Army and the Nazional-VolksArmee, the caps and camouflage uniforms, the binoculars and flags, the gear of the men who had killed those remembered by the white plastic crosses, who had murdered her Hansie.

She reached the small garden. It was on the junction of Prenzlauer and Saarbrucker in the hinterland of the Unter den Linden. A long time ago, she had stood on the pavement beside the garden, and Hansie had given the camera to a stranger. They had posed. One snapshot, a boy and a girl. One picture with which to remember him. For many hours, in the chill wind, Tracy Barnes sat on a bench in the garden. The leaves were no longer swept away, as she remembered they had been. On a crude shaped stone in the garden was the relief portrait of Karl Liebknecht, revolutionary, tortured and killed in the Tiergarten in 1919, on a day as cold as this one. Hansie had told her about the life and death of Karl Liebknecht. His face was marked with bird droppings. Who remembered him? Who remembered Hans Becker? Twice a snow shower came. When it had passed over she brushed the frozen flakes from her chest and shoulders.

She waited for dusk to fall on the city, and the memories danced in her mind.

'I'm very sorry for the inconvenience, but I've given my word.'

'For how long?' snapped Greatorex.

'I know where the daughter will have gone. One night and one day will be sufficient.'

'Who's paying?' whined Wilkins.

'I will. I hope at a later date to be able to recover the expenses.'

'Who's going to handle your workload?' demanded Protheroe.

'I'll work late this evening and early tomorrow before court. If I went tomorrow at the end of the day, then I'd be up and running at the start of the day after, and back that night. I'd seek to cause the minimum disruption.'

Greatorex said, 'As I would hope. Your late wife may have been a valued client of this firm, but you should be damn grateful that we lifted you out of the gutter. Is this the way to repay us?'

After her death, after his collapse and living as a derelict, after he had been taken to a police station and was about to be charged with vagrancy, after Mr Greatorex had seen him and recognized him, he had been given the chance. He was fifty-four years old and he worked as a clerk.

'I have not forgotten your kindness.'

Wilkins said, 'This business, what you've told us, involves Army intelligence, the Germans, our security people. What are you getting into? This has always been a respectable, careful firm and we don't aim now to change that. Are you stirring trouble for us that we'll be left to clear up?'

'There won't be any trouble. I'll just be into Berlin and out, back in twenty-four hours.'

Protheroe said, 'You do realize, Mantle, that sometimes you stretch our tolerance pretty taut? We decide what clients the firm handles, not you. We decide what time and effort we commit to a client, not you. You are a clerk, not a partner. You are aware of that before you go off on this jaunt to Berlin?'

'They never told us what had happened to him. They never brought us his body.'

'I know who killed him. I know the name of that man.'

When the dusk had come, and the high lights had dimly lit the street, she had left the garden and walked along Saarbrucker Strasse, past the big wooden front door of the apartment block, past the small shop deserted and barricaded against squatters; she had turned on the corner at the end by the café with the grimed windows. She had been on the courses and knew what she should do: she had checked that she was not followed, that there was not a tail in place. She had stood in front of the old door and pressed the bell button. It was as she had remembered it from a long time before.

'And it will do you no good, or me, to know the name.'

'You can demand justice.'

She had waited on the pavement and gazed up at the pocked stonework of the block where the shrapnel of the bombs had fallen more than half a century before, and she had seen the rotted old window fittings of the apartments. The façade of affluence might have reached Unter den Linden, but the money had not seeped as far as Saarbrucker Strasse. It was all as she remembered it. He had gazed at her in shock, wide eyes in a white, wearied face, leaning on his stout stick, the same stick. The father of Hansie Becker had clung to her.

'There were a hundred thousand of them, and there were more who informed for them. They have not disappeared. They are here, a rot in the timber. I tried . . . When the new time came, when the city was joined. I went to the government offices, days in queues, I asked the questions. Where is my son? I was shuffled between city police and federal police. What happened to my son? I was passed between the city prosecutor and the federal prosecutor. They are still here, they block the answers, they are a decay. Who wants to see them punished? I ask you, how many did they kill? How many hundreds? How many did they destroy? How many thousands? Then, I ask you, how many trials have there been? How many have been brought to the court? Six or seven out of one hundred thousand, a token, are in the Moabit gaol.'

'If there is evidence . . .'

The room was as she remembered it. Hansie had only brought her to it after dark and taken her fast up the stairs so that the neighbours in the block would not see her, could not inform on her and on him and on his parents. The radio had always been played loudly while they talked. An old stove in the corner of the room, the old smell of gas, the old kettle steaming. The old chairs with the old covers. The old sideboard of dark wood. The old photograph . . . The face of Hansie, where the line of his smile ran at his mouth, had been joined together with Sellotape, as if the photograph had been torn into two pieces

84

and dropped, maybe stamped on, maybe spat on. Beside it was a glass of old, faded plastic flowers.

'You will be disappointed, my dear, if you have come here to find someone who is interested in the past. Believe me. I could not find that person. They are a network, they are an organization, they protect themselves. Twice in fifty years I hear the justification of the obeying of orders. And then, twice in my life, I hear of the need to close the book of the past. Did they hunt the Gestapo men before? Will they hunt the Stasi men now? I tried . . . I was ignored.'

'But evidence cannot be ignored. There must be files, and in the files will be the names of eye-witnesses.'

The mother, older and more gaunt, stood by the stove. She had unwrapped the chocolates but not eaten one; neither had Hansie's father. She had long ago warned her son that meeting with the English student was an unnecessary danger to him. Tracy imagined the trauma it would have been for the mother, her son missing and her home searched. They had owned the barricaded shop on the corner, had sold household fittings when they could get them, second-hand clothes, brushes, and thin paint if it was available. The shop would have been closed down when the Stasi had come to the apartment on Saarbrucker Strasse. Hansie had told her that his mother and father flowed with the tide, supported the regime, would have voiced quiet, mild criticism of its failures, would have existed inside the system. They would have been disgraced, ostracized, after the Stasi had come to Saarbrucker Strasse, destroyed. It was possible that his mother hated her, believed her responsible . . .

'You will not be allowed near the files.'

'It was murder.'

'You will not be permitted near the files.'

The mother lifted the boiled kettle from the stove. Her voice was reedy thin. 'Joachim's daughter works at the Bundesbeauftragte. Hildegard works with the files . . .'

*   *   *

85

'Please try, Doktor Krause. It is necessary, I assure you. Myself, I have served in Washington. I know. To Americans, the substance of the message is important, but its presentation is critical.'

It was the main briefing room of the complex at Cologne. Goldstein stood at the locked door. The room would have seated two hundred, but the room in Washington would be larger and they had been told that 320 invitations had been sent, and that more had been refused. He watched.

'My friend, Pyotr Rykov, used to tell me, when we were together, when we were out on a lake, when we were fishing, that the lifeblood of Mother Russia was the Army. The KGB to him were filth, the word he used, "filth", and it would only have been to me, his friend, that he would have dared such a confidence . . . But the Army was the lifeblood. He would say to me, his friend, that it was criminal of the politicians to have allowed the Army to be weakened, the lifeblood running from a wound. Only when the Army is strong, he would tell me, will Mother Russia be listened to. If the Western powers are nervous of the power of the Russian Army, always his argument, then the voice of Mother Russia will be respected . . . How is that?'

He stood at the podium, erect and composed.

Raub was beside him. 'Brilliant, Doktor Krause, impressive. Please continue.'

Goldstein murmured, 'Perhaps they will keep you to front the network news. God and we will miss you.'

The boom of the amplified voice: 'He despises the politicians whom he regards as responsible for the weakness of the Army. He will work until his last breath to change that weakness into strength . . .'

The head waiter leaned to speak discreetly into the ear of the judge, Court of Appeal, and made the slightest of gestures towards the door. The judge's guests in the old timbered dining room of Middle Temple would not have noted the brief movement of his head. It would be wrong for them to be disturbed,

86

and their conversations rippled uninterrupted around the table. There was a man at the door, hovering, a pale, stoat-faced man with a brush moustache, a black overcoat folded over his arm. The judge took a leather-encased notepad from an inner pocket, wrote, 'Phlegm, you have a visitor – don't bugger up a good evening, Beakie', then tore out the page, folded it for the head waiter, and pointed his index finger across the table.

The head waiter circled the table, handed the note to Fleming. The frown settled on his forehead. The glance arrowed on the doorway, found Perkins. Fleming, so politely, apologized to the lady on his right, a tax consultant with no other avenues of conversation, and left the table.

He didn't have to question the importance of whatever had brought Albert Perkins to Middle Temple. Fleming would have said that nothing in Perkins's working life involved the trivial.

'She's gone, Mr Fleming, good as gold. Of course, I challenged her to produce evidence of murder, and I warned her. The challenge and the warning made it inevitable that she would go – actually she's there.'

'As you said, Albert, she would. Do you know where she'll head for?'

'Yes, Mr Fleming, I think I have that.'

'Our friends and allies, they would be privy to the same information?'

'I doubt it, Mr Fleming. Rostock would only have dealt with the incursion and the death. The follow-up would have been handled from Berlin. I doubt the *Hauptman* would have been told details of the follow-up. My understanding is that that sort of material is long gone from the Berlin files. I don't think they'd have that information. They'd certainly want it but not have it.'

They murmured in the doorway.

'But they are, Albert, friends and allies . . .'

'Exactly so.'

'And, Albert, there is a moral obligation to share with valued friends and respected allies . . .'

'Out of sharing, Mr Fleming, comes the opportunity of barter.'

Fleming mused quietly, 'All that Iran stuff they've gathered . . . If we shared, Albert, the Iran stuff bartered for her location, then would we be cutting her off at the knees?'

'Maybe, and then maybe not.'

'If we share, if they catch up with her – your *Hauptman* said on the tape that he would deal with matters himself, yes? – what would be her position?'

'First they'd warn her – my opinion. If she kept going forward they'd rough her. If she continued going forward and they began to believe themselves threatened, then they would kill her. If it's their freedom or her life, there's no choice.'

Fleming looked into Perkins's eyes. They were the coldest eyes he knew, the eyes of a ferret going into a rabbit's burrow. 'If we shared, Albert, as we should with valued friends and respected allies, just at the start, would we condemn her?'

'Not necessarily. Right now she's out in front, so we might handicap her, but she can still win . . . We would be making it harder for her to win, but still possible. You want my assessment of her, Mr Fleming. She is truly incredible. I hammered her, no sleep, no food, no heat, I was about to drop. Not a single word. She said nothing. People pass through our Resistance to Interrogation course who wouldn't have lasted more than a few minutes alongside her. Her mental focus, her strength, they are fantastic. But that determination will cause her to ignore warnings and a softening beating. She will go for her evidence, she will threaten them. She's driven by love for the agent who was killed. She won't be deflected. She will win or she will be killed. That's only my assessment.'

'Go with it, Albert, share it.'

'What might interest you – her file, the personal one, it tells nothing. Plenty of reports on her work, but inadequate on the personality. Her work is always highly praised, but I don't know her. The person is locked away, kept from sight. You can read a file, most files, and profile an individual – not her. She hid, very successfully, behind her work. Private, alone . . . It makes her so much more interesting, Mr Fleming, don't you think?'

'Share it.'

'So very sorry, Mr Fleming, to have disturbed you.'

Fleming wandered back towards the table. He felt a little sick.

The guests were standing in small knots and talking.

The judge, the host, came to him. They had been at school together, then at the same Oxford college, had played rugby together for Richmond 4th XV, they were godparents to each other's children. The judge advised the Service on legal matters.

'You all right, Phlegm?'

'I'm fine, Beakie, but sometimes I disgust myself.'

'Want the shoulder for the old weep?'

They were in a corner. Fleming's hand trembled around the brandy glass pressed on him.

'Our friends and allies, the Germans, they fuck us at every turn. Our Bank, our City, our food, our EU membership, our diplomacy, our American link – every way we turn they seek to fuck us. Now it's Intelligence. They're looking for a way in, their usual delicate style, kicking and blundering towards influence. They resent that there, at least, we still punch above our weight. They've some dreadful little creature from the old East German secret police and they're trailing him round because he's an alpha-quality source on a particular Russian in whom we have an interest. The Americans are panting because the German source – we cannot match it – is to be paraded before them, which will lead to increased German influence at our expense. I aim to destroy the credibility of that source, but at second hand. I am using a young woman to do my work, a very ordinary young woman, and I am endangering her. Can't dress it up in fancy words, Beakie. In order to maintain correct relations I am sharing information with our friends and allies which will have the certain effect of hazarding that young woman's life. Why will she do the job I want done? Love, boy-and-girl stuff. The target killed the boy she loved. I cannot be seen to help her, not when she works against the agenda of friends and allies, so I have to hope that she is resourceful enough on her own to destroy our mutual target.'

Krause said, pleasantly, 'You had a good journey yesterday, Julius?'

He had discarded his jacket, unbuttoned his collar, loosened his tie. The clothes had been paid for with BfV funds. The organization owned him, dressed him, fed him and put the roof over his family's heads. Goldstein poured the whisky. Raub studied the script and pencilled minute adjustments on it. Sprawled comfortably in his chair, Krause took the whisky and smiled to Goldstein as if he were a servant.

'The aircraft did not crash so it could be described as a good journey.'

'Doktor Raub said yesterday you were in Berlin. In Normannen Strasse? How is it there?'

'Like any other piece of shitty socialist architecture, but still standing.'

'I presume you visited the archive.'

'I did.'

'And I presume you searched for evidence of a criminal act by myself in violation of human rights.'

'I did.'

'And you found nothing . . . nothing . . . nothing.' He rapped his glass on the table, in emphasis.

He rang the bell for the third time. The bastards had checked that he worked late in the office. He kept his finger on the bell until the light came on, sliced between the drawn curtains of the upper window. First Wilkins, then Greatorex and Protheroe, had telephoned him on the direct line with some damn feeble query about the morning. He heard her coming down the stairs. They'd be asleep now in their homes in Gerrards Cross, Beaconsfield and the Chalfonts.

A nervous voice: 'Who is it?'

He called softly, 'It's Josh Mantle. I need to speak. Would you let me in, please?'

A lock was turned. The door with the nailed plywood panel was opened.

'I'm afraid I need some help, just couldn't get away earlier.'

She led him into the kitchen. The cat was asleep in a card-board box on the floor. She went to the cooker, lit the gas ring, put the kettle on it. He smiled. 'Too right, I could murder for a cup of tea.'

She stood by the gas ring, as if to take the heat from it.

'Mrs Barnes, what I agreed to . . . Go to Berlin, yes. Bring back Tracy, yes . . . But I didn't stop to reckon. Where do I find her? Where do I start to look?'

Disappointment creased her face, worried at the wrinkle lines. He thought she was the sort of person to whom promises were made, broken.

'Did Tracy have an address book?'

'Not here.'

'Did she have a particular friend in the Corps, someone she'd have confided in?'

'Not mentioned to me.'

'Are there letters from anyone in the Corps?'

'Not letters.'

'I don't know where to look.'

'There wasn't letters. There was a Christmas card, years back.'

'Who was the card from, Mrs Barnes?'

'From her commanding officer in Berlin. He sent her a card the first Christmas after she came back from Berlin.'

'You don't have that card, Mrs Barnes . . . ?'

She left the kitchen. He drummed his fingers on the table and the cat stared at him. He went to the cupboard on the wall and took two mugs. If he did not know where to look, there was no point in travelling to Berlin. The kettle whistled. He rehearsed what he would tell her. He did not think she would complain that he had promised: she looked to him as though she had lived a life of disappointment. He wondered where her husband was, Tracy's father. Dead or walked out? He would extricate himself from his promise and he would tell the bastards, Greatorex and Wilkins and Protheroe, that it had all been a mistake. He made the tea. They'd smirk, pull long faces, tell him it was for the best, that it wasn't the sort of business the firm went running after.

She laid the bundle in front of him. The Christmas cards were held together with an old elastic band. They were all cheap, except one: pheasants in snow on expensive paper. The Special Branch searchers had missed the collection of Christmas cards.

To Tracy and family,
With all seasonal good wishes,
Col. Harry Kirby DSO . . . and Frances . . .
The Bothy, School Lane, Sutton Mandeville, Wilts.

'He just sent it the once. Just the first year after she'd come back from Berlin, after he'd retired. Didn't send one the next year. Is that any good?'

Yes, he would have owed her a card. She might have won the Colonel – her 'Sunray' – his medal.

'That'll do me fine, Mrs Barnes. That gives me as good a start point as I could have hoped for.'

She had hung back, and Hansie's father had talked with the man, Joachim – low voices as if the danger still confronted them – at the door of the apartment.

Most of the bulbs of the block were gone. They had passed drunks, young men, and her foot had struck a syringe. The lift had broken and they had climbed eleven flights of stairs. She had hung back, not interfered. As if she had brought him determination, Hansie's father whispered at the man, Joachim, and jabbed at his chest with the crown of his old stick. The man, Joachim, spoke, and fear lit his face. He turned away, slammed the door on them, and the lock was turned.

92

When they were in the darkness outside, Hansie's father said, 'Perhaps, Tracy, now that you have seen the fear, you do believe me. There were one hundred thousand of them, they did not disappear. They are here, around you, on the street with you, close to you. They have the network and the organization, and the power – why my friend Joachim still has the fear. I tell you, Tracy, if you threaten them, they will take you between their fingers and break you as if you were a dried branch. It is the way that they know, their old way. There are two thousand people working on the administration of the files. This week she does the night shift.'

The wind caught them. They stood on the pavement near the tunnel down to the U-Bahn of Magdalenen Strasse. The great tower blocks before them diverted the wind into chilling corridors. She held his arm and gripped the threadbare sleeve of his coat. They waited outside the entrance to the old headquarters of the Staatssicherheitsdienst. Past midnight. A trickle of men and women, huddled in heavy coats, scurried towards the U-Bahn tunnel.

The woman was wrapped tight in scarves and a woollen hat and gloves. The light hit the heavy spectacles on her face.

'Joachim and I, we thought once that Hans and Hildegard would come together. It was before we knew of you, Tracy.'

Tracy said, 'Then tell her it's for love, and twist her arm till it hurts, till she screams.'

He sat on his folded coat. The darkness was around him. His fingers brushed the earth in front of his feet. He could feel the strong stub stems of the daffodils that he had planted the last summer and he touched them with a reverence. He only ever came to the grave at night.

'What I'm saying, I was a lamb to the slaughter. The money was the final straw. I mean, she must have got the money from her savings tin, pitifully little, and she's trying to give it me. No, Libby, I couldn't have come and told you about it, about taking her money or about turning my back on her. You'd have given me a grade-one rollicking. I always do that, Libby, wonder whether you'll give me a rollicking or that little tap of the hand, approval. Yes, well, you'll need to know about our Tracy, our Corporal Tracy Barnes . . . She's opposites, you understand. She's sweetness and vilely rude. Sour, cheeky and funny. You like her, you detest her. She makes you feel important, she rubbishes you. Tough as an old boot, small and vulnerable. She is utterly sensible, she is lunatic. It's because of what happened to her, what she lost, that she can be so hideous. I won't get any thanks from her but, you have to understand, I don't have the chance, not any more, to do many things that are worth doing, and she's worth crawling on a limb for. I'm going to Berlin, Libby, to try to bring her home. She has travelled to Berlin to find evidence against the man who killed her boy, but the man is protected . . . It's like she's putting her hand into a snake's hole. Don't worry, I'm not about to embark on anything idiotic. I'm going to Berlin to find her and to frogmarch her to the airport. I'm going to bring her home. She taunted me, Libby, she asked me if I compromised . . . And something else, the only thing we have in common, her and me. The person we loved was taken from us. Before you ask, she's not at all beautiful, not even very pretty, so don't get any dumb ideas . . . Goodnight, watch for me . . .'

He wiped his eyes, once, hard. An owl was hooting in a tree nearby. He picked up his coat. The time he spent at the cemetery, alone, was precious to Josh Mantle. He started to grope his way towards the wall where his car was parked.

5

In the half light of dawn, a smear of red sun behind the trees, the man stood on the lawn and the terrier yapped and jumped against him until he threw the tennis ball. The man's silver hair was unbrushed and wild on his head and fell over the darkened lenses of his spectacles. He was unshaven and he wore his pyjamas, slippers and dressing gown. Josh Mantle watched from the gate on the road at the edge of the village. The dog chased the ball, caught it in the air as it bounced, and ran back towards the man. Josh learned from what he watched. The dog was close to the man and the man bent down but could not take the ball until the dog brought it right to his hand.

Josh took his driving licence from his wallet, held it in the palm of his hand and pushed open the gate.

He went up a narrow gravel path. The scrape of his footfall alerted the man and the dog ran barking towards him.

'Colonel Kirby? Sorry to trouble you so early. I'm Josh Mantle, SIB of the Royal Military Police . . .'

He held up the driving licence as identification.

'I wouldn't have come if it wasn't important. It is correct that in Berlin you were the commanding officer of Corporal Tracy Barnes?'

The frown, like a shadow, slipped on the man's forehead, and Josh again held up the driving licence.

'You'd better come in.'

He was led into a conservatory. Kirby apologized, his wife was away, place a bit of a mess.

The man was alone. Mantle knew he could play the proper bastard. 'We're running an investigation into the involvement of

95

Corporal Tracy Barnes, Berlin 'eighty-eight, with a field agent, Hans Becker.'

Straight in, brisk, with authority, as if he had the right to know. The man seemed to shrivel.

'It was a long time ago. It's history, finished. Who cares?'

'Please, just answer my questions.'

'It'll do no good, should be allowed to sleep. Who needs to know?'

But he talked . . . and Josh let him.

'I'll call her Tracy – you don't mind if I do? – she was a part of my family. She was just past her twenty-first when she came to Berlin, the youngest in the unit. She was, *de facto*, my PA. Always smart, always efficient, good typing and shorthand, buckled down in the evenings to learn good German. I don't think she'd done that well at school but she had the commitment we wanted. She'd work away quietly in the corner and didn't interrupt. I'd hardly be aware of her. There weren't any boyfriends, no tantrums, no sulks – she was a joy to have. If I had to work late, she was there – early start, the same, no problem . . . Tell you the truth, there were plenty of sergeants who tried to get off with her, single and married, and they hadn't a prayer. I didn't complain, she was the best worker I ever had in the military. I said she was a part of our family – she used to help my wife when we had dinner parties, and was paid for it, she used to come in and babysit when we were out. She had nothing else to do and we felt we were really rather doing her a favour, but we became almost dependent on her. Is she in trouble?

'. . . I had a good staff sergeant. We used to go over to East Berlin, once or twice a week, as permitted under the Four Power Agreement and it was important to take advantage of the access. We didn't learn much and were always followed by the Stasi, but we did it. We'd walk around, lean on road bridges and watch for military convoys, look for new cap badges of Soviet troops, pretty mundane but that was the work of I Corps. But one time in December 'eighty-seven, on Leipzig Strasse, the sergeant was bumped. The tail was on the other side of the street, quite wide there. He was bumped by a young man. Actually, he was another hundred metres up the street before he realized that an envelope had been palmed into his pocket. He brought it back, came straight to me and gave it to me. That was Hans Becker's first contact.

'Most of our work in Berlin was debriefing those who had either escaped, youngsters, or been allowed out, the elderly. The Stasi were always trying to plant their own people into our system, to learn about our procedures and to feed us disinformation. I don't deny it, we were truly excited that evening. What we usually handled was so low-grade – what passes were needed for what area of East Germany, where were the passes issued, what colour were they, who signed them. This had the potential of being way ahead of the dross, and it didn't seem like a plant. The letter said that a meeting should take place in Alexanderplatz, that a named song should be played over the forces' radio the evening before; the song was "The Londonderry Air", pretty mournful stuff. I lost sleep over it – it was the staff sergeant's suggestion – but we sent Tracy over. She didn't know, but I sent three Welsh Guards NCOs to have her within sight. I thought she had the ability – she was the only one of us who didn't look like a soldier. I asked a hell of a lot of a girl of that age, but she always seemed so capable.

'We called it Operation Catwalk. She was Traveller. So damn difficult to find a codename. When she was looking after the children she used to read to them, and Walter de la Mare – particularly his "Traveller" – was a favourite for my elder daughter.

'She was a pig in shit – excuse me, a duck in water. Very matter of fact, very calm, took it in her stride. The first time she went over we had back-up and I was down at the Wall. The last time she just slipped out of Brigade, could have been going shopping. She took equipment and material over to him, she had memorized my instructions as to what we needed. We'd give him a few weeks to follow the instructions, then we'd play this song on the radio and they'd meet again the next day. My wife spotted it – not much can be hidden from her. My wife said that something had happened to that "plain little thing". My wife said it was love. Tracy had become a woman, gone confident, more mature – there was another side to her, harder, sharper, quite a savage joker, and then skittish, you know what I mean. We had a good little section that dealt with forged papers. They'd done an excellent job fitting Tracy with a student's pass into the East for the library at the Humboldt, and they did the necessary for getting him over, once, to meet us. You only had to see them together to know that it was love. I should have stopped it then, should have killed our involvement. We were forbidden to run agents, it was thought we weren't capable. Should have been handed over to the civilians. We dressed his reports up as debrief material – that's the way we slid it into the system. We were getting the applause, I wasn't going to pass it up. I saw them together and I could see there was heavy emotional entanglement, and I should have killed it.

'The Baltic was a key, critical zone. All the assumptions were that they would attack, if it came to war, through amphibious forces. We would have tried a counter-strike, which would have meant blitzing the Soviet air defence up there. There was a major concentration of air defence at Wustrow, near Rostock. Prize intelligence was to be able to read their counter-measures. I sent him to Wustrow with the electronics to read the radar. She took it to him and off he went. I was stretching him, too far perhaps. He worked in the marshalling yards at the Lichtenberg rail junction in Berlin and could tell us what tanks were being moved, what units were coming West through the yard, but this was at a different level. I was away that day – a conference or something.

'It was almost a year to the day since he'd bumped my staff sergeant. A quite normal morning. I was in early. Tracy was already at her desk. I asked her if it had gone well, the previous day's rendezvous, she said it had been routine. Would have been about lunch-time that the first reports came through. Our SigInt at Lübeck had picked up heavy Soviet radio traffic from the Wustrow base, indications of a manhunt. Then we had reports via Denmark. One of their ferries, out at sea, had seen flares over the Wustrow area . . . I knew it had gone wrong. I broke it to her, in my office, in private, asked her if she wanted to cut away and get back to her quarters. I thought that was fair. She stayed put, went on with her work. She was very strong. Must have been ghastly for her, the uncertainty. The next month, and the month after, we had that song played on the radio. I didn't send her over, I went myself. He didn't show. What was important, the meeting point was not under particular surveillance by the Stasi. That told me that he hadn't been captured and hadn't talked. The assumption was that he was dead, drowned or killed. I pushed him forward, I was responsible. Do you think I don't know that? Do you think I carry that burden with ease? I was five years in Berlin and in that time he was the only worthwhile source I had. The rest was rubbish, juvenile games. This was real, and it cost a young man, Tracy's young man, his life. For God's sake, what help is it to dredge in the past?'

'Where did he live?'

'With his parents on Saarbrucker Strasse. The staff sergeant checked it to see that we weren't being conned. Apartment nine, third floor, number twelve on Saarbrucker Strasse . . . She's a lovely girl, very kind, very gentle, my children worshipped her. Who's helped by opening the dirty side of history?'

Josh let himself out of the house and walked to his car.

She lay in the bed.

It was as she remembered it. It was narrow, made of heavy wood. She lay naked under the old blankets and she could hear his mother moving behind the thin wood partition. Once, a long time before, in Hansie's bed, there had been no sound from the other two rooms of the apartment, the shop closed and his mother and father away at his uncle's home in Erfurt. Her skin was warmed by the roughness of the sheets and by the weight of the blankets. She had loved Hansie in the darkness of alleyways,

99

in the shadow of deep doorways, but once, when his mother and father were away, he had brought her to the apartment. Crawling on her, climbing above her, loving her. She stretched up her arms, as if she reached for him, as she had reached for him. She held the void, clasped it, sought again to find the love. She had brought the condoms from the lavatory (female) at Brigade . . . She had thought she gave him courage. They had left separately before daylight, walked on Saarbrucker Strasse in different directions and met at the Trabant car. They had gone in the car to Rostock . . .

She remembered the small chest. After they had made love in his bed, he had taken the dark clothes from the drawers of the chest, because she had told him he should wear deep browns, blacks and hard greys that night, and as he had dressed she had reached from the bed, naked, into her bag, which held the electronic monitoring equipment to check that she had the camouflage cream for his face and his hands, for the night . . .

She remembered the dressing gown, hanging on the back of the door, and protruding from under it, slung on the same hook, were his competition swimming goggles. He had a foot problem, right foot, needed a built-up shoe. He could run only with difficulty, was handicapped sufficiently to avoid military service, but he could swim well enough to believe that he could cross the wide water of the Salzhaff.

He had been the only boy into whose bed she had gone naked. She lay and reached for him, to hold him, to smell the sweet sweat of him, to feel him, and her fingers groped at nothing.

In the morning he had done the court, had sat alongside Mr Protheroe and fed him the relevant papers, like a loader at a shoot. He was necessary but unequal.

He had thought that 'Sunray', alone in his garden, would have crumpled under the weight of the responsibility that had won him his medal.

In the early evening, as the partners shrugged into their coats and locked the doors of their offices, he cleared his desk.

'Goodnight, Mr Greatorex, I'll see you the day after tomorrow, first thing.'

'Why do you do this?'

She had come on the U-Bahn. At the top of the tunnel steps she had been met by the woman, Hildegard. A hesitation. The woman looked away, to the snow-brushed pavement, to the high lights and the flat roofs of the tower blocks.

She said, 'You met my father. To you, a stranger, he would appear as any other older man. You came to our home and to you, a stranger, it would have seemed like any other home. He was a poet. He tried to write the poetry of satire, the target of his satire was the regime. Perhaps he was not sufficiently clever. He did not practise self-censorship with expertise. The writers met and discussed their work in the privacy of their homes. They were all friends and he did not believe he could be betrayed from inside the circle. My father complained to his friends, inside the circle, of the denial of his right to publication. You understand, not an angry complaint just grumbling. He was taken by the Stasi, brought here, interrogated, he was charged with "behaviour hostile to the state and characteristic of class warfare". Do you understand that? He was sent to the prison at Cottbus for two years. When he came out it was impossible for him to find work other than as a road labourer, and he had been a teacher, an intellectual. My mother was dismissed from her job in a ministry. She took the work in a hospital of standing ten hours a day in an elevator and pressing the buttons for the elevator to go up or down. I had no chance of going to the university. The Wall came down. We were promised the new dawn. My father was in Lenin Allee. He told me that day it was raining. A car came past him and splashed the water over his legs, a big BMW. It was driven by the man who had interrogated him. My father is the loser, he is now in a ghetto of failure. He is too old to go back to teaching, too old to work as a labourer on the road, and the man who destroyed him is driving in the warmth of a BMW car.'

Tracy said, 'Why are you doing this?'

The woman looked at Tracy Barnes through her thick spectacles, and her eyes were distorted by the lenses. 'Because I loved him, because we worked together in the railyard, because he brought light and laughter to me, because his father says they killed him, because you have come to find the evidence.'

The woman gave Tracy a pair of narrow steel-rimmed spectacles, and a scarf to wear over her hair. She was handed a plastic-coated ID card, and she saw that the photograph on the card was that of a woman with dark hair and narrow steel-rimmed spectacles.

There was a policeman in the shadows, shivering and stamping his feet, and the woman called cheerfully to him. It was a modern fortress complex, great buildings around a wide central open space. They went down a ramp to a steel door, well lit and covered by a security camera, and the windows beside the door were protected by metal bars. The woman rang the bell and held up her card in front of the camera and Tracy copied her. She had memorized the name on the ID. Inside at a desk, behind plate glass, there were two guards. She did what the woman did, and showed the card, scrawled the name, the signature, the time, as the woman had. The woman had moved away from her, to the other end of the desk, and she talked animatedly with the guards, distracted them, then went fast towards the inner door of plate steel. Tracy followed. The door was opened from the desk.

In the corridor beyond, the door slid shut behind them.

'We have six hours,' the woman said briskly. 'Maybe there are a hundred million sheets of paper, maybe there are ten million card indexes.'

They went down narrow concrete stairs, poorly lit.

'Maybe there are a million photographs – I do not know how many kilometres of audio-tape. Everything was filed. They kept, believe me, in many thousands of sealed glass jars the smells of

102

their victims, they stole their socks and their underwear and put them in jars so that later if dogs had to search for those people they would have their smells. Most of all, there is the paper. The dictatorship of today does not need to shoot people, or gas them, or hang them. They do not have blood on their hands, but ink.'

They were at the bottom floor. Ahead was a door of reinforced steel, set with additional bars, opened by a lever.

'You must have names and dates and places. You have that? If you do not then we search for a coin on the ocean floor.'

Tracy said, 'Hauptman Dieter Krause, counter-espionage at Rostock, killed Hans Becker at Rerik, near to the Soviet base at Wustrow, on the evening of the twenty-first of November nineteen eighty-eight.'

The woman wrenched down the lever. The cavern ran as far as Tracy could see. As far as she could see were the metal racks on which were stacked the files. Cardboard file covers neatly tied with string, bound with elastic, as far as she could see. The racks were from the floors to the ceilings, and they had come down two flights of stairs.

'A man was here two days ago, from the Office of the Protection of the State. He had the name of Dieter Krause from Rostock. He looked for evidence of a criminal act against human rights. He did not know of Hans. He had the name of a Soviet officer. He did not have the location of Rerik. He had the officer stationed at Wustrow. He did not have the date. He walked in fog . . . There was a part of the Krause file that was missing, and a part of the Wustrow file that had been taken out. He did not find what he looked for. He was here a whole day, with three assistants. I have to tell you that—'

'How long do we have?'

'We have a few minutes less than six hours, and only the one chance.'

The last flights were leaving Heathrow. Josh Mantle hurried to the check-in. The flight for Berlin was closing. He was in the queue when he heard the voice behind him, 'Hello, Mantle, cutting it fine . . .'

He spun.

'. . . but I didn't expect to see you here. I'd have thought – your track record – you'd have realized this was heavy going and backed off, like you did before.'

'What do you know of me?'

'Not much short of everything.' Perkins was smiling.

'I've never seen you before the gate at Templer.'

'Quite a crowd of folk never looked hard enough behind them, never saw me. Bad business that, Belize, would have thought a chap like you would have showed a bit more spine.'

'Who are you?'

'A government servant, man and boy. I walk the streets with a shovel so that the pretty people don't get shit on their shoes. You were a piece of shit in Belize that I cleared up. Never seemed to find the time to introduce myself . . . Better stir a bit, if you want to get to Berlin tonight. It is Berlin, isn't it? Chasing after the little corporal, are we?'

'Where are you going?'

'As if you need to know. Cologne. Off to see our gracious friends and respected allies.'

The queue lurched forward.

'About her? About Miss Barnes?'

'She's on my Action This Day agenda. You're very sharp tonight, Mantle.'

'Running sneaky messages, piling up the odds. That's work for a proud man.'

The smile had become the grin. 'You used to be bright in the old days, as I recall, when you knew how to back out.'

'You're starting to feel like a boil in my arse. A damn nuisance, but I can ignore it. If anything happens to her, before I get to her, through your hand, I'll . . .'

The smile, which had been the grin, had become the sneer. 'Bit old for her, aren't you?'

The check-in girl had her hand out for Mantle's ticket. He passed it across the counter. He spun again.

'. . . I'll put your teeth through the back of your neck.'

The smile, the grin, the sneer had gone. 'My advice, Mantle. You shouldn't go to Rostock with a boil in your arse. Very painful if your backside were kicked – and in Rostock it will get kicked, hard.'

'Rostock is not a part of it, so fuck you. I'm going to Berlin to bring her home.'

'Of course . . . Oh, and the name is Perkins, Albert Perkins, by the way, a shoveller of shit for Her Majesty's government. Don't forget the name and have a good flight.'

He was given his ticket, his boarding card. When he came away from the counter, his overnight bag slung on his shoulder, Perkins was gone.

He walked towards Departures.

They had both gone to Belize. Captain Ewart-Harries and Sergeant Mantle, the Intelligence Corps presence. Supposed to know their job, supposed to predict whether the Guatemalan military were about to invade. The officer had school Spanish and Mantle had been on a phrase book. Hustling through *Jane's Fighting* books for the strength of the Guatemalan Army, its élite units, its equipment. The Brigadier with his gunners and his infantry demanding an answer, and the Group Captain with his Harrier force. Were the Guatemalans coming? Would they come in force with tanks? Would they probe with reconnaissance units? Who knew more than damn all about the goddamn Guatemalan Army? Every morning at the Brigadier's session, the pressure was growing. Answers, where were the answers? Outside Belize City was a heap of jungle; in the heap of jungle was a mapmaker's line; behind the line was more jungle and the territory of Guatemala. He didn't know, and Ewart-Harries didn't know, what the Guatemalan military had under the triple canopy of the jungle. A patrol on the mapmaker's line had brought the kid in. The patrol's contact had been with three men of the Kaibil battalion, special forces. The patrol had killed two out of three. It had a survivor, neatly tied up and blindfolded, for interrogation. Interrogation was I Corps work. A helicopter ride, from the RAF strip, into the jungle. The prisoner was in a logging shed, no witnesses outside the patrol. The prisoner was just a 'Guat', and the Brigadier was demanding answers . . . Ewart-Harries had called the bet with Mantle for a hundred American dollars to be paid to whichever of them broke the Guat first . . . As if he was a football, a punchbag, taking it in three-hour shifts to work on him. Three hours was the limit for each of them because of the goddamn mosquitoes and the goddamn heat. Going into each shift with the adrenaline pumped at the prospect of an American hundred-dollar bill, coming out and reckoning that Ewart-Harries would win in that session. No gag on the kid, the Guat, because they had to be able to hear the answer when they broke him. Christ, the kid had screamed. Coming out of the logging shed and seeing the contempt of the squaddies who kept a perimeter defence line. Caught in a frenzy because it was just a game, and the kid was just a Guat. The third day, and the kid had died. He had stopped screaming and died in a Ewart-Harries session, and the bet was void.

He walked down the pier to the aircraft.

One of the patrol had gone to the battalion padre. There had been an internal inquiry. If it had ended as a court-martial, the killing of a Guat, then it would have gone public and the Guatemalan government and military would have had a field day of propaganda. As the officer, Ewart-Harries could have fallen out of sight if his sergeant had testified against him. But the sergeant had stayed quiet, as if it should be kept in the family, had refused to give evidence against his officer. A deal done . . . He had been transferred from I Corps to the Special Investigation Branch of the Royal Military Police with no filth on his record. Iain Ewart-Harries, with copybook references, had gone to civilian life.

He had not stood up to be counted, he had walked away, he had not shouted from the Guat's corner . . . It was a part of Josh's history, the day that he had compromised.

Josh Mantle flew to Berlin.

Under the beat of the air-conditioner, Tracy sat cross-legged on the floor between the racks. Untying the string, unfastening the elastic, skipping at the reports filed in the month of November

1988 by Hauptman Dieter Krause. Retying the string, handing the files back to the woman. Reports on environmental campaigners, on three Rostock athletes selected to travel for warm-weather training in Cuba, on the Rostock family of a drowned escaper washed up on the Baltic coast, on anti-social behaviour in the science faculty at Rostock. No report in the files for the dates of 21, 22 and 23 November, the only dates in the month that the busy bastard had not filed reports. She beavered at the paper, and the despair grew as the night hours slipped.

He was a trader. To Albert Perkins, all trade was acceptable. When he came to the trading stall, Albert Perkins was without inhibition. Among the street stalls, Albert Perkins, with quality knowledge of the German language, spoke only in English.

'She is in Germany, seeking evidence. We, of course, in respect of a friend and ally will not help her to gain that evidence. We know where she will have gone. We know her start point. We believe you are short of that information. We believe, also, that should she find that evidence before your prize pig goes to market, before Hauptman Krause goes to Washington, then you will have no option but to slit his throat and hang him up for butchery, charge him, convict him, and wave him goodbye . . .'

The senior official's cigarette smoke wafted between them. They were alone, two easy chairs used. There was whisky in a decanter on the low table between them, untouched. Neither man, when trading, would risk alcohol, would give advantage.

'That we are prepared to offer you that information, where you could find her, should be taken by you as a mark of respect on our side for a friend and ally. Friendships, alliances, thrive on mutual respect, and we would be grateful for reciprocity – sorry, we barter . . .'

His voice was sweet, silky reasonableness. The senior official drew hard on the cigarette. The night air came through the window, opened on Perkins's insistence.

'The little matter we request in return . . . Iranian material, your dossier on Ali Fallahian. You have, last figures I saw, earnings of two point four billion American dollars from equipment supplied to Iran. I want the names of those German companies involved and their British collaborators . . . I want details on all commercial transactions by German companies for equipment sent to Iran that could be utilized in the production of atomic, chemical and biological weapons. I want the surveillance files on all members of the Iranian diplomatic mission in Bonn who have travelled to Britain in the last two years.'

The senior official stiffened. He stubbed out the cigarette and in the same movement was reaching for another, lighting it.

'Did you actually entertain Ali Fallahian in this office? Did you feel the need to wash your hands afterwards, lot of blood on his fists? Must have been a jolly little occasion, entertaining the minister for information and security. Did you discuss the Lockerbie atrocity? I expect you did. I expect he thanked you, as a friend and ally, for refusing us access to those hoods on the Iranian payroll who organized the Frankfurt transfer of the bomb on to Pan-Am 103. Let them go now, haven't you, slipped them beyond reach? I've told you what I want, I know what you want. Do we trade?'

The senior official paused. He held his hands together, over his mouth and his nose as if in prayer. Perkins assumed that he would be travelling to Washington on the back of Hauptman Krause, would take the opportunity to drive to Langley, to meet with the principals of the National Security Council, would be ushered to the big offices of the Pentagon. Another cigarette, half smoked, was discarded. Cancellation would be a bitter pill, would take more than prayer to flush it down.

The senior official went to his desk, telephoned, spoke in a low voice. Perkins heard the murmur of Ali Fallahian's name. He returned to his chair and reached forward to pour the whisky. They both drank, equal measures. The trading had been agreed.

They muttered pleasantries for fifteen minutes.

A young woman brought in the papers, fresh from the computer onto the printer. The senior official passed them to Perkins. He scanned them. He was satisfied and dropped them into his briefcase. The senior official, at the door, gestured for Krause to join them.

To Perkins, the scratches seemed, in those few days, to have healed well. The minders stood back against the wall. The Jewish minder interested him. He would be the token, the symbol of political correctness. He smiled up at Krause and for the first time spoke in German. 'So pleased to note your fast recovery, Hauptman. You were attacked by Corporal Tracy Barnes. You won't need a photograph of her, I'm sure you remember her well. She alleged that you murdered in cold blood, Hauptman, a British agent named Hans Becker at Wustrow on the twenty-first of November nineteen eighty-eight. Corporal Barnes was a girl-friend of Becker. I interrogated her, several sessions. I emphasized to her that should she provide me with evidence of your criminal act then I would use the full influence, not inconsiderable, of the Secret Intelligence Service to see you brought to justice. She has come to Germany, my assessment, to hunt for that evidence. I have no idea whether she knows where to hunt or not, but I assure you that she is a quite remarkable and stubborn young woman. I wouldn't want her hurt, Hauptman, I would take that badly. My opinion, she will begin her hunt for evidence against you from the home of Hans Becker's parents. If you wish to look for her then you should start in Berlin at apartment nine, third floor, number twelve, Saarbrucker Strasse . . .'

They found no files for Krause, or the Wustrow base, or Rerik for 21, 22 and 23 November. The files for those dates in 1988 were missing. The paper bounced before her eyes, seemed to trick, deceive her.

'We have searched, we have to accept it. They are not here.'

Tracy could have screamed in frustration. They had worked in the bottom basement, then the middle basement, then the top basement.

The woman droned, 'If you had not involved him, not recruited him, if you had not trapped him, then he would be alive. You came ...'

Tracy sat on the floor of the top basement, the Wustrow files around her, the cold mischief in her eyes. 'You should know that he never mentioned you, he never used your name. When he was with me I doubt that he remembered your name. He made his statement, many did not. Did you?'

The woman sagged. Tracy said they should look two weeks further ahead in the files, into the middle of the month of December 1988. The woman quietly passed new files to be untied and unfastened. The night drifted.

The taxi had dropped him off at an hotel on the Unter den Linden. He had walked straight across the foyer and found a fire door, pushed the bar and gone out.

Past midnight, long past, and Josh walked slowly up the big street. He checked his map. On the empty road, it would have been easy for him to spot a dawdling car or foot surveillance. He stood at the end of Saarbrucker Strasse. He saw the building. The front, caught by dimmed lights, was scarred from bombs or artillery. That registered with him. The past should be known about: it was right to learn from the past. The third-floor windows were darkened.

He thought it wrong to wake them.

He settled down on the pavement beside the step of the building. Light snow was falling. He was back tight against the wall to keep the wind from him. After Libby had died, after he had gone derelict and dossed and boozed, he had learned to sleep on pavements. He huddled in the shadow beside the step, and waited for the morning.

Her throat was dry from the air-conditioning, her eyes ached and watered. The typed lines on the paper were blurred, merged. The woman stood beside her and bent to pick up the last of the files to place them back on the racks.

'What can we do?'

Tracy squatted on the cold concrete of the basement's bottom floor. Her head was down.

A small voice: 'How long do we have?'

'The early shift comes at five. Before that we have to be gone. We have forty-one minutes. What is the point of having forty-one minutes if we do not know where to look?'

She tried to call him back, the wide smile on his face as he had made love to her, and the pain on his face as they had dragged him off the trawler boat. She sat very still. She gazed at the rough floor of concrete and at the files stretching on their racks as far as she could see. Nobody had cared, as nobody cared now.

'In Rerik, if he had run, if they had hunted him, if people had seen him . . .'

'If people had seen him they would have held their silence.'

Dogged. Clinging to the wide smile, so tired, and the pain. 'If the Stasi had known that people had seen him . . .'

'Their silence would have been gained by intimidation.'

'What would have been done to eye-witnesses?'

'Threats, then moved out of their community.'

Tracy hissed, 'How long afterwards?'

'Three weeks, there was bureaucracy, four weeks, after they had been destroyed, five weeks . . . If there had been eyewitnesses they would have sent them out of Rerik.'

Tracy jack-knifed to her feet. They ran between the racks of files for the stairs, for the middle basement floor.

He had the boy drunk, slumped in the chair at the back of the hotel bar, in shadow. He made the sign to the waiter. Another vodka, double, with ice and tonic for the Jewish boy who had driven him to the hotel, another mineral water with ice for himself. The boy, Goldstein, thought he drank vodka, matched him. Perkins was always patient when sober and listening to a drunk who interested him.

'I joined because I wanted to confront the new Nazis. You live as a Jew in this country, you want to be German and not a

Jew, it is impossible . . . They are neurotic about the past, that the past can come again . . . They try to erase the twelve years of Nazi rule. Ask any old man what he did between nineteen thirty-three and nineteen forty-five, he does not answer . . . They do not trust themselves, they censor the books and films, they need to ban *Mein Kampf*. They take the power from us, Office of the Protection of the State, because of fear that the old abuse of legal process will come again . . . Yet they cry for authority, regulation, as they had it before – no lawn-mower in the afternoon, no children shouting, brought to the court for taking a shower late at night which disturbs neighbours, cannot wash a car on a Sunday, cannot touch vegetables in a public market. You know where my parents met? In Auschwitz. They were six years old, both of them. They survived. Their parents, my grandparents, did not. My father is put on TV each anniversary of the Holocaust. They want to suffer, hear him talk. My father says the same thing for the TV each year. "Our parents just climbed the fence so that they would be shot . . . I never had a childhood, I never learned to play . . . At six years old I was as hard as granite stone." They have purged their conscience because they have watched and listened to the TV, and they can forget . . . My father has invitations to go to dinner as far away as Hannover, because it is exciting for a hostess to have a Jew from the camps at her table. I thought it was my duty to show that I was not a parrot in a cage, that I was a German. I thought that I could be a good German if I worked against the new Nazis.'

The boy gulped at his drink. Perkins sipped the mineral water, and prompted, 'But there are two colours of Fascism. There is the black of the Nazis, there is the red of the Communists. Black or red Fascism, any difference?'

'You know, Perkins, there was an American writer, nineteen forty-five, walked round Germany, never could find a Nazi, the Nazis were always in the next village. People she met told her how they'd suffered. The way she heard it, there was never a Nazi in Germany. Today, you meet a little old man – will he

112

tell you he stood in a watch-tower guarding the camps? Will he tell you he coupled the cattle trucks going to the camps? Somebody did, and they're now little old men and denying it . . . That's good, Perkins, red and black Fascism, the same. You go East, you see the crowds outside the hostels with petrol bombs, where the Romanians are, the Poles, the Vietnamese, old Fascists and new Fascists, the same hatred just new Jews for them to hate. Try to find, in the East, an informer of the shit Stasi. Better, try to find an officer of the shit Stasi. Like they didn't exist . . .'

Perkins nudged him again. 'You'd know an officer of the shit Stasi, you're alongside one.'

'The young woman . . .'

'Don't worry yourself about her.'

'What you've done to her . . .'

Perkins said soothingly, 'She's fine, she can look after herself. About that shit Stasi officer . . .'

Albert Perkins traded. Seven double vodkas to Julius Goldstein for a plate of scum from the file of Hauptman Dieter Krause. Damn good trading.

'I was with that shit, minding him at the trial, a little "grey mouse", foreign ministry. She was pathetic . . .'

The third week in December, nothing. The files were heaped around Tracy's feet, ripped open, grasped at. The second week in December, nothing. She pushed files away from her, grabbed at more.

The woman glanced at her watch, shrugged, passed the files for the third week of December as she placed the others back on the racks. Again, the look at the watch. Tracy scattered the pages of the file as she read, discarded, read.

Who had slept with whom. Who was denounced as being negatively disposed towards socialism. Who was to be taken from the community . . .

The woman reached down to pull Tracy up. Her finger rapped the face of her watch.

Tracy squealed.

She read the names. Brandt, Gerber, Schwarz, Muller.

Her squeal echoed between the racks of files. Brandt, Jorg (school-teacher).

There had been four pages on the instruction order. The fourth page had been missed. Gerber, Heinz (town hall, refuse disposal dept).

Three pages taken from the file, one page unnoticed.

Schwarz, Artur (senior engineer, railways, Bad Doberan).

One page left in the file by the fucking bastards. Muller, Willi (trawler deck-hand).

Tracy held the sheet of paper above her head. She jumped, leaped, danced. Twenty-seven days after the killing of Hans Becker, four men had been forced or sent out of the small community of Rerik. She grasped the paper. She thrust it under her sweater and buried it against her breast. Together they tidied the floor, put the last file together, as they had found it, but for one sheet of paper. They ran up the concrete steps.

They showed their cards and scribbled their initials on the check-out list.

Between the high buildings was the first smear of light. They passed the early shift, coming in cars, on scooters and bicycles, walking.

The woman panted, 'You did not mean that? He never remembered my name?'

'You want the truth?'

'I have to know the truth.'

Tracy gazed into her eyes, into the tears. She said, with sincerity and honesty, to the woman's eyes, 'Of course he loved you. If he had lived he would have married you. We were only a partnership for an operation of espionage, nothing physical and nothing emotional. He would have lived his life with you . . .'

'That is the truth?' The woman hugged Tracy, held her.

'Could I look into your face and lie to you?'

She ran down the steps of the tunnel to the U-Bahn station.

*　　*　　*

The telephone rang on the counter. The café owner picked it up.

'Yes . . . Yes, I can make such contact. Your name?'

He wiped the lead of the pencil on his tongue. He wrote the name he was given.

'Yes, I have that. Krause, Dieter, Hauptman, of the Rostock Bezirksverwaltungen . . . Those you wish to contact, their names. All in Rostock, yes, in November nineteen eighty-eight. Please, the names . . .'

He wrote the names that were given him.

'You should ring again. One hour will be sufficient.'

The owner replaced the telephone. His café was a meeting place early in the morning for the frustrated, insecure and vulnerable old men. They came down the steps from the tower blocks of Marzahn to his café at the same time each day as they had once gone to Normannen Strasse. They wore the same jackets of imitation leather. They were the veterans of the Staatssicherheitsdienst, too elderly and traumatized to find new employment. The state they had protected was gone. They had been the sword and the shield of the state, and they had been betrayed. They gathered in the café each morning to drink coffee, to buy a litre of milk to put in a plastic bag, to talk, to read the day's edition of *Neues Deutschland*, to complain, to dream. The owner's son threaded between them with the note-paper in his hand. The café was a cut-off point for what they knew as the insider network. The former men of the organization hung together in informal contact – better, the grey humour went, to hang together than separately.

There were sixty thousand apartments in Marzahn; a hundred and sixty thousand people lived there. In one apartment, a man had the computer that could summon up the names, addresses and telephone numbers of the former officers of the Staatssicherheitsdienst. The owner's son would be back at the café with the telephone numbers within the hour.

He heard her voice, a song. He blinked awake. He smeared the snow off his face and the ice from his eyebrows. He saw her.

The cold was in his muscles, his bones, his throat. He struggled for the strength to push himself up from where he had slept against the step. She was dancing as she came, skipping like a happy child.

He staggered to his feet. He leaned against the wall beside the door. She stopped and stared.

6

'What the hell . . . ?'
 Josh tried to smile. He was wrecked, chilled, unshaven.
He pushed off the wall and swayed.

'What the hell are you doing here?'

It should have been a big speech, heavy with the older man's
wisdom, the world of experience, the lifetime of gathered knowledge. He stretched his spine, tried to stand upright. He knew
that he should demonstrate, crystal clear, his authority. He
scraped the snow covering off his coat.

He croaked, feeble, 'I didn't want to wake them.'

'That's not an answer. Why are you here?'

He said, quiet, 'I came to bring you home.'

There was an impish light in her eyes. She stood with her
hands on her hips. 'Who bought your ticket?'

'Your mother wanted you brought home. I paid for the
ticket.'

She laughed in his face. 'Bad luck. Bad luck, Mr Mantle,
because you wasted your money.'

'Now, you hear me . . .'

The big speech was beyond reach. He could have made the
speech if she had stood contrite in front of him, if the relief that
he had come as deliverer had been on her face. But the laughter
caught her face, her mouth and her eyes. She made a mockery
of his effort to summon the big words. She had come close to
him and her gloved hand smacked the wet snow from his chin
and his forehead.

'. . . hear me, young woman.' He tried to speak with the stern
tone that he would have used to a sullen kid caught out

vandalizing. 'You should go back inside, get your bag, five minutes, I'm waiting here . . .'

Her fingers caught at his cheek and pinched hard.

'. . . I'm waiting here for you. Five minutes and we leave for the airport. You're going home, with me, first flight.'

'You were an officer . . .'

'The first flight back to your mother.'

'Can see you were an officer.'

'Back where you belong.'

'When they talk balls, officers always shout.'

The anger surged in him. He pushed away her hand. 'Listen to me. You are rude, you are impertinent. Learn to be grateful when people go out of their way to help you. What you are trying to do is beyond the capability of a single person acting without resources. Join the real world.'

'Of course I'm capable – I'm trained.'

'You were just a typist, a clerk. You are not equipped—'

'I got the names.'

'What names?'

'I couldn't just go up there, to Rostock and Rerik, blunder about, bang on doors. No bugger would speak to me then. I had to have the names.'

He felt old, and her laughter mesmerized him. The smile played on her mouth. She pulled off her gloves and unzipped her coat. The smile still played at her mouth, mocking. She reached under her sweater, pushed it up. He saw her navel and the narrowness of her waist and the white skin. She pushed her hand up under her sweater, and he saw, a moment, the material of her bra, a flash. She taunted him. She held the piece of paper.

'There were four eye-witnesses, I have their names. They thought they'd stripped the file, but they missed one sheet of paper. I've been in the archive. Not bad for a clerk.'

Josh Mantle sagged back against the wall. A refuse cart turned the corner into Saarbrucker Strasse. He felt a black gloom of inevitability. He felt the suction force pulling him towards deep currents and fire. The cart came slowly down the street, spraying water on the pavement, rotating brushes cleaning the gutter. She waved the paper in front of his face.

He said, weak, 'You should let me take you home.'

'You go on your own,' she said. She folded the paper, neat movements, slipped it into the inside pocket of her anorak.

'So, you get the bloody speech,' he said. 'The speech is, I will stand in front of you, behind you, right side of you, left side. When they come for you, as they will, they will have to flatten me first. Don't expect the speech again.'

The cart came by them. The water sluiced across the pavement, against her legs. She stood her ground and the water dripped off her.

She said, calm, 'I don't need you holding my hand, trailing after my skirt. You want to come, please yourself. I don't need you.'

'Where is he?'

Goldstein forced the palm of his hand across his forehead as if to drive out the throbbing ache. 'He said he was waiting for a telephone call to be returned.'

Raub snapped, 'Does he think the plane waits for him?'

'He knows the time of the flight because I told him the time. He said he was waiting for a telephone call, then he had to make some calls.'

Raub revved the engine and exploded fumes into the frosted dawn air. 'To whom?'

The ache needled his brain. He knew he had talked into the early morning, could not remember what he had talked of. He could remember lurching to his feet, and remember the realization that the Englishman had been ice sober. But he could not remember what he had said. Goldstein snarled, 'Doktor Raub, I do not know because I did not ask. I just follow after that shit because that is what I am paid to do. He used his mobile phone, digital, so I am not able to check his calls.'

119

When Krause came, he did not apologize. Goldstein scrambled out into the dawn air to open the door for him, because he was paid to do so. Krause settled in the back of the car.

'I cannot tell you, Fräulein, the names of the personalities involved, nor can I tell you the tactics they will use. What I do tell you, Fräulein, those personalities and their tactics are directed at one target. The target is Hauptman Dieter Krause.'

The authorities allowed her to wear her own clothes. Albert Perkins thought her older than himself by four or five years. It was difficult to be exact about her age because her complexion was washed out pallid from thirteen months in the cells. She sat stolid before him in a plain grey-green blouse and a plain grey-blue skirt and plain grey ankle socks inside canvas sandals.

'What you should know, Fräulein, is that I seek specific information that will harm, damage, hurt Hauptman Dieter Krause. The damage to him may not come from you. Perhaps you will give me another name. I want you to believe Fräulein, that in this matter I will walk a long road.'

She was a grey mouse. They were always called the 'grey mice'. She had been a secretary at the foreign ministry in Bonn. She would have been, in 1978, as plain and physically uninteresting as she was today. The grey mice had been in the foreign ministry and the defence ministry and the Chancellor's office in Bonn, in the NATO offices and in the Supreme Headquarters, Allied Powers Europe, in Paris and Washington and, damn sure, in London. They were the spinsters, the plain, uninteresting women fearful of living out their lives alone. They were the women who believed love had gone by them. The grey mice were sought out by intelligence officers.

'You would have been warned, Fräulein, as to the dangers of an association with an East German. But he didn't come in those clothes, did he? Younger than you, good-looking, flattering and considerate. What was he? An academic, import-export? Doesn't matter . . . He told you it was love. And after he'd done

120

the love bit, he asked for those little pieces of unconnected information? By screwing you, Fräulein, he would have advanced his career, he'd have been promoted. I aim to bury him, but I need help.'

For all those years, after the Wall had come down, the little grey mouse would have sat at her desk in the foreign ministry and wondered, as they all did, how long the secret would be kept. Had the file gone to Moscow? Had the file been sold on for hard currency to the Americans? Had the file stayed in the archive for the eventual and inevitable opening by the researchers? God, and the little grey mouse must have sweated, sweated in her heart and her mind and down between her legs. Six years of sweat, waiting for the BfV to come to her desk.

'Last year, wasn't it, Fräulein, that he turned up in Cologne and offered himself as a source? First he had to establish his credibility. Told them all about you. Closed court for the part when he testified against you, yes, Fräulein? After he'd testified, his new friends would have taken him for a damn good meal, and you were given ten years. You were a traitor, he was just carrying out the terms of his job description. You betrayed your country, he screwed you and talked of love, which was all part of a good day's work. Life is unfair, Fräulein, and I'm giving you the chance to make life more fair.'

She spoke quietly.

Albert Perkins had heard that corruption was more widespread in the new greater Germany than ever before. He had slipped a thousand American dollars into the palm of the gaol's assistant deputy director, arrangements made by the embassy staffer, after the boy, Goldstein, had finally spilled the necessary and been expelled into the night.

She spoke of the agent to whom she had been handed after Dieter Krause had gone back to Berlin, drunk, in her bed, boasting of his next posting, in the office of the minister at Normannen Strasse. She spoke of the second agent who had told her that Dieter Krause was too clever for his own good, too arrogant, was being sent to Rostock to kick his heels and scratch his arse.

He'd write a report on the new corruption, something for a wet winter day at Vauxhall Bridge Cross . . . After he left her, after the cell door shut on her, as he was escorted down the corridor, Albert Perkins made a note on his memory pad to have an embassy staffer send her a box of chocolates.

The cold was in him. He lay hunched with his knees up, and the voices were above him.

He was in the cemetery, the worst day and the worst night, a day of chill rain and a night of bitter sleet. Many times in many months he had walked by the cemetery. Once, an evening, he had taken the courage and gone into the cemetery and sat wet by the earth in darkness, he had slept . . . He had told Libby, insisted on it, that he was not to be mentioned in her will, demanded it of her. He had not married her for her wealth, he had married her for love. After the sickness and the treatment, the death and the funeral, he had walked past the cemetery then gone to find a hedge or a shed for sleep . . . The voices were above him, 'A disgrace, Officer, a fit and healthy man, should be working – can't have rubbish like that, Officer, sleeping in a graveyard, a place where people come in grief. Get him out of here, Officer, get that filthy creature out. Disgusting, Officer, when a grown man loses his sense of pride, sinks so low.' The policeman had pulled him up. The women had watched him with contempt as he had been taken to the car, the policeman's hand tight in his damp coat sleeve. He had been driven to the police station, had stood in front of the custody sergeant and been read the charge of vagrancy, and the senior partner had crossed the lobby with a chief inspector and recognized him . . .

'There are four names. Four men were evicted by the Stasi from Rerik village. Hildegard explained it. They would have identified eye-witnesses, they would have destroyed them, then evicted them. Hildegard said it was what they did to people. I have those names. The names are everything. I get to those people, I get sworn statements, affidavits, I have evidence.'

He was on the wide chair of old and worn leather and a blanket had been laid over him. His movement alerted her.

'You've been asleep for three hours,' she said dismissively. 'You snored and you smell. These are Hansie's parents.'

She was at the table, wolfing alternately from bread on a plate and cereal in a bowl. He tried to smile at the elderly couple and he thought their faces were as old and worn as the leather of the chair. The room had been dark when he had come into it: they had been still asleep.

Tracy said, mouth full, 'I told them that you'd come after me, had leeched on to me. I told them that I hadn't thought out how to lose you yet, but I'd work on it.'

Josh crawled from the chair. He stood, stretched. The mother pointed to the food and he shook his head. She tried the coffee pot, and he nodded.

Tracy bored on, 'They can't ignore sworn statements, affidavits. However important the bastard is, they have to respond to evidence.'

He massaged the joints of his knees and his hips, and wondered how many times she had said it.

She had not convinced the old man, Hans Becker's father: 'You do not understand, there has to be will. There is no will in the new Germany to examine old crimes.'

The parents had lost a son, were victims of the past. He looked around the humble, sparse furnished room, and could not see anything that the present had brought them, still victims. He wondered how it would benefit them if they could go to the court and see a former Stasi officer tried, convicted and taken down. In a crappy world where there was no will then old victims, in the passing of time, were new victims.

He watched the mother. He thought she would have wanted to slap her old hand across Tracy Barnes's mouth. She had been in their past lives, made the misery, gone, and come back.

'They can't buck the process of law, they can't block evidence.'

He stood by the window. The frame needed paint. He saw the car turn into Saarbrucker Strasse, a big smart car, black, and it crawled up the street, as if the driver and his two passengers checked the numbers at the doors. It stopped in the street, opposite the window in which he stood.

'You wait.' Krause pushed up out of the car, slammed the door after him.

Raub stared ahead through the windscreen. He despised the East. Everything in the East was rotten. Half a century after the battle for Berlin, and still the stonework on Saarbrucker Strasse showed the damage of bomb shrapnel and artillery fragmentation. Maybe the whole East of the city should be flattened. Maybe it would have been better if the Wall had stayed up. Maybe . . .

'What is he doing?'

Raub turned. He looked past Goldstein. Krause, the jewel, the one they smarmed to please, the bastard, had crossed the street and was at the door of the block, checking the names written with the bells.

'He is doing what he is expert at . . . to warn, to threaten, to intimidate, to identify.'

'Then we are involved. If we are involved then we are responsible.'

'Only today, not after today.'

The life of Ernst Raub was well planned. There was no possibility of involvement hazarding the steady promotion climb that was so precious to him. He understood, because he was from a police family, the small division between legality and illegality, between involvement and clean hands. His grandfather, through involvement, was a failure – a policeman in Munich through the Nazi years, tainted with association, never promoted after 1945. His father, through involvement, was destroyed – a policeman in Munich with the marksmen's group

124

assigned to the shootout with the Palestinians at the Fürsten-feldbruck airbase when they had lost the Israelis, never promoted after 1972. Raub had broken the hold of the family, gone to university, joined the BfV, stepped away from his family because to him they represented shame and failure.

'There is nothing he can do here. And we have no responsi-bility, we are not involved, when he goes to Rostock . . .'

He saw Krause, through the misted window, press his finger on the bell.

The peal of the bell silenced her. The old man looked at the old woman.

Josh snapped his fingers for her attention. She looked at him, caught the tension lines in his face. She came to the window. He pointed to the car, to the two men in the front, and to the man who stood on the pavement. She would have seen his face, his carefully trimmed beard, and maybe the scar lines on his face.

The bell rang, incessant, in the room.

She said, distant, 'It's Dieter Krause.'

Josh raked the room. There was no back-exit fire escape, and no access hatch from the ceiling in the roof. There was a window out of the kitchen – to God knew where. So hard to think . . . The bell howled at him.

He snatched up his bag and looped the strap over his head. He ran into the kitchen. She took the cue from him. He was wrenching open the window. She was heaving the rucksack straps over her shoulders. The wind blistered the outside wall at the back of the block. He looked down at a closed yard, with rubbish bins, lines for drying washing, three floors down. A narrow platform of stone below the window ran the length of the back of the block. He took a huge, deep breath. She was behind him, close to him. The width of the stone platform was the length of his shoe. He looked into her eyes and saw fear and bloody-minded determination. He had done a course, a long time ago, too many years ago, rock-climbing, ropes, instructors and full safety equipment. 'Never look down, old cocker,' the

125

instructor had said. He jerked his head up so that he no longer saw the rubbish bins in the yard and the washing lines. For a moment, Josh Mantle hesitated, then swung his legs out through the window. The wall against him was rough stone set with patches of cement that would have been used to repair the old bomb and artillery damage. The bell behind him rang, and the wind sang against him. He edged away from the window.

'Tell them not to open the door, tell them we need time. Time is critical to us. Don't look down.'

She came after him through the window. He reached to take her hand and she held it so tight that he cursed. He felt her fingers, stiff, free him. He edged away from the kitchen window and faced the wall. His hands splayed as he tried to find security from the wall, to balance himself. He crabbed sideways along the platform. He heard the pant-whistle of her breath behind him.

He felt the bite of the wind because he had forgotten his coat, as she had forgotten her anorak, and he remembered what she had put into its pocket.

There was a drainpipe ahead of him, his target.

He saw where the paint had peeled off it and where the screws that fastened it to the wall had come away. Some years, the drainpipe would have been blocked and the rain would have run down the stonework of the wall beside it. He saw where the mortar between the stones, near the pipe, had cracked or fallen out, and more corrosion from the filth in the rain. There was no turning back. The pipe was inches from his fingers. They brushed against its chipped paint. One more step. The wind gusted. He rocked. One hand against the stone of the wall and finding every crevice and every ridge, one hand touching the drainpipe. He felt the slip below his foot.

The stone hit the concrete of the yard below and broke apart on impact.

He looked back. One stone had gone. Like a gap in teeth. He wanted to talk to her, help her, give her strength, and his voice was stifled dead in his throat. She must step across the gap. He was committed to her. He had made his bloody promise to her. He held the drainpipe with one hand, and grasped her wrist with the other. He steadied her over the space in the stone platform. He brought her wrist to the drainpipe, put her fingers on it. There was terror in her eyes. He looked up. The drainpipe passed the window of the floor above, then the guttering, then the sloping tiled roof above.

He croaked, 'Can you do it?'

'You've all the ideas. Any alternatives?'

'I don't know how secure the drainpipe is.'

'Well, you go first, then we'll bloody well find out.'

She loathed him, he thought, because he had made her show her fear. He loathed her, he thought, because she would not let him help her conquer the fear.

He depended on the fastening of the screws that held the drainpipe to the wall and climbed. His shoes found the smallest indents in the stone. His fingers ached to breaking point. He lay on the tiles and his shoes found a hold in the old gutter. His breath came in sharp pants. There was lichen and moss on the tiles, in the gutter.

'Do I bloody stay down here? Are you having your bloody afternoon sleep up there?'

He was old, stupid, fucked-up – had to have been to have committed himself to her. He wedged his knee and his thigh into the gutter. One hand to push into the gap of a broken tile and try to find a secure hold, one hand to reach for her. He felt her fingers in his, and pulled. He heaved her over the gutter and onto the tiles.

They crawled over them. The lichen and the moss gave them grip. There was the sound of loud, raucous music.

Going slowly, stopping, assessing where the grip was best, where the tiles were damp, treacherous. He pointed to the end of the roof, to the top of a rusted straight ladder.

They were above the window the music came from. He heard the whip crack of a tile breaking behind him and turned. There was something manic in her face. She was standing, swaying to

127

the beat of the music, hips gyrating. She had come through the barrier of fear. She mocked him. Her hips moved as if she was a strip-show dancer.

He went down the ladder and didn't stop to help her. It led to a flat roof. Another ladder at the far end. He heard her coming after him but did not turn to face her. The second ladder, in good condition, came down into the yard of a motor-repair business. He walked briskly towards the open gate, through the graveyard of Trabants and Wartburgs with the wheels off, bonnets up, interiors ripped out, past the mechanics. His chest heaved. She ran behind him, to catch him. They stood on the pavement.

Josh said, grim, as if it hurt, 'You've made a mistake, a bad mistake.'

She caught his eyes, blazed at him, 'Have I? What mistake have I made?'

'He'll break in there.'

'So he breaks in.'

'You left your coat.'

'So I buy another coat.'

'You left your coat for him to find, and I left mine. But in your coat were the names, your precious eye-witnesses. Your coat tells him you were there, the names tell him where you're going.'

'Does it?' The laughter sparkled in her eyes.

'That was your mistake.'

'Was it?' Her shoulders shook gently with the laughter.

'It's bloody serious.'

She took his hand. She gazed into his face. She held his hand across her breast. She ran her tongue over her lips. She forced his hand against the warmth and softness of her breast. She squeezed it tighter on the softness and warmth, and he felt the folded paper.

'Put it there when you were asleep. Needed your sleep, didn't you? I didn't have to sleep.'

'Well done, you did well.'

'You didn't do bad – for an antique.'

They ran towards Prenzlauer, for the labyrinth of streets and the shelter of the tower blocks between Moll Strasse and Karl Marx Allee.

'When do we go to Rostock? Do we get a car? Car is fastest. Do we go now to Rostock?'

'Shut up, can't you?' Josh panted. 'Shut your bloody little mouth so that I can think.'

They ran to be clear of Saarbrucker Strasse, until they could run no more.

They had watched him ring the bell, walk back, look up, go again to the bell and keep his finger on it. They had watched him as he had stood clear of the street door, raised his foot, hit the door with the sole of his shoe. Raub had gasped. The door had swung open. Goldstein had thought that the door of his grandfather's home would have been kicked in.

They had sat in the car in silence and waited.

The engine ran, the heater blew warm air on them.

He came back through the door. His face was ashen.

He walked towards the car and opened the back door, reached inside for his briefcase. They saw the blood on his knuckles.

Raub blurted, 'You have not committed, Doktor Krause, an illegal act?'

Goldstein whispered, hoarse, 'Did you not find her, Doktor Krause, or have you missed her?'

'An illegal act, in our company, is quite forbidden.'

'Is she running ahead of you, to Rostock?'

The face was set, savage. He took the briefcase, slammed the door behind him. He walked away. They watched in the mirror. He was walking towards the junction of Saarbrucker Strasse and Prenzlauer and he had the mobile phone at his ear.

They ran from the car and up the three flights of stairs. The door was open, angled because one hinge was broken free, and there was a smashed chair on the floor, as if it had been used to barricade the door. The food on the table was scattered. There were two coats thrown down on the rug in the centre of the room, a man's and a woman's, and all the pockets of each of the coats were pulled out. There was a photograph on the floor and the wreckage of a frame. The photograph had been torn to many pieces. They stood, rock still, in the centre of the room. The quiet was around them. The far door was open. In the kitchen, the window was open. Goldstein understood and leaned out. He was high above a concrete yard, above the washing lines, and he saw a smashed stone. He looked along the narrow platform below the window and saw the void from which the stone had fallen. He would not have done it, could not have gone along the stone platform. He stared down. His body shook with trembling. There was a man's coat, she was not alone. If she had gone along that stone platform then she must have had the smell in her nose of evidence . . .

'Get to the car. Telephone for the ambulance.'

They were behind the door. Their last refuge had been the space between the door and the refrigerator. Raub was bent over them. They held each other, their hands were together. Blood trickled down their faces.

Goldstein ran for the stairs and the telephone. Raub was close behind him with the two coats that had been on the rug. He did not give his name to the ambulance *Kontrol*.

They drove away.

Goldstein understood that they should be gone before the ambulance came, that they should not be involved in illegality.

Albert Perkins came off the telephone, the secure line, to London. He sat at the desk of the station head, used the man's chair. He could be a pig when he wanted to. What the station heads posted abroad all detested was to have a man in from Vauxhall Bridge Cross who camped in their space, used it as if it were his own. At the station head's desk, Albert Perkins riffled in the drawer and found the Sellotape roll. He sealed the two envelopes, the one containing the Iranian material, the other holding his report on progress concerning the matter of Tracy Barnes/Joshua F. Mantle. The station heads, in Albert Perkins's experience, were from independent schools and good colleges at the universities of Oxford and Cambridge. They had come along well-oiled tracks, of connection and recommendation, to employment with the Secret Intelligence Service. They would detest him as a vulgar little man, a former tea-boy and one-time Library clerk, night-school educated, without pedigree . . . but the vulgar little man had scrambled his unlikely way up the promotion ladder and was now a London deputy desk head and, with tolerable satisfaction, had the rank on overseas staffers, and they'd not be permitted, ever, to forget it.

He smiled his superiority. 'Just get them off to London, please, first courier you've got travelling over. That young fellow, the one straight out of kindergarten, I'll need him up in Berlin. May have to sit on his hands for a few days, but I'll have him there. Oh, yes, and I'll need a Berlin flight soonest, hire car as well at the other end. You won't forget those chocolates I mentioned, not too expensive. By the by, don't go worrying about your Iran file, topping it up, it's all in here. There's a good chap.'

They were in the soundproofed bunker on the second floor of the embassy in Bonn. It was assumed that the steel-lined walls of the room would deflect the listening equipment that was presumably used by the BfV. It was always right to assume that respected allies employed their state-of-the-art electronics to eavesdrop on valued friends. Old Trotsky had known the truth of it, had said an ally had to be watched like an enemy. The station head, flushed, did the bidding, went to the outer office to instruct the station manager to arrange the courier, confirm a flight and a hire car, and to tell young Rogers, who was 'straight from kindergarten' with a first-class honours in ancient history and who was the second son of a brigadier general, that he was off to Berlin, open-ended. Albert Perkins finished the coffee that had been brought to him. He walked at a leisured pace to the door.

'What you're going to do – I've worked very hard for good contact relations here, are you going to wreck them?'

He smiled at the station head. 'By the time I've finished here, your German friends, my German allies, will spit on the ground I've walked on.'

Asked with steeled dislike, 'Am I privy – am I allowed to be told how long you're in Berlin?'

'Berlin is just transit. It's Rostock where it's at. I'll be there.'

Dieter Krause drove fast. He had taken the autobahn 55.

He drove his own car, the BMW 7 series, that they had given him. It was six days since he had flown out from Tempelhof to London and in seven days he was booked on the flight to Washington. There was no speed restriction on the autobahn and he drove faster than 160 kilometres per hour, hammering in the outside lane. In those six days his world had fractured; within the next seven the fracture could be stressed to collapse point.

He went north. The autobahn would take him around the towns of Oranienburg and Neuruppin, it would skirt Wittstock, go past the Plauer See and the Insel See, where he had fished with Pyotr Rykov. It would bypass Gustrow where their families had camped at weekends, and Laage. He was going home, going to face the crisis in his world, going back to Rostock.

They called him as he drove, telephoned his mobile, as he had said they should.

He had the small scrap of notepaper on the seat beside him, with the names.

North of Neuruppin, the mobile rang – Klaus Hoffmann, aged thirty-six, formerly a *Leutnant*.

Klaus Hoffmann did not complain of 'reassociation'. The merging of the two Germanys had been kind to him. He had served twelve years in the MfS, was fluent in Russian, English and Czech. He would have described himself as a pragmatist. The old life had offered opportunities, the new life offered further opportunities. He sold property, acting as a broker for Western companies and international corporations that looked to locate in the East. He had understood the old system and exploited it, he had mastered the new system and made it work for him. He was flaxen-haired, athletic, and tanned from his most recent visit to the Tunisian resorts. He could offer the companies and corporations a detailed knowledge of the necessary procedures to slice through bureaucracy in the matter of planning applications and in the business of gaining federal government grant-aid. He wavered in his business close to the line drawn by the law, crossed it, recrossed and crossed it again. He had knowledge of so many officials: he could provide introductions to those who might be slipped a small brown envelope and he could threaten those who would crumble at the prospect of the unveiling of dirt. Through bribery, through blackmail, he won access to those whose signatures were needed to approve planning permission and to grant funds. He had been taught well in the MfS. He had a fine house in the Wandlitz area of Berlin, once occupied by a senior economic planner. The old wife had gone, a believer in the regime that was washed out, a new wife had been acquired. He had the Mercedes, and investments in the overseas markets and in the safer German companies . . . What he had built was at risk. On the night of 21 February 1988, on attachment from Magdeburg to Rostock, working late, he had been called out by Hauptman Dieter Krause to a shit place on the coast. The kid, the spy, had been on the ground: he had kicked the head of the kid, the spy, he had helped to drag the body back to the trawler and he had helped to weight it. He stood to lose the good life. He confirmed by his car phone that he was coming to Rostock.

Near to Wittstock, Josef Siehl, who had held the rank of *Unterleutnant*, rang at last.

Josef Siehl, on the telephone, complained that it had not been straightforward for him to take time off work, he had had to beg his supervisor. Always, he complained. He had stopped at a filling station and used a public telephone to confirm that he was driving to Rostock.

Past the Insel See, the call came from Ulf Fischer, who had never been promoted beyond *Feldwebel*.

Ulf Fischer, waiting for a fare on Lange Strasse, telephoned Hauptman Dieter Krause from his taxi. It was a good place to wait, near to the Radisson Hotel, which was the best in Rostock, and close to the shops of Kropeliner Strasse. A good place to wait, but the waiting was long, few enough fares to be had from the near empty hotel and shops. He telephoned from his taxi to say that he would be at the rendezvous.

South of Laage, Gunther Peters, once a junior and unnoticed *Feldwebel*, finally called.

Gunther Peters telephoned from his car, ordinary and not ostentatious. He hoped to be on time at the rendezvous, but he was coming from Leipzig and the radio said there would be road works near to Potsdam. He lived in the seat of his ordinary and unostentatious Volvo car. He was a minimum of ten kilos overweight, aged thirty-eight now, and he was pasty pale. He did not run when he could walk. On the telephone he said at what time he hoped to reach Rostock.

Dieter Krause drove on, powering the big car, towards the city that was his home. They were all vulnerable. Each of them was as vulnerable and at risk as himself. Because they were vulnerable and at risk, they would all come that afternoon to the rendezvous in Rostock, as their *Hauptman* had ordered.

'Why?'

They were beside the old Wall, spattered with ugly graffiti scrawl and with technicolor paint sprays. A short stretch had been left for the scrawlers and the sprayers.

'Because I say so.'

They had walked for more than an hour. He never turned to her, as if he knew that she would follow him.

'Why are we here?'

'Because I say so.'

Across the road from the section of Wall, narrow concrete slabs topped by a heavy rubber moon, smooth and of too great a diameter to reach over, was a small circular window with a recessed metal grille, set in the façade of an old building. White

134

and gold lilies were fastened to it. He read the name and the dates that were carved in the stone above the window: Harro Schulze-Boysen, 2.9.1909–22.12.1942. He stood in front of the flowers, gazed at them.

'Why are we here?'

'We are here so that we know why we are going to Rostock.'

She snorted. 'That's just ridiculous. You think I don't know why?'

He said, staring up at the memorial, 'There has to be a reason for going. When I've told you the reason, we will go to Rostock.'

7

'So, who was he?'
     'Harro Schulze-Boysen was a member of the Rote Kappelle, the Red Orchestra. The Communists were against the Nazis, therefore they all became Communists. They spied for the Communists, for ideology. When they were arrested by the Gestapo they were brought here. Schulze-Boysen was brought here.'
     'That's history.'
     'They were in "protective custody". At the end there was "special treatment", days on end of torture. Finally, execution.'
     'What is it to me?'
     She stood beside him, small and playing bored. He faced the open space, large enough for three, four football pitches. There was a raised mound in the centre of the space, surrounded by sparse grass tufted yellow in the carpet of frozen snow. On the far side of the mound were birch trees, gaunt from the winter.
     'What can you hear, Tracy? Sorry, let me do that again. What can you not hear?'
     'That's a stupid bloody question.'
     'You can hear traffic. We're in the centre of a city, of course there's traffic noise. There are no birds. Spring's coming, birds are nesting. It's big ground here, it's where the birds should be, but there aren't any birds. You can't hear birdsong. It was called Prinz Albrecht Strasse. It's where the Gestapo had their main Berlin office. It's where Himmler worked, and Heydrich and Eichmann. It's where they brought people who stood up, who shouted, who did not compromise. It's when

you feel the history in this country, when you can't hear the song of birds.'

The place held him. He wanted to share the feeling of it. Gently, Josh took her arm and turned her round. She was scowling, as if she was tired and cold, as if she had no interest.

They faced the Wall. Below it, half excavated, was a sunken entrance wide enough to have taken a single car or truck. Either side of the entrance were the back walls and side walls of small, compartment rooms.

'They were driven through that entrance. They would have been sweating with fear in the back of lorries and lying in shit and piss and vomit. The small rooms were the holding cells. The people were taken from those cells up into the main building, the top floors, for torture. They were brought back to the cells. They would have sat there, on the stone floors and they would have prayed, cried, for the release of death. They were not there by accident, Tracy. They chose to be there. They made the decision to stand up and to shout, not to compromise. They were ordinary people, from trade unions, from the civil service, from the ranks of junior officers, from the Church. For every man or woman in those cells there were nine hundred and ninety-nine men and women who did not stand up, did not shout, who compromised. If you were in the crowd, Tracy, if your mother and father were in the nine hundred and ninety-nine, would you want it raked over? Would you? You want the bulldozers out. You want it covered over. You want it hidden. Look up, damn you, look up at the Wall.'

He had his fist under her chin. He wrenched her head up so that she had to look above the cell block to the Wall.

'Just as this place killed people, so did the Wall. Behind the Wall, again, history gestating, were those who had the compulsion to stand up and to shout, who would not compromise. Behind that Wall were more cells, more interrogators, more torturers, more executioners working in yards at night. Again, the one in a thousand stood up, shouted, did not compromise. The nine hundred and ninety-nine don't want to know, don't want reminding, don't want the shame paraded. They want history buried, covered up. Look at the Wall. It's a place for scumbags to scrawl inane messages. Shouldn't it be a memorial? Look at the chippings, where bits have been hacked off for sale to tourists like it's damn moon rock, but cheaper. There are places either side of this Wall where the birds don't sing.'

He loosed her chin. He walked to the crude steps set into the side of the mound.

On the top was a viewing platform. He leaned on the rail of weathered wood. She was beside him, and quiet.

'What we're standing on was rubble from the bombing, bad in the February of nineteen forty-five. Prisoners were still held here in the last days, when there was no water, no electricity, but the torture functioned and the killings. Then, it was over. Was there contrition? They covered up the rubble, made the place invisible, hid it from sight. I'm getting there, Tracy. They did not want the past examined. This place was covered with buildings. How many men and women worked here, signed the papers, allocated the cells, organized the shifts of the interrogators, signed the chits for the bullets and the ropes? How many? There was no will. The men and women who worked here went free. History was wiped away. The tens of thousands who compromised did not want the history exposed. There was no will then, there is no will now.'

He gripped the rail hard. He wondered if he had reached her. He looked out over the dead space and the dead grass and the dead trees and the dead Wall.

'They did not have to stand, shout, not compromise, the people who were brought here. They had such courage. They were brought here because of what they believed. Each of them, he, she, could not go on the road of the nine hundred and ninety-nine. They are worth remembering. Am I being stupid or sentimental? They were ordinary people. They were Germans in the Nazi times, they were Germans in the Stasi times. They were the same ordinary people as those in Srebrenica, in the Palestine refugee camps, Kurds. They scream to be remembered with honour. That is why we are going to Rostock, so that history is not bulldozed. Hans Becker was ordinary, and he should be remembered.'

'Have you finished?'

'Don't you want to talk about what I've said?'

'It's a bloody miserable place and I want to get the hell out of it.'

She seemed to shiver. He did not know whether he had reached her or whether it was just the wind across the dead space catching her.

'Come on.'

'Is it Rostock now?'

'We go to Rostock late tonight.'

'Where do we go now?'

'I've a name for you. It's a male name, but it will do for you, just right.'

He had annoyed her and her eyes blazed at him. 'I'm cold, I'm tired, my rucksack weighs a fucking ton. I don't need you.'

'You need me, Tracy. You may be too stupid to realize it. You need me. I brought you here so that you could get into your dumb little brain the importance of what you are doing, and the opposition you will face.'

She was tiny beside him. He could have slipped the straps of the rucksack off her back. He could have carried it for her, but he was damned if he would offer to. They would be expecting him back that evening, and in the office in the morning, and the paper would be piling on his desk. He did not know when it would be finished, but he thought it would go hard before it was. Without history, she couldn't realize how hard it would go.

'What's this fucking talk about a name?'

'We're going to the zoo. You'll find your name there.'

The manager remembered him – a sweet moment for Albert Perkins – and gushed a greeting.

'Doktor Perkins, how excellent. The usual room, of course?'

'Mr Perkins – I'm not a doctor.'

'Everyone in Germany, Herr Perkins, is a doctor, or they are a Turk sweeping the streets.' The manager dropped his voice, mock conspiracy, grinning. 'Or they are an *ossi*, a new brother from the East – and you have a colleague.'

'I have brought Doktor Rogers with me. He'll be here a few days. For me it's just one night.'

He looked around the small reception area. Spotless with fresh paint and clean. The hotel was unpretentious, quiet, discreet. It was three years since he had last stayed there. It was in a street of Savignyplatz at the heart of the old café area of West Berlin. At the hotel off Savignyplatz he had been able to find, in the old days, the anonymity that was valuable to his work, and the inexpensive restaurants that did not challenge his *per diem* expenses allowance. He thought the boy from the kindergarten, Rogers, would have expected to stay in a Holiday Inn or a Hyatt, would have expected porterage and a modern room, stereotyped in design. He'd not get it here. Perkins tramped up the stairs to the first floor, his usual room, the view over a yard and a car park and over the back of another block. Rogers came after him.

He said, 'What's the plan, Mr Perkins?'

'I unpack, I make a few phone calls, we collect the hire car. We go visiting.'

'It's just, Mr Perkins, that I don't really know what it's about.'

Perkins went sharply to the door, closed it. He drew the curtains at the window and turned on the bedside radio before taking the slim file from his briefcase. He tossed it casually at the young man.

Perkins rang a number from his personal directory, a number from way back. He murmured into the telephone, against the music from the radio.

'Mr Perkins, am I being an idiot? I understand the position of Corporal Barnes. I understand why we're targeting Krause. What I don't understand is the reason that Mantle has involved himself.'

'You've the file.'

'Doesn't help me, Mr Perkins, doesn't tell me why he's pushed his nose in.'

'Read the file – read it to me.'

The life of Joshua Frederick Mantle, as known to Albert Perkins, was a single sheet of paper. The boy from kindergarten, Rogers, had a good voice, well-articulated, quiet against the music.

Born: 27 March 1942. Parents: Frederick Mantle and Emily Mantle (née Wilson). FM served Royal Engineers, Military Medal in North Africa, twice promoted to Sgt and twice demoted for persistent alcohol abuse. Served post-war in Catterick, Plymouth, Colchester, Palestine and Malaya. EM shot dead by CCT (Chinese Communist Terrorist) in Penang, 1953.

Perkins said, 'The file always tells the story, rare when it doesn't. His father was a drunk with a career saved by one daft moment with a bazooka. The child had little contact with his father, his mother was everything. She was shot dead in a street market in Penang. The night she was killed, his father wasn't in the barracks comforting his son, he was pissed and out wrecking the Chinese quarter with his mates. It would have been, aged eleven years, the end of his childhood.'

Education: Army schools, Army Apprentice College (Chepstow).

'There were no relations to dump him on so he was carted round his father's postings. One school after another, no permanence and no stability. A lonely and self-contained teenager. Would have thought he was unloved, would have been damn sure he was unwanted. Went to the Apprentice College as soon as he was old enough to be taken in. His father came out of the Army in nineteen sixty and headed for South Africa, his latest woman in tow. Mantle told a man I spoke to that he never heard from him again. The last time he saw his father, in a pub at Chepstow, the old bugger was in his cups and yakking on about building pontoon bridges, under fire, over the gullies, in front of the tanks in the desert. The truth is his father dug latrine pits and plumbed in the field showers, but just had the one glory moment with the bazooka. The Army, his own service, was the only horizon he had as a youngster.'

Army career: Joined I Corps as clerk, 1961. Stationed at Templer, Ashford. Aden, 1966/1967. Osnabruck (Germany) 1972/1975. Staff Sergeant 1981. Belize 1982. Transferred out of I Corps.

'He started at the bottom of the heap. Not particularly sharp, but dedicated. He was pretty typical. Had made corporal by the time he went to Aden, based at the Mansoura gaol where the FLOSY and NLF guerrillas were held. Would have done a bit of native bashing in the interrogation sessions, would have been able to justify it. Then to Quebec barracks in Osnabruck. He was pushing paper with the rest of them, waste of time, analysing the Soviet order of battle. Quite a shy man, I was told, made his work everything. I don't think there was anything in his life but his work. What he owned fitted into the suitcase under his bed. He went to Belize with an officer . . . A prisoner being interrogated died. A soldier reported the death to his unit padre. There was an inquiry. I was sent to minimize the fall-out. If Mantle had made a statement indicting his officer, who had tortured a prisoner to death, then the officer was gone and we were knee deep in propaganda shit. He didn't, he was sensible, kept his mouth shut . . . Frankly, at that time I reckoned he hadn't the bottle. He's regretted that act of compromise ever since. We bought him off with a transfer and a commission. He left I Corps as a changed man.'

Joined SIB, Royal Military Police. Commissioned 1984, rank of Captain. Served RMP Hounslow HQ and Tidworth Garrison. Left Army in 1989.

'He went into Special Investigation Branch. He was chasing squaddies for petty pilfering, for being drunk louts on Saturday nights, for flogging equipment out of the stores. They made him up to a commission. He would have been a cuckoo in the mess, too old for his junior rank, never works. I saw him at Tidworth camp . . . I was told he was very cold and very bitter, poor company. Actually, he was ostracized, ignored like he didn't exist. There had been a touch of a scandal the month before, a major who was popular had a finger pointed for pocketing a very small amount of money. Mantle had played it by the book, and the regiment involved thought it should have been handled internally. Mantle went for prosecution. He'd gained that awful bloody sense of duty that afflicts bitter men, everything lined up against him. When the downsizing started at the end of the Cold War, he was top of the list.'

Civilian occupation: Social Worker 1990/1994. Unemployed 1994/1996. Solicitor's clerk, qualifying as Legal Executive, 1996 . . .

'He came out. He would have been a lost man. He would have thought that the Army had rejected him, and he'd have been right. He worked with juvenile offenders, car thieves, yobs, but to him they'd have been disadvantaged by the system. A police officer in Thames Valley told me about him. Then he was married, a very wealthy woman. She died. Don't expect me to score points. He would have crumpled. He went right off the rails, went downhill, lived rough . . . He was lifted out of the gutter by the solicitors who had handled his late wife's affairs. Outwardly he'll have pulled himself together. Inwardly he'll have blamed the world, every symbol of authority, for what has happened to him.'

Status: Married Elizabeth (Libby) Harris (née Thompson), divorcée, 1994. No children. Died 1996.

143

'That was bad luck. Up to then, his marriage, he'd seemed like one of those men who just couldn't make it with women. No girl-friends before. One plunge, and again the failure. He has no-one to love, and no-one to love him. At his age, now, he's left on the shelf. As a substitute, he will attach himself to any cause and to any unfortunate that happens along . . .'

The city had been the gateway to the world. But the gate of Rostock was now rotten and decayed. In medieval times, under the same grey-black clouds of late winter, Rostock had been the trading gateway to the Baltic but the Hanseatic League had fallen apart under the spite of war and been rebuilt. It had been destroyed again by the grey-orange tongues of flame in the fire of three centuries ago.

The great churches and the university and the timbered homes of merchants had risen again in Rostock and then collapsed, lost, under the incendiaries of the bombers flown from Britain to target the shipyards and the submarine pens beside the grey blue of the sea.

The Soviet Army had come. On the coat tails of the Soviets had been the Party, the German Communists, the Stasi and the lorry convoys bringing the grey dull concrete for rebuilding the shipyards. Rostock was once more the gateway.

All crashed down again, as surely as if the bombers had returned to the city sprinkled with grey-white snow. The bureaucrats and business men had travelled from Bonn in the wake of 'reassociation', from Kiel and Hamburg and Bremen. They spoke of 'self-determined democratic renewal', and for every ten jobs in the shipyards they took nine men and threw them on the refuse tip of unemployment. In the grey, tired and suffering city, fragile hope again fell, as it had through history.

Each morning of late winter the grey-brown mist was settled on the Warnow river that split old Rostock from new Rostock. The city, the people of Rostock, suffered again, sullen and hostile to the disasters brought by strangers, as they had been through history.

Under the cloud bank, by the sea, in the mist, spattered with snow, the city struggled for survival.

The city, Rostock, its people, would fight to hold the little they had. Each man for himself in the grey cold jungle. It was a bad place for strangers who came to throttle the little that was left, as it had always been.

She heard the key in the door. He had been gone a week. He had not telephoned her.

She sat in the comfortable chair, new, and watched the television, new, and slipped her feet into her shoes, new. The programme on the television was a game show, new, imported from America. She switched the programme off with the remote control, new . . . Everything around Eva Krause was new. The house in the refurbished terrace beside the Petrikirche was new for her.

In their generosity, they had allowed her to choose her new clothes and had provided the money, but everything else around her had been chosen by them, by the man from Munich and by the little Jewish shit, as if Dieter and Eva Krause were not permanent but only on trial. If Dieter failed in what they wanted of him, a removal van would come and carry away everything that was new and provide it for the next manipulated man and his family, and the house would be closed to them, locks changed.

Eva Krause stood. She smoothed her dress and touched the styling of her hair. She tidied the magazines.

He came into the living room. They had been married for fifteen years, the wedding a week after she had passed her vetting, after he had been told she was suitable. She gazed at his face. He had been told that, as a full-time official of the Freier Deutscher Gewerkschaftsbund in the shipyard, she was acceptable as the wife of a Stasi officer. He came across the room. She saw the tiredness, and she saw the scars. He bent to kiss her and the thickness of his trimmed beard brushed her chin.

She twisted her face away so that his lips, beside the raked scars, touched her cheek and not her mouth. They had been

145

equals, she in the trade union office at the shipyard, he at the headquarters of the Staatssicherheitsdienst on August-Bebel Strasse; they were not equal now because there was no job for a trade unionist in the castrated shipyard. She had only the money that he gave her, that they gave him. The scars were alive, knitting angrily, raw dark red. Now that she no longer had a position of importance, she had the time to manicure her nails. She understood the scratch scars on his face, either side of his mouth. Her nails used to be pared short: now she had the time to grow them, shape them.

'A good trip, a good journey?'

He would not try to kiss her again. He looked into her eyes.

'You were made welcome, you met new friends?'

His eyes seemed to yearn for her, not wanting love but comfort.

'The one who made you welcome, why did she scratch your face, Dieter? Was that part of the entertainment provided for an honoured guest? But did the young woman not like you, Dieter?'

He turned from her. He had the palms of his hands against the wall beside the oil painting of the nude bathers on the beach at Rugen Island. They would mark the clean paint.

She no longer taunted. She spat the accusation: 'Is that the life when you go with them? Do they find you whores? Were you too clumsy for the bitch? Did you come too early for her? Couldn't you do it for her? Does the Jew have a whore? Does Raub? Or is it only Doktor Krause who must be amused when he goes to talk of Pyotr Rykov, his friend? How will it be when you come back from America? Will you be more marked?'

He lifted his head. He shouted to the ceiling, 'You do not understand.'

'I understand that some whore, a bitch, has scratched your face. Did you pay extra for that? Did they pay extra? Do we have, from England, presents to compensate for your time with a whore? What, Dieter, with their generosity, have you brought us?'

146

'There was no whore. I have brought you nothing.'

'Nothing? No rubbish from duty free, no trinket from the airport, nothing? Could you not go to the shops because you were too busy with whores? You promised Christina—'

'If you let me tell you—'

'—promised Christina the new racquet. For tonight – the tournament starts tonight. You promised.'

He took her shoulder, he forced her down into her chair. She was strong. He pushed her down and told her of the way it had been, of the young woman soldier and the rake of her nails. She held his hand tight.

'Why?'

'Because of what happened a long time ago.'

Eva Krause listened. In the apartment on Augusten Strasse, behind the headquarters at August-Bebel Strasse, they never talked of his work. It was not accepted that an officer of the Stasi should talk with his wife of his day, of his problems, his successes. But now he told her that a long time ago a spy had been killed at Rerik and that the woman soldier had attacked him because of the spy who had been killed. 'People have come now to look for evidence. I apologize, I have to go out.'

'Where? What evidence? Where do you go? Christina's match . . . Who are the people? What is there to find?'

He broke the hold of her hand, left her. She felt as if a darkness closed in on her. She heard the cough of the engine of the big car driving away from the house which had been provided for them.

She sat in the dim light of the room. She thought, for something to cling to, of Pyotr Rykov.

The minister spoke on the telephone.

'Don't interrupt me. Don't threaten me. I have the facts. On my staff is Colonel Rykov. Colonel Rykov tells me that thugs answering to you have arrested a Major Ivanov who serves in the Pechenga garrison in the St Petersburg military district. I am informed by Colonel Rykov, in whom I have total and absolute confidence, that Major Ivanov was pulled from his car this morning by your criminal thugs in connection with a falsified charge of defamation. You will hear what I have to say.'

The minister talked to the General who headed Directorate Z of the Federal Counter-Intelligence Service. Before 'reconstruction' the General had headed the Second Chief Directorate of the KGB. Pyotr Rykov had rehearsed his minister well: it was not necessary for him to prompt.

'The alleged defamation was obtained by the illegal use of a telephone intercept on the home line of Major Ivanov. Hear me, you bastard, never again do you order a telephone intercept on a serving Army officer. You claim that, in talking to his father, Major Ivanov – who is a hero of Afghanistan and who did not stay at home like the shit that your thugs are, who served his country with distinction in combat – referred to the State President as 'that obese cunt who is in the coat pocket of the Mafia'. Hear me. Within one hour, Major Ivanov is to be returned to his garrison camp at Pechenga, a free man. I believe your people to be stupid and also cowards. If, within one hour, Major Ivanov has not been returned to his camp then he will be taken from your custody by a unit of the Zenith team. I promise you – I honour promises – such action by Special Forces would result, inevitably, in your thugs at Pechenga requiring the attention of nurses or a mortician.'

The Major was a good and valued friend of Pyotr Rykov, had acted as second-in-command of his paratroop company at Herat. And the Major had spoken the truth to his father: the Mafia owned the politicians; without the politicians the Mafia could be crushed by the fist of the military. The Federal Counter-Intelligence Service was the tool of the politicians, the bumboy of the Mafia. Politicians, the Federal Counter-Intelligence Service, the Mafia, all were cancers of corruption eating at the strength of Mother Russia.

'Major Ivanov, on his return to barracks, should confirm his freedom by telephone to Colonel Rykov. One hour.'

The minister put down the telephone.

'It was as you wanted?'

'Better than I wanted it. Rumour moves, whispers speak, word travels. In three days, perhaps a week, it will be known in every camp, garrison and base that you stood down those bastards. You will have earned the loyalty, unquestioning, of the corps of officers. That is important for the future.'

'And earned enmity.'

'You have the power.'

The minister put his hand on the arm of Pyotr Rykov, gripped it tight. 'I have the power to confront enemies. Do you? Be careful . . . Be careful of that enmity.'

He did not think he had reached her on the dead space of the old Prinz Albrecht Strasse, and he was bewildered. It was not possible, to Josh Mantle, that a person could not be moved by the imagining of the fear, the bravery, the isolation, the courage and the hopelessness of those brought there. He had walked her by the entrance to the courtyard of the old war ministry building where Claus von Stauffenberg of the '44 bomb plot against the Führer had been executed, and had not spoken of the place and the history. He could not face again the realization, after the pouring out of his emotion, that he could not reach her.

He could not reach her because he did not understand her.

They walked. They were on the wide pavements of the Kurfürstendamm. Just another European city, where history was no longer required, where history was bulldozed. They were among the great blocks of glass and steel, among the hotels of luxury. The past was contaminated, so the past was shut out. Perhaps he was trapped by history, neurotic in his allegiance to the past, perhaps he should have gone home, alone, on the evening flight to be at the papers on his desk in the morning. But he was trapped by the history, by her.

Perkins drove. What he liked about the boy fresh out of kindergarten, Rogers, was that he didn't talk. He disliked talk for the sake of it. The quiet in the car helped him to wallow in the nostalgia. He had known Berlin as closely as he knew the back of his hand, the wrinkles on his face, as he knew the hairs of his trimmed moustache. It had been his city, on both sides of the Wall. He had the address. He thought he kept good time. The nostalgia flowed, like the good days gone . . . Spittelmarkt was devastated, whole blocks destroyed. Bulldozers and lorries dispersing rubble, as if it was his image of 1945 all over again. A few isolated buildings were left, dark and smoke-grimed, like lost teeth in an old mouth, waiting for the demolition men. He squinted in the gloom to see the number of the block he wanted. He pulled up. The air was choked thick with dust from the lorries and the pile hammers.

'You'll wait for me. While you're waiting, get me the times of the last trains this evening from Berlin/Lichtenberg, to Rostock.'

He paid for the two tickets.

The light was sliding, throwing the big shadows across the far trees of the Tiergarten.

He had made a child of her.

When she sneered she was foul. Happy, young, without care, to Josh Mantle she was captivating. He gave her the book, let her skim it for the map. He wondered when she had last been in a zoo park. She made a grimace at the unblinking amber eyes of the brown fishing owl. She stood in awe to gaze at the bulk of the American black bear. She watched and squealed as the keeper, final feed of the day, threw fish for the leaping sea lions and was cascade-splashed. She grabbed his arm to point to him where the jaguar slept. As if without thinking, natural, she had taken his hand and squeezed it, excitement, when she saw the panda. It was the end of the day. The crocodile columns of schoolchildren were being marshalled by their teachers, the zoo park was emptying. She hurried him, seemed frightened that it would be closed before she had seen everything. He wondered about her childhood.

She faced him and giggled, the child. 'But you haven't told me – which of them has the name you want to give to me?'

A hooter sounded. The zoo park was closing. He checked the map he had given her. He strode forward.

'Have you ever seen them, for real, the animals?'

'Once.' His guard had slipped.

'Where?'

'It doesn't matter.'

'Africa, India, America, where?'

'It's not important.'

The lump, the specialist's diagnosis, the holiday, the first failed treatment. A week's holiday with Libby in the Tanzanian game park at Serengeti, sandwiched between diagnosis and treatment.

He had drained the excitement from Tracy, as if she recognized that he did not trust her with confidences. He could have kicked himself, so savagely, for having let his guard slip, for having broken her mood of child's happiness.

She no longer held his hand and sulked beside him.

He took her to the hippopotamus house. The keeper eyed them, as if they were too late in the afternoon. The heat in the glass-sided house brought out the sweat in them. The creatures were in a wide pool topped with green slime and the stench of their excrement was sucked to his nose. There were limp-leafed plants in tubs beside the pool, to give it a fraudulent impression of African water, where he had been with Libby before the treatment started, and when they had known it was short time, borrowed time.

'You'd better tell me,' she said. 'What's my bloody name?'

It was ten years since he had been in the zoo park. He'd assumed that the hippopotamus was dead and commemorated.

'I'm sorry, I was married then. I went with my wife to Africa, just once. I'm sorry that I was foul with you. The memory hurts . . .'

She said, sour, 'Don't mind me. I'm only a bloody clerk.'

He pointed to the tooth. It was in a cabinet on the wall. An immense curving tooth was all that commemorated the animal.

He smiled, weak. 'More history, Tracy. Don't interrupt me, I'm not in the mood. I wanted somewhere good for you while we used time. The history. The zoo park was one of the last battlegrounds for Berlin in nineteen forty-five. It was the final line protecting the bunker where Hitler was. There were young guys in trenches, kids, fighting till they'd no more ammunition. There had been bombing as well, but the real killing was in the close-quarters fighting. There were five thousand creatures when the battle started, and ninety-one still alive when the final line broke. There was this big hippopotamus, monstrously big – he weighed several tons. When the shooting stopped and the smoke cleared, he came up to the surface of his pool. All through the battle he'd been down at the bottom in the mud. He was starved, thin, if you can imagine it. He was called Knautschke. He was a survivor. He stayed down in the mud, underwater, while there was all the shit and chaos up above. He became famous, a symbol of the spirit of isolated Berlin. He waited for the right time, the good time, then he came up from the mud . . .'

She pulled a face, mock grotesque. 'I'm Knautschke?'

'Right.'

'I'm a big hideous bastard with a tooth a foot long, stinking of shit and mud, with a mouth you'd drive a bus into? Is there any more history?'

'No.'

'Can we go to Rostock now?'

'Yes.'

A wizened little man, with a cat that stank on his lap, in an uncleaned room, faced Albert Perkins.

'A thousand American dollars, yes? You have to understand, Doktor Perkins, that these are hard times for persons such as myself. I am an expert on matters of security, on the gaining and analysis of information, on the administration of any large corporate body – I cannot find work, Doktor Perkins. You would imagine that a person with my skills would not face a problem of poverty. Many of my illustrious colleagues, they have not

152

faced a problem as I have, but they did not operate from inside the personal office of the minister. I think I am a very few years older than yourself, Doktor Perkins, but I am in the graveyard of life. You hear much talk of victims of the old regime. I myself am a victim. You agree, a thousand American dollars? I thank you, Doktor Perkins. I believe you are a very sympathetic and understanding gentleman. Cash, yes?

'Hauptman Dieter Krause? It is right that you should know why I talk of him, not only because you pay me one thousand American dollars in cash, why I talk frankly of him. I had no feeling for that woman, she was a fuck, she was information, it was mechanical, it was a good source. But, believe me, I refused the offer to go to Bonn and give evidence against her. They came here, the supercilious pigs of the BfV, to ask that I travel to Bonn as a state witness. I refused them. I have my pride. My pride told me that, by expertise, we had destroyed the security of the West's government. To us, they were donkeys, rubbish, quite lacking in the imagination necessary for intelligence officers. They wanted me to help to clear their garbage, and I refused. Krause offered himself, named the woman, sent her to prison, to ingratiate himself. The killing was on the twenty-first of November nineteen eighty-eight, Doktor Perkins. I have a very clear memory for dates and places and situations.

'I was the personal assistant to the minister, I was in his office in Haus 1 at Normannen Strasse. The report had reached Mielke when he arrived at his desk the following morning. A spy intercepted and killed, and no opportunity for questioning the spy. Krause was summoned to Berlin. He came that afternoon. He was an arrogant bastard, but not when I met him in the corridor outside the minister's office. I can picture him. I walked him through the outer offices, to the presence of Erich Mielke and I thought he might break his bladder on the carpet.

'The old man saw him, and told him that he was stupid enough, if he killed a spy before questioning, to push his prick up his own arse. He cringed in front of Mielke's desk and I thought he might cry . . . You would want to know, there were four men with him when he killed the spy. They were Leutnant Hoffmann and Unterleutnant Siehl and Feldwebel Fischer and Feldwebel Peters . . . He told his story and he was dismissed by Mielke and I thought he might run clean out of the old man's office. He was a suspicious old goat, Mielke, he demanded to know more of Krause. Had he killed the spy through incompetence, or killed him before he could be questioned? That was the way old Mielke's mind worked. He had me examine the file on Krause. There was a particular aspect of the file, gone now, I am sure – Krause was here in the last hours, in Berlin, with many others doing the same work, cleaning their files – and the file dealt with the IMs of Krause. I direct you towards one *Inoffizielle Mitarbeiter*, who had a position at the university in Rostock. He reported to Krause on his academic colleagues. To another officer, he reported on Hauptman Krause's wife, was given for that work a different codename, and Krause would not have known of that file. I see you smile, Doktor Perkins. We were very thorough. We were the best . . . I shall write you the name of that IM. He will still be there, he cannot leave the city. If you want amusement at the expense of Hauptman Krause, and I think you would be most amused, then you should go to see that man and hear about Krause's wife when you travel to Rostock.'

The thin hands grasped the banknotes, the fingers flicked them and counted. The pen was given him, the receipt for a thousand American dollars in cash was already made out, and he signed for it.

Josh had bought her the food, a takeaway burger and fries. Tracy had paid for the taxi in the bloody shivering cold, on the pavement outside the station.

When she had eaten the food on the street in the old west of the city, when they had waved down the taxi, when the taxi had dropped them at Berlin/Lichtenberg, Josh had checked they were not followed, or watched.

They joined the queue at the ticket counter.

* * *

154

He parked the car in a side street, two hundred metres from the station. He snapped his fingers for Rogers to walk beside him.

'Just a few things that you should take on board, young fellow. This isn't the Great Game. Don't expect to spend your life creeping up the Beka'a Valley, or cuddling with Yemeni tribesmen. It's idiots, not us, who do the graft. We send them off through the wire, across frontiers and through the mines. We don't go sentimental, we don't get involved. We just give the idiots a good push and send them on their way. We use them indiscriminately against friends and enemies, if you can tell the difference. If they want paying we pay them, if they want flattery we flatter them, if they want kicking we kick them. They are idiots and they are workhorses and we use them to move us a little closer, usually a fractional step, towards a successful conclusion of policy. What you have to remember, young man, the greater Germany is the most stable, wealthy, sophisticated, politically democratic country in Europe, but that is only the surface spectrum. Underneath, where the idiots go, it is as dangerous to them as Beirut in the old days. These idiots, tonight, are taking a train into man-trap country. We don't cry tears for them if they lose, we walk away. If they lose we start again, look for other idiots. I didn't ask them to step into man-trap country, it's their decision, but I'll damn sure take advantage of that decision. That's the way it is and don't ever forget it.'

The young fellow, the boy from kindergarten, walked silently beside him, head down, considering.

It had been Perkins's intention to shake him, with his first-class honours in ancient history. He would have moved paper and tapped the keyboard of a computer at Vauxhall Bridge Cross, and believed in the romance of his work. In Bonn, first posting overseas, he would have scanned documents and met low-grade sources, and believed in the ethic of his work. In the bright-lit hall of the Berlin/Lichtenberg station, it was time for the boy from kindergarten to see, close up, the idiots who went into man-trap country.

155

He went forward, the young fellow close to him. He saw them. They were in a short queue at the ticket desk.

'Evening, Tracy, evening, Mantle. Thought I'd find you here.'

156

8

He spun. The movement of turning, fast, buffeted Josh Mantle into a woman standing behind him, pressing close to him in the queue. He had been far away, his mind, in the last moments before the voice had cut into his consciousness, in the office in the high street of Slough – the morning, the partners, his desk empty, the papers for the day's court appearances not laid neatly out. It took him time, two seconds or three, to locate the voice.

'Thought you'd be here. The obvious way would have been to hire a car ten hours ago and get straight up there, or to take the first train. Good thinking, Mantle, and what I'd anticipated.'

The old railway station had been cleaned. There was a polished floor, flowers in pots, new counters and computers for issuing tickets, fast-food stalls, newspaper and magazine stands. Progress had reached the railway station of Berlin/Lichtenberg, so that a veneer covered the past and obliterated history.

'Always best to make your own agenda, not to let the opposition set it for you. Smart thinking . . .'

Perkins was close up to him.

He had looked right by Perkins. He focused. The pale, drawn face, the thin moustache, the evening stubble greying on the cheeks, the half-drawn cold smile, and the eyes that twinkled bright from the reflection of the strip lights. There was a young man behind Perkins, but hanging back as if he were not a willing player in the game. He felt a loathing for Albert Perkins. In the queue, behind his back, Tracy would have turned, would be watching him, judging him.

'You called them "gracious friends and respected allies", and told them where to find me. You fucking nearly killed us. You are disgusting.'

'Steady on, Mantle. No call to be wound up, stay calm. Tell him that, Tracy, shouldn't ever lose your calm . . . Actually, I'm not with the hare and I'm not with the hounds. Done my bit in the market-place, very satisfactorily. I'm here to watch the chase.'

'Get off my back.'

The queue shuffled forward a pace.

Perkins said, 'I've warned you once, but I'll warn you again, the last time. You go to Rostock and you will upset people. For those people there is a great deal at stake. For Hauptman Krause – by the by, Tracy, his scars are knitting quite well – at stake is his future. He's in from the cold, the future looks comfortable, there's no shortage of federal money in his wallet. Don't think he's going to hand that over, without a fight, for ten years in the Moabit gaol. His former underlings – they'll be verminous – will have built new lives, too, and if Krause goes to the Moabit gaol then they go with him, as accessories to murder, and they won't take kindly to it. There's the BfV, my esteemed colleagues, who reckon that Hauptman Krause is their invitation card to top-table intelligence evaluation, and they'll tell you that for too many years we and the Yankees have treated them as kitchen staff. They'll not be pleased to see him wiped away. They will close their eyes and turn their backs on little matters of illegality. It will get bad up there in Rostock.'

The queue slouched forward another pace. Josh didn't turn to face her, he did not look to see the effect on Tracy Barnes of Albert Perkins's poisonous tone.

Perkins said, 'You should know, the man I report to, he asked me what would happen if you, Tracy, were damn fool enough to go to Rostock. Only my opinion, I told him that first they'd warn you, very clear, no misunderstanding, and if you persisted they would rough you – that's a quick ride to hospital Casualty – and if you still went forward and threatened them and it's their freedom or your life, they'll kill you. I hope you listen to the radio, you always should when you're abroad, keeps you in touch. It only made two or three lines. An elderly couple beaten up in their home on Saarbrucker Strasse, unknown assailant, unknown motive. That'll be the warning. After the warning they'll go more physical, then they'll kill. You go to Rostock and you're on your own.'

Her voice, behind him, was clear, matter-of-fact.

'Two persons, adults, one way, to Rostock.'

He saw the slow smile, so bloody cold, break at Perkins's mouth.

He turned towards Tracy. She was shovelling banknotes out of her purse, and the computer was spitting out the printed ticket. Her face was quite set. He did not know whether Perkins had frightened her, or whether she hadn't even bothered to listen.

Through the late afternoon, through the evening, Dieter Krause sat in his car and watched the slip-road. It was at Rostock *Sud*, the most direct turn-off from the autobahn into the city. Of course, they could have come off at the Dummerstorf-Waldeck slip-road up the autobahn, or they could have driven on to the Rostock *Ost* turn-off, but this was the best place for him to wait. He had the heater on in the car. In between the cigarettes he took a strip of gum and chewed incessantly, and every few minutes he used his sleeve to wipe the car's windscreen. He looked for a hire car – a Ford, an Opel or an Audi. There were high lights over the slip-road, bright enough for orange day. He would recognize her, but he had no face, no build, no features for the man travelling with her. He would know her if he saw her, her face had been close to him. He could recall each bone and each muscle of her face. He watched the cars brake, swerve and slow as they came off the autobahn and onto the slip-road. When he had headed the section on the second floor at August-Bebel Strasse, when he had targeted environmentalist shit or the crap people with religion, then he would have had the authority to call out twenty men for a surveillance operation of such priority. He was disciplined. He studied each car for Berlin plates, and every woman in those cars. He looked for the gold of her hair and the small face and the bright eyes. The cigarette, the latest, was stubbed out, and he took the gum again from the dashboard beside the radio where he stuck it each time he smoked.

In the apartment on Saarbrucker Strasse, when the old people had found their last hiding place behind the kitchen door, when he had beaten them in his frustration, the wind and the cold had come through the opened window. He had seen the platform of stone and the distance of the platform between the window and the drainpipe, and he had looked down to the concrete of the yard. If she had gone along that platform to the drainpipe, so high above the concrete, then she was hard. If she was hard, then, certainty, she would come to Rostock. The headlights of each car, each truck and lorry, speared into his face, dulling his sight, as he searched for her.

'What confuses me, Mr Perkins, you warned him and you spelled out the dangers of the course he was following.'

'How is that confusing, young fellow?'

'Frankly, Mr Perkins, I don't see what more you could have done to persuade him to pack up and go home.'

'Are you so very naïve?'

'The policy objective, Mr Perkins, is fulfilled by him going, but you were telling him to quit, walk away.'

'That's the nature of the beast. The beast is embittered, contrary, hostile. You tell the beast to go back and he will go forward, tell him to go right and he will go left, tell him the colour is black and he will say it is white. Tell him not to go . . .'

'Then you manipulate him?'

'Quite right. You can always get an idiot to dance like a marionette. Part of the job is jerking the strings, you'll learn that . . . He's predictable. But you're wrong to focus on old Mantle. It's the young woman who's interesting.'

'Is it real, the danger?'

160

'Oh, yes, very real. As real as the minimal enthusiasm there will be from our friends and allies to accept evidence unless it's served up *cordon bleu*. What have they done about the Stasi crimes? Listen, Erich Mielke was minister for state security for more than forty years, responsible for the psychological destruction of thousands of lives, responsible for the taking of hundreds of lives, and he was given six years' imprisonment for killing two policemen at an anti-Nazi demonstration in nineteen thirty-one, believe it. Nothing, for their convenience, in his time as head of that despicable organization, was deemed criminal so they raked back sixty-six years, a farce. Hans Modrow was the last Communist prime minister, sat for years at the Politburo meetings that legalized repression, and his only crime was falsifying voting results, suspended sentence. A Stasi major presented the Carlos terrorist group with the bomb detonated at the Maison de France in West Berlin, three deaths, three persons murdered, as a direct result, and he was given six years, out by now. A hundred victims shot trying to scale the Wall, two border guards given decent sentences for firing at point-blank range on unarmed youngsters, nine suspended sentences so they walked free, thirteen acquitted. There was murder, unpunished, assassination squads roaming abroad and unpunished, wholesale theft of monies sent to relatives living in the East, unpunished, torture in the Stasi cells, unpunished. They don't want to know who was guilty, they want it forgotten. If she is awkward and if she threatens, then it gets dangerous.'

He left the boy from kindergarten at the outer door of the hotel. He wouldn't see him in the morning, would be off early. He wanted to walk around Savignyplatz, to be on his own, to sit in a café late in the evening and hear the talk around him, as he had walked and sat long ago when Berlin had belonged to him.

In his taxi, the 'Free' light off, Ulf Fischer watched the forecourt of the Rostock *Hauptbahnhof*.

Twice, passengers off the trains had sworn at him because he would not take them. It was a hard life, driving a taxi in Rostock, and it hurt to turn away money. It was not his own taxi, and when he had paid for its hire, and the hire of the radio, and the fuel and the insurance, there was little enough left at the end of each week. He was a warm man, though, not greatly intelligent but cheerful. Once or twice a month, he was a professional mourner. The ethic of the family had broken down in the new Germany – money ruled, old people died alone. They needed, the old-and-alone dead, a small show of affection at their funeral. He made an oration at such people's funerals, spoke well of them when no-one else did. It brought a little more money into his life – as did the earnings of his wife, who went five evenings a week to clean trains at the *Hauptbahnhof* – but too little to hold the love of their two sons. His boys were beyond his control, without discipline, were in love with the American culture. In his plodding way, the way that he had learned from twenty-seven years in the MfS, he tried to merge into the new life, but he had wept the night that the mob had broken into the Rostock barracks building.

He had been the driver for Hauptman Dieter Krause. On the night of 21 November 1988, he had driven the *Hauptman* to Rerik, at panic speed. He had been the driver and confidant of Dieter Krause, he had done shopping for Eva Krause when her work at the shipyard did not allow her time and when the *Hauptman* was tied to his desk, he had been like an uncle to the little child, Christina. That night, his boot had been across the throat of the kid, the spy, to steady the head and make it an easier shot for the *Hauptman*. He had last seen Hauptman Krause in Rostock nine months before, and the *Hauptman* had walked past him and not seemed to recognize him, but there must have been some reason for it.

He had been at the station since the late afternoon, and all through the evening. He knew the times of the trains arriving from Berlin/Lichtenberg, and when each train was due he left his taxi and went to stand at the steps to the tunnel from the platform so that he could see the faces that passed him. He had been given a good description of the face that he watched for.

Hauptman Krause had always been careful with detail. There would be a man with her, and Hauptman Krause had told him that the man would be about 1.85 metres tall and might weigh about 90 kilos. The *Hauptman* had found the man's coat and made his estimates from it. It was English made. Later, after the last train had come, if the young woman and the man were not on the train, he would go to the meeting that the *Hauptman* had called. He still did not understand why the *Hauptman* had walked past him those months before on Lange Strasse.

There was a rap on the passenger window.

He saw the skinny, poor face of Unterleutnant Siehl. He unlocked the door for the *Unterleutnant* to join him. It was necessary, in these days, to lock the taxi's doors while it was parked at the kerb, because of the violence of the new bastard undisciplined skinheads of the city. They shook hands formally. In the taxi, the *Unterleutnant* ate a sausage with chilli from a small polystyrene tray with a plastic fork. It was not possible for Ulf Fischer, the *Feldwebel*, to tell Josef Siehl, the *Unterleutnant*, that he did not permit food to be eaten in his taxi. The next train from Berlin would be arriving in six minutes, and two hours after that the last train of the night would arrive.

She slept.

The train clattered north in the darkness. They were alone in the compartment. Ahead, in other compartments, were the Scouts with their adults, singing lilting songs in treble voices. Behind them the compartments were used by drab elderly people, their small cheap suitcases on the floor by their feet. He had the window blind up, and when the train slowed, the light from the carriage spewed over the snow-specked ground beside the track.

She slept, so peaceful, so gentle, her shoes kicked off, her feet on the seat and the weight of her body against the carriage wall.

The light showed him the frozen ice at the rim of the lakes beside the track and once he caught the eyes of a deer startled by the approach of the train. They went through the small towns

163

and villages where there were illuminated advertising hoardings for new cars and new supermarkets and new soft drinks from America. They went past an old barracks of the Soviet Army, light and shadow from the train meandering over the vandalized buildings where once the big tanks had been serviced. It was Mantle's nature to look out over the barracks. In the days when he had been stationed in Germany, days that were twenty years gone, on a few occasions he had been tasked to take the British military train from Helmstedt to Berlin. Every time it ran, most days of the week, an I Corps sergeant had travelled on it. From the West, across the Soviet zone, to West Berlin. An hour in West Berlin, then back on the train across the Soviet zone, through Potsdam and Brandenburg and Genthin and Magdeburg, peering over the walls and through the trees at Soviet camps, at tanks, at artillery, trying to spot cap badges that would say a new unit had arrived. Pitiful, small beer. He now rated the work of I Corps, scratching for information on the military enemy hidden behind the great fence of wire, mines and watch-towers, as pathetic.

She slept without care.

The train rolled on the track. Cattle trucks had come this way. They went by the town of Fürstenberg, sandwiched between lakes, ringed by forests of straight pine. Going slower, pulled by steam, the cattle trucks had come, doors bolted. Would there, then, have been young people on the blacked-out platform at Fürstenberg, waiting for a train north, or a train to Berlin, who had watched the cattle trucks slink noisily by, smelt the bodies and heard the cries? Would there, now, be old people on the bright platform at Fürstenberg, waiting for a train to Rostock, or a train south, who remembered the roll of the cattle trucks, the smell and the cries? Past Fürstenberg, as the train gathered speed, he saw the small narrow branch line disappear into the web net of the forest. The branch line had carried cattle trucks to Ravensbruck.

She slept beside him, as if his history was not important to her. He let her sleep.

*   *   *

164

West of the city, from the Reutershagen district, a narrow, unlit road straddled open ground and ran towards a wooded area of birch trees. Klaus Hoffmann had sited the pit and dug it seven years and four months before. In darkness, using only a small-beam pencil torch to guide him, he blundered and stumbled away from his car towards the dark outline of the trees. He carried with him a short-handled spade, kept in the boot of his car every winter as precaution against being marooned in blizzards. He remembered the track and the line of the trees ahead. He had taken trouble that night to site the pit. The path meandered close to a ditch. He had to stay on the path until he reached the line of trees, then backtrack for twelve long paces, a dozen metres.

Standing on that point, his feet either side of the scraped mark, he must search with the torch beam for the shattered tree across the drainage ditch. The bearing he must find was eighteen paces from the mark towards a direct line with the shattered tree. There was ice on the ditch. He tried to jump it but one leg fell short and the ice gave, cracked like a pistol shot beneath him. Frozen ditch water up to his knee, soaking his trouser leg and his sock, filling his shoe. Klaus Hoffmann swore. He pulled himself, heaved his body, scrabbling at the grass fronds, up the bank of the ditch. He made the measurement. His shoe squelched.

The night, over seven years before, that the mob had come into the building on August-Bebel Strasse, was the night he had come and made the siting and dug the pit. He breathed hard. He rammed the blade of his spade down into the earth. He dug, and failed to find the rubbish bin. He took another pace, on the same line, dug again and failed again. He dug the third time, his foot cold and sodden. The blade of the spade hit the buried plastic cover of the bin. It was near to an hour after he had left his car that Hoffmann lifted the top from the bin. As he had left it, the guns and the files were wrapped in greased paper and in sealed plastic bags. Wrapped against the wet were three Kalashnikov rifles, the magazines and bullets in smaller plastic bags knotted at the throat, hand grenades and gas canisters, four pistols and more ammunition, and the two shopping bags that held the files. He took the Makarov pistols and the ammunition. He searched for the names on the files, as he had been told to, and selected those that were required. He closed the rubbish bin, covered it again and stamped down with his cold numbed foot on the earth. He tore up grass, yellowed in his torch beam, and scattered it over the scar on the ground.

She moved. She did not open her eyes. She swung, so casual, still sleeping, away from the compartment wall. For a moment her body, her head, wavered upright, then she slumped, her head against his shoulder and her body against his arm.

He could not move. If he moved he would wake her. He thought it would be criminal to wake her.

The short spread of her hair was splayed against his collarbone. She slept on and the train gathered pace, its motion rocking her head on his shoulder. Josh Mantle felt a great tenderness towards her. He could have woken her, thanked her, because in sleeping against him he thought she showed her trust . . . Coming back from the specialist, after the diagnosis, as he had driven the car, Libby had rested her head against his shoulder and closed her eyes, and that, too, had been a gesture of trust. His arm was numb but he did not dare to shift it, to risk disturbing her sleep. She breathed smoothly. There was no panic in her breath, no nightmare. He saw the cleanness of her face, clear skin. He smelt the chilli sauce. He could not imagine living with himself if he had abandoned her. He was old enough to be her father. He felt as if it were demanded of him that he should protect her.

She slept. His arm ached. Her head was on his shoulder.

Coming fast off the autobahn, on to the slip-road, Gunther Peters saw the parked car. He flashed his lights. The headlamps lit the face of the *Hauptman*, whom he had not seen since the collapse of the regime. He pulled in his small Volvo behind the

BMW. He was given the description, height, weight, build and hair colour, told what he should look for, and told at what time he should leave the slip-road and come to the meeting place.

The *Hauptman* was gone, driving away into the night. Peters settled low in his car, and watched and waited.

There had been an Armenian who had taken money up front for the supply of spare engine parts for Mercedes cars, and not delivered, and the Armenian's body was now deep in an earth-fill site where rubble from the rebuilding of Leipzig was dumped. There had been a businessman from Stuttgart who had claimed to have the right contact in the Ukraine for the supply of infantry weapons, mortars, machine guns and wheeled 105mm howitzers, and there had been a suspicion that he doubled with the BfV; he had gone, weighted, into the Rhine river at Bingen, west of Wiesbaden. The Armenian, before he had died, without his fingernails and with a pain-shaking hand, had written the account number at the Zurich bank and the letter of authorization for its transfer. The businessman, before he had gone, alive, gagged, into the river, had spelled out in staccato gasps the limited information he had passed to the agency.

He watched the cars come past him on the slip-road. He thought the *Hauptman* a fool to have killed the kid, the spy, before interrogation. Now the history of that night was churned up again, debris left on a beach, stones turned over by a plough. If he was threatened, he killed.

He watched for the face of the young woman who had been described for him by Hauptman Krause, a fool.

He checked his watch.

The feeling in his arm, against which she slept, had died. His shoulder was warmed by her head.

He felt almost a sense of fear because she slept against him as if she gave him her trust, and yet ahead of him was the earning of the trust.

*   *   *

167

He eased into the seat beside her.

'You are late.'

'I came when I could.'

'You have missed most of the game.'

'I came as soon as it was possible.'

'If she wins this game she has the match.'

She sat high in the stand beside her husband. If Christina survived to the final for under fifteens of Mecklenburg-Vorpommern, and won, she would go to the under-fifteens all-Germany championship at Munich. The coach said that Christina had the ability. The club where the coach worked was a thousand Deutschmarks a year. The coach's time was priced at seventy-five DMs an hour. When they had paid for the membership, the entry and his time, Ernst Raub had written the cheque. Without the cheque from Raub, her daughter would not be playing in the championship for under fifteens of Mecklenburg-Vorpommern. She served for the match in the first round of the championship.

'The problem, it is still there?'

'I don't know.'

'The woman, has she come to Rostock?'

'I don't know.'

'What do you know?'

'It is about the collection of evidence.'

'You told me that all the files were destroyed. What evidence?'

'There were witnesses, that is the problem. The files were destroyed, I do not know if she can find the witnesses.'

'What will you do?'

'I have to finish with the problem before I go to America.'

Their voices murmured. They watched their daughter below. They applauded the point that was won. Eva heard the quiet, cold certainty of her husband's voice.

'If you cannot . . . ?'

'Cannot what?'

'If you cannot finish with the problem before you go to America . . . ?'

'If I cannot finish with the problem, if she finds the witnesses, if the witnesses talk to her, then I am named . . .'

'Then?'

'I am arrested. I am tried, am convicted. I would go to prison.'

'You will fight?'

The past clung to her. The past was Pyotr Rykov. And the past was also her husband coming home in the night with the wet salt smell on his clothes and the sand on his shoes and undressing in silence. The past was poverty, boredom, when she had been unemployed because the FDGB had closed down as an irrelevance, and it was four years of him struggling to find work. The past was him seeing the picture in the newspaper of a Russian general, and behind the General had been Pyotr Rykov, and driving to Cologne to offer himself, and coming back with Raub and the young Jew, and the move into the new refurbished home in the *Altstadt* near to the Petrikirche and the new clothes and the new furnishings. The past was ghosts . . . The overhead smash shot, the victory, their daughter leaping in cele-bration on the court with arms and racquet raised . . . All in the past if a young woman came to Rostock, searched for, and found, witnesses.

'You ask me if I will fight. Yes, I will fight.'

He was gone from the seat beside her.

The train slowed. He broke the dream. They had gone through Malchin and were past Teterow. He moved his arm, edged it from behind her body. The train lurched on its brakes. Her eyes opened, blinked, stayed open. Her face was close to his. She didn't shift her body from against his.

'How long have I been there?'

'A bit less than an hour.'

'Enjoy it, did you?'

Josh said quietly, 'I didn't want to wake you.'

'Got a thrill? Grope me, did you?'

He thought trust was beautiful and precious, and that he was old and stupid. He jerked up off the seat. He pulled her rucksack

169

and his own bag down from the overhead rack. He did not care to look at her. He did not know which of her was real. The train was slowing, crawling. He did not know which of her was the core, when she was asleep and lovely, when she sneered and was ugly. Was he trusted, was he a convenience? Out of the window, slipping by, were small homes.

'Is this Rostock?'

'This is Laage, about fifteen miles from Rostock.'

'Why'd you wake me?'

He felt the anger and tossed the weight of the rucksack onto her legs.

'Do the obvious and that's the way to get hurt. The obvious ways to reach Rostock are by the autobahn or through the railway station. This is the last stop before Rostock, so we get off.'

'No call to be so bloody grumpy. I just asked.'

The train stopped.

She shrugged away from him, heaved the rucksack onto her shoulders and avoided his help. They went down the corridor, past the Scouts, quiet now and sleeping.

They walked out of the empty station and waited across the road at the deserted shelter for the bus to Rostock.

He had driven to a petrol station where there was a photocopier and reproduced the file, a dozen pages given him by Hoffmann, the reports of an *Inoffizielle Mitarbeiter*, codename Wilhelm, on the community in which he worked. In the payphone, he had called the directory for telephone numbers, and then the number of the IM, codename Wilhelm. He had pretended he was trying to reach another man with an offer for double-glazed windows, had checked the address, and apologized for the disturbance.

He drove into the small community, clear roads at that time in the night.

There was a storm out at sea, beyond the darkened peninsula, and the wind came in over the Salzhaff, the spray climbing over the piles of the piers where the trawlers were tied. The file would turn the mind of the man, would destroy the man who had been, many years before, an *Inoffizielle Mitarbeiter* of the Staatssicherheitsdienst. Where the man lived now, there would be a fine view of the shore and the sea.

He put the copied file in an envelope, gummed it tight, and wrote the man's name on it. There was no need to write a message. He walked from his car to the door of a small house and the box beside it for post and circulars. The man who lived, in retirement, in the small house close to the sea at Rerik had known the names of all the witnesses. The man would have friends, would be respected, would be destroyed if it were known that he had been listed as an *Inoffizielle Mitarbeiter* of the Staatssicherheitsdienst, if it were known that he had informed on those who befriended him and respected him.

Dieter Krause swung his car away from the sea and away from the beat of the surf on the shingle shore.

They walked out of the bus station.

There was a whiff of the sea scent in the air. He chose the side streets and the back streets, where the lights were sparse, where they could hug the shadows. She murmured her bloody song . . . The bloody song, played on the forces' radio, was hers and her boy's. He was not a part of the bloody song. It was all for love, her love and the boy's love. He was not included in the love . . .

The last train of the night reached Rostock.

The passengers spilled down onto the platform.

The two men waited at the top of the tunnel from the platform, scanned each half-asleep face, beaded their eyes on each young woman who scurried with her bags from the platform to the tunnel.

They waited for the platform to clear, threw down their cigarettes, and turned away.

It was an old house, three storeys high. The façades of the houses on either side had been pressure-cleaned, but the house with the *pension* sign was grimed with old dirt. He waited at the door. She had dropped back. Through the glass he saw a man at the desk, reading, oil-slicked hair, wearing an overcoat, and behind the man was the row of keys hanging in front of the letter rack. She reached him.

'Gold medal for picking luxury.'

'There's a Radisson in Rostock, and a Ramada, and there's a new hotel at the railway station, and they are where they would expect us to go.'

'Don't be so bloody scratchy.' She grinned.

He pushed open the glass door. The man looked up from the magazine. The reception desk was worn, unvarnished, and there was the smell of cabbage and boiled sausagemeat. The man shivered in his overcoat. Around the letter rack, where the keys were, the wallpaper was wrinkled, faded. The man greased them a smile.

It was obvious from the keys, hung unevenly from nails, but he asked if the man had accommodation available.

The man leered. 'One room or two rooms?'

She laughed out loud behind him.

'Two rooms,' Josh said.

The man's hand, the nicotine-stained fingers, flitted over the keys. He took two keys.

The man winked. 'Two rooms – adjoining.'

She laughed again.

The man asked for documents. Josh took his wallet from his pocket and slid a banknote for a hundred DMs onto the palm of the man's hand, which did not move. Another banknote. The hand slid with discretion towards the man's hip pocket. He gave Josh the keys, pointed to the staircase, picked up his magazine again.

They climbed the stairs, up the threadbare carpet. The smell of cabbage and sausage was replaced by the must of stale damp. It was colder on the stairs than at the reception desk. They stood in the corridor on the second floor in the low light and he gave her the second key.

'Is it off and running in the morning, Mr Mantle?'

172

'We don't run anywhere, at any time. We plan. We take it slowly. Step by step, so there are no surprises. I need to think it through.'

'Goodnight, Mr Mantle.'

He needed to sleep and, in the morning, he needed to think . . . and in the morning he needed to tell her that he was Josh and not Mr Mantle. So damn tired . . .

'Goodnight, Tracy.'

He had been the first to reach the café. Krause had taken a seat in an alcove where he could view the door. They drifted in from Augusten Strasse. He stood, correctly, for each of them, for the taxi driver who came with the building-site security guard, for the criminal, the property developer. The woman who now owned the café had once managed the canteen in the building on August-Bebel Strasse, she would once have run to take the orders of Hauptman Krause and Leutnant Hoffmann, even Siehl, Fischer and Peters. She had closed the café, kicked out her customers. She had put beer on the table and gone to her kitchen area.

Hoffmann said, 'I can be away for two days. Too much work for me to be away longer.'

'I am building a new life.' Fischer shrugged. 'In three years I hope to have my own taxi, but I have to work.'

Peters had a meeting in Warsaw the day after tomorrow.

Siehl whined that if he were not back by tomorrow night then he would lose his job, and did the *Hauptman* know how hard it was to find work in Berlin?

Krause wondered if they had walked past the old building before coming to the café and looked for the darkened windows above August-Bebel Strasse that had been theirs, remembering how they had walked with pride, anonymous, through the big door. He wondered if they had glanced down at the windows flush with the pavement behind which had been the interrogation rooms.

'Can I tell you, my friends, the reality? You stay, we all stay, until the matter is completed, until the problem is finished with.

We have one week. It is necessary for it to be finished in one week. If you do not stay, you will not be doing anything from a cell in the Moabit gaol . . . That, my friends, is reality.'

'Because of one girl, height a metre sixty, weight sixty kilos. Not to forget the russet hair. It is just one girl. Easy to recognize her. Ask her to hold up her hands, look at her fingernails, scrape under fingernails for the skin of Hauptman Krause.' Peters led their laughter.

'It is amusing? It is the big joke? It is funny? We are together, as at Rerik we were together.'

Hoffmann hesitated. 'I didn't kill him.'

Siehl flushed. 'You killed him and we only obeyed your orders.'

'So, let me tell you more of reality. The kid, the spy, was chased. Who chased him? He was caught, felled. Who caught him? On the ground, he was kicked. Who kicked him? He was kept still on the ground by a boot across his throat. Who wore the boot? He was taken back to the boat. Who dragged him? He was weighted, he was put into the water. Who lifted him over the side of the boat? More of reality, it would be a common charge. It would be an accusation of conspiracy to murder. We were together at Rerik. If we fail we will be together in the gaol at Moabit. Do you now believe?'

Fischer said, loyal, 'We did our duty. Again we will do our duty, whatever is necessary.'

He told them where they should watch in the city, what times and at what places, and repeated his description of the young woman. He took the Makarov pistols from his attaché case, each still wrapped in the plastic bags, and passed them over the table, with ammunition and magazines. He handed them the mobile telephones he had hired in the afternoon and had them each write down the numbers. He passed a file to each of them – Jorg Brandt's to Hoffmann, Heinz Gerber's to Siehl, Artur Schwarz's to Fischer, and Willi Muller's he slipped between the beer glasses to Peters. For each of them there was a responsibility. He laid his hand, palm down, on the table. Hoffmann's covered his. Siehl's covered Hoffmann's. Fischer's covered Siehl's. Peters' covered Fischer's. He felt the weight of their hands on his.

They went their ways.

He walked in the shadowed streets towards his car.

He could see the body of the boy, moving in currents of water, held by the weighted pots, flowing against the sand bottom of the Salzhaff. There were crabs crawling at the eyes of the boy, and molluscs fastened to his lips. Eels writhed on the legs and arms. For six nights now he had seen the body and heard the laughter of the boy, mocking and taunting.

He ran, as if when in his car he would no longer see the boy.

Josh slept. A ragged, tossing, restless sleep. He was too tired to dream.

9

The banging split his mind. He hadn't dreamed. He was dead to the world. He jerked, like a convulsion. The sheet and the two blankets came off his body, along with the coat that had been on top of them. The banging belted at the door.

'Are you in there, or aren't you?'

He yawned, gulped. The cold of the room came around him. Bright, brittle sunlight streamed through the thin material of the curtains. He shivered. There was no heating in the room. He blinked, tried to focus his eyes, looked at his watch.

'If you're there, then bloody well say so.'

It was past ten o'clock. God, he'd slept nine hours, dead, without a dream. He had been able to do without sleep in Ashford or Osnabruck, when he'd worked the night shifts merging into the day shifts at the Mansoura prison in Aden . . . but Josh Mantle was fifty-four years old and he had missed a whole night's sleep on the step beside the door at Saarbrucker Strasse. He checked that he was decent, that he wasn't hanging out of his pyjama trousers, had his coat wrapped tight around him. He turned the key.

She stood in the corridor. She looked at him, made him feel so feeble. She looked from his unshaven face to his coat tight around him, to his waist, to the pyjamas and down to his bare feet.

She grimaced. 'Christ, that's a pretty sight.'

'I'm sorry, I overslept.'

'Old for it, are you? Need your sleep, do you?'

He bit his lip. 'I apologize. I've slept three hours longer than I intended.'

176

'I've been sitting in that damp, grotty, freezing bloody room and waiting. What you've done, *sir*,' she sneered on the word, 'is bugger up the day, don't you know.'

'I said that I was sorry.' She was dressed in her heavy walking shoes and jeans, the thick sweater and the new anorak. He stood aside so that she could come into the room. He went, dazed, across the room and moved his clothes from the one wooden chair. 'Anyway, it doesn't matter, I hadn't intended that we'd do much.'

'That's good, "intended". That's bloody rich. "I hadn't intended" – great, terrific!' She had mimicked his words in a west London whine, the drawl of an officer thrown in. 'You're taking a bloody liberty.'

'What I was trying to say ...' He stood in the centre of the room, clothes of two days' wear in hand. 'I was trying to say that I hadn't intended we'd do much today – get everything in place, think through ...'

Her face lit, mock amazement, savage. 'You have a misapprehension, *sir*. Do you think I came out here, one hope in my mind, that *Mr* Mantle would come running after me? *Mr* Mantle, bloody white armour, shining, and necessary to me? Can't do it without *Mr* bloody Mantle, after he's had his sleep.'

He said, 'It's right to plan, take time over it, plan routes and schedules. You work it out, don't just pitch in, you weigh the options. We plan today, work it through, we go to Rerik tomorrow. Have to have decent maps, have to know what we're doing.'

'I'm going out.'

'That's not clever.' Trying to be reasonable and patient.

'Then I'm not clever, but I'm going out.'

'Where? Where are you going?'

'Where I'm not suffocated by you. Where you're not breathing down my bloody neck.'

'You want to be stupid and unprofessional, see if I care.'

The sneers had gone, the taunts were wiped away. She said, 'We were in Rostock a few hours before we went to Rerik, before it was dark and he took the boat, before Hans went ... We went from here up the river to Warnemunde, and we walked on the beach there and on the breakwater. Do you know about being in love, Mr Mantle?'

'Not a lot.' His temper had melted. She was the child, the innocent.

'I want to go on the beach, on the breakwater, where we were. I want to be alone, just with him. I want to be with him, alone with him . . . I had to drive, after we'd been on the beach and the breakwater, to Rerik because he was too screwed down tight, clawed up, to drive himself. He was dead a few hours after we'd walked on the beach and the breakwater.'

She told him where she would be, and he would get a map after she'd gone and find the place. She had sledgehammered at him, the emotions rioted in him. He wished he could take her in his arms, comfort her, hold her, but he was fifty-four years old and knew so little about love.

'Just give me two or three hours . . . It's where we were . . . Come and get me. We'll talk it through, your plan. We'll have a bloody great meal, and double chips, and a bloody great big bottle. I have to be with him.'

He said gruffly, choked on it, 'Fine, that'll be fine. And go carefully.'

She smiled, sadness and youth, a love that he was not a part of. He heard her go away down the corridor and listened for her singing until he could hear her no longer. He stripped and washed in ice-cold water. The sunlight had gone from the window, the clouds massed low above the roof tops. The room was greyer without the sunlight, without her.

He had made good time. He had left Savignyplatz too early to disturb Rogers: he had paid his bill and slipped away.

He rather enjoyed the quiet of the car, the radio turned low.

As he drove towards the outskirts of the city, ignoring the Dummerstorf-Waldeck turning, he considered the priorities of his day. First priority, a good hotel, if that were possible in Rostock. Second priority, to telephone Helen. Couldn't remember, not to save his life, whether this was a day on which she had morning, afternoon or evening classes. He tried to call most days when he was abroad. Third priority, to telephone Basil. He called Basil his best friend, and Helen called him his only friend. He sat next to Basil in the Riverside Stand, season-ticket holders. He would not be back for Fulham against Bristol City, division two. He disliked the thought of Basil sitting next to an empty place and, if he was away over a home game, always rang him at the car-repair yard to suggest that Basil should call by at Hampton Wick and collect his ticket and take someone else. The fourth priority, to telephone Mr Fleming, just a progress report. Fifth priority, to search out the man who could tell a story, guaranteed to amuse, about the wife . . . It was important to Albert Perkins to have a day ahead of him filled with priorities. He braked hard, swerved for the slow lane at the sign for Rostock *Sud*. He saw the parked car. With a slight gesture, insufficient to arouse attention, he raised his hand so that it would block a view of his face. He noted the man with the trimmed beard and the scars.

He had heard, walking on empty streets away from Savigny-platz, in his imagination, the night before, the howl of a wolf. He smiled, satisfied, because his prediction had been proved correct. The pack had gathered. He drove towards the towering spires of the old churches, and the old walls of the city. The car at the slip-road, watching the traffic off the *Autobahn* from Berlin, told him that they had slipped through in the late evening. The young woman, if she listened to Mantle, stood a chance of achieving the policy objective, if she listened . . .

He headed past the *Rathaus*, onto Lange Strasse, towards the heart of Rostock.

He was not certain.

The former *Feldwebel*, the taxi driver, eased the vehicle into gear. The hair was correct, but there were many with hair that colour in the city. He thought the height was near to correct, but it was an average height for a young woman. He had been told that the target woman was of slight build, but she wore a heavy sweater, he could see the neck of it and a quilted anorak, and he did not know whether she was slight or heavy.

He passed her, idling in the road, drove by her and then stopped so that he could see her in his mirror. In former times, when Ulf Fischer had served as a *Feldwebel* at the headquarters on August-Bebel Strasse he had not been required to make a decision, to act on initiative. As a taxi driver he did not make decisions, went where he was told to go. The *Hauptman* would be on the far side of the city, on the slip-road. He was nervous of alerting the *Hauptman* and being wrong. He rang Hoffmann on the mobile phone.

She came past him, but her head was turned away. He thought she walked towards the *Hauptbahnhof*.

The second secretary (consular), each week and alternating between their Moscow embassy offices, met the cultural attaché for lunch. It was a source of some small annoyance to the London man from the Service that the Washington man from the Agency had the resources to serve up the better meal.

'This Krause guy, the one your lady soldier rolled over, they've gotten into heavy excitement about him back home.'

'Soon be there, the warrior wearing his wounds.'

'They've moved the auditorium for him, at the Pentagon. He's going where they can fit another fifty seats.'

The annoyance, to the Briton, was that the American was provided with quality equipment for his kitchenette – gas rings, a microwave and a fridge-freezer large enough to store half an ox, a coffee-bean grinder and a percolator. The room at the American embassy where they lunched was metal-walled, sheet steel plate on the windows, secure against electronic audio surveillance.

'The man of the moment, the good Colonel Rykov . . . I can tell you, Brad, there's a monumental inquest back home. Heads will roll for what happened to Krause. Is it right that the Germans are going over the pond mob-handed? It's what I heard.'

'Chipping away at the cement of the special relationship, David. What I hear, at Langley there's a powerful number enrolling for German classes – hey, David, that's intended as a joke. These days, for all the kids, the clerks, who go jogging in the lunch hour, Elgar is strictly dated, they've all put Beethoven tapes in their Walkpersons. OK, so that's not funny, but can I hint to you, prickly Brit, that the special relationship still lives?'

'I feed from the floor under your table.'

It was usual for them to share at their weekly lunches. Half an hour later, the Briton was on his way back to his embassy and formulating in his mind the text of the message that would go in cypher to Vauxhall Bridge Cross. Colonel Rykov, through his minister, had kicked with accuracy the testicles of the 'reconstructed' KGB, which was a dangerous old game, a game where the kicker might incur a serious hurt. It would go as a priority signal.

'I think you did well, Fischer.'

'I was not certain. I didn't wish to waste the time of the *Hauptman*.'

They stood beside a café, closed for the winter. The sun had gone. The sleet came in the wind from the low cloud merged with the sea and whipped the beach. Hoffmann held his hand flat above his eyes to keep it from his face, to see better. She was a small grey figure holding bright flowers and she sat on the dull sand near the water line.

'I think the *Hauptman* will be pleased with you, Fischer.'

'Thank you.' Ulf Fischer flushed with pride. She sat alone on the beach. Hoffmann made the call to Krause on the slip-road. Hoffmann had met him at the *Hauptbahnhof*, they had tried to track the train on the S-Bahn line north from the city to Warnemunde, had been held at red traffic lights behind a police van. They had seen her, for a few seconds, at a distance, near to the Hotel Neptun, had lost her because they could not park the car, found her again. The flowers moved, bobbed, carried by the faint figure as she pushed herself up from the dull sand. She was against the sea and the cloud and the sleet. She walked slowly on the beach, meandered, towards them, towards the breakwater over which the waves burst.

He used to tell his wife, when he came home in the evening from August-Bebel Strasse, each time that the *Hauptman* praised him.

He had the route, not the direct way, down the E22, the main road, through Bad Doberan and Kropelin. On the map he had marked the minor roads through the villages skirting the two towns and then coming to Rerik from the south, using Neubukow as the crossing point over the E22. Slower roads and a greater distance, but safe. Painstakingly, using a sliver of rolled paper, he measured the distance on the minor roads, so that he would know how long the journey would take. It had to be thought through. It was important to know the detail. He had telephoned for a hire car, using the trade directory, not a company from the centre but a small business in the *Sudstadt*, and he would pay extra and the car would be delivered to the *pension*.

When he was finished, Josh folded away the map and went methodically through his room, through the pockets of his clothes, through his bag. He left nothing that identified him. With his nail scissors from the wash-bag he cut out the label tabs in English on every item that would be left in the room. He satisfied himself. When he brought her back he would do the same in her room, bully her into allowing him to destroy her identity. His telephone rang, his hire car was downstairs. He checked the money in his wallet. It was later than he had hoped to be. She would have longer to walk on her beach and her breakwater.

The breakwater ran two hundred metres into the sea.

The base of it was huge quarried rocks, some as big as a saloon car, cut rough and jagged edged. To the west was the sand beach, scattered with debris seaweed, ice and snow packed solid at the tideline. To the east was the channel for the fishing boats of Warnemunde, and the river passage running the few kilometres to Rostock and the shipyards.

More snow, more ice had gathered in the rocks of the breakwater. It would melt in the next month, but the bitter Baltic wind and the harsh frost nights would keep it in place for the next few weeks.

There was a concrete walkway on top of the rocks and a single strand of metal tubing made a barrier to save the unwary from being blown by the gale, or slipping on the ice, and falling onto the rocks, onto the snow and ice, into the pounding sea that smashed on the breakwater.

At the end was a squat lighthouse, paint peeled by the force of the winter's sea spray, daubed with the names of the summer's tourists. There was no fence around the base of the lighthouse, only a low wall less than half a metre in height. Below it the rocks fell sheer to the foaming motion of the water.

The sleet in the wind had driven visitors from the breakwater. Years ago, before the day of 'reassociation', before the day that the crowd had pushed and elbowed their way into the headquarters of the Staatssicherheitsdienst on August-Bebel Strasse, there had always been people standing on the breakwater, whatever the weather, huddled close to the curved wall of the lighthouse, to watch the big ferries sail for Sweden, Denmark, Norway, and to dream.

The low cloud, carrying the stinging sleet, made a short, grey horizon.

The breakwater and the base of the lighthouse were deserted, empty, but for one small splash of colour.

They stood at the south end of the breakwater, bent forward against the wind. They narrowed their eyes against the driven sleet.

Fischer said, 'We should wait for him, we should not take action until he is here.'

Peters jabbed a finger into the taxi driver's arm. 'We don't wait for Krause – you guarantee me a better place and a better time, do you? Can you?'

The year after the anti-Fascist barrier had come down, in the Sicilian town of Agrigento, Gunther Peters had been given advice by an old man with a weathered walnut face. Never, in a matter of importance, hesitate in the taking of action. He had accepted the advice, and the proof was in his wealth held in numbered accounts in Lichtenstein and in the British-administered Channel Islands, in Gibraltar, in the investment companies based on the Caymans, and none of that wealth was flaunted. He moved money for the Sicilians. He moved cars, stolen in Germany, for the Russians and the Ukrainians. He moved weapons, bought at a knock-down price in Russia, for the Chechens, the Kurds and the Palestinians. He forswore a top-of-the-range car, gold necklaces and gold bracelets, a penthouse apartment in one of the new blocks in Leipzig, following more of the advice of the man from Agrigento. It was his belief that he figured on no police computer. On the night of 21 November 1988, clearing his desk, about to go to his home, Hauptman Krause had seen him. Krause, running, had seen him, shouted, given the order. He had been in the car before he had even known the cause of the emergency. It was he who had first caught up with the kid, the spy, grabbed him and flung him down to the ground and held him in the moment after the kid, the spy, had lashed with a boot into the balls of the *Hauptman*. He had his freedom to lose, and his anonymity, and the wealth that he did not use, and his power.

Two hundred metres from them, away up the length of the deserted breakwater, was the young woman.

Peters jabbed again with his finger. 'You are chicken shit. I do it myself.'

He went forward. Hoffmann ran, bent against the wind, to be alongside Peters. The young woman sat on the low wall at the base of the lighthouse and her legs were above the foam of the sea. Siehl, his hand protecting his face from the sleet, hurried to catch them. The young woman threw, one at a time, the bright flowers into the rising, falling, pounding spray below her feet. Fischer looked a last time behind him, as if hoping to see the *Hauptman*, and scurried to reach them. The young woman, above the rocks, above the sea, gazed down and did not look up.

They made a line and walked with purpose towards the light-house, and the spray rose around them from the rocks and the ice.

He came to the start of the breakwater. He peered the length of it, searched for her.

He had driven from Rostock, a fast four-lane road, bypassed the housing blocks on flat, windscaped ground, and the ship-yards with the idle cranes.

He had checked the beach, looked as far as he could see, and the sleet in the wind had dampened his trousers and soaked his shoes.

He blinked. She was a small, blurred figure. He saw her and the colour of her flowers. She would be wet through because she was a lunatic to have gone in that weather to the end of the breakwater. He was old enough to be her father, feeling the responsibility of a parent for a child. He began to walk briskly, into the sleet wind, along the breakwater. Half-way, the spray wall climbed and fell, and he was aware of the men.

Josh saw four men.

They made a line across the width of the breakwater's path-way. They were in front of him, and he had not noticed them, only her. It was where she had been with the boy, giving her love, frightened, kissing the boy and holding him. He saw them, the two of them, loving and kissing and holding. He seemed to see the boy, clear images, rattling through as if shown on a fast-changing projector, swimming and bleeding and staying afloat, sinking and rising again, and hands reaching for him from over the side of a small trawler.

Four men moving forward, striding in step. It was a cordon line. There could be only one purpose for it. Either side of them was deep water, and rocks and ice with snow. Holy Christ . . . His old, slow, numbed mind churned. So bloody obvious. He started to run.

She did not seem to see them. She was looking down into the breaking waves at her flowers.

He ran, and the wind caught him. The sleet cut at his face and blinded him, the spray fell on him and drenched him. He slipped as he ran, legs splayed by an iced footfall, and he fell, his trouser knee ripped. He pushed himself up and ran again.

They were across the breakwater's pathway and closing on her. He could not have shouted to her, not while he ran and sucked for breath. He saw the sea, rising and falling and hostile, and the rocks, hard and jagged and cruel. The four men would have turned if they had heard him, but he came into the wind and the sleet and the crash sound of the sea on the rocks.

Josh ran. As he ran he ripped down the zipper of his coat, which billowed out, a sail against the wind and the sleet, slowed him. He sobbed for breath. He reached with cold dead fingers inside his jacket, to the inner pocket. It was the only fucking answer in his head. He was near to them and they were unaware of him.

He dragged the gold-plate fountain pen from the inner pocket, the pen that Libby had given him, their last Christmas, held it in his fist. He could see the backs of their necks.

She looked down at the sea. There was one flower left in her hand and she threw it to a wave crest.

He came behind them. He chose the one with the black hair falling on the collar of his coat, the one with the longest hair. He grabbed it. He rammed the metal, gold-plated end of the pen against the nape of the man's neck, pulled him back, in one movement. The line broke, they were turning on him, swinging to him. He was behind the man. They could not see the end of the pen, cold metal, against the man's neck.

Josh shouted, good German, 'Get back or I shoot. I shoot to kill.'

He felt the tremble-shiver of the man's fear. The three faced him. He must dominate and fast. He must use the shock of the three and the fear of the one.

He hissed, 'Tell them, bastard, they back off or I shoot. Tell them.'

She was forty paces from him. She stared at him, at the men. He yelled against the wind, fought for breath for his voice: 'Tracy, come to me. Come on.'

The man croaked, pleaded, to the three.

'I shoot, bastard, I shoot through your fucking spine.'

One, the youngest, with a cold face, thin lips, took a half pace forward. The man Josh held shook and cried, and the two older men grabbed the youngest, held each of his arms.

Josh shouted at the wind, at the spray, at the sleet, at the cloud where it merged with the wave caps behind her: 'Come to me, Tracy. Move!'

God, and she was so bloody slow, pushing herself up as if she did not understand.

He hissed again, into the ear of the man he held. 'They interfere with her, they stop her, you are dead. Tell them.'

The youngest was trying to break free and his hands flailed towards the inside of his coat. The two older men hung grimly to his arms. She reached them.

'Come on past. Then run.'

She went by them, past him and the man he held.

'Run.' He shouted again, at the three: 'Stay your ground, stand where you are.'

Josh backed away, hanging on to the hair, pressing the metal end of the pen deep into the flesh, smelling the lotion on the man's body, and the scent of sweat.

He backed, in steady movements, to prove control, twenty-five, thirty metres from them. There was only the rail beside them and then the rocks, the ice and the sea. He thought the man's legs gave out on him and he had to hold him up by the hair. The man screamed. He manoeuvred him to the side of the pathway, and pitched him over the rail. Over the rail and onto the rock. His hand caught at a rock edge and Josh stamped hard, frozen sodden shoe, on it. The man slipped on the rock, on the ice, towards the water.

187

Josh ran until he caught her and grabbed her arm. He turned once. They were on the rocks, three of them, holding hands to make a chain, trying to pull the man back from the sea and the spray.

He ran with her until the breath died in him.

Krause had come.

Hoffmann was soaked, incoherent. 'He would have shot me. Peters would have had him shoot me.'

Fischer, shaking, blurted, 'I said that we should wait for you.'

Krause had gazed at the waves and the rocks, through the sleet, and at the small colour points of flowers in the water.

Siehl, shivering, whispering: 'There was nothing we could do, we did the best that was possible.'

Peters, defiant, storming: 'We had the chance. If through losing the chance it goes against us, then remember it was me who was prevented from taking the chance.'

Krause felt the cold strip his flesh and walked back up the pathway of the breakwater.

'You were aged twenty, serving in a signals unit based in Heidelberg. It was forty years ago. You were that rare American who reckoned he had principles. You defected, took the big step and crossed the line, and you never knew how to retrace the step.'

Albert Perkins had driven into the Toitenwinkel district. The blocks of homes, with stained and weathered concrete outer walls, were sandwiched between the *Autobahn* and the railway line on one side, and bog marsh on the other. The damp was on the outer and inner walls of the stairway. The apartment, also wet, was a bedroom, a sitting room with a kitchen corner, a bathroom where he couldn't have swung a cat with an out-stretched arm. He had found the American. He had been told that the American would amuse him.

'Famous for fifteen minutes, and that was forty years ago. One news conference and photocall. One debrief where you coughed out all you knew, and that was not much because a private first class, conscript, twenty years old, knew sweet damn all of anything classified that mattered. You'd have become like those Catholic Church converts, so sincere, so fervent and so boring. You embraced this awful quasi country like it was God's gift to social engineering.'

There was no sign of a woman in the apartment on the sixth floor. The room was bare, bleak. The ashtrays were filled. There were books on the table, on shelves, on the floor.

'It's one thing to believe at the age of twenty in the interests of world peace being best served by the balance of military power, but at the age of twenty years plus fifteen minutes they'd squeezed out everything you knew about signals in Heidelberg. You had to start to make a new life here. Bright lad, graduate material if you'd been able to go home, but you couldn't. Educated here, yes? Learned German, learned Russian, became more native than the natives. You were given a teaching post at the university in Rostock. What did you teach – English literature, American history? Found a little place, and convinced yourself you were a champion of peace, and that two Germanys would last for ever.'

Albert Perkins had kept his coat on. The American sat in an old armchair. He had a small body. His legs seemed scrawny thin in his shapeless grey trousers. He hunched his shoulders forward and rubbed his hands incessantly as if that were the way to warm them. His head was big, the scalp shaven, and the veins ran riot patterns in his cheeks. He had thick pebble spectacles and one arm was held to the lens frame by Elastoplast. He smoked acrid cigarettes. Perkins bored on, never hurried himself to get to the point.

'I expect you were quite a celebrity in the common room at the university – an American, gave the department a little international status, they'd have hung on your words. And you had the ideology, you believed in the rotten little neo-state. Natural step, wasn't it, to inform on your academic colleagues? Not for money, not for privilege, not for power, but because you believed, in sincerity, in the need to protect the state from Fascist renewal. You'd have informed on anyone idiot enough to trust you, from the head of department to junior staff, from full-time students to part-time students. You had your codenames and your contact men in August-Bebel Strasse and the safe houses where you'd go, once a week or once a month, for the debriefs. Eva Krause, wife of Hauptman Dieter Krause, Stasi officer, was a part-time student.'

The big head jerked up and the stinking smoke from the cigarette billowed into Albert Perkins's face.

'Never bank on permanence, eh, that's what I say, fatal to believe anything lasts for ever. The Wall came tumbling down. The wonderful little state ended in the gutter. Files were opened and identities were matched to codenames. You would have been slung out on your ear. Big job, big status, down the tube. What do you do? A bit of translation work if you can get it? You're sixty years old, on the scrapheap because you backed the wrong horse, miserable mean little pension. Not much thanks for dishing the dirt on a part-time student – Eva Krause. What's keeping you here? Let me list what you resent, shall I?'

Albert Perkins smiled, icily. It was not in his nature to feel pity. A man made his bed, he must lie on it. He stood in the American's damp room and his presence emphasized the man's failure.

'You resent the new unemployment – two in five Rostock males, from the *Rathaus* statistics, out of work or being trained for work that does not exist. You resent the new poverty – the city is the poorest, as measured in *per capita* income statistics, in Germany. You resent the dumping of immigrants – gypsies, foreigners – in hostels in housing estates like this crap place. You resent the new crime – muggings, beatings, thievings, pickpocketing, prostitution, protection racketeering. You resent the new drug culture – cannabis available and Ecstasy, crime syndicates bringing in the heroin and cocaine. You resent the new men in town – the *Wessis* come to take over the *Rathaus*, the police, the schools, business. Most of all, what you resent is the big message – everything you did in forty years was second rate, was rubbish, should be replaced. I think, my friend, that you should go home. Where is it? Is there an old mother there who's never had a letter? You need me, my friend, because I can speak on your behalf to my American colleagues. I trade, life for me is a market-place. You talk to me about Eva Krause, and I talk to colleagues about forgetting the dumb stupidity of a twenty-year-old signals kid forty years ago.'

Albert Perkins believed the screw should be turned tightly, but always slowly. The maximum pain, the greatest hurt, was in the slow turning of the screw. He would come back the next day for his answer. A discussion on Eva Krause in exchange for letters being written to Immigration, Defense and the FBI. The American would brood on it overnight. He would be washed in sick sentimental memories of his mother and white bloody fences and apple bloody pies. The room was darkening. There was the glow of the single bar of an electric fire.

'I'll see myself out. You shouldn't think of me as an enemy, was once but not now. You should think of me as your last best chance. There's nothing left for you here. I'm trading that chance for the dirt, what'll make me laugh, on the wife of Hauptman Krause. Have a good evening.'

'Where is he?'

'I don't know.'

'He said he would drive us.'

'Yes, he said that.'

'Where the hell is he?'

'You do not, Christina, have to use foul language.'

'He said he would drive us and he isn't here. He said he would watch every match I played and he was late last night and went early. He said he would bring me a racquet from London and there was no racquet.'

Eva said flatly, 'Your father is very busy.'

'What does that mean, "busy"? Why does he lie?'

'You should not speak of your father like that. Are you ready?'

The girl, her daughter, with her ugly, snarling face, flounced up the stairs. Eva Krause stood by the front door and put on her coat. He had said there was a problem that could lose them everything. She checked in her handbag for the car keys. He had touched the sleeve of her coat and the gold bracelet on her wrist, as if they, too, could be lost. She waited and flicked her fingers in impatience.

Christina stamped down the stairs, her bag scraping against the paintwork of the wall, and she carried an armful of racquets. When Eva Krause had been a girl of fourteen years old, her sports kit would have gone into a big paper bag and she would have been proud to own one racquet.

'You have everything? You have checked?'

'I have everything except my father, who has lied to me.'

Eva Krause locked the door behind her.

Through the late afternoon, through the evening, the five men searched the city and watched the roads out of Rostock. Two at any one time on the exit roads to the south and west that could lead to Bad Doberan and Kropelin and on to Rerik, three at any one time cruising the central city streets. Easier for them to watch and search now because all of them knew the face of the young woman. For Krause, the time for the tennis match, second round, came and went. They watched the exit roads, they idled in their cars in the old city and the new city of Rostock. Each yearned to see her, recognize her, to have the second chance to finish with the problem.

He knocked. He gave his name quietly.

There was loud music and shouting and laughter from the floor above and the floor below. Seamen filled all the rooms of the *pension* except those on their floor. He thought the crew big enough to have brought a bulk carrier or a container ship to Rostock but he did not know whether their language was Swedish, Finnish or Norwegian.

Josh knocked, gave his name, unlocked the door.

He had, in the Army vernacular, torn a strip off her. He had put her in the car, swerved off down the road, come close to crashing a lorry because the tension was still eating into him, driven back to the *pension*, and marched her up the stairs as if she were a foul little brat spoiling a family outing. He had taken her to her room, given her his tongue, and locked her in. He had sat in his own room, cold and damp, on the bed, gripped his hands to contain the trembling, and failed.

He turned the key and carried in the food boxes and the beer cans, his bedding, the mattress and a pillow.

He dropped the bedding and the mattress, used his heel to close the door behind him. He groped for the light switch. She was in bed, where he had told her to be. She had found more blankets from the shelf at the top of the wardrobe. Her clothes were scattered on the floor, her underwear, jeans, sweater and walking shoes. Only the shoulders of the pyjamas showed above the sheet and the blankets. He had made, again, a child of her. She hadn't spoken to him in the car, hadn't bloody thanked him, or apologized to him for rubbishing his advice. He had gone out only when the night closed on the city. She looked up from the pillows.

'Have to eat – have to eat something, damned if you deserve anything.'

He was stern because he had been frightened fit to crap and angry because he had been frightened fit to piss. The big eyes gazed at him from the pale face, from the pillows.

He put the food boxes on the bed. She sat up for him and he rearranged the pillows behind her back, as he would have done for a sick child. The burgers would have cooled and the sauces would have congealed. He opened the boxes. She wore thin cotton pyjamas and he could see the shape of her beneath the material. He gave her the coat from the floor and she hooked it round her shoulders. Her face was filled with the burger and chips. He pulled the ring on a beer can, passed it to her, and she lifted her knees, gripped the can between them, against the blankets. He sat on the end of the bed.

Her mouth was full. She pointed with a chip at the bedclothes behind him, and the mattress.

'What's that for?'

He flushed. 'I am sleeping in here.'

Her eyebrows arched, as if the life returned to her, the mischief. 'Please yourself.'

He said, as if it was another speech, 'You are not alone again, you are not out of my sight again.'

She ate, she thawed, she drank.

Through a full mouth, swallowing, 'What do you do with yourself, when you're not working?'

'Don't seem to have much time.'

'I was only asking.'

'I read a bit, in the evening, if I've the time.'

'What do you read?'

'Military history, and my law books – work for the morning.'

'Is your work good?'

'It's dismal, but it's what I have.'

'What's important to you?'

'Important to me, Tracy, is to be my own man.'

She grinned, first time. 'That matters?'

'Some people, not many, say it does.'

'Is that why you came here, to be "my own man"?'

'Have you finished?'

She nodded. The last of the sauce from the last of the burger dripped onto her blankets. She reached for another can and he passed it her. He took the boxes, squashed them small and shoved them into the room rubbish bin. She watched him. He laid his mattress across the doorway. He came close to her, her eyes following him, and he bent and switched off the light. It took him moments to accustom himself to the light in the room, faint through the curtains. He sat on the end of her bed and pulled off his shoes and socks, his shirt and trousers. He folded each item and placed them next to his pillow, with his shoes. He stripped to his vest and underpants. He crawled into the cold of the bed, hugged himself for warmth. Her arm hung from below her blankets, near his head.

'Josh . . .' A whisper.

'Yes?'

'You didn't tell me. Is it why you came here, to be your own man?'

'I'm pretty tired. Keep it till the morning.'

He heard the rhythm of her breathing.

'Josh . . .'

'Yes?'

'What sort of team do we make?'

'Pretty bloody awful.'

'Josh . . .'

'For God's sake.'

'A good enough team to break the bastards?'

'Maybe.'

He rolled over from his back to his side, away from her and her hanging hand. He shivered.

'Josh . . .'

'I'm trying to get to sleep.'

'Josh . . . If anyone ever called you a chatty old bugger, they lied.'

'Goodnight, Tracy.'

He heard her finish the second can. She threw it away over the floor of the room. It clattered against the wall by the window. He pulled the blankets tighter on his shoulders.

10

'I can't help you. You have travelled from England? A great journey. I have been here for three years only. I was a church youth leader in Schwerin.'

He was a pleasant-faced young man. He shrugged. He stood at the gate across the road from the church. By the side of the house his wife hung washing on a line. There was a good wind off the sea and sunshine. Small children played at the woman's feet.

'I can't help you because I have never heard such a business spoken of in Rerik. I know the names of those who come to my church and they are the few in this town, the majority do not care to come. Those who worship with me have not talked of it.'

Josh sensed that, beside him, she sagged.

She had needed the help so that she would not have to bang on doors and traipse from road to road. They had talked about it in the car, the long drive on the small roads to the south, past the lone farms and the cranes pecking in the fields, the need to find the pastor because he would be able to unlock the doors.

'I have to tell you, the past here, and everywhere through the East, is a closed book. You will not find people who wish to talk of the past. They were dark times and there are few who want light thrown on those times.'

He looked at her.

She was turning away. Her chin jutted in determination. It was a small community in a half-moon around the inner sea, bordered to the north by the peninsula. They had laid too great a weight on the pastor, at the heart of the community, opening doors that would otherwise be locked to them. She was walking away. He nodded to the young man, thanked him, for nothing, and there was pain on the young face that recognized the failure to help. Josh grimaced. He followed Tracy.

The voice called from behind him.

'I came here three years ago when my predecessor died. There is somebody else who could perhaps be of assistance to you. There was a pastor who came to Rerik when my predecessor was away, he lives here now. He came every year to Rerik for twenty years. I cannot say that he would wish to talk of this matter.'

She was rooted still. Her head turned. She demanded and was given the name, the address, the direction.

'People do not talk of the past, there is nothing of pride in the past.'

They left him frowning and walked by the old red-brick church with the steep tower where there was a nest box for kestrels. An elderly woman in a formal coat sat on a bench in the sunshine in the graveyard past the church. They walked on the small main street and a shop-keeper was sweeping hard at the snow on the pavement. A woman was pushing up the shutters from the front window of a craft shop. A workman from the council shovelled rubbish from the gutter into his wheeled bin. Josh could not sense the past here. Neat small homes and precious tidy shops. He could not sense that this was a place of murder in cold blood. They walked by the fenced gardens and the little wired compounds for chickens, and the sheds where a single pig was kept or a ewe or geese. It seemed to him to be a place of peace, but when he looked across the water, to the peninsula, he saw the faint shape of buildings among the trees.

They came to a bungalow, small and humble, facing the water and the peninsula and the wall of trees. It was newly painted. An old woman, grey-haired and small, was sweeping the path. Josh smiled at her and gave the name that he had been told. She was so helpful, so keen to please. Her husband, the retired pastor, was at the dentist in Bad Doberan and would return in two hours. He thanked her. The sun shone on the small bungalow. He felt foul: he blasted his way, her way, into a place of peace, where the past was forgotten.

He said briskly, 'We've two hours to lose.'

Tracy gazed into his face. 'You don't believe it, do you? It's like you don't believe it happened.'

Josh said, 'People go to old battlefields – Waterloo or the Somme, Sedgemoor or Culloden. They see farms and fields and woods. Yes, it's hard to believe what happened.'

There was the hardness on her face, as if she thought him weak.

'You were here?'

'I was here, if you can believe it.'

'Where? In the car? In a lay-by? Down the road by the shore where he launched from?'

She faced out and gazed on the inner sea, the Salzhaff. Short piers jutted into the water against which small fishing boats were tied. The light sparkled on the water and swans cruised.

'No, I was in those bloody trees, if you can believe it.' She jabbed her finger towards the line of poplars beside the road, and the bramble undergrowth between them. 'I saw him taken from the water and brought back here, and I saw him fight from them and run. I didn't see him again . . . I didn't see him after he ran. I had to go to the car, drive to Berlin, drop the car, go through the checkpoint before midnight. I had to get out of this shit hole, if you can believe it.'

She took his arm and propelled him away from the piers, and the peace that denied the history. The spring sun was warm on Josh's face. They went to lose two hours, went towards the gate of the base and the fence of rusted wire that straddled the narrow point of the peninsula.

'It was sex. It was physical sex. I did not have to be an expert to learn what it was. Not love, I do not think it was anything more than a lust for the physical business of sex. It was not necessary for her to tell me, she wore it like the clothes on her. The desire for sex with the Russian was in her eyes and her hands.'

The sunlight came through the window, filtered by the dirt on the glass, and fell on the floor, which was filthy, and on the table, which had not been cleared from his morning meal, and struggled through the smoke of his cigarettes. Albert Perkins paced the small room without comment. He let the American sit and talk.

'When she first came it was to regular classes in the evenings. Her husband handled me – that's how she would have known about me. No, she did not know that I informed to her husband. He would have sent her, and it started out as the regular classes, English literature. But she was a busy woman, and it soon had gotten that she couldn't make all the classes, she had meetings half the night, half the evenings of the week, something with the FDGB down in the shipyard. She asked if she could come here, fit in one-to-one classes when she didn't have meetings. She paid. She was working, her husband was a top cat, she wasn't short of money. She paid me and she came here. About a month after she'd started coming here, because of the way her talk was, liberated, I went to another officer who had handled me when Krause was away, sort of signed up for him with a different codename and a different file, and talked about her to him. It wasn't a big deal, at least I didn't think so.'

Perkins wore his coat. The bar on the fire was not lit. The grimed dirt in the apartment seemed worse when the sunlight splayed on it than it had the evening before. Probably it was good that the wretched little man smoked because the cigarettes were strong enough to wipe out more pungent smells.

'You said what you would do for me. It was South Carolina where I was raised, near to Summerville, up the river from Charleston. It was a crappy little place. You know, where we lived half the community turned out to see me head off on the bus to Charleston and the military, and half of that half wouldn't have known where Germany was. I hated that place for its ignorance. My father had a bronchitis problem, he won't have lasted. I think my mother would still be there. There were two sisters I had, younger than me, and I think they'd still be there because people from that sort of place don't go far. It would have been about the day after the Wall came down that I stopped hating that place. What could I do? I could get on a train to Berlin, and another train to Bonn, and I could walk into the embassy and tell the marine guard that I was AWOL, that I was a deserter. You said you'd speak for me. Did you mean that? You'd speak to Immigration and Defense and the FBI, would you?'

Perkins nodded gravely, with sincerity. His wife, Helen, said he was as trustworthy as a second-hand dealer in Ford cars.

'It came out when we were talking English literature. I'd gotten her on to D. H. Lawrence. Well, she was a spiky woman. We'd gone through *Women in Love*, then *Sons and Lovers*. She was sort of giggly about it. I sent her home one evening, she'd good enough English, with *Lady Chatterley's Lover*. Krause was away. She came back the next evening. Shit, her clothes were a mess, crumpled like she'd been rolling, creased like they'd been on the floor. She might have reckoned I was some sort of monk, or maybe I was a eunuch to her, maybe she reckoned me one of those castrated creatures she could spill it all out to. What I gathered, she and her guy had screwed all afternoon trying to do what Lawrence described. The next time she came I was at the window. She was dropped off from a Soviet military jeep and she wanted to know if *Lady Chatterley* was in Russian. How the hell would I know? I said it was in German, but that wasn't any good – sort of slipped out that the guy didn't read German. It became confidential. She'd talk to me like I was her goddamn shrink.'

Perkins paused by the window and considered the wording of the letters that would be sent to Immigration and Defense and the FBI. He thought, after they had read his letters, that Immigration and Defense and the FBI would shred them and leave the wretch where he was, to rot in a damp, cold room.

'He was a major, commanded a small outfit down the coast, west, an unimportant little place. You said that you wanted me to make you laugh – the Major was rated by her husband as his best friend. Does that make you laugh? I told you it wasn't love,

200

or even romance. It was about sex and fucking. She told me the size of him and how often he managed it and how long he did it. I didn't feel bad about the telling of it, what I said to the handler, but I didn't feel good that they'd gotten to film it. They had a department that did covert filming . . . You'll write those letters, I've your promise? I'm washed up here, I'm old and I want to go home. You gave your promise.'

He nodded again. He might not even send the letters that Immigration and Defense and the FBI would shred. He thought it would be harsher punishment for the wretch to sit inside the walls of the apartment with the dirt and the damp until the end of his days, suffering betrayal at first hand.

'Does that make you laugh, Mr Perkins, knowing that Lady Chatterley was squashing down daisies with the gamekeeper who was Krause's best friend? The gamekeeper was called Rykov, Pyotr Rykov.'

The guide was a small man, perky, enjoying the reciting of history.

'It was built as a school for recruits to learn the use of the air-defence guns. The base was opened straight after Hitler had taken power. It was the principal *Flakartillerieschule* in all Germany.'

It was a desolate, quiet place. They had come through the outer gate with the guide, who escorted half a dozen of the first tourists of the year. Mantle had been told that it was possible to enter the base only with the guide. The trees grew wild with bramble thorns and long grass.

Tracy said, 'It was so bloody important to get in here that they didn't care a shit if Hansie was killed. Now it's just for tourists to have a laugh at. He waited till it was dark – he'd brought a little inflatable in the car, the sort that kids use on the lakes in Berlin, with a little bloody wooden paddle. He didn't know what defences there were, whether they had infra-red. He went off the beach back there. I saw him go into the sea, I blew him a kiss and waved until I couldn't see him any more. There wasn't a man about, not a dog. He was going to go three hundred yards out and then paddle for a mile, it was a right foul night. The planes came over, then there was the first shot, then there were the flares.'

'Sixty years ago, on the twenty-sixth of September nineteen thirty-seven, Adolf Hitler came to the *Flakartillerieschule* and was accompanied by the *Duce*, Benito Mussolini. They inspected an honour guard and they watched a display of the firing of the air-defence guns.'

They walked behind the guide and his small party, and slowly separated themselves from the group. Every window in every building was smashed. All around was the wreckage of cannibal-ized trucks rusted from the weather off the sea. The trees grew around a watch-tower where a sentry, that night, would have peered out into the spitting wind. She pointed, for him, towards the low-set concrete bunker where the radar dishes that control-led the missiles had been, and beyond the bunker was the brightness of the Baltic sea. It was criminal, he thought, to have sent the boy, as criminal as his murder.

'On the second of May nineteen forty-five, the base at Wus-trow was occupied by the troops of the *Roten Armee*. There were two and a half thousand men here with air-defence capability, also a small naval force, also aircraft, also a tank unit . . .'

Tracy said, 'Can you imagine it, what it was like for him? He was blocked from the dinghy and bloody running. Flares going up, shooting, sirens going. Couldn't go back towards the open sea, had to cross the base. Blundering through the base and troops spilling out from the barracks huts. They had dogs, I heard them. He was running blind.'

They walked on the potholed tarmac of the roads through the base. Cats followed them, hissing and snarling and running on their bellies, the cats of the Soviet troops that had been aban-doned so many years before and that now ran wild. He thought of the work he had done in I Corps, checking hazy telephoto pictures and satellite images, poring over Red Army magazines, all useless work when set against the chance to put HumInt into the heart of a base with radar, missiles and tanks. They had played God, those who had sent him.

'In the last days of the occupation of Wustrow by the Soviet troops, the people in Rerik brought them warm clothes and food. The position of the Soviets was desperate as their government collapsed in confusion. We saw little of those troops, but they were not regarded as an occupying force. They were seen as protectors. At the end there was a great sympathy for them.'

Tracy said, 'God, and he must have been so bloody frightened. He was alone. In front of him was just this bloody great space of water. There wasn't another way for him but into the water. He could have seen the lights of the town. It was the only chance he had, to go into the water. They didn't care, back in Berlin. Afterwards it was like a stray dog in Brigade had been run over, no bugger cared.'

There was a small drill area, weeded up and covered with the autumn leaves, and round the area were figures, life size, showing how to march, how to salute, how to stand at attention. Paint had peeled off, leaving them grotesque and amputated. There was a board for aircraft-recognition classes, silhouettes in all profiles of British and American attack aircraft, Harriers and F-16s, Tornadoes and F-15s, Jaguars and the A-10 tank busters. It was all rotten, dead, decayed history.

'Before they left, the Soviet troops tried to take from Wustrow everything that was of value. They stripped electric fittings from the barracks rooms, they took the stoves from the sleeping quarters, they removed the concrete slabs from the pavements, and they even tried to lift the street lights in the base from the concrete by helicopters.'

Tracy said, 'Those buildings, over there. It's where the senior officers were. And just there, past the big house, he'd have gone into the water. Look, damn you, look – how far he had to swim. Did anyone care then? Does anyone care now? If it had happened to someone you loved, wouldn't you, damn you, want to see the bastard responsible smashed?'

Josh gazed out over the water. They stood near to the commanding officer's house where a door hung loose and flapping. Between the birch trees, beyond the beach, the water in sunlight stretched across to the small homes of Rerik and he could see the church tower beyond the roofs. He shuddered. He was pleased that she had brought him to the deserted base: it was as if she shared with him. The tour was finished.

'It is dangerous to go off the hard roads in the base. We have found unexploded mortar bombs and tank shells. There is the possibility that chemical weapons were stored here and not removed. The place is now a nature reserve and we have seen the sea eagles here and know they nest and make young.'

They walked behind the group and the guide back towards the gate.

It closed behind them, shutting them out from history.

The sun warmed them. He was thinking of the young man and the terror. His commitment was made.

She breezed into his office.

He stood. Fleming always stood when Mrs Olive Harris came visiting – most of the other desk heads did. She was junior to him, only the deputy on Soviet Desk. He did not stand out of any sense of antiquated courtesy – there were women in Vauxhall Bridge Cross, the modern ones, who took offence if a man stood aside for them in a doorway, in a corridor, at the elevator. He stood because she made him, like many others, nervous.

No preliminaries: there never were with Olive Harris.

'We're working up a paper on Russian military morale. Interesting stuff. Reports of small-scale mutinies because of critical shortages, seen as Government's attempts to subvert military power. Stories of malnutrition, poor discipline, morale on the floor, funding suppressed, had it before but it's in greater detail. You know, up in the Arctic some units are said to be starving. That means there's a right dog fight between Government and the armed forces. The Federal Intelligence Service, of course, sides with Government against the military, and that's a choice little spat.'

There was a husband somewhere, rumoured to be a lecturer at University College – he probably stood up when Mrs Olive Harris came into the room – and there were rumours of children . . . never could imagine her on her back with her legs wide. A few, from the dark recesses of memory, claimed to have seen her smile. She was small and had grey-white hair tied at the back with an elastic band. She wore, each day, a plain, laundered blouse, a straight skirt and flat black shoes. She was an institution with the Service, part of the fabric of each building it occupied.

'We've a lazy bastard on the desk in Moscow, not for much longer – spends too much time hoovering crumbs from under the Americans' table. The latest crumb . . . The minister at Defence rang an FIS general threatening that Special Forces would be sent to liberate an Army officer if the FIS didn't free him soonest. The said officer is a close friend of Colonel Pyotr Rykov, the minister's *éminence*. You're into Rykov, aren't you? You've things running along the rails with Rykov and his Stasi friend, haven't you? That reptile Perkins is in Germany, isn't he? You can call up the full text on your screen, reference RYKOV 497/23. Know how to work it, do you?'

Actually, he had been on a residential course, two weeks, and had attended evening classes to learn mastery of the damn thing.

'Marry it up. See if there's useful progeny.'

She was gone to the door. Fleming stood.

He would have been a brave man, the lecturer, when he had served Mrs Olive Harris, and it would have been in the dark and he wouldn't have been thanked for the sweat.

When the door closed after her he sat.

'I have nothing to tell you.'

'You know what happened to them.'

They had waited in the road for him. He came back to the small bungalow with his old face swollen from the dentist's drill.

They had let him park and lock the spotless, polished, ten-year-old scarlet red Wartburg car. Mantle had intercepted the pastor at the low front gate to his handkerchief garden and had explained, curt and brusque, from where they had travelled and why.

'It is a liberty that you make, to come, to bully.'

'You know the community, you know what happened to the witnesses.'

'It is finished. There is no benefit in the resurrection of the past.'

'The present is only cleaned of the past if there is punishment.'

As the sun had dipped so the cloud had gathered from the north and the wind had grown. They stood inside the gate. Tracy was close behind him and Josh blocked him from going up the path to his door and safety.

'Do you think of me as a coward?'

'It is not for me to make that judgement. What I want—'

'You want to dredge what is in the past.'

'There were four witnesses. They were sent out of Rerik. I want to know where they went.'

The face of the wife was at the window. She had waved to them when she had first seen them. Anxiety now lined her face. She would have seen the hostility of the young woman's expression and the way that the older man blocked her husband from his door, and she would have seen the way her husband stabbed his finger into the man's chest for emphasis.

'And you require us to feel a shame for what happened that night.'

'Where they were sent. There was murder done that night and it should be punished.'

The growing wind flailed the pastor's scarf, dislodged his cap. He was a small man, little flesh on a pale face, and poorly dressed. Josh knew about interrogation and disorientation, knew about building the stress. He had forbidden Tracy to speak and told her he was the expert.

'You judge our morality, our shame and our fear. We are a people that learned compromise. Better to know nothing and hear nothing. Do you understand, Herr Mantle, the psychology of fear? We were born into fear, we were children in fear, and, as adults, we are old in fear—'

Josh snapped the interruption. 'Where are the witnesses?'

'The fear is like the clothes against your skin. The fear does not disappear because we now have fast food and big cars and Coca-Cola in tins. With the fear is the shame and the act of compromise.'

'Your way, the guilty go unpunished.'

'You make a big statement, but it is the statement of a bully. I tell you the first day that I learned to compromise. It was the day that my bishop told me that I was not of sufficient intellectual value to be worth the government in the West paying thirty thousand Deutschmarks to buy my freedom. The freedom of some was bought but they were of greater value than me. That is the day you learn to compromise. Do you accuse me of cowardice?'

Mantle thought he was losing. His voice rose. 'You know the names.'

'I know the names of each of the men who witnessed . . .'

'And they have never returned.'

'They have never come back to Rerik. I tell you when, again, I compromised. I wanted to come here to live the last years of my life. I informed. I supplied gossip on my church, my church leaders, on my church congregation. I was promised in return that I would have the permission to come to live here. The regime ended one year before my retirement and I did not need permission to come here. That is my personal punishment. I live here quietly in my shame and my fear. If it were known . . .'

Josh caught at the buttoned coat of the pastor. He was losing, he must savage him. 'Tell me where they bloody went.'

'If it were known here that I had informed, then we would be, my wife and myself, like refugees. We would be put out of our home, we would be friendless, we would be pariahs.'

The frustration welled. Josh shouted, 'I'm giving you the chance to conquer the shame and the fear. Where are the witnesses?'

'I tell you . . . A man came to my house. He put through my door an envelope. In the envelope was a photocopy of my Stasi file, the file of an *Inoffizielle Mitarbeiter*. If I should direct you to the witnesses . . .'

Josh thought he had lost. The pastor smiled, grim and sad, as if he knew he had won.

Tracy said, small voice, 'The boy who was killed, Hans Becker, was my lover.'

'. . . the file would be sent to the church . . .'

Tracy said, quiet voice, 'Hans Becker was the only boy I ever loved.'

'. . . and to the town administration, and to my wife.'

Tracy said, with no passion in her voice, 'I fucked Hans Becker because I loved him.'

The pastor rocked. The voice was behind him, soft and quiet and gentle. His shoulders, thin under his coat, shook. He turned to face her, turned to the wind that ripped at his scarf, and turned his cap.

'My dear, you try to shock me. I am hard to shock. You try to make a volcano of my mind . . . I was conscripted into the Army in nineteen forty-five. I fought in the battle for Berlin. I know what it is to be shelled and bombed. I know what it is to hear my father has been killed. My mother was raped by the Red Army. I know more of shock than the vulgarity of the words you use. I know also the shock of the realization that I was frightened, that I would compromise. Come . . .'

As if his mind was turned . . . Josh recognized it, Tracy had turned the pastor's mind. The pastor looked into her face that was simple, clean, without complication.

He ignored his wife at the window.

He led them back through the garden gate and out into the road. He walked with a good stride, as if a weight were lifted from his back, and Tracy skipped to be alongside him.

208

'I know what happened. I saw it. I was not sufficiently close to recognize the faces of the men who killed your lover. Perhaps in the vulgarity of your words you have given me a small courage, and for that I should thank you. I said a prayer for him. I did not go out into the night and kneel beside him and make my prayer, I was too frightened of the consequences. I said my prayer in the secrecy of my home. There were four men and myself. We shared the fear, we did not have the courage to help him.'

They had walked along the shore path. Dark cloud hovered now above the trees on the peninsula across the water. The waves hammered onto the pebble and sand beach, flowed to the rotted seaweed and fell back. The pastor led Tracy past the pier, then turned inland onto a track through the bare poplar trees in which the wind sang. He stopped outside a brick-built house and the front door was flush to the road. Josh trailed behind, as if he were no longer relevant to their business.

'Jorg Brandt, he was the eldest of them. He was a schoolteacher in Kropelin, a Party member, a respected man. When the boy had broken free of them on the pier he tried to find a house where he would have protection. At Jorg Brandt's house the door was shut on him. He was denounced by colleagues at the school for the abuse of children. His wife left him, his community shunned him. He suffered psychological collapse. He went to live with old relatives in the Lichtenshagen district of Rostock where he was not known. He cannot return home because it is believed that he abused the children.'

The pastor spoke only to Tracy, ignored Josh. He went on up the road past the small gardens that were fenced, past the homes. He stopped in front of a house of dun concrete-rendered walls. There was a raised patio at the front, a low trellis fence and a window above the front door framed in modern plastic.

'Heinz Gerber, he would now be fifty-seven years of age. He had the job of administrator in the town hall for the collection of refuse, and he worked also for the church in Rerik. It was the second house the boy went to, and he was losing strength and

209

Gerber came to the window and saw him, and did not open the door. He was denounced by his brother as a thief of church funds, and as there was little money in our community, money was precious. He was thrown out by his family, he was disgraced. He went to work as a gardener at the base at Peenemunde, and is still there.'

Behind them, Josh, in his mind, could see the boy who was wounded and exhausted and running at the limit of his strength. It was the last house before the square, well-built with a good garden to the front of pruned roses.

'Artur Schwarz was a senior engineer on the railway working from Bad Doberan and responsible for the line between Rostock and Wismar. His was the last house that the boy came to. Schwarz saw him from an upper window, drew the curtain and turned his back on him. The rumour was spread that he was an informer. His wife was beaten by the Stasi at a protest at the environmental damage caused by the chemical works at Neubokow. He was blamed for the beating of his wife. He works now as a common labourer on a farm near to Starkow, which is between Ribnitz-Damgarten and Stralsund.'

They were in the square. On three sides around them were low two-storey blocks of cheap-built homes. The grass was yellowed grey and sprinkled with the old leaves that the wind curled. They stood among the washing lines and the parked cars that scarred the grass to mud. Josh stood back from them. It came stark to him. They had walked the route of Hans Becker's flight, and he had not seen a man or a woman or a child. Did they hide? Did they crawl behind closed doors? Did they not dare to look down from their windows? He felt the weight of the fear . . . The pastor stood and looked around him as if he stretched far into his memory and then he moved a single short pace to his left, to be exact.

'Willi Muller was then just a boy. His father had a fishing boat. His father's life was the fishing in the *Ostsee*. He took the trawler out for them, when they pulled the boy from the sea. He was with them when they killed the boy, here, at this place, where I stand. He took the trawler out again when they put the weighted body of the boy in the sea. All of the fishing people of Rerik know where the body was put into the Salzhaff, without charity and without decency, and they never run their nets there because they have the dread that they would bring up the body and the past. There was a family meeting. His father had been told that he would lose the boat if the son did not go away and swear to stay silent. He went to Warnemunde and took work as a deckhand on a herring boat. If he were to return he would have to confront his father's bargain. He would be ashamed of his father and ashamed of himself. He has never returned, and never will.'

The pastor took Tracy's hand and ducked his head, chin against his chest. His eyes were closed. The quiet was all around them.

Tracy let his hand fall free. 'Thank you.'

'Let me tell you, if a man is sentenced to death then he has an hour, a day, a week, to gather his integrity. If a man is sentenced to prison then he has a month, a year, to find a true dignity. Where is the integrity and true dignity of a man denounced as a paedophile, accused as a thief, rumoured as an informer against his wife, suffering shame for his father and himself? They were more intelligent than the Gestapo – they did not leave a trail of martyrs behind them. They destroyed but they did not permit their victims to hold the small light of dignity and integrity.'

Tracy stood her full height. She put her hand on the pastor's shoulder and her lips brushed against his cold, lined cheek. Josh shook his limp hand, and said, 'I wish you well.'

'You should not take loosely the responsibility. There is little left for these men and the little left them is what you now hold in your hand. You should be careful with your responsibility. He was a brave boy. I saw his bravery.'

Mantle took Tracy's arm. He led her away from the pastor and out of the deserted square. He understood. The wet blinked in his eyes.

* * *

They sat in the car and ate the sandwiches he had bought for both of them. He had gone as far down the coast as it was possible to drive, a kilometre beyond the last of Rerik's houses. She gulped the bread slices, filled with sliced sausage and salad. He had parked the car so that it faced out over the Salzhaff and across to the trees masking the buildings on the peninsula.

Josh said what he felt he needed to say.

'It's where you were, yes, when the flares were going up, when you could see the tracers, when the trawler came in. I tell you, Tracy, when you couldn't intervene, when you had to back out, that must have been worse than anything I can imagine. To leave him, to have to get back to Berlin for that bloody midnight curfew, that is a definition of hell.'

She choked. A piece of sausage fell to her lap. He thought it would help her to cry. She would never have cried before on a man's shoulder.

'To drive away from it, with the bastards after him, him running, for the bloody curfew. What was his car? A wretched little Trabant? Nothing you could have done for him. To have to drive back alone, not knowing . . . God . . .'

The tears streamed on her face, made rivers on her clean scrubbed cheeks. He groped in his pocket for his handkerchief.

'I want to see him in court, Tracy, begging, and sentenced. It is more hideous than anything my imagination is capable of.'

He wiped her eyes and her cheeks. She stared straight ahead at the dark water. He gunned the engine.

'Come on, girl. We're going, together, to hack it.'

He swung the car off the grass, onto the road. He drove through the back lanes of the town, towards the myriad side roads that would keep them safe on the journey back to Rostock. Clumsy, awkward, he had made his commitment. In the morning they would begin their search for the witnesses.

He came in the darkness into the town. It would have been good for him to have been in the town all through the day, but not possible. Dieter Krause did not possess the resources of manpower to have watched Rerik through the day and the early evening. The old goat would tell him if they had been to Rerik. The old goat would know who had come, who had asked, as he had always known, and would tell as always. He drove down the hill, the central road of the town, towards the sea. The road was deserted.

Not a soul alive on the road, not a car, no-one walking the pavement, not a curtain undrawn or a door open. He could remember it and yet he could not place the image of the memory. He drove towards the shoreline, then swung left and drifted the car past the piers. He could see the roll of the fishing boats in his lights. He came to the small, darkened bungalow. Only the wind for him to hear, and the rustle of the sea on shingle and the flap of tossed paper.

He stepped from his car. He opened the gate and walked up the path. The street lamp threw enough light for him to see the paper that was nailed to the woodwork of the door. He snatched from the nail the pages of a file identifying an *Inoffizielle Mitarbeiter*. He ripped at the pages with fury. It was the first time that Dieter Krause had ever known the fear to be broken. He tossed the torn pages up into the wind and they scattered from the light to the darkness.

In his car, as he left the town, drove away from the sea and the pier where the trawlers were tied and the church, he placed the memory. That night, he remembered, after the chase and the shooting and the taking of the body out on to the Salzhaff, it was as though the town had emptied.

The policeman lit the cigarette for the lorry driver. There was no smell of alcohol on his breath but it would be tested. The lorry with the trailerload of steel construction girders being transported from Rostock to Wismar had been recently checked by a garage, but that would be verified. It was slewed onto the grass at the side of the road, but the radiator grille was barely marked. More policemen and men from the fire brigade were setting up lights around the wreckage of the car. The ambulance men sat in their parked vehicle, relaxed, because there was no need for their intervention. The policeman, newly posted to Rostock from Kassel in the West, went to the second vehicle involved in the accident. It was difficult to recognize it as a scarlet Wartburg car. It was mangled, concertinaed, crushed. He shone his torch into the interior. Their faces, extraordinarily, were unmarked. Their bodies, an old man's and an old woman's, were pressed back against two aged leather suitcases that had burst at the impact. The fire-brigade men were preparing the cutting equipment that would be necessary to recover the bodies. From reporting the registration of the scarlet Wartburg, from his radio, the policeman knew their names, that the man was a retired pastor of the Evangelical Church, that they were resident in Rerik on the coast. Tiredness, a heart attack, the glare of the oncoming lights of the lorry were equal possibilities, the shit engineering standards in the building of East German cars was most likely, but there was nothing of fact to tell the policeman why the Wartburg had come over the central white line of the road and into the path of a lorry carrying forty tonnes of steel girders.

'You're quiet, Josh.'

'Just thinking.'

'Thinking about what?'

'What he said about responsibility, Tracy. About the responsibility we have to those four men.'

She snorted. 'You think too much.'

'For each of them we are a hand grenade rolled across the floor of a room, into their lives.'

'That is crap.'

'Tracy, listen, you have to know about the responsibility.'

'You were better quiet, Josh.'

She never opened her eyes. Her head was against the back of the seat, as if responsibility was not important to her. He drove back into Rostock. The beginning ended that night. In the morning, the end would start. He did not know where it

214

would lead and his mind tossed with the burden of his own responsibility.

Siehl listened.

'We try to avoid the use of extreme measures. We aim not to use extreme measures.' Dieter Krause rapped his knuckles on the table. 'We employ extreme measures only if the alternative is the Moabit gaol.' He stared each man in the face. 'She has nothing without a statement from one of them. If it seems likely she will gain a statement then we must take extreme measures.'

Josef Siehl, now forty years of age, believed himself to be a victim, a casualty. He had supported the old regime and never doubted the legitimacy of the Party. He had accepted his orders, placed bugs, met the informers, interrogated men and women, followed targets in careful surveillance, had broken up the meetings of the environmentalists. He had only done what he was told to do. If he had been ordered to fire on the mobs in the last hours of the regime, then he would have done so, and he did not understand why the order had not been given. He lived now high in a block on the Hohenschonhausen complex of Berlin with the new filth around him. He had been driven from his apartment in Rostock by scum who did not realize that he had dedicated his life to their betterment through the socialist ideal. In Hohenschonhausen, he was surrounded by drugs and thieving and vandalism. He had been married twice before, divorced twice before, and the woman with whom he lived shared his aptitude for complaint. Each night, back from work, skinny and sallow, poor and bitter, he and the woman shared complaint about the new life, the new indiscipline, the new hardship. He worked as a security guard on a building site for the new Sony tower. He had been an *Unterleutnant*, he had twice in Rostock been personally commended by Generalleutnant Mittag, and now he was a security guard on a building site . . . He had been given, once a month, the duty of supervising the cell block at Rostock. Always correct, of course, but harsh in his administration of the prisoners. His nightmare, the role reversal, that he should be a prisoner in a cell block. On the night of 21 February 1988 he had been ordered from his desk by Hauptman Dieter Krause, he had driven one of the cars. He had dragged the body back to the trawler, he had roped the lobster pots to the body. He stood to live the nightmare, to be locked in a cell as a prisoner.

They left Krause. By dawn, Siehl would be in Peenemunde and Hoffmann would be in Lichtenshagen and Fischer would be on the road from Ribnitz-Damgarten to Stralsund and Peters would be in Warnemunde. They would all be in place at first light.

It was the last point of the last match of the evening.

Eva Krause sat in her seat with her fists clenched. She was breathing hard. Her daughter served for the match . . . Ace . . . The opponent never moved. The service ball thudded from the court into the back netting. Her daughter stood proud on the base line with her arms, her racquet, raised. The opponent was a gawky, gangling girl, limbs too long for her body, and for a moment she hung her head, then trotted to the net, held out her hand and waited. She wore an old costume, handed down, and held a racquet that was reinforced with binding tape. Eva stood and clapped, forgot for the moment that the seat beside her was empty, and watched her daughter, who savoured the applause and took her time before advancing to the net. The handshake was cursory. Christina Krause did not even look at her opponent as she shook the hand offered to her but gazed around her as if to enjoy the triumph.

Eva gathered up her daughter's tracksuit and the spare racquets. She was pushing them into a bag.

He came from behind her.

'You are Frau Krause? It is your daughter that has defeated my daughter?'

She nodded.

He was tall, as his daughter was. He had sparse hair, prematurely grey, uncombed. He wore trousers without creases and old trainer shoes. The elbows of his coat had been ripped and were sewn, and the cuffs were frayed.

'You should be very proud, Frau Krause, of your daughter's ability. She looks to be well coached. It is a beautiful outfit she wears. There is great power in that racquet, yes, but expensive. I was here last night, Frau Krause, to see my Edelbert play and I stayed to see the girl who would be her next opponent. The man who came to join you, last night, that was your husband?'

He gazed at her. His eyes never left hers. She thought it was as if he had waited a very long time, as if he would not now be deflected.

'Your husband, yes? The name of your daughter was announced on the loudspeaker and I saw her wave to you and you waved back, so I knew it was your daughter. The man, your husband, came and joined you, I saw that. I did not know that his name was Krause, but I knew his face. Do you have a good memory for faces, Frau Krause?'

The row of seats behind her ran to a wall. He stood between her and the aisle steps of the stand. He spoke with a soft, reasonable voice that was without menace, and the voice chilled her.

'Eighteen years ago, I was a student at the university, my first year. My course should have led me to be a constructional engineer. You would say, Frau Krause, that I was stupid, but in my defence I would say that I was young. On a wall in August-Bebel Strasse, opposite the building they used, with my girl-friend, I painted the slogan "Old Fascists, New Fascists – Old Nazis, New Stasi". It was scrubbed out by dawn the next morning, but I was very stupid and I returned the next night with my girl-friend and we painted the slogan again. We were caught and arrested. Your husband, Frau Krause, was in charge of the investigation. Did he ever tell you about the conditions in the cells at August-Bebel Strasse? Did he tell you what was done to those charged with being "politically negative"? I was sent to the prison at Cottbus for three years and my girl-friend was sent to the prison at Bautzen for one year and a half. That is why I remember so well the face of your husband. You should not be afraid of me, Frau Krause . . .'

Her daughter, Christina, was waiting at the bottom of the aisle steps and waved peremptorily for her to come.

'The day I was released from the prison at Cottbus, the day I met again with my girl-friend, our Edelbert was conceived. I did not have a university degree, nor did my girl-friend, but we could do the arithmetic, it was that day in 1983. For both of us, there was no possibility of returning to the university. Our futures were destroyed because we had painted on a wall. I swept the streets, my girl-friend scrubbed the floors at the offices of the Freie Deutsche Jugend. Our futures were destroyed because of the thoroughness of the investigation of your husband, Frau Krause. When the Wall came down, when your State was finished, I believed a fresh opportunity would come for me, for my family. But I had no qualifications. I have gained nothing from the new freedom. You should not be afraid, Frau Krause, I will not beat you as I was beaten in the cells at August-Bebel Strasse . . .'

Below her, her daughter had her fingers in her mouth and whistled piercingly for her to come.

'I am pleased to see that you have done well from the new times, Frau Krause, and that your daughter wears a beautiful costume, that you can afford for her to be coached, that she has expensive racquets. Remember me to your husband – the name is Steiner, but perhaps he will not recall me. Frau Krause, believe me, I have to be very disciplined so that I do not put you on the floor and kick your face, as your husband kicked my face in the cells at August-Bebel Strasse. Will your good fortune last for ever, Frau Krause, or will the day come when you are destroyed as I was? Goodnight.'

He was gone. Her daughter whistled again. She saw the man go to his daughter near to where Christina stood, hands on hips and pouting, and put his arm around the girl, who kissed him, and they left arm in arm.

She felt so cold. She went down the steps.

'Who was that old drone?'

Eva Krause said, 'It was the father of your opponent.'

'What did he want?'

She took her daughter's bag, carried it for her. She said, wearied, 'He came to me to congratulate you.'

'She was useless, not coached. Did you see her gear? Rubbish. Where is my father?'

II

'Right now . . . What would you be doing . . . ?'
    'What do you mean?' She lay on the bed, on her stomach, chin resting against her fists.

'What would you be doing, if this hadn't happened?'

'Does it matter what I'd be doing?'

He was on the hard chair, bent forward and polishing his shoes. 'Of course it doesn't matter. I was just making conversation – you know, communication. But if you don't want to tell me, if it's a secret . . .'

Josh had slept poorly. He'd had a wretched night on the mattress against the door. Each time he'd been awake, each time he'd drifted back to consciousness from the dreams, images, moments of half memory, he had heard the sweet regular breathing of Tracy. She had slept, an innocent, a child, beside him while he had been tossed by the image of the young Guatemalan soldier with the ropes round his ankles and his wrists and the blood dribbling from his nose and from his lips.

He slipped his feet into the polished shoes, began to lace them. The top buttons of her pyjama jacket were unfastened. He could see the hang of her breasts. His fingers fumbled with the laces. She would have wanted him to see the hang of her breasts. He felt the blood rush through him. She rolled over on to her back and stared at the ceiling and the single burning bulb under the plastic shade. He could see the outline of her breasts and the drop of her waist and the rise of her hips.

She glanced at her watch. She said, 'About this time, I'd have been heading down to G/3 . . .'

'A bit early.'

'. . . I like to get in early. Got G/329 to myself if I'm in early. The rest of them are filling their faces at breakfast then . . . Check the messages in overnight on the printer, do the decipher if it's necessary. Sort out the Major's day, can't wipe his bum unless it's down on his schedule. Put the Captain's programme in place, useless and idle sod . . . Sorry, shouldn't talk like that of officers, 'cos you were an officer . . . Best time of the day, early, before the Major and the Captain come in. Sort everything out so it's tidy, so there aren't surprises . . .'

'Why didn't you get to sergeant?'

'Is that your business?'

'No, it's not my business . . .'

He frowned. He didn't understand why she kept him far away, beyond arm's length. He thought she believed her privacy was her strength.

'Are you just going to sit there and watch me dress?'

He muttered something about needing to get to the bathroom. He folded away his bedclothes, took the mattress from across the door and dragged it down the short length of the corridor. He unlocked his own door and dumped the mattress on his own bed with the folded sheets and blankets and the pillow.

Josh went back into her room and said coldly, 'We leave it about another half-hour, then we go. Time for him to be up, about . . . I talk, I ask the questions. It'll be time for a bit of sensitivity. You write down everything he says, down to the last word, and he signs each page of the transcript . . .'

She was dressed. He had never known a young woman who took so little care of her appearance, no make-up, no comb or brush through her hair, no effort in style. She wore her jeans and the shapeless heavy sweater and she picked her anorak off the floor. He handed her a notepad and two ballpoint pens and she pocketed them.

He let himself out of the apartment on the tenth floor of the block. Jorg Brandt suffered claustrophobia so he did not try to use the lift. He left the apartment high in the block early each morning to go to the home of the Schultz children. Each morning he left behind him his uncle, who sat in the chair by the window, and his aunt, who groped around in the half-light of the room. His uncle, confined all day to the chair, and his aunt, who suffered severe and untreated cataracts, were the only people he had known those many years ago who would have accepted under their roof a man denounced as an abuser of children and who had been evicted from his home and abandoned by his family.

The agony of leaving the apartment did not end when Jorg Brandt reached the block's litter-strewn, paint-daubed hallway. He also suffered from agoraphobia. He shuffled on his stick as close to the walls of the apartment blocks as was possible. Sometimes, if the kids were going to school, if they saw him, they would jeer at him. A long time ago he had been the headteacher and a man respected for both kindness and discipline. This time of the morning, early, was the most precious in his day as he made his way amongst the apartment blocks to the Schultz home.

He went slowly and sometimes he stopped as the clammy fear of the open spaces between the blocks gripped him. He would stand then, the perspiration running on his locked legs; the agony was the struggle to overcome the phobia. This was the daily nightmare of Jorg Brandt. The nightmare after darkness gathered around the tower blocks of Lichtenhagen was the memory of what he had seen when the young man had come bleeding to his door and had pleaded for help. With the nightmare, each evening when the small bed was unfolded in the corner of the living room of the apartment, were the memories of the denunciation and the impact of a stone thrown at him from behind by a child as he left. The rabbits were the only peace Jorg Brandt knew.

The Lichtenhagen housing complex was built on flat land between the bog wilderness to the west and the An der Stadtautobahn linking Rostock to Warnemunde. The front façades of the blocks were of brick with small balconies, the sides were featureless concrete and the backs were pocked with small windows. If it had not been for the Schultz family's rabbits he would never, day or night, have left the apartment. The hostel had been six floors below the apartment of his uncle and aunt. They had been trapped for two days in their apartment when the crowds had gathered to burn out the foreigners from the hostel. The skinheads and the neo-Nazis and the people of Lichtenhagen and the neighbours from the block had bombarded it with petrol bombs to drive out the immigrants. They had been trapped for two days in the apartment that was his refuge.

At the broken perimeter fence around the housing complex was a cluster of houses with small gardens. Jorg Brandt came each day to the Schultz family garden to feed their children's rabbits and to escape the memory of the boy at his door and the sight of the men who had chased him. He cleaned out the rabbits' hutches, and in those few minutes he forgot the nightmare of his denunciation. They were fine rabbits, black and white and heavy with flopped ears. He told the rabbits the same stories each day, of Rerik and of his home, and of what he had seen from an upper window.

Klaus Hoffmann watched the door of the apartment through the closed window of his car, and he shouted in growing fury into his mobile telephone.

'. . . You don't have to cry, weeping doesn't help. You tell them to go screw themselves. I bought that house. I paid 700,000 DMs for that property . . . I don't give a fuck what they say . . . I bought the house in good faith . . . No, you listen – see if I care if a smartarse man comes from Stuttgart and claims his grandfather ran from Wandlitz in 1945, that the Communists had no legal authority to expropriate the freehold of his home. I paid in good faith, it is my home . . .'

A family had been evacuated from Berlin as the Red Army closed on the city. A house had been locked, in the spring of 1945, abandoned and taken by the Party to become the residence, for thirty-eight years, of a senior official in the department

223

of economic planning. When the Wall had come down, the official had produced papers of ownership for Klaus Hoffmann and had sold the property. Hoffmann had paid cash. It was said that two million properties in the East were subject to ownership claims by the grandchildren of original residents, and the courts backed them with restitution orders.

'What do you mean, he has documents? What shit court in Berlin? See if I care about a "restitution order" . . . They were all bastard Nazis in Wandlitz . . . When? I'll come back when I can, as soon as possible . . .'

He cut the call, and the sound of his wife weeping. He watched the door of the apartment block. The house in Wandlitz for which he had paid 700,000 DMs was collateral for his business. It was the new fear in a district such as Wandlitz, the big car with *Wessi* plates. Smart bastards from Frankfurt and Cologne and Hamburg searched the streets of districts such as Wandlitz for the homes of Nazi grandparents, and the lawyers came with them.

He watched for the girl with the russet-copper hair, and for the man who had thrown him onto the rocks and into the sea.

It was without thinking, but Josh had slipped into the old habit. He was the officer, she was the corporal. The glove fitted. In the car he talked to her as though he were an officer explaining procedure to a corporal.

'We go the long way round, we do nothing that is obvious. They have lost us so they can only stake out the places that they believe we will come to. They know we have to come for the witnesses. You understand that, Tracy?'

'Yes, "sir".'

'There's no call for impertinence.'

'No, "sir".'

'And you can cut the bloody "sir" nonsense . . .'

'Is it because you're frightened?'

'Is what . . . ?'

'That you're so bloody pompous.'

She was grinning at him. She'd read him; he was frightened. He didn't think she was. He thought that under the mischief, behind the grin, an excitement bounced in her. He wished it were the same with him.

'Can we start again?'

'Be a good idea.'

'Without "sir" and without "corporal"?'

'Shoot, Josh.'

'We watch the backs and we watch the sides. It's where the bastards know we have to come.'

'I worked that much out.'

'I do the talking . . .'

'I'd have been here, come here, whether you'd been with me or not. I'd have done the talking.'

'I really think it's better, Tracy, if you leave the talking to me.'

She shrugged.

The estate stretched away to the right of them, and beyond the estate was the main road, the obvious route into Lichtenhagen. It was hard for Josh to accept that he didn't matter, that his experience didn't count, and that the streetwise craft of a lifetime was unimportant to her. He was frightened, he didn't know what they would find. He carried no weapon, not a screwdriver, not a hammer. He felt, the truth of it, so bloody, God Almighty, involved.

He drove into the estate . . . Of course, they would be watching. He had planned the route in so that when he reached Lichtenhagen, he would not be going slow and looking for the block as any stranger might have been. He didn't know how the man, Brandt, would be. He could be hostile, could be servile, could be co-operative. He looked for a man, or two men, sitting in a car. There were old Audis and Volvos and Renaults parked up outside the block, and there were older Trabants and Wartburgs. He looked for a car with steamed windows, for an engine spiralling exhaust fumes.

'When we go out, go fast, direct.'

225

'Back at it again – yes, "sir".'

'For Christ's sake . . .'

'Listen, I'm not your bloody corporal.'

She was out of the car and walking away towards a darkened alley at the corner of the block. He didn't lock the car, thought it sensible not to. He hurried to catch her in the dirty, paint-daubed alley. It was where the graffiti smearers worked and over grotesque faces had been sprayed the slogans. *Nazis Raus. Stoppt Den Nazi-Terror.* The inner garden of the square was strewn with wind-whipped paper. It seemed to Josh, and he knew Slough and a dozen barracks towns, a place without hope. He had caught up with her. He took her arm as if to propel her forward, faster, across the garden square, and she shrugged his hand off. He went to the back entrance, where the communal rubbish bins, stinking, were stored. There was a hallway, and an elevator. He pointed to the stairs. After six flights Josh stopped. Tracy strode on ahead of him and waited for him on the land-ing. He went past her and paused by the door. He breathed hard and then hammered on the door.

'I talk,' he hissed at Tracy.

He looked around him. He looked for discarded chewing-gum wrappers and for a little heap of cigarette ends stamped out on the concrete floor in front of the door, left by men who watched and waited. He heard the scrape of slippers behind the door and the turning of a key. The door opened. He saw a small woman, bent with age, dress hanging loose on her body under a heavy wool cardigan. He saw the opaque glaze of her eyes. He saw, past her low shoulder, an old man hunched in a chair by the window.

Josh said, gently, 'My name is Josh Mantle. I've come from England. I've come to see Jorg Brandt . . .'

The small woman gazed, unseeing, past him, through him.

'I've come with a young lady who wishes to meet with Jorg Brandt, your nephew.'

'He's not here, the idiot is not here.'

'Will he be back soon?'

226

A whistle sang in the voice, through mucus. 'Nobody wants to see the idiot. Why do you come to see him?'

Josh said softly, 'It's about what happened a long time ago.'

The voice reeded from the chair by the window in contempt. 'He's not here, the idiot goes each morning to feed rabbits.'

'When, sir, will he return?'

'Perhaps he is an hour, perhaps less than an hour. How long does it take for a grown man to feed rabbits?'

'May we wait for your nephew?'

The old man sat at a grimed window, in a threadbare chair. His life, handicapped, would revolve around what he saw from the window. The old woman saw nothing.

The smell of the room hit Josh and he choked. 'We'll wait outside for him. We don't wish to disturb you. We'll wait by the elevator . . .'

'He does not use the elevator.' The voice of the old man cackled in derision. 'The idiot is afraid of the elevator. The idiot is afraid of the stairs, but less afraid of the stairs than the elevator. The idiot is afraid of everything except the rabbits.'

Josh leaned against the wall in the hallway. He thought of what the pastor had said. The woman shuffled from the door back into the room. The pastor had spoken of the dignity and integrity of a man sentenced to a prison cell. Tracy squatted down on to the dirt of the floor, back against the wall.

'Are you OK?'

She looked up at him. 'Of course I'm OK.'

They waited.

He was parking his car when the local news bulletin began.

Albert Perkins eased into the space. The rain had started and perhaps there would be sleet or snow later . . . The owners of the shipyard voiced concern at its future profitability . . .

He had made his telephone calls. His wife had complained that the man who did the garden was hiking his prices. Basil in his repair yard had babbled that Fulham had won 2–0, a goal in each half . . . The mayor of Rostock feared that further

227

redundancies were necessary among the city's employees, already slashed to a third of what they had been . . .

He had eaten a good breakfast, and driven south on the auto-bahn from Rostock Sud to this bleak and functional collection of shoebox offices. Down the road, beyond the trees, was the new prison. The old fence remained around the shoebox offices. The administration centre of the Stasi had moved here as August-Bebel Strasse had become too cramped . . . Two muggings on the S-Bahn the previous night on the line between Rostock-Bramow and Evershagen . . .

Near to him a bus had parked and he saw the schoolchildren jump from the bus and run to escape the rain . . . An elderly couple, a retired pastor and his wife, travelling from Rerik on the Wismar road had collided with a lorry, both dead . . .

He switched off his radio.

He followed the schoolchildren towards the nearest of the shoebox offices. The files of the Staatssicherheitsdienst of Rostock were kept here in the care of the federal authority. He hurried against the spitting rain towards the doorway. He told the guards that he was a research academic from Britain and needed to find the curator of the archive. He was directed upstairs, the third floor. The children were ahead of him, babbling, as if the shoebox was a place of fun. He gave his name to a secretary on the third floor and was told that the curator would not be available for several minutes. Would he care to inspect the museum while he waited? He joined the schoolchildren as they clustered round a guide. The museum was only three rooms, a token, but the walls were closely covered with mounted and photocopied Stasi documents and the rooms were edged with glass-top cabinets displaying Stasi equipment. 'Go on, sir,' Perkins murmured, 'show the little beggars what it was all about.'

The guide told the schoolchildren, 'We have here what we believe to be the most shocking case of informing in the Stasi time at Rostock. A young woman from a Party family, so she would have been brought up without religion, but she enrolled as a theology student at a college in the city. She went to

228

the college with the express intention of informing on the other students, on the lecturers and pastors, on their families. She was given the codename of Gisela. During the 1980s she submitted more than three thousand pages of reports to her Stasi handler. The betrayal was for money. She was paid five hundred east-Marks each month by the Stasi, nearly as much as a skilled worker in the Neptun yard, and after her graduation she was paid by the Church. She was dedicated, motivated solely by greed, and because of her avarice there were many who were sent to gaol. But after 1990, after her actions were revealed, it was decided by the Federal government that such people were not criminals and we were not authorized to release even her name. She still lives in Rostock . . .'

The guide moved on. The class teacher, an earnest young woman with her hair tied loosely in a ponytail, shepherded the schoolchildren to the next room. Some wrote copious notes, some merely jotted headlines, and one gazed out of the window in blatant boredom. She was a pretty girl, tall and athletic, haughty-faced. Perkins was close to her and saw that the paper on her notepad was blank.

'. . . The Stasi office in Rostock was the biggest Bezirksver-waltung in the old DDR. Because of the long state border of the Baltic coast there were many who attempted to escape into the international sea lanes. It was extremely difficult for them to gain access to proper boats, most took to the water at night on rafts they had made or on children's inflatable sunbeds. In their search for freedom they paid a heavy price. We know of at least seventy-seven persons who were drowned in the attempt to flee the oppression of the DDR. Their bodies were washed up on these shores, on those of the Federal Republic, on Danish beaches. We believe there were many more whose bodies were never found. There were more persons drowned, many of them young, a few of them as young as yourselves, than were shot on the Wall in Berlin or the inner-German border fences. Your generation should remember their courage – they were a witness to the bankruptcy of the state and its Stasi servants . . .'

'Doktor Perkins . . . ?'

'That's me.'

'I am the curator, the director. I understand you are from England and interested in research . . .'

He was leaning against the wall. Tracy, on the floor, sat close to his feet. He heard the reedy voice of the uncle through the open door, 'He is coming, the idiot is coming back from feeding his rabbits.'

Josh started away from the wall. In his mind he had rehearsed the questions. He heard the groan of the window being opened. The wind came through and caught a newspaper on the table, battering it out through the opened door until it wrapped against Josh's leg. He heard the shout.

'Brandt, there are people here to see you. Hurry, idiot.'

He heard the cackled laughter from through the open door. Josh thought that only the old knew how to be truly cruel.

Tracy looked up at him. 'What do we do?'

Klaus Hoffmann heard the shout.

He pressed the button to open the misted window on the front passenger door. He leaned forward and saw the tight, smirking face at the high window. He looked in the mirror. A man came towards his car, hesitant, hugging against the walls of the block as if they were safety, reliant on the support of a stick. It was what he had come for. He saw the man's anguish as he struggled to cross the empty road. They would have come in at the back. It was what Klaus Hoffmann had waited for. He felt the bile rising in his throat.

'What do we do? Well, we don't take him inside there, we don't talk to him in front of that vicious bastard. Go and meet him, take him somewhere. Have you a better idea?'

He heard the clatter, far below, of elevator doors opening.

She shrugged. 'That's OK.'

He heard the rumble of the doors closing. The sound

echoed up to him. Josh led down the flights of stairs, taking them two at a time. The strategy was to go gently, go slowly with the poor devil because he was sick. They were on the third flight from the ground when the elevator climbed past them. He thought Brandt would have managed three flights by now. He ran down the last flights and burst into the ground-floor hallway. The elevator moaned high above him. The fear caught at him. He looked out through the doors, into the road and saw the back of the man as he reached his car. The car's windows were misted and the engine spurted exhaust fumes. The man turned and leaned his elbows on the roof of the car. God Almighty. Josh recognized the man he had pushed down on to the rocks.

He looked at the elevator doors and above, the numbers of the floors. The light came on for the seventh floor, then the eighth. He didn't tell her, didn't try to. The sense, disorganized in his mind, was of catastrophe. A woman with shopping bags was pressing, in irritation, at the call button of the elevator.

He bullocked past Tracy and launched himself at the stairs. He charged up the first flight. She was coming after him. He heaved for breath. At the seventh-floor landing, running past the elevator doors, he saw the light slip from the tenth floor to the eleventh. His legs were leaden. She was coming after him, easily. The light had gone from the eleventh, the last light was for the roof. He fell. His feet slipped back and hit the edge of a step, caught the bone of his shin. The pain shimmered through Josh's body, and he struggled up the last flight of stairs. The elevator door was open, the elevator empty. The door for the low shed structure housing the elevator shaft and the stairwell hung free and rapped in the wind.

Josh stepped, panting, on to the roof of the block, and saw Jorg Brandt out on the roof, away from the shed structure. He stood as if marooned on the puddled asphalt.

He saw the terror on his face.

His coat billowed in the wind and the force of the wind

seemed to drag him further from Josh. Brandt edged backwards as if the control over his legs was gone, lost.

There was no rail at the edge of the roof and no wall. Josh saw, behind the man, the town of Warnemunde laid out as a model would have been, the shipyards, the beach, the sea stretched limitless to the cloud horizon. The man dropped his stick, as if the hand which held it was lifeless.

Josh pushed away from the door. He thought Tracy was behind him and moved forward.

'You have nothing to fear from me, Herr Brandt. I've come to help you . . .'

The man who had been a schoolteacher edged a pace back.

'Please, Herr Brandt, just come to me. If you cannot come to me just sit down, let me reach you. Please . . . They cannot get to you, Herr Brandt. When you are with me then they cannot harm you, I promise.'

The man who had been denounced as a paedophile wavered and lurched back.

Josh shouted into the wind, 'I have come, Herr Brandt, to free you from them. They have no power over you. Their ability to hurt is gone, believe me.'

The man who had been rejected by his family, evicted, destroyed, was at the edge of the asphalt roof.

'They are finished, Herr Brandt. They are gone, they are history.'

Josh's voice died. He saw the slow smile settle on the man's face, as if from turmoil a last peace had been found. Josh crouched and had no more words. The smile was calm. Josh wanted to close his eyes and could not.

The man, Jorg Brandt, turned. It was so quick, two paces, as he stepped off the roof of the block.

Josh stared at the space where Brandt had been. There was no scream. He shook, and wished he could have wept. Tracy walked past him to where the stick lay and kicked it hard and it rolled and teetered close to the edge of the roof.

She faced him. 'Are you going to stay here all day or are you going to shift?'

He felt so small and so weak and so much a failure. He wanted her comfort.

'I couldn't reach him . . .'

Tracy said, brutal, 'You were never going to reach him. He would never have let you. The bastard was too yellow ever to have let you reach him.'

She was gone. When they reached the ground floor she did not hesitate. She did not go to see the body, or to join the small knot of a crowd that gathered. He watched the car with the misted windows pull away. They went out into the back, into the inner garden of the square.

She said, without looking at him, 'You don't have to blame yourself. It's him that's to blame. He was a coward.'

His fist clenched. He could have hit her. They reached the car and he threw her the car keys. They were already on the road when the ambulance passed them, siren wailing.

He had the section and he had the name.

Even by the standards of Albert Perkins, a quality practitioner, heavy flannel bullshit had been needed to win the interest of the curator of the archive – an international affairs research unit, funded by a Cambridge college, a centre of excellence, an acknowledgement that the Rostock archive at Dummerstorf-Waldeck was the most helpful in all the former DDR. He had the section that dealt with surveillance filming, and now the name of the former *Oberleutnant* who had headed the section in the late 1980s. He left a note of thanks, on the desk they had offered him, for the curator. He slipped away down the corridor. The tour of the schoolchildren continued. He saw the earnest teacher and the youngsters who took notes, and the one girl who did not care to hide her disinterest.

'Those who collaborated with the Stasi have built a great lie. These weak and manipulated people tell the lie now that it was not possible to refuse the Stasi. They try to explain their betrayal of friends and family by spreading the lie. There were enough who refused to kill the lie. It should never be sufficient again in

233

Germany for a man or woman to claim that he or she merely obeyed orders . . .'

She came to the door. She had already laid out her daughter's kit on the bed, laundered and ironed.

Christina was lying on the bed in her tennis costume. She had the phones of her stereo in her ears.

'You're resting . . . ?'

'Trying to.'

'What sort of day did you have?'

'Boring.'

'What was boring?'

'It was compulsory, because of the new teacher. We had to go to Dummerstorf-Waldeck, to a boring museum.'

'What museum?'

'The Stasi museum. The new teacher is from Hamburg. She says we have to know about the past. The past is boring. I missed tennis practice. The past is gone, why do we have to know the past?'

'What were you told about the Stasi?'

'We were told what they'd done. It was boring, it has no relevance to today. I'm not to blame for what happened before. It has nothing to do with me. I don't have any guilt. The new teacher asked us whether any of our parents had been victims of the Stasi.'

'What did you tell her, Christina?'

'That I didn't know. That I'd never heard you or Poppa talk of the Stasi. The man who took us round the museum, he said the Stasi suffocated under the paper they made. They spent all their time writing reports, so they had no time to read their reports, all they did was write them. That was why they did not know the revolution was coming until it was too late. They sounded to me to be stupid and boring. Momma . . . I need to rest.'

His car took him from the Kremlin gate.

The minister had told the cabinet meeting that the armed forces were short of funds to the extent of one hundred trillion roubles

– Pyotr Rykov had given him the figure, and made the exchange calculation for his minister – twenty billion American dollars. The minister had told the politicians that a minimum of 100,000 troops lived in sub-human conditions of poverty – Pyotr Rykov had provided him with the statistic and the fact that soldiers sold their equipment into the black market so that they should not starve.

He always sat in the front passenger seat, beside the driver.

He would trust his driver with his life, with his secrets, with his future. He had clung to his driver because the grizzled elder man, long past the date of retirement, had been a true friend from the second tour in Afghanistan and through the German posting, and during the years at Siberia Military District. He had brought him to Moscow. Pyotr Rykov had always shared his inner thoughts, confidences, with his stoic quiet driver. 'It's the funding, or it is mutinies . . .'

A frown slowly gouged at the forehead of his driver.

'Either the funds are provided or the Army disintegrates . . .'

The driver squinted from the wet, icy road ahead up to his mirror.

'We cannot, will not, tolerate the destruction of the Army.'

It was the fourth time the driver had checked the mirror, and in response he had slowed for a kilometre, then speeded for a kilometre, and repeated the process.

'Without the strength of the Army, if the Army is neutered, then the Motherland collapses.'

The driver gave no warning but swung the wheel from the main highway and cut into a side street that was half filled with the stalls of a vegetable market, scattering men and women.

'Either they make the funding available or the Army, to save itself, must take decisive action . . .'

The driver pulled out of the side street and accelerated into a two-lane road. His eyes flickered again towards his mirror and his frown deepened.

'There is money for the politicians and for their elections, there is money for bribery and corruption, there is money for schemes to win votes to keep the pigs at the trough . . .'

The car crawled. Pyotr Rykov glanced at his driver, and finally noticed the anxiety. He swung round in his seat, stretching the belt taut, and saw the car that followed them. Two men in the front of the car, a man in the back.

'How long?'

The driver said, grimly, 'The whole of the journey.'

'All of the way?'

'Fast when we go fast, slow when we are slow.'

'Not before today?'

'I would have told you, Colonel.'

'Who are they, the shit fuckers?'

He regarded his driver as a mine of information. His driver sat each day at a centre of learning, as he many times had joked, in the car parks of the ministry or the Kremlin, the foreign embassies or the city's major military barracks, talking with the other drivers. They were the men who knew the pulse and movement of Moscow. They were the men who recognized first the shifting motions of power.

'They change nothing but the name. It is a new name but the old way. When the KGB wishes to intimidate then it drives close. It lets you see them, lets the anxiety build, lets you know they are close and merely await the final order.'

'You have no doubt?'

'They want to be seen.'

He reached between his legs and pressed the combination numbers of his briefcase lock. He took his service pistol from the briefcase and checked the magazine and the safety. He slid it into his waist, cold metal against his skin.

'Stop.'

His driver braked. The black car with the three men inside stopped a dozen paces behind them.

'Pull away.'

They eased away from the curb. The black car with the three men inside followed behind them.

'What do I do, friend?'

'It is what you have already done. You have bred enemies.'

The fear winnowed in Pyotr Rykov's mind. It was the fear he had known when he had walked in the villages of Afghanistan, when he had been in the street markets and bazaars of Jalalabad and Herat, when the threat was always behind him.

'I am protected.'

The driver smiled mirthlessly. 'In Russia, through this century, Colonel, men have believed they were protected.'

'I am protected by the minister.'

'The minister is not in the Kremlin, Colonel. They are in the Kremlin.'

'They can fuck themselves.'

'It is a warning. They will watch to see how you respond to the warning.'

They reached the apartment. The apartment was in an old building in a wide street. He stood for a moment on the pavement and the black car accelerated away. None of the three men looked as they passed. He told his driver at what time he should be collected after lunch. He was alone, and exposed.

'I wouldn't have believed it of you, Phlegm – diffidence sits uneasily with you.'

They lunched in the judge's chambers. A man-servant waited at the table. No guests, only the judge and Fleming of German Desk.

'It's not a state of affairs I enjoy, Beakie.'

'Do I have to spread the towel on my shoulder again, or is it time for confidences? Is it about that business, the young woman and the Stasi thug?'

In the good old days, the lamented old days that were gone, there would have been brandy with the coffee. Not any more. Fleming refilled his glass of gassed water.

'How long have you got?'

'Not more than ten minutes. Bounce it at me.'

Fleming said, 'It is extraordinary, certainly beyond my experience. We are not in control, but we have what we regard as important policy riding on it – yet, we are reduced to watching.

Our allies, the Germans, equally have policy at stake and they, too, are not in control. Our two policies are set against each other. We're like two commanders, each on our respective high ground, looking down into a valley. That valley, into which we respectively look, was once a superpower confrontation zone – not any more. The valley, the battlefield of our policies that conflict, is the city of Rostock and the small communities around Rostock. It's a minor provincial city, stultifyingly dull. In that valley are our respective shock troops – don't laugh – engaged in combat to the death. On their side is Hauptman Krause, and any allies he can muster. On our side is an abject failure of a man and a junior NCO, a young woman. Either of us, on the high ground above the valley, can lose the policy we seek to achieve but neither of us can intervene. It is as if the valley were covered by the fog of war. I've never felt so helpless about something that matters to me. I assume my opposite number in Cologne feels precisely the same way. We must wait for that fog to clear to see who holds the valley, who are the casualties. Good to get it off my chest, Beakie, thank you. It's a unique experience for me to feel so helpless. You'd better get back to that bloody court-room.'

12

'. . . because he was a coward . . .'

He walked on. Josh Mantle had never in his life hit a woman.
He walked fast, tried to leave her behind him. He wished he had
hit her. If he had turned to look behind him then he would no
longer have seen the low buildings of Warnemunde and the
breakwater going out into the water and the squat lighthouse.

'Josh, you are being ridiculous. It wasn't your fault. He
couldn't face it, he was a coward . . .'

There were low scrub trees at the top of the beach beyond
the bent grass of the dunes. He walked beside the last strips of
the winter's grey-brown ice and close to the grey-green sea that
came white-flecked to the ice line. His head was down, his chin
was on his chest. Sometimes he closed his eyes, squeezed them
shut, but he could not lose the image of the man, or escape the
terror of Jorg Brandt.

'Josh, will you stop, will you listen . . . You don't blame yourself, you blame him. He was a coward.'

He saw only the terror of the man, not that last moment of
peace on his features.

But for the hectoring voice behind him, Josh was alone.

He sought a solitude. He was, had always been, his own man.
He had been his own man when they had brought him home
from the school in Penang to the stinking heat, wet, insect-
ridden home, and his father had sat with the whisky bottle and
told him that the 'fucking slit-eyes' had shot his mother, and had
then left him alone and gone with the rest of them to wreck the
Chinese quarter. His own man at barracks schools, and at the
Apprentice College, alone on the train with the small suitcase,

239

alone in the classrooms and in the dormitory. He had been, for ever, alone. He had been his own man, alone, in the I Corps postings . . .

Except the once when he had followed his captain and the Guatemalan had died, and he had compromised.

. . . and in the Special Investigation Branch, alone in the mess at Tidworth when he had demanded that a thief be prosecuted and branded; alone in the bar of the mess half an hour after the call for free drinks to see him on his way, after the second in command had made the speech, perfunctorily, and dumped the cheap carriage clock on his lap. His own man on the streets, alone . . .

Except for the meeting with Libby and marrying Libby, and better that he had been his own man, alone, because she was taken from him and the pain of it was his cross.

Each crisis that came to Josh Mantle's life battered a message to him: better to be his own man, better to be alone.

'Are you going to stop? I can't help it if he was a bloody coward.'

He pounded the beach, empty ahead of him, because he yearned to be alone. If he had been alone, if she had not been behind him, if there had been no witness, if there had been only the company of the sand and the sea and the grey black clouds and the wind, then he would have gone down on to his knees. He would have talked to his Libby, would have told her everything . . .

'Look at me. Bloody well look.'

He stopped.

'Come on, look at me.'

He did not kneel.

'Do it, Josh, turn round. Look.'

He did not know how he should escape from her. He had walked an hour and a half on the beach, round headlands, and she tracked him. He could not escape from her. As if she held him, Josh turned.

Her coat was furthest back, discarded by the ice line, a speck.

He saw her sweater, left on the sand and lying across the track of their footprints. Her blouse and her bra were caught by the wind and rolled towards the grass of the dunes. Her shoes were behind her, abandoned, and her socks.

She hopped on one foot, she kicked off her jeans. He had turned as she had known he would. She threw her jeans away from her, over the bare white skin of her shoulder. She wore only her knickers. Her legs were a little apart and she stood defiant with her fingers at her hips, resting on the waistband of her knickers. She challenged him. She would strip to nothing if he did not come to her, as she ordered him to. He could not turn away. The gale came off the sea and ruffled the clothes scattered behind her and caught her hair and beat at her nakedness. He wore, against his chest, a vest and a shirt and a pullover and a jacket and his outer coat, and Josh still shivered. She did not flinch in the cold of the wind.

'Come . . . Come here, Josh.'

He started to walk towards her. She stood on the beach, so still. His eyes never left her. His eyes searched across the nakedness of her body. He unzipped the fastener of his coat, peeled it from his chest and shoulders. He saw each line on her skin, each spot and blemish and mole. She held out her arms. He saw the straggling hair in the pits of her arms. He slotted the sleeves of his coat over her arms and he stood in front of her and fastened the zip, and then he buttoned the coat over the zip. He retraced their footmarks in the sand, picked up her trousers, then her shoes and her socks. He shook the sand from her bra and her blouse, from her sweater and her coat.

He dropped the clothes at her feet. 'Get dressed.'

'I'll get dressed when you've spat it out of your system, Josh.'

He looked into her face. He wanted to hold her and warm her. There was no scorn in her face, only the innocence.

'You never, ever again call a man a coward. You call a man a coward and you strip him bare. To call a man a coward is to make a judgement on him. It is the worst of arrogance to believe yourself qualified to call a man a coward. He would have been soaked from the sea, bloodstained, he would have been in shadow, incoherent, but you say that the man who slammed the door on him was a coward. Your Hans was a goddamn problem. We all do it, every day, I do it, you, everybody, we cross over the street to avoid a problem. Jorg Brandt suffered, he didn't have the memories of love that you had, but you call him a coward.'

'Should have stayed at home, should I?'

'Just get dressed.'

'Don't fucking lecture me.'

'I walked away from you because otherwise I would have hit you.'

She tore his coat off. She crouched over her own clothes. 'Your wife, when she left you, did you hit her?'

He rocked.

'When she left you, did you lecture her?'

He clasped his hands together so they should not be free to strike her.

Josh said, 'I'll see you at the car. You should get dressed.'

He went back, away, along the beach.

Albert Perkins walked on Kropeliner Strasse in search of a former *Oberleutnant*. He was inside the old city walls. The street was a pedestrian precinct, at the core of Rostock. There was, he thought, an air of prosperity about Kropeliner Strasse, new paint, new shopfronts, new pavings, but he knew the prosperity was a mirage because the interiors of the shops were empty. Women queued to be served at the fruit and vegetable stalls and kids lounged by the fast food outlets, but the boutiques and the hardware stores and the interior furnishing businesses were empty. There were people at the well stocked window of the camera shop, but inside the shop was empty. He looked through the window, past the shelves of cameras and lenses and tripods and binoculars and bags, and he saw a middle-aged man and a girl who sat languid and under-employed.

He pushed open the door.

The smile of welcome lit the man's face. He was a customer,

an event. The girl straightened. Albert Perkins wandered to the far end of the shop and the man, predictable, followed him. He had led the man out of earshot from the girl. There were times when Albert Perkins lied with the best of them, and times when he discarded untruths for frankness.

'Good afternoon. I am a busy man, and I am sure you would like to be a busy man . . . You were the *Oberleutnant* heading the *Abteilung* responsible for covert surveillance filming. I come as a trader. If you have what I want then I will pay for it. Life, as I always say, is a market-place. You don't need my name, nor do you need to know the organization that I represent, and if the merchandise is satisfactory then I pay for discretion. There was a Hauptman Krause at August-Bebel Strasse. The wife of Hauptman Krause was Eva, and the lovely Eva enjoyed the favours of a Soviet officer, a Major Rykov. An *Inoffizielle Mitarbeiter*, overwhelmed by his ideological duty, reported these sessions in the art of copulation to a handler. The bed play was filmed. Now, if I am not to be disappointed and you are to be paid, those films will have been preserved. I wish to buy the films of Eva Krause coupling with Major Rykov.'

The man, the former *Oberleutnant*, chuckled. The mirth ripped his face. 'People want only, today, what is new. I could fill my shelves with cameras, lenses, produced in the old DDR, and people will walk past them. They demand only what is new, which they cannot afford to pay for.'

'No money orders, no travellers' cheques, banknotes in the hand – if you have the film I want to buy.'

The man waved to the girl, she should mind the shop. She was unlikely to be trampled by a stampede. He had keys on a chain and he walked through to where the stock was piled in boxes. Albert Perkins was pleased to see the quantity of the boxes, unpacked, as he had been pleased to see the quantity of cameras and lenses on the shelves. He thought the account books would make stark reading. The man unlocked a steel-plated door at the back of the shop. He led Albert Perkins down gloomy old stone steps.

The cellar was a small shrine dedicated to the past. The present and the future were at street level, where the Japanese cameras and lenses were displayed, and kept out by two sets of double-locked doors and a poorly lit stone staircase. Heavy timbers had been brought in, old wood, and were used as props between the floor and the ceiling, and Albert Perkins thought the cellar must have once been a shelter against the bombing. There was a good armchair on a square of good carpet. The man gestured that he should sit. In front of the chair was a television set, large screen, and under the television was a video player. He sat. The man ignored a shelf of video-cassettes and knelt in front of a wall safe and used his body to prevent Perkins seeing the combination he used. The exhibits, for the shrine, were on a shelf behind the television, and each was labelled as if the pride still lived.

There was a camera the size of a matchbox, what the 'grey mouse' would have used for the photography of documents; an attaché case, and it took the trained eye of Albert Perkins to see the pinhead hole in the end of it; a cooler bag, and he saw the brightness of the lens set where a stud should have been for the holding strap, good for the beach in summer; tape recorders for audio surveillance; button-sized microphones for a man to wear on his chest; long directional microphones for distance; a length of log, the bark peeling from dried-out age, and he frowned because he could not see the lens; electric wall fittings and plugs for hotel rooms, in which a microphone or a camera could be hidden . . . The safe door was shut. The man had lifted out three video-cassettes.

He said, briskly, 'Could you, please, my friend, stand up.'

Albert Perkins stood. The man came behind him and quickly, with expertise, frisked him. The man tapped with the palms of his hands at the collar and the chest and the upper arms and the waist and in his groin and at his ankles. Albert Perkins had never carried a firearm. Firearms were for the cowboys in Ireland. It was a good search, professional.

The man said, 'Please, sit down.'

A video was placed in the cassette player. The television was switched on.

Monochrome . . . A cramped, tight bedroom, filled with the width of the bed, and the angle wide enough to show the wallpaper above the bed. She was a good-looking woman. Agony and ecstasy on her face. She had a strong body.

Perkins watched. The warmth came through him.

'Fifty thousand DMs . . .'

'Fifteen thousand.'

She was on her back. Sharp focus. He was on her. Her knees high and tight against his hips. His hands on her shoulders and his back arched.

'Forty-five thousand DMs.'

'Twenty, top.'

She squirmed under him, she lifted her ankles and closed them round him. It wasn't the sex that he knew, what Helen allowed on his birthday or her birthday, or on their anniversary, or when, rarely, she had drunk too much. She rolled him. 'Forty thousand DMs, that is final.'

'Twenty-five thousand is where I finish.'

He saw Rykov's face. His mouth was open, as if he gasped. He was on his back. She rode him, bucked on him as if he were a steer and her breasts bounced and she seemed to cry her rioting pleasure to the ceiling.

'Thirty-five thousand DMs, and that is my absolutely final—'

'I said twenty-five thousand was where I finished.'

'You have seen five minutes, it is a three-hour tape, and there are two more tapes . . .'

'Twenty-five thousand, cash.'

His eyes never left the screen. He wondered whether the old bastard had stayed home on the day the *Oberleutnant* had come to install the camera, or whether he had merely left the keys under the mat. She sat across him and she stroked the hairs of his stomach and his chest and he cupped her breasts. There wasn't shyness between them, and the old bastard had said it wasn't love.

'Thirty thousand DMs; that is quite absolutely the final—'

'Twenty-five thousand – be a shame to go to insolvency when you've worked so hard to build your business.'

245

She was off him. He was limp. She wiped a tissue between her legs. They didn't kiss. They dressed fast, as if he had to get back to commanding a missile and radar unit and she was headed for her office or for a meeting or for collecting the child from the minder. The room was empty and the film ended. 'Twenty-five thousand DMs, cash.'

'Twenty-five thousand, cash, for three tapes, agreed.'

Albert Perkins stood in the street. Behind him the man pulled down the shutters, obscured the window of unsold Japanese cameras.

The cold of the evening settled on him after the heat and warmth of the cellar. It was always a mistake for a man to insert himself into forbidden territory, he reflected, but Albert Perkins never ceased to be amazed at how many men jeopardized their future in sweaty copulation.

He murmured, 'Might have been good at the time, Colonel Rykov, might have been brilliant, but did you ever consider that you might live to regret it. Did you?'

He left his apartment in the early evening to go back to his desk in the ministry. His wife, Irina, had watched him change. Pyotr Rykov crossed the pavement with a firm step, and the driver hurried from the car to open the door for him. His wife had watched him take the best, most recently acquired, uniform from the wardrobe and change into it, and she had not asked him why, that evening, he chose to wear his best uniform and why he went back to his desk. He paused at the open door. His minister would have left the building, and the aides and clerks from the outer offices. It was, to Pyotr Rykov, an act of necessary defiance. Down the road, misted windows, was a stationary black car. It was important to Pyotr Rykov that he should not believe he was intimidated.

She braked sharply outside the *pension*. He had not spoken all the time she had driven back to Rostock.

She turned to him. 'All right, you want to bloody sulk, but do it on your own. Piss off.'

246

He looked into her face, contorted and ugly. Josh said, slow and deliberate, 'I don't find this easy, but I'll say it because it has to be said. Today you have been more cruel and more vicious than any woman I have ever known. Beside that, you can be more gentle and more caring, and I include my wife, than any woman I have ever known. Tracy, I do not understand the depth of the scar . . .'

She said, cold, 'I lost the boy I loved. Isn't that enough for you, "sir"?'

'No, not enough.'

She spat, 'He was murdered.'

'Not enough. People cope, they're hurt but they live with it.'

'What do you want?'

'I want the truth. I want to know the truth so that I can help you cut out that viciousness and cruelty before it destroys a very worthwhile person – you, Tracy.'

'Loving a boy who's murdered, that's not enough to scar?'

He shook his head. The traffic went by them. 'No, sorry, not enough.'

'If I told you that I was going to have his baby, Hans's baby . . . that it was when I loved him in the early morning before we went to Rostock, and I didn't use anything, when he needed all the courage I could give him . . . If I told you that two months after he was murdered I found that I was carrying his baby, that I went to a place in Kreuzberg, just a stenographer so I couldn't afford a clinic, and had the baby aborted, and that Hans's daughter would now be nine years old, that there isn't a day when I don't live with the guilt . . . Would that be enough?'

Josh shook.

His laundry was back in his room.

He caught the radio news – statistics released from the finance ministry put the cost of seven years of unification at a thousand billion DMs, he made the calculation in his mind, 418,410,040,000 pounds sterling . . . He put the laundered clothes in the drawers of his room.

On the radio news – the chief executive of a chemical plant at Dortmund warned that labour costs now ran at 44DMs an hour in Germany, and at 3.36DMs in the Czech Republic . . . He tried to call his wife. There was no answer.

A statement from the *Rathaus* predicted there could be no further funding for the infrastructure development of Rostock . . . He brushed his teeth, washed his hands, changed his shirt and pondered on what he would say to Mr Fleming. He sat in his chair and made notes, because it was, in his opinion, always best to know clearly what to say.

In the Lichtenhagen suburb of Rostock a former schoolteacher from Rerik had fallen to his death from the roof of an apartment block . . .

He reached for the telephone and unscrewed the cover of the voice box and the ear piece and fastened the coiled wires that ran from a small plastic box. It was one of the better devices, originating from the Technical Section at Vauxhall Bridge Cross. It had been tested, as they said, to destruction and the guarantee was given by the engineers responsible that the equipment made a call proof against a tap.

He dialled the number for the head of German Desk in London. He remembered talking with an Israeli officer a few years before, when relations had been tolerable. French officers and Americans from the Agency and the Israeli of the Mossad section in the London embassy had been hosted by British officers for a weekend at that awful country place down in Surrey. Disgusting food, an old house that was an icebox, and a weekend to discuss the movement of nuclear materials from the Eastern Bloc through Germany and onwards to Iraq, Iran, Libya, wherever . . . Late on the Saturday night, with a shared whisky bottle, the Israeli had made his confessional to Albert Perkins. A Jordanian airforce pilot, young, was being trained under contract by the Germans. A lonely man, far from home. The Israeli officer, tongue loosened by the whisky, had said he controlled the targeting of the trainee pilot. The usual story, an introduction to a female agent, an isolated

248

man finding sex and comfort, his entrapment. The pilot had completed his course, had gone home, and the contact had been renewed, and the threat of disclosure had been made. The pilot's cousin ran Jordanian vegetables and fruit, every week, across the Allenby Bridge, to the market at Jerusalem. The produce was never stopped, never checked, and his business flourished. The cousin carried, with the vegetables and fruit, reports on the Jordanian airforce and its Iraqi ally to the Mossad. Couldn't last, such business had only a short shelf life. The pilot and his cousin were arrested in Amman. They were tried for espionage, and hanged. The Israeli's confessional, slurred through the whisky fumes, was poignant still to Albert Perkins. On the morning of the executions, the morning the pilot and his cousin had been frogmarched to the noose, there had been no remorse in the Mossad offices in Tel Aviv. They were casualties of the game . . . A retired pastor from Rerik was dead, with his wife, from a collision on the road. Now a former schoolmaster was dead, a fall from a high building . . . He had created the situation and made the casualties of the game. Albert Perkins, waiting for the connection, wondered if ever he would feel remorse.

'Evening, Mr Fleming, Albert here . . . Yes, thank you, it's been a good day, very good actually . . .'

Josh sat on the bare mattress with the pillow beside him and the folded bed clothes. Of course, she would have gone alone to the house in Kreuzberg. A woman would have used pills or alcohol or needles. A minimum of recovery time. She would have gone alone, unsteady and shaken, back to Brigade and her room. His head was in his hands. He thought that she had the right to be scarred, and the right to viciousness and cruelty. He had prised the story from her and he felt a cringing shame.

He vomited over his trousers. The tears streamed down Klaus Hoffmann's cheeks. He coughed the sick from his throat and it fell over the steering wheel on his car and onto his trousers. He was parked up to the west of the city, alone in his car on a farm track, vomit spewed on his trousers.

'That's good Albert, that's well done . . .' Praise always went a long way, Fleming reckoned, with a dogged foot soldier of the Service. And a joke was useful. '. . . My advice, Albert, after what you've had to sit through, take a cold shower . . .'

He had written the note on his pad. There were three cassettes on offer. The sale price of the cassettes was, the calculation given him by Perkins, sterling pounds 10,460. He wrote now the names of those who would be needed to authorize a payment of that size, and the names of those who would wish to consider the potentials of the direction in which the matter now ran. And he wrote the name of Dieter Krause and his pen scratched three lines under the name.

'. . . Oh, and, Albert, shouldn't have forgotten them. What news of our intrepid pair . . . I see. Yes, I have that . . . A pastor and a schoolteacher, from Rerik – you don't have the connection? . . . I see . . . Well, we have to hope for them, don't we, that they stay sensible, yes? . . . Forgive me, Albert, but I need to push on if I'm to get the authorization. It's about the time that people go home . . . I'll call you in the morning.'

It was so peaceful on the river below, and so quiet behind the double glazing around him in his room. He found it difficult, in the peace and the quiet, to imagine, in distant Germany, a small car impacting against the radiator of a heavy goods lorry and a man spiralling down to his death from a great height . . . It was a question of policy. Policy ruled, policy did not permit imagination.

'Violet, a moment, please . . .'

He called through the door. She had her coat on, a scarf round her head, and carried her collapsed umbrella and a shopping bag. He didn't have to apologize. It was not necessary to apologize for destroying Violet's carefully constructed timetable. It was general talk that she lived alone, had no life outside the Service. He knew the way to soften her.

'Albert's done well . . . I need a meeting in an hour. I'll want the assistant deputy director, someone from Resources, Russia Desk should come and American Desk, and someone to take a note . . . would you emphasize priority, it doesn't wait till the morning . . . Albert's done very well.'

She turned away. Already she was awkwardly shrugging out of her coat, then loosening her scarf. They'd have made a good item, the dogged Albert Perkins and the ever dependable Violet. They'd probably have found a little space in the building to bunk up so they'd never have had to leave Vauxhall Bridge Cross, two devoted servants of the Service, perpetually on call for times of priority.

'Oh, and please . . . Dig me what we've stored on Dieter Krause, former MfS, Rostock, so I can have a fast hack at the guts of the brute's life . . .'

KRAUSE, Dieter Friedrich.
Born: 11.9.1952, at Hessenburg (n.e. of Rostock).
Father was horticultural worker, amputee from Normandy 1944. One sister, Petra, born 1954.
Mother was horticultural produce packer. Unremarkable childhood. Joined FDJ in 1966.

It was not the influence of his father. His father, without a right leg, was a survivor. His father came through the Nazi childhood, the wound, the arrival of the Red Army, the coming of the Communist regime. His father, the survivor, was *brav*, believed in obedience and correctness towards power. The influence on the child, Dieter, came from the man he called his uncle. The uncle, too, was a survivor and spoke with the guttural accent of an ethnic German from northern Yugoslavia, and had been three years in Tito's post war prison camps. The uncle taught the child, Dieter, aged twelve, the twin arts of survival and advancement as he had learned them in the prison camp near to Novi Sad. He had also taught young Dieter to understand the mind and character of the Slav Russian without which the distant

251

friendship could not have been bred. He informed, after his first FDJ summer camp, on the other children, on the brigade leader, on what the other children said about their parents. He was given coarse chocolate, and made a unit leader. He had a handler, he was noticed, he tasted power . . . And he had learned to fear the loss of power . . .

Volunteer to Border Guard, 1970. Volunteer for additional six months service. Doctorate of Law, University of Potsdam (MfS sponsorship). Joined MfS, 1976, Normannen Strasse HQ, Berlin. KGB fast track promotion course, Moscow, 1979. Bonn (import-export cover), 1980. Posted to Rostock, 1981, rank *Unterleutnant*. Married Eva (née Schultz), FDGB organizer at Neptun shipyard, Rostock, 1981.

On the horticultural farm, a friend of his sister, the daughter of workers in the tomato houses, was Annelore. He had promised, dishevelled, wet, naked, that he would love Annelore all of his life. When he had gone to join the Border Guard, Annelore had come with him on the bus to Rostock, and walked with him onto the platform of the *Hauptbahnhof*, and waved to him until the train had curved away on the tracks. Sex in the seed store with Annelore when he had returned on leave from the Magdeburg sector. Sex in his mother's bed, through long afternoons, with Annelore when he had come back for the vacations from the university at Potsdam. There were many girls he could have fucked, sucked, stroked, in Potsdam and when he was posted to Normannen Strasse, but he had stayed faithful to his Annelore. And he had come back to Rostock, and they were to be married. It had been a summer's evening when he was ordered to the office in August-Bebel Strasse of the *major* who headed the internal security *Abteilung*. Annelore was not suitable. Annelore's cousin was associated with an environmental action group. Annelore, if he wished for a career in the MfS, should be dismissed from his life . . . He had written to her that evening, four lines . . . He had been introduced the next month to a quite pretty FDGB organizer. He had chased the power, clung to it. He would not lose the power . . .

Promoted to *Oberleutnant* 1984, transfer to Counter-Espionage. 1986, authorization for 'friendship' with Major Pyotr
Rykov, Wustrow Base, w. of Rostock. Promoted to *Hauptman*
1987. Following incursion of UK agent, Hans Becker, to Wustrow Base (run, non-authorized, by I Corps, west Berlin) shot
agent dead after capture – 21.11.1988.

There had been sufficient light for him to see the way that the back of the boy's head, against the dirt and the grass of the square, had exploded. Before they had dragged the boy away, they had all knelt on the ground and picked in the earth for the tissue of the boy's brain and for the fragments of skull bone. Earth was kicked over the blood . . . He had had the pain in his groin, and he had not felt bad then at shooting the boy or drop-ping the body into the night sea . . . He had felt the pain, the next day, when he had been called to the office of the minister, Mielke. Made to wait in the outer corridor, eyed with contempt by officers who used the corridor and the secretaries at their typewriters in the outer office. Marched into the inner office, as if he were a prisoner. Standing, the ache still in his groin, blurt-ing answers to the questions of the old man. Then the monologue of abuse from Mielke. Through the cigarette smoke, he was an incompetent cunt. He had shivered as the smoke had played at his nose, trembled, because he had thought he had lost his power . . .

Believed to have sanitized personal MfS file, and Becker file,
Dec. 1989. Unemployed. 1992, worked in Rostock bank (four
months), dismissed. Unemployed. 1995, hardware salesman
(on commission). 1996, offered himself to BfV, Cologne.

He had sat for two hours in the public hallway of the BfV complex. He had himself typed the letter he had handed in at the desk, and with the letter had been the torn out photograph from the newspaper. He had sat there for two hours, a man forgotten, without status. A secretary, a plump and grey haired woman so similar to the one he had slept with in Bonn so many years before, had come to the public hallway and given him a security pass and escorted him to the elevator. The faces had been suspicious and sober. He had talked of his friendship with Pyotr Rykov as the spools of a tape recorder turned. He had given the name of a secretary in the Foreign Ministry, and many years before the woman had played her fingers in the hair of his chest and whispered love. They had changed the tape three times . . . A week later he had been called back to Cologne, escorted with deference to the room of a senior official. There had been sandwiches of Scotch smoked salmon and white wine from the Rhine. He had been welcomed, his power had returned. He remembered the sick feeling of relief as he had driven back again to Rostock. On the autobahn he had made the pledge to himself, over and over, repeated and repeated, that he would never, a second time, lose the power . . .

'. . . Thank you, Fleming, very concisely put. I feel all of us now know Dieter Krause, share his skin with him . . .'

It was a short meeting and would produce, as the assistant deputy director was to inform the deputy director, Olive's finest hour.

'. . . To draw it together – Albert Perkins, in Rostock, provides us with back-up should the pair, Mantle and Barnes, fail to provide evidence of murder against Krause. The indication, as of this moment, they are not close to that evidence. The back-up, the cuckolding of Krause by Rykov, could be used to discredit Krause's address in Washington next week . . . of course he knew, he was a ranking intelligence officer, he would have known. Vindictive, bitter, humiliated, spreading lies . . . Not much of a back-up, but perhaps enough to throw doubt on his veracity. Is the back-up, a salacious film, worth that amount of money?' The assistant deputy director was due at

254

the ballet and would have to join his wife after the performance had started.

'I can push it through the books, no problem, bounce it out
of any number of budgets. But, it's more than half a year's salary
for a junior executive officer. Personally, I'd say there's better
things to spend our money on.' The woman from Resources was
anxious to be home to relieve the child minder of responsibility.
It was the third successive evening that she had telephoned to
beg the girl to stay the extra hour.

'If you believe a little extramarital on the part of his wife with
Rykov is going to faze our American friends, then you are on
another planet. I see no reason, none at all, why such nonsense
would diminish Krause's standing in Washington. They're all at
it there, screwing like rabbits. Sorry, but the money would be
wasted.' From North America Desk.

'My own view, it would be cheaper for Perkins to get his kicks
down in Soho, give him a bunch of luncheon vouchers and pack
him off to get an eyeful if it's films he needs. I vote against.' The
head of Russia Desk was due to collect his serviced car from the
garage, and if he were not there in 25 minutes the garage would
have closed.

'Sorry, Fleming, but that's the verdict of colleagues. Perkins
shouldn't take it personally, it's been good ferreting. Thank you
all for your time.'

The assistant deputy director shovelled his papers into his
briefcase. Fleming stood grimly. The head of Russia Desk
scraped back his chair. The stenographer folded away her pad.
Resources was half way to the door. The head of North America
Desk smiled sheepishly at Fleming . . . and Olive Harris still sat
and she rapped her pencil hard on the table.

'I'll take them,' she said. 'I'll take those videos because they're
cheap at the price . . . I find it sad and extraordinary that none
of you recognize their value.'

He heard her footfall, and the knock.

'Josh.'

'Yes.'

'Have you been having a good cry?'

'Actually . . .'

'It wasn't true, Josh, not a word of it, but it was what you wanted to hear. Right? You wanted a bloody good sob story, and I gave it you. I am what I am, Josh, take it or leave it. What you see, Josh, is what you get. You fell for it, Josh, all gift wrapped. So, don't try again to package me, put me in a little slot where you can get all bloody sentimental. There was no baby, Josh and no abortion. Because they killed Hans Becker, and that's going to have to be good enough for you, I'm going after those bastards. And, I'm hungry . . .'

He heard her go back to her room.

He had watched Christina's victory. He had kissed her, had congratulated her, had left Eva to take her home.

Dieter Krause was not more than five minutes late at the meeting in the café on Augusten Strasse. Siehl was there, and Fischer, and Peters. They smoked and drank beer. They had all heard on the radio that a man had fallen to his death in Lichtenhagen. He had tried, himself, a dozen times to ring the mobile telephone of the former *Leutnant*.

He sat with his back to the door, and had not heard the door. He turned because of the smell. It was a moment, in the half-lit corner of the café, before he recognized Hoffmann.

Klaus Hoffmann's hair was messed across his forehead. His eyes were reddened, those of a man who has wept without control. The vomit stains were on his jacket and across the thighs of his trousers.

'You smell like a fucking pigsty,' Peters said.

'Where have you been, Klaus?' he asked. There was, in that second of time, a hesitation in Dieter Krause.

Hoffmann said, a distant voice. 'I walked. You see, friends, I saw him fall. It was not I that pushed him. I spoke to him, a few words, as he went into the block. I knew it was him because his name was called from the apartment, there were people to see him. He broke away from me and took the elevator. I saw him on the roof . . . I have to go home because people have come from the West and attempt to claim our house . . . The man who threw me onto the rocks from the breakwater, he tried to reach Brandt on the roof. They have come from the West and have an order from the court for the restitution of the property that their grandfather abandoned in 1945. When I spoke to him at the door of the block he had such terror. I told him that we watched him. I made the terror real for him. I did not know we could make such fear, still . . . They have come to take my house and I am going, now, home to Berlin . . .'

Dieter Krause said, chill, 'You walk away from us, Klaus, and you are walking to the Moabit gaol.'

Klaus Hoffmann's manic laugh rang through the room. 'Still, the threats, as if you believe that nothing has changed. Too much has changed. I walked and wept and was sick because I realized what had changed . . . Then, I had an order. Then, I could hide myself behind the instruction of my *Hauptman*. Then, I could say I was doing my duty as told me by my superior . . . Now, I have no order and no instruction and no duty, and I am going to my home in Berlin.'

He turned on his heel. He took his smell into the street. He left them, stunned and silent, behind him.

Only when the black shadows came to the streets had Josh left his room to get fast food for the two of them.

He had taken the food and his bedding to her room.

They had not spoken as they had eaten, nor as he had made his bed up.

He lay on his back in the darkness and stared towards the ceiling he could not see.

'For God's sake, Josh . . .' The night sounds of the city murmured through the window, through the curtains. He lay on his back with his head in his locked hands.

'For Christ's sake, Josh – so, the man fell . . .'

He watched the man go over the edge of the roof.

'So, you wouldn't talk to me and walk with me, and I made you by stripping . . .'

He watched her body hit by the wind on the beach.

'So, tomorrow is another day, maybe tomorrow we get lucky.'

Josh said, quietly, 'You have to earn luck.'

'Have we? Have we earned it?'

'Not yet,' Josh said.

13

J osh drove.

They had come over the heavy wood bridge at Wolgast, crossed the wide Peene-Strom. He had driven for an hour and a half east from Rostock. She checked the map. She told him where to turn off the big highway that headed for the Polish border.

Until then the talk had been desultory, as if both were too bruised from the day and the night before. But when the forest closed around the road, high, dense pines, straight, towering trees that hid the light, Mantle told her the history of the place.

'On the night of the seventeenth of August nineteen forty-three, five hundred and ninety-six aircraft were sent here, everything that could fly from the bomber bases in the east of England. The target was Peenemunde where there was the pro-gramme for the development of the V2 rocket. There was a clear moon, a rotten night to come. If the target of Peenemunde had not been so critical, they wouldn't have been asked to fly on a night like that. They were told that if they didn't crack the target then they'd have to come back and do it all again, face the air defence again, and keep coming back till they'd cracked it. There were three target areas at Peenemunde, pushed up close to each other. The strike had to be really exact.'

'How do you know all this?'

'I read about it. The pilots of the bombers, of course, had never heard of Peenemunde. They weren't told what was on the ground, just that it was important. There was a firestorm, the casualties were horrendous. But the bomber crews took bad casualties as well, because of the moon, lost forty-nine aircraft over the target and on the way back.'

'Is that how you spend your evenings, reading about what's gone?'

'I read history because it's important to me. The target area was comprehensively hit. The best of the German rocket scientists were here, and they were creating what was to be the best weapon of the war. Even though the target was pulped, the science survived. The scientists, after nineteen forty-five, were snatched by the Russians and the Americans. Neal Armstrong's walk came from here, and Apollo and Challenger and the shuttle, and Gagarin and the space stations. It's all about Peenemunde.'

Tracy said, distantly, 'Did your wife leave you because you lectured her on what's gone?'

He said, quietly, 'I can't help what drives me. Out of history comes everything. Codes, morals, ethics, they're all learned from history. Why we're here today, why we have to be here, is because of the need to learn the lessons of history.'

'You were better quiet, better when you didn't lecture.'

'Please, Tracy, listen. History breeds principles. The history of Peenemunde is about fantastic scientific achievement, but it's also about slave-labour compounds and about starvation and about men working until they died of exhaustion. That was wrong. The people who were here then, they closed their eyes to what was wrong, believed the wrong – slave labour – did not matter. They wanted to ignore principles, but principles are the core of life.'

'Did she have to listen to your lectures before she left?'

'You come to Peenemunde, Tracy, and you learn what was wrong, you learn about when principles were ignored. To get the rockets to London, to develop the science to put a man on the moon, slave labourers died of starvation and exhaustion. It's the same story. It's why I'm here. It was wrong to shoot Hans Becker. That is a principle and I try to live by it.'

'Me, I only want to see the bastard hammered.'

'You have to know why. You have to hold the principle as faith.'

She closed her eyes and turned away. They went through Trassenheide and Karlshagen, and he saw the cemetery with the exact lines of the stones, and he came to Peenemunde where the bombers had flown. Without principles his life would have been emptied.

'I talk,' Josh said, cold. 'We are quite close. There won't be any more lectures or much more history . . . I talk and you write it down.'

The man walked away, his hands thrust deep in the pockets of his old coat, and was lost among the first tourists of the day.

Heinz Gerber had been sweeping the roadway that led past the scale-sized model of the Vergeltungswaffe 2, past the old Me 163, the MiG-21 and the MiG-23 on their concrete stands. It was his job, each day, to sweep the roadway from the *Feld Salon Wagen* that had been used by the former ministers and generals, and which was now a café, and clear the rubbish and wrappings all the length of the roadway to the harbour where the Type P21 gunboat was moored. He was qualified to sweep the roadway because he had once been in charge of the refuse collection of a small town. The people he worked with did not know of his former life. It was his nightmare, lived alone in the dark hours of the single room he rented in Karlshagen, that it should be known he was a man accused of thieving precious money from his church . . . He could never go back. There had been silence in the street when he had left his home. They had all believed it, that he had stolen from the church box, because it was what they had been told.

When he had first come to Peenemunde it had been to clean and scrub the sleeping quarters of the conscript soldiers of the military base. When they had left, he had been given the work of sweeping and brushing the roadway of the new museum.

He had finished the work, brushed the small heap of paper, dirt and wrappings on to his shovel. He had tipped the heap into his wheelbarrow. The roadway behind him was cleaned. He had left the wheelbarrow there, near to the model of the Vergeltungs-waffe 2, with the brush and shovel laid neatly on it. He loved his work. He had gone to the store shed, near to the models of the SA2B and SA5 ground-to-air missiles, and lifted a coil of rope down from a nail. He loved to work with his brush and shovel and wheelbarrow, and he did not care whether the heat stifled him or whether it rained or whether the snow came.

He walked out, past the big Soviet troop-carrying helicopter, towards the pine forest and the path he took each day to and from his single room in Karlshagen. He loved the daylight: the nightmare only came with the darkness. He carried the rope into the forest, where the light was shut out by the high canopy.

Josef Siehl watched them pay the woman at the kiosk and take the tickets. He recognized her because he had seen her sit beside the lighthouse on the breakwater and throw flowers into the sea. He watched from his car. He recognized the man who had held the *Leutnant* and threatened to kill him, and he had believed the man. He watched them speak to the woman in the kiosk, who shrugged and pointed towards the roadway and the aircraft and the models of the rockets.

The brevity of her note was typical of Olive Harris.

An hour before the meeting she had circulated it to the personal assistant of the deputy director general, with copies to the assistant deputy director and to Fleming of German Desk. She had sat at her desk late into the previous evening, and she had come again early to Vauxhall Bridge Cross to check the note and make some, few, slight revisions to the text. Olive Harris succeeded, in a man's world, by the clarity of her thought and by the instant dismissal of what she regarded as unnecessary.

She explained the concept of her plan.

'The so-called seekers after truth – the young woman, Barnes, and the man who has tagged on to her, Mantle – they are unimportant. She is directed by sentimentality, he is governed by naïve notions of retribution. They are a minor sideshow and should be ignored.'

The deputy director had come down from his quarters high in the building to the office suite of the assistant deputy director. He listened without comment, his angled chin supported by his fists, his elbows on the table. It would be his decision.

'Krause is irrelevant. He is a small-time bit player. Whether he committed murder in cold blood is of no concern to us.'

The coffee provided by the assistant deputy director remained untouched, the biscuits uneaten. He would never interrupt Olive Harris and would seldom contradict her.

'The carping between the German agencies, BfV and BND, and ourselves on the issue of influence in Washington is frankly demeaning. It may be sustainable by dwarf-sized minds. If we seek a position of supremacy then we should justify that position by achievement, not by whining.'

Fleming sat beside her. He had sniffed when she had sat down and he reckoned that she wore no scent.

'But Perkins, plodding in Rostock, has provided us with the ammunition for sniping at a target of consequence. The situation – we have the growing restlessness of the Russian military, we have a defence minister being kicked towards action, we have a minister gaining increasing popularity from the officer corps of the military, we have the ever present frustration of the military for the current civilian leadership. That is the situation. Behind the minister, with obvious and dominant influence over him, is Colonel Pyotr Rykov. He is a target of consequence. Do they want – in Downing Street, in the White House, the Elysée, in the Quirinale – a military government in Russia? Do they hell. They prefer civilian corruption, political inefficiency, the chaos we have at present. I want those video-tapes for myself. I have explained how they should be used, because they provide us with the opportunity to target Colonel Pyotr Rykov.'

She looked each of them, in turn, in the eye. Fleming looked away. The assistant deputy director dropped his head. It would be the deputy director's decision.

'Thank you, Olive. It can be assumed that you're known in Moscow?'

She said, scornful, 'Of course I'm known.'

'It can be assumed that you would be recognized?'

She said, proud, 'Of course I would be recognized.'

Then, on a misty dank morning, in the cream and green building that dominated the southern bank of the Thames river, they diverted attention from the former Hauptman Dieter Krause to Colonel Pyotr Rykov. It was done with effortless ease.

The meeting broke.

Fleming walked back to his office. He felt crushed and knew it was because he had not spoken out.

The woman in the kiosk had said that they would find Heinz Gerber sweeping the roadway. There was no-one sweeping the roadway. They had waited by the abandoned wheelbarrow.

The man who painted the aircraft had said that Heinz Gerber might have gone for his *Pinkelpause*, and explained how long in each hour it was permitted to go to the lavatory. They had stood outside the toilet block at the front of the power station.

'Where the bloody hell is he?'

'I don't know – how would I know?'

'If you hadn't spent so bloody long jerking off with all that crap about principles, boring the arse off me—'

'I want to find him, Tracy, as much as you want to find him – maybe more. And your foul little mouth won't help me to find him.'

She sagged. 'Where is he, Josh, please?'

'We just have to look again.'

Albert Perkins walked from the bank near his hotel back into the old walled city. The street, leading up from the mighty shape of the Marienkirche, was filled with old men and old women. Little slipped by the eyes of the intelligence officer from Vauxhall Bridge Cross. He thought that the faces of the older men and women showed the despair that came from a lifetime of

264

sustained defeat. The oldest men would have gone from these streets to the battlefields of Stalingrad and Kürsk and north Africa and France, and defeat. The oldest women would have seen the Red Army come, and the Stasi and the *apparatchiks* of the Party, and would have hugged their thoughts to their chests, and known the fear that was defeat.

The shop was empty, again. He walked inside.

He was led to the back. The former *Oberstleutnant* unlocked the heavy door and led him down the steps into the museum cellar.

'You have the money?'

'You wish to check?'

Each of the video-cassettes was inserted into the player and the first thirty seconds of each was shown on the screen . . . More than a flight of fancy for Albert Perkins. God's truth, they had kept him awake and aroused and tossing. They were wrapped in brown paper and put in a plastic supermarket bag. He handed over the envelope and watched the man count the money, hundred-DM notes, interminably slowly, with concentration. Perkins's eyes meandered. It was the weathered log that intrigued him most, with the peeled bark. If it had been by his feet, in Bushy Park close to his home, if the grass had grown around it, he did not believe he would have noticed it.

There was a chuckle behind him. 'It is good, yes? I think you copied it, I think you used a copy in Ireland. I think we were the first. I think we were the best, yes?'

Perkins smiled, so friendly. 'You were the best, yes, which is why you now sell Japanese cameras that cannot be paid for.'

The former *Oberstleutnant* grinned cheerfully. 'I do not take offence. The world changes, we adapt or we die. I do not complain. You should know I have a great pride in the quality of material on those three tapes. I went, a year before the end, to Leipzig to help with their surveillance techniques. It was two days before the Christmas of nineteen eighty-eight. There was a party that night and I showed my material. I received a standing ovation, I was applauded for its quality. Why do you wish to hurt them?'

'Hurt who?'

'When you buy a ten-year-old film of Frau Krause fucking with a Russian officer, then you go into the gutter to hurt either Frau Krause or the Russian officer. What have they done to you that they deserve to be hurt?'

Perkins turned away. He climbed the steps out of the cellar, he crossed the shop, he did not wish the man a good day. He walked out onto the street.

A week before, seven clear days, if he had been told that he could go to Peenemunde, Josh Mantle would have hugged the man who gave him the invitation. It should have been the place where the bare pages of books took life. He would have yearned, seven clear days before, to walk in that place of history.

It was the fourth time that they had tracked the length and breadth of the museum area.

He no longer cared for the history.

He had been through the smaller museum that housed the wartime exhibits – and his eyes had not caught the photographs of the V2 development, or the encased slave-labourer's uniform that dressed a dummy, or the little personal possessions of the test pilots who had flown the Me 163 jet prototypes, or the artist's impression of the Lancaster bombers over Peenemunde.

The wheelbarrow was still in the roadway, filled, with the brush and shovel placed carefully on the rubbish.

He had scrutinized the tourists on the benches and at the picnic tables beside the aircraft on their stands. He had gone into the graveyard area of the helicopters that needed renovation before they could be displayed. He had walked among the missiles. He had been through the power station building that proclaimed the site as the 'Gateway to Outer Space' where the displays boasted 'Peenemunde to Canaveral'.

A man with a wet cloth cleaned pictures on the stairs. He had wiped the portrait photograph of Walter Dornberger, then soaked his rag, squeezed the moisture from it and started on the portrait of Wernher von Braun. Josh hadn't seen him before.

Did the man know where Heinz Gerber could be found? He would be sweeping the roadway. No, not in the roadway, Josh told him, and not in the lavatory, not anywhere.

The face of the slow, dull man shook, as if he were puzzled that he had forgotten. Methodically he rubbed at the glass over the portrait of Wernher von Braun. 'I remember . . . He was the start. Doktor von Braun was the beginning of everything the Americans have done. All of their rockets start with what Doktor von Braun created here . . . I remember. He was going to the path. I think he was going home. I remember that I wondered why he was going home. He goes home on the path through the forest.'

'I am so sorry to trouble you. You are very gracious, Doktor . . . A man yesterday fell to his death from the roof of a block in Lichtenhagen – one of those awful places built by the old regime, a desert of concrete. I would not have thought the matter involved the BfV, except that two foreigners had visited the apartment in which the fatality lived, British foreigners. That is peculiar because Lichtenhagen is an extraordinary place for foreigners to visit. He was a retired schoolteacher from Rerik, which is west along the coast, but was now living in Lichtenhagen.'

He was young for the job. All through the morning he had hesitated from making the call. If he had stayed in Dortmund, he would have been, with his experience and seniority, the third man in the chain of command. He had gone east, joined the migration flood of *Wessis*, gone on the fast run of promotion and extra salary, taken the position of police chief for the city of Rostock. All morning the report had been on his desk and he had hesitated before ringing a senior official of the BfV in Cologne. With greater age and greater experience he would either have made the call two hours before or dumped the report in his Out tray. His deputies were all *Ossis*, men of greater age and greater experience, and all had been passed over for the job of police chief for the city. He rarely asked them for advice: to have done so would have seemed to confirm their prejudice against him.

'There is a problem with descriptions. The tenants of the apartment are elderly, one handicapped, one sighted, they were the uncle and aunt of the fatality. Neither can offer descriptions beyond that one was a man and one a woman. No, no, there is no evidence of homicide. There is no evidence of a crime . . . I forget it? I confirm your suggestion and apologize, Doktor, for wasting your time.'

The forest closed around them. They walked on the pine-needle path in the gloom. Only the cold drifted down from the canopy. Among the pencil-straight trees were the stunted, angled shapes of broken concrete. He thought it was the true museum, not the museum in the sunlight fashioned for the tourists. The true museum was the cracked and disintegrated shapes of concrete that had been the buildings of the experimental-rocket works, where the scientists had been and the Polish labourers, where the bombs of concentrated explosive had fallen. The concrete shapes were covered with lichen. The needles had gathered on them and softened the angles of their destruction. The craters had survived half a century of the dark gloom below the forest canopy. Impossible for Josh, who had read the books, not to imagine the carnage hell of those who had run in their terror where he now walked, when the forest had burned and the buildings had come down as the bombs had fallen. She came easily behind him, light feet on the cushion of needles. They walked past the great façade of a building that had been taken by the pines. Only the façade survived, still fire-blackened. The pines were the roof and the interior of the building. It was the true history.

He saw the hanging body.

Josh stopped. He stared at it. She cannoned into his back. Tracy had not seen the body. He held her close against him.

There was no wind in the forest, under the canopy. The rope was over a branch and knotted. The hanging body rotated so slowly. He saw the back of the man and the collapsed shoulders, his side and the outstretched arms, the stain at his groin. He closed his eyes. The man had climbed the tree, struggled to gain the necessary height, clawed his way up the rough, scaled bark of the tree. He had climbed to the first branch that he would have judged could take the weight of the rope under strain, tied the rope to the branch and slipped the noose over his head. He thought of the man for whom the terror of living was greater than the fear of death.

He opened his eyes. He held her as she shook in his arms. He kept her head, her neck, against his chest.

The man's shoes were on the path, had been kicked off. He saw the worn, holed socks of the man. He judged the terror that had been brought to the last moments of the life of Heinz Gerber . . .

'Good to see you, young man, and how is Berlin?'

'Cold, Mr Perkins, very cold. I'm sorry, I'm very pushed for time on the schedule they've set me. Have you the package?'

It gave Albert Perkins perverse pleasure to hand to Rogers, when the kindergarten kid was fresh from the Portsmouth recruit courses, a frayed supermarket bag containing a package loosely wrapped in brown paper. They were in the car park, broad daylight, in front of the hotel.

'That's the package. Going this evening, is it?' He grinned. 'If they get their eyes on that lot tonight, in London, when they get home their women can expect a pretty fearful time.'

He saw the confusion on the young man's face. 'London?'

'London, yes, that's where it's going.'

He saw the flush on the young man's face. 'Weren't you told, Mr Perkins, what was happening?'

'Where's it going, if not to London?'

He saw the young man flinch, blink, then summon the courage. 'If you'd needed to know, Mr Perkins, I'm sure they'd have told you. I'd better get on, sorry.'

Young Rogers, kindergarten kid, ran to his car and he clutched the supermarket bag to his chest. Perkins's breath spurted, steamed in his face.

The car of the kindergarten kid accelerated away, out of the car park.

Dieter Krause, in his car in the parking area outside the tennis hall, heard the news bulletin.

The radio said that, in Gustrow, a hostel for eastern foreigners had been firebombed; in Wismar, the chemical factory was to close with the loss of 371 jobs; in Schwerin, the tourist authority for Mecklenburg-Vorpommern reported that advance bookings for the summer were down on the previous year . . .

The police chief, driving in his chauffeured car to his new home in the *Altstadt*, heard the news bulletin. In Rostock, the transfer of the reserve-team striker to Werder Bremen was confirmed with a fee of one million DMs; in Peenemunde, a former *Rathaus* official from Rerik had been found hanged in the forest near to the space-exploration museum . . .

Albert Perkins, in his hotel room, in shock, lying dressed on his bed, heard the news bulletin.

'Where is Siehl?'

Fischer said, 'He waited for you. He waited a long time for you.'

Peters said, 'I told him not to bother to wait longer. I told him that watching your bitch daughter play tennis was more important to you.'

The match had gone on. Christina had lost the first set before he had reached the stand and sat beside his wife. Christina, rampant, hugging him, at the end had said that she would not have won if he had not been there to watch her and she had babbled about the racquets that she should be brought from Washington. When Christina had gone to shower and change, Eva had asked him . . . No, the problem was not solved. No, the problem continued. She had stared ahead of her in the emptying stand and bitten at her lips. Her fingers had worried on the new bracelet of gold chain on her wrist.

Peters said, 'The bastard quit on us.'

* * *

270

It was the first time in the three years that his career had so far run that young Henry Rogers had felt true involvement in a mission of importance. Everything before had been analysis and the interminable work at the computer screen. His pride mingled with apprehension. He had followed, most exactly, the detailed instructions he had received from Mrs Olive Harris in London.

He stood on the north side of the Unter den Linden.

The man, in front of him, crossed the wide street, went to the south side, walked towards the floodlit grey granite façade of the Russian embassy. Mrs Harris would have known of the man, Rogers assumed, from Mr Perkins's daily situation reports. He had been to the apartment near to the Spittelmarkt and paid the wizened little man who stank of cats the sum of one thousand American dollars. He had given him, as the instructions of Mrs Harris had demanded, an airline ticket to Zurich, valid for the last flight of the evening with open-dated return, and had driven him to the Unter den Linden. He had written a Russian name, from Mrs Harris's instructions, on the brown paper of the package, and handed it to him.

In the bright flush of the embassy's security lights, he watched the man ring the bell at the heavy door.

He fished in his pocket for his car keys. He watched the man cross the Unter den Linden, scurrying to avoid the cars, not waiting for the pedestrian lights. It would be only a twenty-minute drive to the Tempelhof airport. He felt pride at his achievement in carrying out Mrs Olive Harris's meticulous instructions, and he lost the apprehension of failure. He did not know his part in the destruction of a target of consequence.

Josh would have said, normal times, that he could accept silence.

He lay on the mattress and the blankets were tight around him. He lay on his side and faced the wall. He could smell the damp of the wretched little room they shared. The party of seamen from Sweden, Denmark, Norway, wherever, must have sailed that day. Down below, in the reception of the *pension*, his key and her key would be the only ones missing from the hooks. He could hear her breathing behind him, and he did not know whether she slept or whether she lay awake, and he did not know whether images of the body, the shoes, the terror of the man obsessed her as they knifed him.

He had held her close, tight, against him all the way back down the path through the forest. The moment that they had broken clear from the dull light and the sun had fallen on them, she had shouldered herself free of his arms, pulled away from him.

In the faint night light of the room he saw her hand hanging careless at the side of her bed, near to his face.

'Are you awake, Tracy?'

'Trying to sleep.'

'You know that if we fight, Tracy, we fail.'

'I didn't ask you to be here . . . and I didn't ask for lectures.'

'Do you know how much you hurt, Tracy? Does it bother you?'

She murmured, savage, 'God, are you going to moan again, again? Is that why your wife left you?'

Josh pushed himself up. He sat against the wall. He heaved the blankets around him.

'We'll start there. That's as good a place as anywhere. Don't interrupt me. Don't open your horrid little mouth . . . I was out of the Army. I was a social worker. I worked with kids for three years. Can I say it, so it's on the record? They were thieves and vandals and joyriders and none of them had the quality of viciousness that you parade, that you find so easy to justify.'

He heard her breathing sweet and regular. He saw the outline of her body and her hand careless beside his face.

'There was a boy, Darren. He was on the pills. He thieved to get the money for the pills. I quite liked the kid, I thought I could break him off them. He thieved from this house, big place, smart road in the Chalfonts, he was all dosed up when he went in and he didn't do the necessary with the alarm. The police picked him up outside the house. He was in the cells when I saw him and he was going back, as night follows day, to Feltham Young

Offenders', and he was sitting on the bunk bed and the tears were streaming down his face. I thought he was worth the effort, and the custody sergeant told me I was an idiot. I went to the house he'd broken into. She was Libby Frobisher, stinking rich, divorced, and I told her about Darren and what the custody sergeant had said and that the kid was in the cells and weeping his heart out. She withdrew the charges. The kid, Darren, walked free. I drove him round to see the woman and made him stand in front of her and apologize and mean it.'

He did not know whether she slept or whether she listened.

'She rang me a month later, she wanted to know what had happened to the kid. She said I should come round, have a drink, tell her. Six weeks later we were married. I was fifty-one years old and she was the first woman I had loved. There was only her accountant and her solicitor at the wedding and they thought I was into her life for the easy ride. I made her – insisted on it – write a will where nothing was left to me. Until I met her, I was not a man who cried or laughed or knew happiness or understood pain. I learned them all from her. For a year I knew happiness, and then she found the lump.'

Josh reached out and took her hand.

'For half a year I cried and understood pain. She went through the treatment. She died.'

He brushed his lips against her hand and opened his fingers and allowed her hand to drop back, careless, beside the bed.

'I tell her about you each day. I went to see her the day I left to come to find you. I told her then that you put your hand into a snake's hole, that you weren't beautiful, weren't even very pretty. I told her about the killing of Hans Becker, your boy, and that the only thing we had in common was that we had both had the person we loved taken from us . . . I tell her, each day, how we're doing. I tell her that we're frightened, that we don't know where it's leading us.'

He thought she slept. He saw the calm stillness of the profile of her face.

'I tell her that, thank God, tomorrow is always another day.'

14

Josh had tried to think, in his methodical way, while they had dressed in the gloom of the room at the *pension*, still dark outside the window, and then she had sung the song. Whether she sang it, whether she whistled it, whether she murmured it, the one bloody song with the words or the one bloody tune, it scraped through his mind and deflected him, breaking his train of thought. They had left Rostock early, before the traffic was on the main streets. The irritation grew in him because he had not made a plan in his mind. It was another day, the day for Artur Schwarz. Time was so precious, and was running, sand grains from the upper bowl slipping steadily into the lower . . . but the bloody song, the tune, hacked at his ability to use the time. His irritation surged.

'Can you leave it?'

'Leave what?'

He said, ponderous, 'Can you leave that noise?'

'What noise?'

'Can you, please, stop whistling, singing, whatever, that puerile dirge?'

'What's the harm of it to you?'

'Just that I can't think.'

She lifted her eyebrows and made a face at him that was grotesque. She closed her eyes and pursed her lips shut as if to show him how idiotic she thought his irritation. The song was her anthem. She would have lain in her bed at Brigade in Berlin and heard it played on the radio and known that her boy, beyond the Wall, heard it too.

He had the wipers on now. The light was a grey smear ahead, to the west. The sleet storm burst over the car, was running free over the flat expanse of the fields either side of the road. They had driven through the last village before they came to Starkow. He had not used the main road from Ribnitz-Damgarten to Stralsund, the obvious way to Starkow. He tried to think. He could see into the low cloud of the storm. He could see the dulled shapes, far away, of rectangles of planted forestry, and at the fringes of the trees were timber-built platforms for the marksmen who shot deer in summer. Cranes were feeding in the yellow weed grass close to the road, tall, elegant birds who seemed not to notice the blow of the sleet storm against them. He wanted cover from which to watch the farm, high ground or hedgerows or a plantation of forestry . . .

There was only one farm at Starkow. The village was a main street of old houses, a post office, a shop with a new front and a church. From the main street he could see the farm. Up a long lane, between open fields, was the huddle of buildings. There was a rectangular block of trees away to the left, and a marksman's tower, but nowhere to leave the car where it would be hidden. There was no way to the forestry and the marksman's tower but across the open yellow weed grass of the field. He parked the car at the end of the village main street, and saw a curtain flicker. He stood beside the car and shivered. The sleet blew into his face and settled on her hair. He looked at his feet.

'I'm sorry.'

'Why are you sorry?'

'Because I didn't think it through. Because we don't have the right footgear.'

'Is that why you're so miserable?'

He stamped away ahead of her. There was a hawk in front of him, blown by the storm, careering in flight, not able to hover and hunt. The mud was a slippery carpet to the frozen ground. He plodded forward. It caught at his shoes, clung to them, weighted them. Once, he fell and slithered to the ground and she stood over him and grinned. He hoped, the night before, that she had slept and had not known that he had held her hand

and kissed it. He went across the open field towards the block of forestry. He was near it, close to the marksman's tower, when he saw the car leave the farm, bump away on the potholed track from the buildings of grey-red brick and grey-brown wood. He was too far from the track to see who was driving behind the misted windows. The wind swayed the high trees above.

'How long are we staying here?'

'Long enough to see who comes to and who goes from the farm.'

'What about the taxi?'

'Was it a taxi?'

'Didn't you see that? Of course it was a taxi. It had the sign on it for a taxi.'

He felt the cold. He huddled behind the trees. He stared at the farm buildings away across the open fields and tried to scrape the mud off his shoes.

He wondered if they had come to the farm too late. Nothing moved. There were dull lights in the windows of the farmhouse and in one of the barn buildings but he did not see the signs of man, woman or child.

'We wait and we watch,' he said. 'We wait and watch until I am satisfied.'

He had wept the night that the mob had entered the building on August-Bebel Strasse. Ulf Fischer, the former *Feldwebel* who was now a taxi driver and the maker of orations at the funerals of old people, had stood on the far side of the street, on the fringe of the mob, and he had watched the clamouring, jeering crowd beat on the doors of the building and hammer at the shuttered windows. It was said, among the lowly ranks of the Stasi, that the *Generalleutnant* had forbidden the guards to use their weapons, that the senior officers had argued bitterly on whether they should open fire on the mob. The 'realists' had wanted to shoot and the 'idealists' had wished to capitulate. He had not, that night, seen Hauptman Krause. He had thought it the worst hour of his life.

276

He sat in his taxi outside the one small bar in the village of Starkow. Before he went back to the rank for taxis on Lange Strasse, he would need to hose off the farm mud from the wheels and bodywork of his Mercedes taxi. He had not felt guilt when he had pushed his boot down on the throat of the young man so that the *Hauptman* could have the easier shot at his head. He was with, then, the power of the Staatssicherheitsdienst. The power had protected him from guilt. Sitting in his taxi, going to the farm at Starkow, he had decided, with personal anguish, that he no longer believed in the protection. He would make one last action, and he had agonized on it in his taxi, in defence of the power. He could see, from where he was parked outside the bar, the hire car in which they had come. His last act, before he went back to Rostock and found a car wash at a garage and took his place on the taxi rank, would be to telephone the *Hauptman* and give him the make, colour and registration of the hire car. He had no more fear of the cells of the Moabit gaol. He held the telephone in his hand and the tears coursed down his cheeks, as they had done on August-Bebel Strasse when the mob had come in. Afterwards, he would go to the car wash and clean his taxi and take his place on the rank, and in the evening he would go home, as Leutnant Hoffmann had gone home and as Unter-leutnant Siehl had gone home.

She said, 'Do you chase the tail of the beast or do you chase its head?'

Dieter Krause sat in his chair in the living room of the new house.

She said, 'You can forever cut the tail of the beast but you do not kill the beast until you cut the head.'

Dieter Krause sat in his chair and held the telephone. It had been ringing when Eva had come back to the house. She had been in the hallway when he had answered it. She stood in front of him, above him. The shopping bags were by her feet.

She said, 'You have to cut the head of the beast or the beast is with us always, will take everything and break us.'

Dieter Krause looked up into her face. There was a hardness that he had not known before, a pitiless contempt that he had not seen before.

She said, 'If you do not cut the head from the beast then it will be behind you for ever, and for ever you will look over your shoulder for the beast.'

Dieter Krause put the telephone into his inside pocket. The tail of the beast was the witnesses. The head of the beast was the man who had come from England and the young woman with the copper-gold hair who had kicked and scratched and bitten him. He tapped, a reflex movement, at his waist, and he felt the shape of the pistol lodged there by his belt. He picked up the car keys from the table beside the door.

She said, 'You have to be there tonight, when she plays . . . First you must cut the head.'

The sleet storm swirled around the farm. He had seen no movement, but there were short times when the storm was so intense that the blizzard took from him the view of the farm buildings. He had heard, faint, a man's shouting but he had not seen the man. He had heard the noise, distant, of a tractor engine starting up but he had not seen the tractor.

The sun came out abruptly, great pillars of light that fell on the fields and onto the buildings, as if a curtain was drawn back. The cold was gone, and the driving sweep of the sleet, but still Josh held his arms across his chest for warmth. Away to the right, from the forest block, a young deer with stubbed antlers came cautiously from the cover and tried to find food in the yellow weed grass. The light played on its back.

He took Tracy's arm, squeezed it hard. He started to walk across the field towards the farm buildings, lit by the sun.

The mud clogged on their shoes and smeared their trousers. They walked, slow going, towards the buildings.

He could smell the farm, old hay and new manure, and hear the faint sound of a radio playing in the farmhouse and the bellowing of cattle as if they demanded attention. The farmhouse was at the side of a courtyard of buildings. It was a building, centuries old, that decayed. He thought the great armies passing this way would have seen that same farmhouse of brick and timber beams – the guards of Napoleon and the grenadiers of von Hindenburg and the panzer men of Mannstein and the artillery men of Zhukov. The radio played light music behind the heavy door. Water dripped on the step from broken guttering above. He rapped the knocker. He expected to hear a footstep, a grumbling complaint from a man or a woman that they were coming, but heard only the radio. They walked together, close to each other, around to the back of the farmhouse, past abandoned kids' toys and a tricycle, past a small garden where winter cabbages grew in neat lines. The door at the back of the farmhouse was wide open.

He knocked with his fist on the opened door. There was food on the wide wood table and two mugs of steaming coffee. The pages of a newspaper were scattered on the table, as if discarded in haste. A cat slept in a chair and ignored his knocking. He called out, and the cat opened its eyes, scowled and closed them again. He called again, and only the bleat of the radio's advertisements answered him.

In the courtyard of farm buildings, the outer door of the cattle shed was open. The animals shouted at them for their attention.

There was a light trailer of manure with a fork set in it, as if work had been interrupted. The sunlight came down into the courtyard and caught the old gold of the hay bales that had been moved from the open barn and left. A horse was wandering free in the courtyard with a halter on its head and a trailing rein.

She took his arm and pointed.

Josh followed the line she made with her arm.

A mud track led from the courtyard out over the yellow weed grass of the fields. He saw why she pointed.

They ran, slipping and slithering, along the track, between the deep ruts that the tractors had made.

279

The wind blew against them and the low sun was in their eyes.

The small, slow-moving procession edged towards them. A tractor pulled a trailer at the head coming steadily. He saw two men walking beside it, heads down. He saw four women, in pairs, walking alongside the trailer and none had coats against the wind and the cold. There was a tractor at the end of the procession and it dragged a muck-spreader through the ruts of the track.

He stepped into the mud of the field so that he should not impede the path of the procession. He slipped his hand into the bend of Tracy's arm; she jerked it away from him.

The tractor at the head of the procession came past them. Mud clods were scattered from the big tyres and thrown against their bodies. He saw the lined, weathered faces of the man who drove the tractor and the men who walked beside the cab, who had left their cattle in the courtyard barns and left the horse free. He saw the women who had come from the warmth of the kitchen.

He looked for the body on the trailer.

He looked for Artur Schwarz.

He saw on the trailer a small load of winter turnips.

He caught the sleeve of the coat of one of the men, and asked where was Artur Schwarz, where could he be found. He was told . . . Josh closed his eyes, so old and so bloody tired. He heard the grating voice of one of the women talking to Tracy, but could not distinguish the words against the roar of the tractor engines.

He let the procession move away from him, watched them go all the way to the old courtyard.

He stumbled across the open emptiness of the field and she was behind him. Her shadow danced ahead.

Tracy shouted, 'Their shit-spreader's broke. That's what they all came out for. Dropped everything because the shit-spreader's buggered. A bust shit-spreader is their definition of disaster. Did they tell you where we'd find Artur Schwarz?'

* * *

280

Albert Perkins so rarely lost his temper.

'Is that what the bloody woman called us, me and them? Are you telling me, Mr Fleming, that the bloody woman said I, they, were a minor sideshow?'

He sat on the unmade bed. The wires for the equipment that made the call secure were tangled in his arms.

'And Krause is an irrelevance? And our operation is demeaning? How, in God's name, did you let her get away with that fucking talk? Don't you understand, Mr Fleming, what is being played out here? Four eye-witnesses were evicted from Rerik in nineteen eighty-eight. I don't know their names. What I do know, in the last several days two men, formerly from Rerik, have died. That's what is being played out here, bloody cruel warfare – and that is a sideshow, a minor sideshow? I am listening to hourly news bulletins for more deaths, damn it. There are two left, I don't know who they are or where they are. What should I do, Mr Fleming? Should I place an advertisement in the local newspaper calling on these unnamed, unlocated individuals to dig a bloody hole in the ground and sit in it, because it's not worth them getting themselves killed for a minor sideshow? How's that, Mr Fleming?'

He heard the chambermaid's trolley in the corridor and the knock at the door. He held his hand over the telephone and shouted at her that she should come back later. His bitter temper brought the sweat to his forehead.

'No, I am not coming home, Mr Fleming. In case you had forgotten, Mr Fleming, the matter of agreed policy is as important now as it was before Mrs bloody Olive bloody Harris inserted her unwanted nose into my mission. And I hope, Mr Fleming, that you will make my views known to the ADD with clarity, and tell him there is blood spilt here and that there will be more spilt before it's over. Good day, Mr Fleming.'

Albert Perkins so rarely lost his temper. He had never before spoken with such vehemence to a man of seniority. If Corporal Barnes and Mantle did not succeed, he would be crucified for what he had said to his senior, and out on his arse from the front

doors of Vauxhall Bridge Cross. He sat alone on his bed and the
radio played jazz music. He sat quietly.

The wooden cross was at the back of the churchyard, where the
grass was longest and the weeds thickest.

The legend had been written in black paint, flaked, across the
arm of the cross: Artur Schwarz 1937–1995. It was the only
grave in the cemetery over which there was no headstone. Josh
thought the man had lived his last years alone and died alone
and now rested alone. He stood by the cross.

'Have you seen enough?' she called.

'Yes.'

'It's like he cheated us.'

'Yes.'

The car was where he had been told it would be.

He had driven at the speed of a lunatic, taking the fast road
out of Rostock, through Ribnitz-Damgarten, and the needle
had showed that his speed had reached 180 kilometres per hour.
He had gone on the grass to pass a lorry and had swerved savagely to avoid an oncoming van. He had gone on the paving to
pass a pick-up pulling a trailerload of pigs.

They were walking to the car. He saw her. She was with an
older man. He saw the mud that was smeared and spattered
over her legs and across the front of her coat. He had no plan.
The Makarov pistol was out of his belt under his thighs on the
seat. Dieter Krause had reached the rank of *Hauptman*, and if
the regime had survived, in another year, he would have
expected promotion to the rank of major, it would have been
expected of him that he could act without a plan.

He drove past them, braking.

The man led. He was a big man, a man older than himself,
with a short, old-fashioned, military haircut, and the hair was
dark but peppered with grey. The man's head was down, as if
despairing, and his clothes, too, were mud-smeared and spattered. He drove on up the main street of Swarkow, then turned

282

in front of the village's small school. He had a clear view of them. She seemed to him more substantial than he remembered her, but that would be because she wore the heavy coat.

She could destroy, with the man beside her, everything he had built. She could put him into the cells of the Moabit gaol. She could humiliate him. She could turn his Christina from him. She was, with the man, the head of the beast. He watched. There was only one way out of the village of Swarkow, and he could recall the detail of the road.

They were cleaning their shoes against the wheels of the car and the man tried to scrape the mud from his trousers. He reached into his pocket. Dieter Krause saw him toss the car keys to the young woman.

She sang as she drove. Josh sat and sulked.

The road was straight, fast, and she drove easily. He glanced at the vanity mirror in the sun visor and saw the big BMW closing on them.

Beside the road, straight ahead, against the fields of yellow weed grass, was the narrow ribbon of the river. Between the river and the road was the line of poplar trees. He touched her arm, gestured with his hand that she should slow, pointed to her mirror. She should slow to let the big BMW pass them. They had reached the line of the poplar trees. Beyond the trees were the steep, snow-flecked banks of the river of dark, listless, flowing water. She was slowing. He checked the mirror again. It was filled with the black shape of the BMW's bonnet.

Suddenly, the scream of the impact behind them. He was jolted forward. The belt held him, but his head whipped towards the dash. He had his arms out in front of him, trying to cushion the blow. The small hire car was tossed ahead. Josh gasped. In the mirror, the BMW had slowed, slid back, now came again. There was nothing he could tell her. First rule of military command: a subordinate is given authority, a subordinate cannot be second-guessed, a subordinate must be left to sort the shit. She clung to the wheel. He saw the whiteness of her fists as she hung on to it and fought to keep them on the road.

He could not help her.

The BMW, again, filled the mirror. He braced. She was braking. The trunks of the high poplar trees were beside his window, then the darkness of the water, then the steepness of the banks . . . Christ, this was where it ended. She stamped on the accelerator a moment before the second collision, deflected the blow. He thought she'd lost control. The road was wet-greased. The trunks of the poplars were white where the sleet was frozen to them. He thought it was where it ended, going off a treacherous road and into the trunk of a poplar and into the dark water of a river.

She held the road.

The BMW came again for them.

It was alongside them, edging past. There was the tear of the metal of the BMW against the door of their car. He saw the face of Dieter Krause. There was no anger on it, no hatred, but the calmness of a man who follows an instruction. The weight of the BMW, shrieking against them, forced them towards the side of the road, towards the trunks of the poplars and the steepness of the river's banks. She fought to hold the wheel steady. It was unequal. The weight and power of the BMW were driving them towards the line of trees, towards the river. He thought it was all for goddamn nothing, another road-accident statistic . . . She seemed to stand in her seat as she drove down the brake pedal.

The BMW was past them.

'Get your coat off.'

She drove behind him. Krause braked. She braked.

'Get your bloody coat off.'

He struggled out of it. It was habit, but he stripped the contents from the pockets. She snatched it from him and wound down, furiously, her window.

He did not understand her. She went after the BMW.

She squeezed level with the big car, half on the road and half on the verge. The door beside Josh scraped a tree. The cars were locked together. She threw his coat from the window. The coat, ripped open by the wind, spread right across the windscreen of the BMW. He heard the squeal of the brakes. He could not see the face of Dieter Krause. He could imagine the panic of the darkness and the obliterated vision.

They were past. They were clear.

He turned.

He saw the BMW, going slowly, lurching under the power of the brakes, slide between the trunks of the poplar trees and topple without dignity down the steep bank of the river.

She drove on.

He was incoherent. 'That was fantastic . . . fantastic and incredible . . . Christ, I thought . . . I didn't believe . . . Dead, I thought we were dead . . . for nothing, all for nothing, I thought . . .'

'We are going to Warnemunde, Josh. Not tomorrow, now.'

'Ribnitz-Damgarten, that's first. Go to Ribnitz-Damgarten, then go to Warnemunde. You were incredible.'

'Will you tell your wife?'

He had thought she slept when he held her hand and kissed it, when he had talked of Libby. She laughed and there was the bright light on her face.

She came on the early flight from London. The documentation for her visa, to be inspected by the passport officials at Sheremetyevo-2, described her as a publicity officer for the British Council. Mrs Olive Harris was known in Moscow, where it mattered, in the Lubyanka building, as a senior officer of the Secret Intelligence Service. The British Council cover was merely to see her without hindrance through tedious scrutiny at the passport desk. She was quite fond of the city. In the early 1970s, she had spent four years of her career in Moscow. She gazed from the window of the second secretary (consular)'s car at the first familiar landmark, the tank traps of rusted steel marking the furthest point of the panzer advance on the city, and they eased onto the St Petersburg Highway and went at speed towards the Circular Road. There were good memories for her.

'I expect it's all pretty different, Mrs Harris.'

She detested, when she was quiet, to have the quiet broken.

'All pretty different from your day, Mrs Harris. I'm right, that was a while back?'

She asked the sharp question. 'Is he under surveillance?'

'I checked this morning, as you instructed. There was a car up the road from his apartment. When exactly, Mrs Harris, were you here?'

She said quietly, 'I had an early start this morning. I am quite tired.'

Mrs Olive Harris, intent on the destruction of a target of consequence, laid her head back in the Rover, let the station chief chauffeur her into the city. She was pleased to hear the surveillance was in position because that would give the matter a much greater authenticity than if it had been necessary to take their own photographs. Her plan, as she had conceived it, did not trouble her. This was the city where she had cut her working teeth and learned, as a colleague had so eloquently put it, to be as hard as barbed wire. She was seldom other than at ease with herself.

The first Aeroflot link of the day from Berlin had brought the three video-cassettes, hand-held by courier, to Sheremetyevo-2. The courier inside the customs area had handed the package, with an attached explanatory letter, to an official of the counter-espionage section of the renamed but former KGB. It had been driven into the city and delivered to an office high in the yellow-walled, handsome Lubyanka building.

Three men watched the video-cassettes, settled in their chairs, sipping their coffee. Each, in turn, had read the attached letter from Berlin. The videos concerned Colonel Pyotr Rykov, who served on the minister's staff at Defence, and Frau Eva Krause who was the wife of a former officer in the Staatssicher-heitsdienst now collaborating with the BfV in Cologne. The videos had been delivered to the embassy late the previous evening by a man, identified from the security cameras as a former personal assistant to minister for state security Mielke. The man was not at his home address early that morning and therefore it had proved impossible to learn his motivation for providing the cassettes.

The snowstorm slipped from the screen. Monochrome pictures flickering then steadying ... She stripped. She groped for him as he dropped his trousers ... The room was filled with their raucous, bellowing laughter. All day, and into the evening, long after brandy had replaced the coffee, they would watch the cassettes and know that the career of Colonel Pyotr Rykov was damaged.

He had in front of him a facsimile message, For His Eyes Only, from the police chief of Rostock. The message that had arrived on the desk of the senior official in Cologne, brief, reported the death at Peenemunde of a former official of the *Rathaus* at Rerik, by hanging, and a British man and woman had been asking for him.

The senior official telephoned Raub across the city at his home.

The world of the senior official closed on him. In two days, he checked the wall clock in his room, less a few hours, he would be airborne with his *Direktor*, with colleagues, with Raub and Goldstein, with the man they regarded as a jewel.

The senior official telephoned Goldstein, in Berlin, at his apartment.

He saw the face of Pyotr Rykov enlarged on a screen. He saw an audience of eminent and influential Americans rising to their feet to applaud, and saw the handshakes and the backslapping for his work. He saw opened doors at the Pentagon and at Langley. He saw the livid lines of the scratch scars on the face of Dieter Krause. His world closed on him, in darkness.

They passed the big airbase. There was little to see of the base the Soviets had used, from which they had flown the MiG-29s. Josh had read in the last year an assessment of the MiG-29's performance by the Luftwaffe, who had inherited a former DDR squadron. What had been designated by NATO as 'Fulcrum' was damned as unstable in advanced air combat, with poor navigation and lacking the required look down-shoot down capability. A bit bloody late – nine years late in the making of the assessment. Everything was history. It was history that the British had allocated fifteen billion pounds sterling to the development of the Eurofighter as a counter to 'Fulcrum', and history that the MiG-29s had flown, from Ribnitz-Damgarten, mock attacks against the missile and radar base at Wustrow. And that was the reason Operation Catwalk had been launched, and Traveller had been sent through the Wall with the gear, and the boy had been pushed towards the coastline of the peninsula at Wustrow. History, pure and simple, had killed the boy, and history lingered to the present. He told her where to turn and where to stop.

She braked. She parked. She switched off the engine. She quizzed him with her eyes.

He pointed.

She looked at the door of the police station.

She frowned, not understanding.

'It's because, Tracy, I believe I'm beaten. I'm beaten because I believe I have the responsibility for two men's deaths. Today he escaped us, he was so bloody lucky. Being dead already made it his lucky day. I cannot fight against a criminal conspiracy on this scale. I can't.'

He opened the door of the car, had to force it open because it was buckled from the scraped impact against the trunk of the poplar tree. She folded her arms across her chest, stared straight ahead.

'They won't listen.'

Josh bent at the open door. 'It's their job to listen. Hear me . . . This is a democratic country. It has laws and a constitution. It's not Iraq or some other shit hole. Tracy, I'm sorry but I'm out of my depth. I'm sinking.'

She didn't look at him. 'They won't listen.'

He stood straight. 'They have to.'

He walked towards the door of the old brick police station that served the town of Ribnitz-Damgarten. He turned at the door. He watched her get out of the car, cross the road and go into a pizza bar.

He pushed open the door and went to the reception desk. A policeman folded away his newspaper, pushed aside his coffee mug and smiled a welcome as he had been taught to. The mud weighted Josh's shoes, caked his trousers, spattered his coat, flecked his shirt and was smeared on his face.

'I would like to talk, please, with a detective.'

15

'Good, they brought you coffee. I apologize for the delay. I have tried to make a judgement on the accusation you have made, Herr Mantle. I hope the coffee was satisfactory.'

He had been taken to an interview room. The detective was young, fresh-faced, and dressed neatly but casually. He had sat across the bare table from him and written notes as Josh had blurted an accusation of criminal conspiracy and murder. He had not interrupted, not passed comment, and Josh had stumbled through a brief, chaotic version of the deaths. The detective would have registered the filth on his clothes and the exhaustion on his face. He had then been left in the interview room for five minutes short of an hour, alone in the bare room with the white-washed walls and the wood table and the hard chairs and the concrete floor and the electric fire. He knew that he had wasted their time and his own. He had heard the voice, away behind the closed door, of the detective on the telephone.

Finally the detective eased into the chair opposite him.

'You have mentioned, Herr Mantle, three situations. I have only a short digest of the facts involving the first two of those matters, but the third is more clear.'

The detective spoke slowly and was careful with his pronunciation, as if he believed that he spoke to an idiot who needed patient calming.

'I have spoken with Rostock. You are correct, a man fell to his death, but the man, unfortunately, had a previous history of mental disturbance. I have to tell you, Herr Mantle, there are many sad people in our Eastern German society who have been severely traumatized by the pressures of "reassociation".

They have seen the pillars of their lives removed, cradle to grave dependency on the state, and are unable to adapt. It is unfortunate.'

The detective turned the page of his notebook.

'I have also spoken with Wolgast, where the police deal with matters affecting Peenemunde. Again, you are correct, a man hanged himself. For my generation, Herr Mantle, there are only advantages and opportunities to be taken from "reassociation" and a higher standard of living. Older people, I regret, find the self-reliance of the new society most stressful. That generation has no knowledge of pensions, social-security payments, the new costs of a capitalist society. This individual, we understand, had allowed himself to fall heavily into debt. For that reason he took his life. Many gain from the modern greater Germany, but there are casualties.'

The detective closed his notebook.

'And you have referred to a death two years ago on a farm at Starkow. I have spoken to the relevant local authorities. The deceased, it seems, was an elderly agricultural worker who chose to live in a conversion of a cowshed. He did not know how to look after himself, he had poor habits of personal hygiene. The conditions he chose to exist in were, to be very frank, similar to those of the animals he cared for. He died of pneumonia. There was a full investigation at the time by the health specialists, and it was found that no-one, other than himself, could be blamed for his premature death. I cannot tell you why he made that choice, to live in filth and cold, but I can say that many of the older generation in the East have suffered from mental collapse. It is tragic, but . . .'

Josh stood. He knew that she would laugh at him.

'I have to tell you that there have been three deaths, but that there is absolutely no evidence of murder.'

He turned towards the door. She would laugh in his face.

'You spoke of the Staatssicherheitsdienst. I am afraid that I did not understand you. There is no Stasi now in Germany. The Stasi was dismantled in nineteen ninety, it does not now exist.'

He walked out of the room.

'Please, Herr Mantle, how does a foreigner become interested in these matters?'

He went down the corridor towards the light and the street. By the reception desk, he saw the grin as the policeman looked up from his newspaper. The officer would have heard that a foreigner, dirty as a vagrant, talked of the Stasi and murder. He blinked, the sun shone on the street.

He looked for her.

Dieter Krause rode in the cab of the recovery truck.

He had used his telephone, sitting against the trunk of a poplar tree, and had waited. When the recovery truck had come, he had supervised the hooking of the cable rope to the chassis fender of his BMW, giving orders as he used to give them. The mechanics had said that they thought the car might be serviceable, that they would need to lift it onto the ramp at their garage for checking.

The car had been his pride. The car was, to Dieter Krause, the symbol that he had reached the new stature. The car told him, shouted at him, that he was accepted by the people in Cologne. He could have, perhaps should have, abandoned it. If he had abandoned the new car then he would, also, have abandoned the symbol of the new life. The sides were scraped and dented, the paint had been torn away. The river water had poured from the engine when the cable had dragged the car clear. The engine had started – coughed, choked, belched – started, and then died. The men had said that maybe his car could be rescued from the breaker's yard, and maybe not. There was always, they'd said, the possibility of electrical failure and fire after a car's engine had been in the water.

If he had not brought the car back to Rostock, Dieter Krause would have accepted failure, defeat . . . He had seen her face when he had rammed the tail of her car, and as he had accelerated past her to drive her off the road. He had seen the strength and determination in her face and there had been the moment, so short, that she had turned to him and seemed to laugh.

He sat in the cab of the recovery vehicle as it trundled towards Rostock. By his feet was the coat she had thrown across his windscreen.

He had walked up the street and couldn't find her.

The car was where she had parked it, near the police station, but empty and locked.

The panic swirled in him. He had turned again to retrace his steps, and he saw her.

She was on a bench, a filthy, mud-encrusted urchin in the sunlight. He must have passed her when he had gone up the street, and she had not called out to him. She had let him walk, search, and let the panic rise in him. She was grinning. The sun fell on her face and on her hair. He stamped towards her.

His voice was shrill. 'Don't say it. Don't, please, give the smug "I told you", just don't. It seems the new Germany is stuffed to the nose with mental disturbance, with debt, with good old decent tragedy. Didn't you know it? Trauma caused a man to jump off a roof, debt caused a man to hang himself, tragedy caused a man to live in cow-shit and catch pneumonia. Of course, no-one is to blame. Isn't that sad? And, surprise, there is no Stasi. I'm at the end . . .'

She pushed herself up. He did not know whether she despised or pitied him.

Josh was turning away. He saw the man, half view, at the edge of his vision. The man stood near to the side of the bench. He had not noticed him before, only seen Tracy on the bench with the sunlight on her. The man had his back to them. The man wore smart jeans, was heavy-built, wore a full leather jacket. It was the uniform, what they'd worn on the breakwater, and worn going to the steamed car on the Lichtenhagen estate. The man was a dozen paces away and his back was to them.

Josh hissed, 'How long has he been . . . ?'

'Who?'

He shook. 'That bastard. How long . . . ?'

'No idea.' She didn't seem to care.

They were all around. They watched him, played with him. He was exhausted and panicked. The aggression drove him forward, they'd no fear of him, anger fuelled him. One arm straightening to turn the bastard, one fist drawn back and clenched to punch the bastard, and if he went down there was the mud-caked shoe to kick him. He caught the shoulder of the leather jacket and spun the man. He saw the shock. He saw the baby the man held. The man cringed away. Josh loosed the hold on the leather jacket, and reeled away, mouthing apologies.

He stumbled back down the street towards the car. He would say it, did not know when he would dare to say it to her. He was at the end . . .

'I dislike him because he is coarse and vulgar, and he is arrogant, but not because of what he did in the past. I dislike him because I do not believe he is properly a German as you and I are Germans, not because he shot an agent of the British. I have my job, I must do my job, I must suffer in his company.'

Ernst Raub packed his suitcase and his wife passed him, from the wardrobe and the chest, the clothes he would take. The plan that was now discarded by the senior official of the BfV had been for him to meet the man he disliked in Frankfurt for the flight to Washington. He was directed now to go to Rostock, and there were precise instructions as to what was expected of him in the Baltic city before escorting Krause to Berlin and the connecting flight to Frankfurt for the link to Washington. He packed carefully.

'It is unimportant to me, what he did in the past. Julius, my little comrade, he sees Krause as the incarnation of the Gestapo, detests him. Little Julius wraps himself in the past, so self-righteous, so sickening. Not me . . . There are too many who seek to blame us for the past. In the old past, my grandfather, a policeman in Munich, would have helped with the round-up of Jews, gypsies, Communists. He would have been on the detail that took them with their bags to the railway station. Does that mean I do not love the memory of my grandfather, that I will not permit our children to go to his grave, when we travel to Munich, and lay flowers on it? I heard it said that there were gypsies, men, women and children, once at Munich who tried to break away and flee from the platform as they were driven towards the rail trucks, and the police shot them. I have no idea whether my grandfather was there, whether he fired, because in his life I never asked him. We cannot, should not, any more be required to carry the burden of the old past.'

He folded his dinner jacket into the suitcase, and she passed him his dress shirt. He smoothed it carefully. It was for the dinner at the Pentagon, and the following evening they would be the guests of the Rand Corporation. And then she gave him his pre-knotted black tie.

'What did your grandfather do in the old past? He was at Krupp in the Ruhr, he had a good position in management. At Krupp, the production was maintained, in the last eighteen months, by slave labour. Did your grandfather take responsibility for the slave labour? You did not decline to send him an invitation to our wedding. By us he was treated like any other grandfather, given our love and our welcome on the day of our marriage, because the past should be forgotten . . .'

They would eat together that night as a family. The excursion with the children, the next day, on the river, was cancelled. He would be gone early, while the children slept.

'If I do not accept the guilt of your grandfather and my grandfather in the old past, then I cannot accept the guilt of Dieter Krause for what he did in the new past. He shot a young man – it is not confirmed to me but I believe it – shot an agent in cold blood. I believe, but it is not confirmed to me, that my grandfather fired on gypsy children at the railway station in Munich and that your grandfather used slave labour to maintain the armaments output from Krupp. If I do not have to carry the burden of guilt from the old past then I don't carry that burden from the new past.'

He closed the suitcase, pressed it shut, fastened the small padlock to the central leather strap.

'It is my job to disregard the past. It is policy that I protect him from guilt . . . and he is, forgive me, my dear, a total piece of shit.'

They were close to Rostock.

Ahead of them was the junction, Rostock-*Ost*, for the *Auto-bahn* to Berlin, anywhere. If she drove under the *Autobahn*, it was the road north to Warnemunde and the fishing harbour. He had to dare to say it to her. He searched for the courage.

She drove, didn't look at him. It had been an agony to Josh, with him all the way from the police station at Ribnitz-Damgarten.

'Tracy . . .'

'Come alive, have you?'

'I have to say it . . .'

'Say what you've got to say, spit it out.'

'Tracy, I cannot live, not any more, with the responsibility.'

'What does that mean?'

'We should go to Berlin. If we hadn't come those men would be alive. That is responsibility, and it crushes me. We should go to Berlin, the airport, and take the next flight out. The alternative is too much for me.'

Her lip curled. 'If you forgot, he murdered my Hansie in cold blood.'

'It is men's lives, and I can't carry that weight, Tracy, not any more. There is a man at Warnemunde, like he's waiting for us, Tracy, and we are bringing him his death, bloody wrapped up in ribbons and shiny paper.'

'Quit, if that's what you want. I'm staying.'

He had no power over her. He was familiar with issuing an order, and that order being obeyed.

'We should go to the airport, to Berlin. Believe me – for God's sake, *listen* to me. Listen, forget about the poor bloody wretches that you and I have intruded upon and hammered and broken. Think about yourself, Tracy. We can be in London tonight. You have nothing to be ashamed of. You did what you could. You tried. You cared when nobody else cared. You lost and you can be proud, you can walk tall with yourself. You stay, and you carry the responsibility. What will that have done to you, Tracy? If you win, *if*, have you thought how it will leave you? That responsibility, those lives taken, it will leave you old and crabbed and bowed. Accept failure, accept you're beaten, accept that you have humanity, and begin to live again. Your way, staying, killing another man, taking that responsibility, is to turn your back on everything precious. Love is precious, and fun and happiness – God, Tracy, they are worth reaching for – it's what your Hansie would have wanted. Me, I'm bloody well finished, won't ever be love again in my life, but, listen, you have youth. I plead with you to listen. Don't let what happened destroy you. You can be in London this evening and maybe you will have given a man his life.'

She pulled up onto the hard shoulder. Ahead the road split between the slip-road for the autobahn and Berlin and the route straight ahead, under the bridge carrying the autobahn, to Rostock and Warnemunde.

'A man, a woman, can be frightened, Tracy, and not be ashamed. Being frightened isn't weakness. Admit it, Tracy, you're driven by fear – why you're so bloody cruel. Too frightened of failure to tell Hans Becker that he should refuse the Rostock job and walk away from it. Too frightened of falling off your little pedestal at Brigade to tell Hans Becker to quit on the Rostock job. And, Tracy, too frightened to do anything but crouch in cover and watch as they dragged Hans Becker off that boat, before he ran . . . But, Tracy, you have no call for shame. People push agents beyond the limit because that's their bloody job. People hide in cover and don't intervene because that's their survival route. You don't have cause for guilt, believe me. It's just that you're the same as all the rest of us, frightened. You've done what you could, and more. Please, come back to Berlin . . .'

She reached across him, unfastened the door beside him and pushed it wide open. She loosed his seat-belt. On the autobahn the traffic thundered by, going south for Berlin. There were kids on the slip-road, with their rucksacks beside them, holding pieces of cardboard on which they had scrawled the names of the cities of Berlin and Düsseldorf and Leipzig and Schwerin and Hamburg.

Josh asked, 'Is that it?'

'You wanted an answer. That's it.'

'Then your answer is selfish, conceited, egocentric.'

She said quietly, 'You never listen, and you understand nothing. I will say it again, the last time, I don't quit.'

He could get out of the car. He could hitch a ride into Rostock and collect his bag from the room at the *pension*, and take the train to Berlin. He could sit on an aircraft flying high in the evening darkness, and know that she searched in the fishing harbour at Warnemunde for a trawler's deck-hand. He pulled the door shut. He fastened his seat-belt.

Her hands rested loose on the wheel. He saw the jut of her chin.

He took her hand from the wheel. He was his own man. He kissed her fingers as he had in the night when he had thought she slept. It was his own decision. She stared ahead.

'Thank you,' she said, small voice. 'Thank you for staying.'

He said, gruff, 'Time we were getting on, light's going.'

She took the car off the hard shoulder, past the slip-road, under the bridge, towards Rostock and the fishing harbour at Warnemunde.

'I couldn't, if I left you, live with myself.'

Albert Perkins felt, from his telephoned harangue of his superior, Mr Fleming, a slightly light-headed excitement, and that was as rare to him as had been his loss of temper. He walked the length of Kropeliner Strasse. He imagined, and took a certain pleasure from it, that through the day his superior would have been badgering Violet to use her supremely oiled inter-office communication lines to arrange a meeting, one to one, for Fleming with the ADD, on high. He paused outside the camera shop. The window was empty. The stock of Japanese cameras was gone. He laughed out loud. Done a runner with a vanload of stock and a bagful of banknotes. Good that one bastard had won. Who else would win? The slight young woman with the copper-gold hair? Dreary old Mantle? The former *Hauptman*? One of them must win . . .

He walked briskly, a sharp stride, past the low arches of the old gateway at the *Altmarkt* and headed for the Rostock police headquarters. He was thinking that it could, of course, be himself who would win.

In the embassy on the Sofiyskaya Embankment, in a small room on a high floor, Olive Harris dozed.

She felt at ease, the matter was in place, her schedule was organized. She would rest until the middle evening.

She was grateful that she would not have to refuse the ambassador's invitation to dine. Ambassadors seldom issued dinner invitations to travelling guests from the Service. They regarded the presence in the embassy of the likes of Olive Harris as pure potential for broken fences and expulsions. She did not expect, or wish, to meet with the ambassador during her short visit to his territory, but he would know she had arrived and he would be fearful of what she might achieve and what rocks might fall later on him.

She disliked being so far from home. Few at Vauxhall Bridge Cross would have believed it, but she missed sleeping with her husband close to her. She would be home the next evening, when the business was done. The local file on Pyotr Rykov, unread, was beside her on the bed. Where she lay, on her side, catnapping, she could see the small photograph frame she always carried away with her, the picture of her husband and her children. It would be a triumph, and the pity was that they, most precious to her, would never know of it.

'Have another, why not? I always feel that sherry soothes . . . Fly it by me again, the basis of Perkins's tantrum . . .'

The assistant deputy director filled Fleming's glass.

'. . . The wickedness of sherry, it's never too early. I always feel like a guilty schoolboy if it's gin before six, but any time after five seems decent for sherry. Perkins may be totally disreputable but he is a damn good officer and it would be sad for him to harbour grievances.'

The afternoon had slipped away and the street lights across the river played on the water far below the office.

Fleming said, 'The usual thing, disjointed nose. The feeling that the dragon woman has hijacked his act, that Moscow Desk is walking over German Desk.'

'I wouldn't want a niggle, not about something essentially trivial . . . Now, don't get me wrong – I'm not in the business of buying off Perkins's temper, but he's well due for a step up the ladder.'

'Always the tried and trusted way, a Special Responsibility peg to hang his coat on.'

'Special Responsibility for Iran matters in Europe, right up his street.'

Fleming smiled. 'Go up a grade with that, wouldn't he? It's rather a good sherry. Go to grade seven, wouldn't he?'

He tapped slender fingers on his desk calculator. 'God, how did we ever do without them? An additional annual increment of, what? £4,597.78 should straighten out his nose. I've been discussing reorganizations with the DD and we're thinking about a European Desks supervisory grade, sort of pulling the strings together. This little spat would not have boiled if one man had been in the co-ordinating seat. Your name's been pencilled in, would be a grade six position.'

'Just a pencil, not ink?'

'Early days . . .' The ADD refilled Fleming's glass, and smiled. 'Well, that's that, then. Let me just confirm – Perkins, he's not on a principle kick? It's merely that Olive elbowed him off centre stage?'

Fleming chuckled. 'Principle? Perkins wouldn't know what it means, certainly wouldn't know how to spell it. I'll tell him what's been decided. It's just about played out over there, and he can see it through, can start his new position on Monday.'

'First class. You've reassured me – I'd have thought we had a real problem if it was the principle thing. It will be a good day tomorrow, I've that feeling.'

He had brought the bottle of Scotch whisky and a carton of Marlboro cigarettes. That a degree, small, of civility was shown him was because of the whisky and the cigarettes.

They queued to complain.

'We're treated as if we were without value. We're treated as trash. This garrison camp, and every camp you might care to visit, Colonel, is like a dumping ground for rubbish.'

A long-standing commitment, it had been in his diary for seven months that on this day he should travel to Kubishev and watch the annual showpiece exercise of a motorized rifle division of the strategic reserve based at Volga Military Headquarters. What he had witnessed, in Rykov's opinion, was a complete and unprofessional shambles.

'You saw, Colonel, a divisional scale live firing exercise. You would have asked yourself, Colonel, where was the artillery. The absence of the artillery was not because they had no shells to shoot – they did not have shells but they could have gone along for the walk without shells as women who push prams. The regiment of artillery was not present, Colonel, because they were in the fields picking cabbages. If they do not pick their own cabbages they starve.'

He had stood in a bitter wind on a viewing platform and could have wept at what he saw. He had asked the General commanding the division what message should be carried back to the minister in Moscow, and the response of the General had been to gather a group of officers into a small room off the mess. The whisky had been put on the table and the carton of cigarettes had been ripped open. What hurt most was that each of the officers, the most senior to the most junior, spoke as if he believed that Pyotr Rykov had the power to change a situation of desperation. It was as if a message had been telegraphed ahead of him, that he was a man of unrivalled importance.

'It was a live fire exercise, Colonel, an exercise for the division in manoeuvre, Colonel, but the tanks were static. Why? Because, Colonel, we had enough fuel to send the armoured personnel carriers forward with the infantry, but the tanks use more fuel. We do not, Colonel, have sufficient fuel for the armoured personnel carriers and for the tanks. What is the point of a divisional exercise where the tanks do not move?'

There was a small paraffin heater. He was their guest, and he had brought whisky and a carton of cigarettes, and was given the place of honour closest to the heater. Even the small warmth that it threw was insufficient to stop the shivering tremble in his legs. He thought them proud men. Some wore the ribbons for gallantry in Afghanistan, as he did, and some wore more ribbons for bravery in the pointless farce of Chechnya.

'When the division attacks, Colonel, there should be supporting fire from the mortar units and from the RPG-7 and the Schmel and Falanga missile units. There was none. May I tell you why they did not fire, Colonel? There are no mortar bombs and no rocket-propelled grenades and no ground-to-ground missiles in the division's arsenal store. We have sold them, Colonel. The divisional commander ordered it, and I arranged it. Perhaps, now, they are in Palestine or in Somalia or in Iraq, I do not know and I do not care. They were sold so that the division could buy heating oil, so that our soldiers did not die of hypothermia in the winter. I offer no apology, because that is what we are reduced to.'

He had written the statement of concern for his minister, given at a news conference. He listened. He had not known the half of the Army's despair. It would have been better than anything his minister could have uttered if he had brought these officers to Moscow, given them a bottle of Scotch whisky and then wheeled them in front of the television cameras to speak to their countrymen. The Army had been the strength of Russia, her defence, and now it was humiliated. Pyotr Rykov felt the sting of the shame.

'We sell, Colonel, to anyone who can pay. If the man who can pay is a criminal, then so be it. Where did the weapons of the Chechen bandits come from, Colonel? Why did they always have adequate reserves of ammunition when they fought us? They had our weapons, Colonel, they had our munitions. Our own weapons and our own munitions, sold to those shit bastards, killed our own troops.'

He was humbled by their belief in him. There was an Antonov transport waiting at the airfield for him. The ground crew, on the apron spraying the de-icing fluid on the wings, could wait. They believed him all-powerful and able to fashion change. He did not interrupt. He did not tell them, look into each of their faces and tell them, that he was now a target for surveillance, or that his driver, waiting for the arrival of the Antonov at Moscow Military, had told him that they waited to see how he responded to a given warning. He did not tell them of the fear that had settled at his back, lain on his stomach, the same fear he had known in the street markets and bazaars of Jalalabad and Herat.

'My own unit, Colonel, in the exercise today, performed poorly. I can admit that. It performed poorly because it is short of officers. On paper I have under my command forty-seven officers. In the exercise, today, I was deprived of the use of fourteen. They were at work, Colonel. They are attempting to feed their families. They are many things – market traders, salesmen, security guards, taxi drivers – but they are not, any more, soldiers. In addition, adding to my shortage, three of my officers, in the last eight months, have shot themselves because of their sense of humiliation at the state to which the Army is reduced. Do they care in Moscow, Colonel, what they do to the Army?'

Outside the door of the small room off the mess was an armed corporal of the Military Police. Invitation to the room was personally given by the divisional commanding officer. At Kubishev, old practices in new times, there remained the political officers. They would be in their heavy coats with their vodka

303

at the bar of the mess. They would know that Pyotr Rykov listened to chosen officers, and they would report that. It would be known in Moscow before the morning how Pyotr Rykov responded to a warning.

'I read, Colonel, that when I was a captain we were the equal of the Americans in military technology and we were superior to the British and the French. I was a captain ten years ago. Where are we now? It is not just that we are behind the Americans, we are out of sight. We are no longer on the same playing field. We are the Army of a republic that grows bananas.'

The whisky was finished. The ashtrays were filled. He stayed silent. If he had interrupted, Pyotr Rykov could have told these men that their arsenals were empty, their weapons obsolete and their troops starved because of the cancer of corruption that had eaten at the body of the state. With the cold and the whisky and the cigarette smoke a great tiredness came to Pyotr Rykov. They told him what he already knew, and what they added was only the passion of detail.

'I do not believe, Colonel, that the Army will mutiny. It has lost even the cohesive organization to take such dramatic action. It will melt away, it will go home, it will cease to exist, it will be snow in sunlight.'

The paraffin heater spluttered, gurgled, coughed, and went out.

They did not attack him. If any of them had accused him of complicity in the catastrophe, the litany would have been easier for him to accept.

It was their trust that weighed him down.

He could fly back to Moscow through the night and be at his desk in the morning. He could seek out his minister and report that the division at Kubishev was guilty of gross defeatism, and he could walk away from the trust. But they knew he would not betray them. He stood and rubbed his hands together for warmth. They pushed around him.

'Colonel, you have the influence to force through change. How long before we see that change?'

'When does that cesspit in Moscow get cleared out, Colonel?'

'They say, Colonel, that you control the minister. They say you are not afraid to fight the enemies of the Army. What do you offer us?'

Finally, Pyotr Rykov said, 'I offer you my respect. I offer you my guarantee that each word you have said will be reported to my minister. I offer you my promise that the scum who betray the Army will not sleep easily. Trust me . . .'

He walked out into the night to the car that would take him to the airfield. The evening frost glinted under moonlight.

They drove into the small community of Warnemunde. It was the last throw, the last chance. They were quiet in the car and they harboured their own thoughts. It was the same small community, pretty and tidy, where he had saved her from the sea crashing over the rocks of the breakwater and the same small community to which she had come with her boy, so many years before, to build the boy's strength and to give him courage. If he touched her, as he believed he did, then she would now be thinking, quiet in her mind, of when she had come here with her boy. He loved her as she had loved her boy . . .

She drove past the police station. The shops had closed for the evening. It was too cold, too early in the year, for tourists, and the pavements were empty, the building sites of the new holiday hotels silent. She parked at the railway station, from which the S-Bahn trains ran to Rostock, in shadow, the furthest place she could find from the lights. The wind came harsh off the sea channel and across the quayside and tore at them. He had told her where she should park and for once there was no trace of scorn at her lips. He had found again his strength, because she had thanked him, and she was beside him, walking from the car, elf small and tired, and he thought she now depended on him.

She slipped her hand onto his elbow, and they walked together towards the bridge over the smaller channel.

On the plank bridge, flanked on the far side by the old houses of Warnemunde that were now painted, chic and the homes of new money, and on the near side by the fish harbour where the boats were, they stopped.

The fleet, tied up with heavy ropes, was of small boats all painted in a uniform red from bow to stern with a white flash running their length above the water-line and with white wheel-houses. Men in dark heavy coats and boots worked on the decks by the light of small arc lamps high on posts above the quay. They coiled ropes, scrubbed decks and stowed nets.

Beside the moored boats, above them, was the drab concrete of the quayside. From small stalls on the quay, gross large women, swaddled in stained aprons, sold raw herring-fillet strips and bread, or shredded crab and bread, or smoked fish and bread, or pickled onions and raw fish, and *pils* beer. They did poor trade because the men were still at the boats and the tourists had not yet come.

Along the quay and the stalls was a concrete shed, bright-lit, and in it were men and women, old and young, gutting the fish catch, which the kids brought them from the boats, on wide bench tables. Cats howled by their booted feet, screamed for carcasses. Beyond the brightness and movement in the shed was the dull greyness of the quay, and beyond the quay was the blackness of the water.

Josh took her hand, where it rested on his elbow. He squeezed it, held it tight.

They walked down the ramp towards the quayside, the boats and the gutting shed. A man lumbered towards them, a rolled wool cap on his head, a beard darkening his face and a loose dark coat on his body, carrying a box of gutted fish and powder ice.

'Excuse me, *mein Freund*, where do I find the boat on which Willi Muller works?'

The man did not look up, paused bent under the weight of the box, and jerked his head backwards, directed them towards the long line of boats moored to the quayside and riding on the blackness of the water. The pastor had said that Willi Muller would now be twenty-four. They went by the end of the gutting shed and he could see no young man, dressed in the dark clothes and boots of a fisherman, with a box of fish or a bucket of powder ice, among the white-coated and white-aproned men and women at the work benches.

He came to a stall. Moths bounced in the wind around a naked bulb hanging above the raw fish fillets and the smoked fish fillets and the bread.

'Excuse me, *meine Frau*, where do I find the boat of Willi Muller?'

The woman buttered bread and she did not look up from her work. She made the gesture with the knife, away down the quay, away towards the darkness at its end. They walked past stalls, past small unused tables, past men working on their boats, past the kids who carried the fish catch from the boats to the gutting shed.

A man worked at the repair of his net, fast gnarled hands made good a rip. He leaned against his wheel-house and the net was gathered up across his knees. Josh asked, again, for Willi Muller. The man flashed his face, away, towards the far end of the quayside, towards two boats, empty, in the last fall of the light. He held her hand, crushed it . . . Step quickening, stride lengthening, holding her hand and dragging her behind him . . . Past the boats that were empty, towards the boat that was a rocking shadow shape beyond the point where the light failed. It was the last chance.

Nothing moved on the boat but the slow tossing of the mast and the waving of rigging in the wind. He stood on the quay, his body thrown against the wheelhouse, giant-sized, by the high arc lights far behind him, grey black on grey white. He looked the length of the boat, over stowed netting, coiled rope and stacked boxes. She jerked his arm, she pointed. He looked down into the blackness of the water.

He saw the darkened figure floating there. The figure moved so slowly, so gently, half submerged against the angled bow of the trawler. It wore the dark coat of the fishermen on their boats behind him.

307

Josh screamed out loud.

The figure rose and fell on the swell of the channel.

He screamed because it had been the last chance, because it had all been for nothing . . .

16

The trawlermen on their boats, at their nets and ropes and buckets and brushes, would have heard his agony cry, and the women at the stalls, and the fish gutters in the shed.

Josh pushed her away from him.

He pulled off his coat, and his blazer jacket. They would have seen him stand for a moment on the quay above the darkened boat and the black water. They would have left their boats, their stalls, the gutting shed, left their boxes of fish and powder ice, and have come to the end of the quay where the light did not reach. A narrow, rusted ladder was fastened to the quayside wall. It went down, twice a man's height, into the darkness, to the black water. It disappeared in the water, close to the bow of the boat, to the figure, half submerged and half floating.

He was a driven man. He did not look back, not at her, not at the men and women and the kids coming from the lit end of the quay. He went over the side, down the ochre rusted rungs of the ladder. It sagged. A bolt into the wall was torn clear by his weight.

The water came chill into his shoes, gripped the legs of his trousers. He shuddered at the cold.

He could see the figure, the back of the torso. It was an outline against the oiled black water that slopped against the bow angle of the boat. The water was against his chest and lapped into his armpits. He held the rung that was level with his head, left hand, and he reached out, right hand, towards the figure that rose and fell in the motion of the water. He stretched, but could not reach it, could not hook his fingers, frozen wet, into the coat.

His hand thrashed in the water and the eddies took the figure a few more inches, so tantalizing, away from him. He reached out and there was only the water for his fingers to snatch at.

The rung, rusted, that he held, gave and broke. He was pitched into the water. The foulness of the oil, the sharpness of salt, was in his eyes and mouth and nose. He kicked, gasped, and came up. It was years since he had last swum, and then in a heated pool. He spluttered, choked. He had to reach it. It was his obligation. His shoes were against the wall of the quay, sliding on underwater weed. He pushed away from the quay wall. Three strokes, four, and he would be within reach, if he stretched. He coughed the oil water clear from his throat, his eyes were closed. He lunged. He could not see ahead.

His hand caught it.

He smelt the stench of it.

It came so easily to him, it had no weight.

He pulled it to him. He trod the water. He lifted above his head a black coal sack from the blackness of the water and rotting herring heads spilled from its neck. Around her, above him, were the trawlermen and the stall women and the fish gutters and the kids who carried the boxes. He saw the glistening light of the eyes that gazed down on him. His screams that had brought them had been of agony and pain. At that moment, Josh screamed with hysterical, lunatic laughter. He threw the sack and its debris away and out beyond the bow angle of the boat. He swam back to the ladder. Hands reached down for him. Men knelt to help him. Hard rough hands caught his wrists, caught at the shoulder of his shirt. He was heaved up. All the time they lifted him he laughed. They pulled him over the broken rung of the ladder. He had no control over his arms, his legs. He shook with the cold and the laughter burst through him.

Below him, the sack drifted away towards the current.

The water spilled from his shoes and ran down his body.

All around her, they laughed with him, as if an idiot should be humoured.

Tracy said, 'He's at sea. He's safe. He's up the coast and after the herring. A man just told me. They're due back in tomorrow afternoon. He's safe from them.'

The words came through his chattering teeth. 'Wouldn't have minded knowing that earlier.'

'He was due in today – stayed out another twenty-four hours. Only the crew of the sister ship knew it.'

He kicked off his shoes, peeled off his trousers and dragged off his shirt. He stood, a moment, in the evening air, in his sodden underclothes and soaked socks. The laughter convulsed him. He shrugged into his blazer jacket and wrapped the arms of his coat around his waist. The body of the coat hung over his legs as an apron would have. He picked up his shoes and shook the last of the water from them.

They walked away. She carried his trousers and his shirt. He hobbled in his socks on the coarse concrete of the quayside and she left a dribbled trail of water behind her. He led her past the back of the gutting shed, where they could hug the shadows of the harbour's lorry park and slip unseen back towards the car.

Josh said, 'It was the moment we won, Tracy. Can you see that? It's the first time that it's turned for us.'

Willi Muller's life was the sea and his family were the crew and his home was the boat. On a small stove, powered by kerosene fuel, in a wide pan of sliding lard fat, he cooked porkmeat sausages. On the second hot ring of the stove he poured milk from a bottle and water from a kettle on to the dehydrated potato powder. They were far out in the *Ostsee*, east from the Wittow peninsula of Rugen Island, and north from the island bay that was called Tromper Wiek. They were at the limit range of the trawler boat that carried the designation WAR 79 on the white strip above the red-painted hull. The sister boat, WAR 31, in the early morning, had sailed for Warnemunde with its hold not yet filled with herring, but WAR 79 had stayed out as the wind had freshened and the sea had risen. His life was the sea and he had no fear of the sea wind and the sea waves. The wind hit the boat and the waves made it shudder, but the only fear he knew was when the memories came of the men with the guns dragging the body back to the pier, and aiming the guns at him and ordering him again to start the engine. The guns had been against his neck and his back, and he had helped to pitch the weighted body into the waters of the Salzhaff. He did not believe, ever, that the wind and the waves would make a worse fear for him than the guns had made . . . They drifted on low power, rolling in the water. The sea spray came across the windows of the small wheelhouse. It would be the third night they were out but the herring run, at last, was good. Because it was the third night, there were only sausages to eat with powdered potato and one apple for each of them. There would be old bread for breakfast in the morning and more coffee. They would fish through the night and before dawn they would head back west for Warnemunde.

His family were the skipper and the mate. They were brothers. They had been at sea together for fifty-two years. They had gone to sea together, the skipper and the mate, in 1944, in the submarines from the port of Brest, out into the dark Atlantic waters when the codes were broken and the enemy's bombers and destroyers had hunted out the wolfpacks. They had taught him, as fathers and uncles teach, that the sea was not meant to claim them. The old brothers, wizened, thin, gaunt, bent, were the family he loved. There had been another family, long before, and he was shamed by his mother, who had said her son should swear his silence so that she would not lose her house, and she had kept the house. His father had said that he would lose his boat in Rerik unless his son went away, and his father had not lost his fishing boat. He would never go back to them. To go back was to face the shame of them. The old brothers' boat was the only home he now knew. When they were tied to the quay at Warnemunde, sheltered from the wind and the waves, he slept on the boat. The frayed quilted sleeping bag came out at night, in harbour, from his wood chest below the wheel. His home was a place streaked with engine oil, where the paint flaked loose, where the floor was splintered planks, where all the possessions he owned fitted in the rough-built wooden box that the skipper and mate had made for him. The sea was the life of Willi Muller, and the crew were his family, and trawler WAR 79 was his home.

He knew no fear here because the fear was in the past, with the shame.

He had paid a Turk for the use of her. She was 175 DMs for an hour and a half. There would have been a Turk pimping for her in Leipzig and, in Leipzig, a Turk would have charged him 250 DMs, minimum. He had found her on the Am Strande, and he had paid the Turk and driven her, followed her directions, to an apartment in a block in the *Sudstadt*.

Gunther Peters thought she was new to it. She had the gear, open blouse under a windcheater, and the short skirt, riding high on her thighs, hair rinsed platinum blonde, mouth coated with mauve lipstick. The gear was right but she didn't know her trade. She wore a wedding ring, a television was playing in the living room, and children were sleeping in the other bedroom. He had done it twice and he had felt nothing. He thought that her husband would be out cleaning streets or polishing cars or washing dishes. She lay on her back and she had her legs still stretched wide as if she thought that necessary. She was skinny, white-fleshed, and dark-haired where it wasn't rinsed from the bottle. He had come to Am Strande to look for a tart because it was not important for him to watch the harbour at Warnemunde that evening. Tomorrow was important . . . To use his hour and a half, he had thought about tomorrow, when the boy came back on the boat. Gunther Peters dressed slowly. He had time to kill.

Hoffmann had quit, and Siehl and Fischer, coward bastards. Only himself and the *Hauptman* would be there tomorrow, at the harbour at Warnemunde. He felt no hostility to the tart because she was useless.

When he was dressed, when the Makarov was back in his tight, stretched belt, he gave her a good tip and said that he would drive her back to the Am Strande. After he dropped her, he had forgotten her thin white body within five minutes and was thinking only of tomorrow . . .

'We are off the record, nothing is attributed to me?'

Albert Perkins nodded his agreement. It had been a long wait outside the office of the police chief. It would have been worthwhile. It was his luck that the police chief had served in Dortmund and, there, had worked closely with the British military, had been liaison officer between the German authorities and the British intelligence people trying, fingernail stuff, to keep a track on the Irish bombers targeting the British bases.

'This is not a conversation that is happening?'

Albert Perkins tapped his lips with an index finger. He had already flattered the younger man: without the excellent cooperation of the German police the Irish shits would have had free rein to bomb and kill.

'The correct procedure would be for me to report your arrival to BfV in Cologne, and to seek guidance, but I do not think you wish that?'

Albert Perkins shook his head and a grimace of mock pain crossed his face.

The police chief for Rostock said, 'I went two years ago, Doktor Perkins, to Berlin. There was to be a seminar on the investigations into criminal acts by the former officers of the Stasi. There were two days of lectures and, I tell you very frankly, the two days passed slowly. It was the evening between the days that was interesting, my eyes were opened. I went to dinner that evening with an officer from Berlin on the special-investigation team, codenamed Zerv, and I met with a bitter man. The unit was denied the federal funding and the manpower it needed to be operationally efficient. A combination of covert obstruction and lack of a political will created, my dinner guest told me, a *de facto* amnesty for the Stasi. He said the attitude of government was that the prosecution of the Stasi for criminal offences would lead only to a further alienation of the people of the eastern part of our country. He was a disillusioned man – twice in a lifetime the German nation was confronted with the crimes committed by a totalitarian regime, and twice the blind eye had been turned to illegality. You give me the opportunity, Doktor Perkins, to stand beside that bitter and disillusioned officer.'

Albert Perkins ducked his head, the motion of respect. He could have done without the lecture, but listening to it was his route towards the facility he required for the next day.

'The failure to prosecute the Stasi left the organization intact and emboldened, my dinner guest told me. He listed for me the prosecutions that could, should, have been brought. The theft of twenty-six billion DMs that should have gone to the treasury of a united Germany, four hundred cases of murder, torture and kidnapping, the destruction of the personality of many thousands of innocents. But that is the cold world of statistics. It was a good meal, we had the opportunity to eat well. But one story he told so disgusted me that the meal was an irrelevance. My guest investigated the death of a young man in the Stasi prison at Jena. He killed himself after the interrogation during which they played him a tape of the screams of a young woman and told him the screams, under torture, were those of his nine-months-pregnant girl-friend. There have been no prosecutions of the Stasi officers responsible for driving that young man to the despair of suicide.'

A deep frown of concern cut Albert Perkins's forehead.

'They are intact, Doktor Perkins. They have a network, an organization, to which we give the name of Seilschalften. They are the source of organized crime in the old East. They have links with criminals in Russia. They are behind the illicit movement of arms, the narcotics trade, the theft of cars, they are expert in the recycling of fraudulently obtained monies. Through inaction, when the chance was there, Doktor Perkins, we have made a monster. I offer you co-operation.'

Albert Perkins reached across the table and, with warmth, shook the hand of the police chief.

'If the politicians can determine who is to be prosecuted, and who is not, then they have destroyed a cornerstone of democracy. You say, Doktor Perkins, that tomorrow is the critical day in this matter. I wish to help. I wish to do something in the name of that officer who was my guest at dinner in Berlin. Tomorrow you are welcome to sit with us.'

Albert Perkins went on his way, out into the night.

'I think it is necessary that you lose him, for a month, for two months. I think he is damaged.'

The three video-cassettes, copies from the originals, had been couriered from the Lubyanka to the minister. He had watched the first fifteen minutes of the first cassette, then turned away, his face a lined, wearied portrait of pain. The General of military intelligence, GRU, his friend, had switched off the video player.

The General said, 'He climbed too fast. He is a shooting star, brilliant in the night sky but burning out fast as it falls. He takes to bed with him the wife of a Stasi officer. That Stasi officer is now a prize exhibit of the Germans and talks to whoever will listen of his knowledge of Pyotr Rykov. Did the German share his wife with Pyotr Rykov? Was there compliance? If there was compliance where does it end? Or does it continue? Is he still linked with the German who calls him his closest friend? You would trust Rykov with your life, and I believe I would, but the cassettes ask questions that we cannot answer. If you protect him you make yourself vulnerable. He has damaged himself but he should not be permitted to damage you. You should lose him. If there is nothing else to compromise him, in a month or two months, you might call him back, with discretion. You should not seek to help him, if there is anything else. For now, you must distance yourself from him. It must not be you who is vulnerable.'

They cruised on the wide street.

Olive Harris was tolerably rested. She had read the local file and thought it inadequate. She had eaten, alone, in the

316

staff canteen, apart from the security men and the night-duty secretaries and the communications team who worked late. The food had been indifferent.

They passed the surveillance car. She was pleased to see it in place. The city, until the moment she saw the car, had seemed disappointing. It was without threat, until she saw the car with the misted windows and the fumes spilling grey-white into the night air and the glow of the cigarettes. She had thrived on that feeling of threat and danger, half a career ago, when she had been here before and run agents and sidled to the dead letter boxes and played games with the tails. In London, she missed, more than anything else, that feeling. In London, in her small personal office, on the train and the bus that took her to and from work, she made a fantasy each day of threat and danger, as if to fill a void. They were ahead of the surveillance car and he murmured the number of the floor on which the target lived. There were three windows. Two were darkened; in the third a dull light speared the gap in the curtains. It was a shabby little block of apartments, which told her something of the target man. He was pulling away, one run down the street only. It was all in her mind, the street door, the width of the pavement, where they would stop in the morning and the position of the surveillance car. She eased back in her seat.

'May I, Mrs Harris, ask a question of you?'

'You can try.'

He stared straight ahead, eyes on the road, and his voice was clipped. 'I'm just wondering what Rykov has done to us that he deserves our targeting him? That's my question.'

'For God's sake, have you a problem?'

His voice was quiet and without emotion, and she thought he had stored the question through the day. 'It's pretty straightforward. What has Rykov done to deserve the action we are taking against him?'

'Where are you starting from?'

'Starting from? I've never met Rykov. I've only watched him from a distance and evaluated him. I listen to what people say about him. Actually, Mrs Harris, I've not heard a bad word said of him. He's a patriot. He's a man who cares about his country. You saw that grubby little apartment block – that's not the home of a man on the make. With his position, his connections, he could live in style, snout in the trough, hand in the till, running rackets. What's evil in this country is the degree of corruption and criminality. He's not corrupt, he's not criminal. That's where I'm starting from. Why are we mounting a hostile operation against Pyotr Rykov?'

She said, tried to cut him down, 'Been here a long time, haven't you, David? Started to get to you? Going native, are you?'

He said, without anger, 'I quite understand, Mrs Harris, if you are not willing to answer my question. I think he's a good man. I think he's a brave man. Of course, Mrs Harris, you have no obligation whatsoever to answer my question. I think also he was doomed before you came here. I think what he has fought against here would have beaten him anyway within a few months. He'd know that. Without you, in a few months or a couple of years at maximum, beaten, he'd have been pushed aside, shoved off to some mission in Ulan Bator or some crap job in Transbaikal, put out to grass. But that's not your game, Mrs Harris. Your game is the immediate destruction of a fine man. You won't mind me saying it, Mrs Harris, but I find your game distasteful and immoral. Well, here we are. I'll see you in the morning.'

He stopped the car. The policeman at the embassy gates eyed them.

'Not just gone native, gone squeamish.'

'If you say so, Mrs Harris. You do know what will happen to him – yes, you'd know that . . . Sleep well, Mrs Harris.'

The wind on the street buffeted her. She gathered her coat around her and ran across the pavement on clattering heels, through the gates towards the lights and the warmth of the doorway.

* * *

'What do you do, Josh, afterwards?'

She sat cross-legged on her bed. The carton of chips was on the blanket beside her hips, an opened can of Pepsi between her bare feet, and the cardboard tray for the pizza was on her lap.

'There's a bit has to happen yet.'

'You said it, Josh, wasn't me that said it. It was you said it had turned.'

'Guilty, I said it. Probably shouldn't have. When you've been kicked – we've been kicked – you need a light to walk towards. Just have to hope that was our light.'

He was hunched down on his mattress beside the door. He wore a clean white shirt that was already specked with leaked chilli sauce from his hamburger. He had already brushed the mud off his blazer jacket, as if it were important to him that he should smarten himself for a dinner of a hamburger with a young woman who had chosen pizza, fries and Pepsi.

'Tomorrow it's over – win, lose or draw,' Josh said. 'I shouldn't dare to, but I believe it turned for us this evening. What you've waited for, nine years, tomorrow it's over.'

'What do we do tomorrow, when he comes in?'

Josh hung his head. He held the remnant of the hamburger. 'Don't know . . .'

She grinned, not cruel. She mocked so gently. 'But you always know what to do, Josh.'

'Not this time.'

She ate the last of her fries, crumpled the carton, threw it at the rubbish bin, then wiped her mouth on her sleeve. The empty rooms of the *pension* below them, were cemetery quiet, with only the far murmur of the streets' traffic.

'Why did you go into the water, Josh?'

He blinked. He chewed the last mouthful. With a clean hand-kerchief he dabbed the sauce from his shirt. 'Because of you, because of him, because of where your love for him has taken you, because of what you've given me . . . because you have shown me a road of honesty and truth and courage. I try to live on a creed of principles, and of course I fail. I try to be, and I can never achieve it, my own man. You gave me the strength, Tracy, to go into the water. I owed it to you.'

'What will you do, afterwards?'

He spoke slowly, thoughtfully. 'I go back. I have a couple of rooms on the top floor of this house – not too far from your mother's street – and I'll dump my bag. It will be precisely and exactly as I left it. I'll load up my dirty washing and go down the stairs and if I meet anyone they'll nod to me, but they won't have noticed I've been away. The woman at the launderette will see my stuff through. I'll walk over to the high street, the office of Greatorex, Wilkins & Protheroe, and I'll look contrite and I'll say it won't happen again and I'll grovel for my job. They'll puff a bit, there'll be a deal of talk about last chances and ingratitude, and there will be a pile of work about a mile high on my desk. At the end of the day I'll go home past the launderette. In the evening, when it's dark, private, I'll go and talk to my wife and tell her about it. Back home, I'll do my ironing, and I'll go to bed and read a book, and I'll sleep. Next morning, back to work – the magistrates' courts, police interview rooms, the Britwell Estate, and the morning after, and the morning after that. That's it, that's afterwards.'

'It's not much, Josh.'

He pushed himself up. The rueful smile played at his mouth . . . It wasn't much, it was sweet bugger all, but it was the truth of afterwards. The memories would be precious, and he would tell Libby, in the dark of the night, of his memories before he went back to the lonely solitariness of the rooms on the top floor of the house behind the London Road. He picked up her chips carton and her pizza tray and put them in the bin with her Pepsi can. He loosed his tie, pulled it from his collar and unbuttoned his shirt.

'I'm sorry, Tracy, I'm dead on my feet, and I'm bloody poor company.'

She sat cross-legged on her bed and watched him.

*   *   *

'It is policy and it is principle. When they go together it is when we walk with honour. When they are apart, conflict, then we crawl on our guts, in confusion.'

Julius Goldstein threw clothes from the drawers and wardrobe on to the floor. She walked the room and smoked. What she smoked, Moroccan stuff, was enough to have him thrown out of the BfV without question. They lived together in the Kreuzberg district of Berlin, in her apartment, alongside the immigrants, the students, the artisans and painters, because his girl said it was a stimulating place for her work. The apartment was her studio. She worked big canvases with oils and next year, maybe, she would sell one.

'When they walk together, policy and principle, then I am happy and I applaud. This time they don't, this time they fight, so we are in shit. The policy is easy. We have a man who gives us status. We take the man to America and feed off the status of the man. We are maggots, we wriggle around and we are happy little maggots, and the Americans love us and give us more status, and we are happier.'

He loved her, part for her mind and part for her body. She wore only her knickers and her roll-neck sweater, the bed was, as always, unmade, and her canvases were propped around the walls. She came from a big-shot family, industrials, from Frankfurt, and she didn't have to live in a dump in Kreuzberg, and she didn't have to live with a Jew. He was a token of fair-mindedness at BfV, and a token of her goddamn obstinacy. He didn't know, didn't ask, but he thought she might screw around while he was away. He began to throw the clothes, haphazard, into the bag.

'The principle is not easy. It is full of shit. Our valued asset is guilty, unprovable but guilty, of murder. Never mind that he is an arrogant fuck-pig, he is a killer. We protect him, don't investigate him.'

He had no dinner suit. For the Pentagon speech, and at dinner afterwards, he would wear a crumpled jacket and an open shirt. He believed he was safe from censure, whatever he

321

wore, because he was the token Jew. His passport and the sachet of travellers' cheques were on the table with her paint tubes and rags.

'He should be investigated, prosecuted, locked up. All right, I am a Jew, but I don't have the heavy thing. I am not obsessed with the camps, but . . . I go and buy a lottery ticket from an old man in a kiosk and he smiles so kindly at me – was he on the trains that took my grandparents to the camps? Was he in the camps' watch-towers when my grandparents came off the train? I don't know. I only know that the guilty were protected then. I see any old man who smiles at me and I have no trust for his smile. It is the same now – there can never be trust unless the guilty are prosecuted. Same then, same now, conflict of policy and principle, and it makes for a shit time.'

She stubbed out the joint of Moroccan stuff. She pulled on paint-smeared jeans. They liked a little Vietnamese place on the Mehring Damm. They'd eat there, and then he would drive to Rostock. That conflict, policy and principle, would be decided the next day.

'I detest him. He is the same man that killed my grandparents. The same man . . . I try to be, first, a German, but for me it is impossible. I try to do my German duty and to obey my German orders, but it is impossible. Before I am a German, first I am a Jew. I detest him, and I will never forgive him and never forget what he has done. I am a Jew, I walk in the shadow of such a man. It does not mean that I am obsessed, as are my father and my mother, but it is inevitable. It is what I cannot escape from. I cannot forgive, as a Jew, and I cannot forget. Let's go . . .'

He went past the lines of the unlit windows.

He had taken them back from the tennis, after the applause. His daughter had punched the air in victory and the coach had come to congratulate him and Eva. The final of the under-fifteen tournament, girls, for Mecklenberg-Vorpommern, would be played the next evening. He had driven them home in his wife's car and left them.

322

Dieter Krause did what he had never done before: he sidled, walked slowly, past the unlit windows of the big block of red brick and dun concrete on August-Bebel Strasse.

He had never before felt the need to catch at the past. It was, to him, an act of weakness. His window had been on the second floor, the fifteenth window to the right of the main door. The building was now a district court for family and commercial affairs. There was a light in the hallway, behind the main door, but the windows of the second floor were darkened.

He lingered. He stared up. On a Tuesday night, nine years before, the panic call had been switched through to the room on the second floor. Eva had said she was working late that night at the shipyard. If she had not said that she would be working late, he would have been at home when the panic call had come through and the Duty Desk would have handled it, and there would have been delay in finding him. If there had been delay in finding him, if he had been later at the seashore at Rerik then, perhaps, the boy would have drowned in the Salzhaff or, perhaps, the boy would have been taken from the water by the Soviets or, perhaps, the boy would have come ashore and staggered away into the night, but the past could not be altered ... The telephone had carried the call, a shrill bell of panic, into his office as he had been slipping on his coat, and he had answered it ...

He gazed up at the window, on the second floor, fifteenth on the right from the main door.

He was the prisoner of the building on August-Bebel Strasse.

If he had not interrupted the shrill call of the telephone so long ago ...

Josh lay on his back, the mattress on the floor hard under him.

He tried to think it through and make a plan for the morning, when the trawler boat returned to Warnemunde.

He heard her turning in her bed, and he knew she could not sleep.

There must be a plan for the morning, but he could not make the plan because his mind was cluttered with the day gone by, and the day before that, and the day before that. She heaved on the bed beside him, sighed, grunted as if a decision were made. Her blankets and sheets were pushed back, and he sensed the warmth of her foot close to his head. Her hands lifted the blankets that were tight around him. She snuggled against him, the heat of her body was with him, raw heat. He lay on his back and he clenched his hands tight together.

'Is it wrong? It can't be wrong.'

'I don't know whether it's wrong or whether it's right.'

'You think of her?'

'Only the bloody bad times. Only the times I was foul and shouldn't have been, like it's guilt. Calling back the good times gets harder.'

The warmth of her was against him. 'She doesn't own you, Josh, not now.'

His fingers were locked, entwined, hard as he could hold them. 'She is all that I have to hold to.'

'What you said, about afterwards, it doesn't have to be that.'

Josh said, 'Her funeral, I can remember it. It's like it was an hour ago. There was the vicar, the box, the men who carried the box, the solicitor and the accountant, and there was me. We had two hymns and only the vicar sang. They carried the box out and put it in the ground and there was a man behind me with a long-handled shovel and a cigarette cupped in his palm. I wasn't supposed to see the cigarette. I didn't want to go, to leave the box, but he coughed, like he was telling me that it happened every day and he'd a bloody schedule to keep to, and would I, please, let him get on? The vicar knew the schedule, he shifted me.'

'Your wife was lucky to have a proper prayer said over her, luckier than my Hans . . .'

His hands broke apart. He stretched out and she wriggled over his arm. Her head was on his shoulder.

'It was the little that I knew about love, and it was the little that you knew, Tracy, about love.'

'You're making bloody speeches, Josh.'

324

'Sorry.'

'It can be better, afterwards . . .'

He held her. He felt a fear of her. The fear was that she would laugh at his clumsy love of her. He held her, small, against him. He heard the chuckle murmur from her, and she kissed his neck below his ear and her fingers unfastened the buttons of his pyjama top. He clung to her. He found the small shape, squashed against his chest, of her breasts where the fingers of the boy had been, and the boy was the past, and he believed himself to be the future. The blankets climbed above them. She kissed his mouth and seemed to take from him the oiled salt stench of the water and the cold. He whispered, apologized, that he did not have anything. She whispered, cheerful, that it did not matter. They loved in quiet deep desperation. She was, to him, a child, and his hands moved with gentleness down from the smoothness of her stomach, and he no longer thought of the boy. She was the love light in his life. She gripped, narrow, muscled, small legs, around the width of his hips and across the breadth of his back. Her nails raked his back. He was deep within her. The sweat warmth of his stomach and her stomach shut away the cold. It was love, it was beauty, it was together. She shouted his name . . . his name, not the boy's name . . . He had reached her and touched her . . . He felt a great slow growing sense of pride, because they were together, because they shared love.

'You are brilliant, you know that? Not just now, all the time, you are fantastic.'

He came off her, out of her. She lay with her wet warmth on him.

'Thank you, Knautschke, for giving me happiness, thank you little hippopotamus for coming out of the mud.'

She giggled, 'Daft bugger.'

She broke his hold. Her thigh was across his waist and her heel massaged between his legs. She leaned across him, her breasts hung fluttering on his chest.

'What's afterwards, Josh, for us? Not the crap you told me. What's afterwards, Josh, for you and me?'

325

17

She lay on him, snuggled on him. The clock on the Marien-kirche chimed midnight, big bells. He wanted, desperate for it, the warmth of her to last.

'There is an afterwards, for us, for you and for me?'

'It's what I'm saying.'

He lay on his back on the mattress and he held her tight against him and his fingers played patterns on the small of her back, and her fingers made tangles with the hairs of his chest. To be his own man was to protect himself. He wanted to trust in the afterwards, to believe that it was not a fraud. He had seen it so many times before in the camps in Germany and the camps in the UK, men under stress and women under stress coupling together for strength and deluding themselves that there was an afterwards when the stress time had passed. He had seen the hurt that was left, two people broken, because the stress time was gone and there was no reality of afterwards. She had told him that before he went on the last bad one, the last bad mission, she had loved the boy to give him strength.

'Is it enough, Tracy, after what we've shared, to make an afterwards?'

She kissed him. 'It is for me, yes.'

He jerked, pushed himself up on his elbows.

She had offered him the prize, the trophy to be won.

He leaned against the cold damp of the wall and he took her face in his hands. He held her cheeks, gripped them, and against his hands was the smoothed narrowness of her neck.

'I can't talk about it.'

'Afterwards is babies, Josh.'

'I shouldn't talk about it, because it isn't finished.'

'And puppies, Josh, little black bastards, peeing . . . And a place that's our own, babies and puppies and fields . . .'

'If I don't have a plan then we lose.'

'And no people, just a home and babies and puppies and fields . . .'

'I love you, Tracy. I'm so thankful to you. I want it, your afterwards, I want to be with you for it. Can you understand? I'm so frightened. I don't have a plan, I can't think . . . I don't delude myself, Tracy. If we don't win tomorrow, there is no afterwards. Loving you, loving me, and I didn't think it possible that I would find happiness again, find what you've given me, but it doesn't count tomorrow. Have to think, can't, have to have a plan . . .'

She slipped off him. The warmth was gone.

Her bed creaked, took her weight.

He tried to think, tried to make the plan. He could not find it and ebbed towards sleep.

'Did she win?'

'She won.'

'You were proud of her?'

'I was.'

'Would she be proud of you, Hauptman?'

Gunther Peters oiled his smile. Only the two of them that night in the little annexe corner of the café. Peters let his hand, long thin fingers, rest on the fist of Dieter Krause, and asked his questions with a familiarity, as if the old ranking of *Hauptman* and *Feldwebel* was no longer of importance, as if they were equals. Peters' fingers held tight on Krause's fist.

He hesitated, uncertain. 'I don't know.'

'A man is privileged when his daughter is proud of what he does.'

'That is shit.'

'I have had several days to think, Hauptman.' Peters rolled the word on his tongue. He mocked. 'Over the last several days I have thought of the future . . .'

327

'Tomorrow it is finished, tomorrow is the end of the future.'

'Tomorrow I go home, Hauptman? Tomorrow, after it is finished, I go home and you pretend I never came? You go to America, you are the big-shot man, you are free to fuck with your new friends, and I go home and you forget me? You don't believe that, Hauptman, you cannot believe that.'

Krause tried to break the hold of the fingers on his fist. 'We came together in common purpose and you go when the matter of common purpose is finished.'

'I come at a price, Hauptman.'

Krause gazed into the eyes of the former *Feldwebel*. Peters had been just a face in the corridors, another junior who had snapped smartly to heel-clicking attention each time they passed, just a face sitting at a desk and the order had been shouted through the open door. They had been chosen, grabbed, commandeered, at random. He gazed into the face and the fingers relaxed on his fist.

'What is the price?' Krause growled.

'That is not gracious, Hauptman, that is not generous.'

'Tell me what is the price.'

'I come from Leipzig. I leave my affairs, I cancel a business opportunity. I stay, I don't run, I stand with you.'

'What is your price?'

'You give me orders and I obey them. You involve me, I do not complain . . . and then you wish to forget me, as you would drop the wrapping of a cigarette packet.'

'What is the goddamn price?'

'I can do as Hoffmann did, as Siehl and Fischer did. I can walk away. I was only a simple *Feldwebel*, I was carrying out the orders of my superior officer. That is the usual defence, yes? It does not suit me but it is an option. I can go to my car, I can be on the road, I can reach Leipzig by the morning, if a price is not paid.'

'Tell me the price.' Sweat beaded on the forehead of Dieter Krause.

'You have new friends?'

328

'I have.'

'Your new friends have influence?'

'They have influence.'

'They value you?'

'What is the fucking price?'

'Do you want to be alone tomorrow, Hauptman, when the trawler boat comes in? Can you do it yourself, Hauptman, remove the problem? You want to go to America with the problem behind you?'

'Name the price.'

He talked softly, silky smoothly. 'You have new friends with influence who value you. They would protect you. You are the ideal partner for me.'

'Partner in what?'

'I put cars out of the country, I put munitions into the country. I move money into Germany and out of Germany, and your new friends, if you were my partner, would protect me.'

'That is criminal activity.'

'What is it you do now?' He laughed quietly. His laughter was without noise, without mirth. 'Without me beside you tomorrow you fail. If you fail you go to the Moabit gaol. That is the price.'

He was trapped. He squirmed. The rat eyes faced him, and the thin fingers were held out to him. He would be, in the Moabit gaol, with the scum and the filth and the addicts and the foreign pimps. He thought he plunged over a cliff and fell, and fell.

Krause took the hand that was offered to him.

There had been no car to meet him at Moscow Military Headquarters.

He had rung the drivers' pool office at Defence, and he had won no sense out of an idiot: the idiot did not know why he was not met at Moscow Military. He had telephoned his driver's home and the call had rung out unanswered.

Pyotr Rykov had hitched a lift into the city. A drunk sergeant, veering over the roads, losing himself, had taken him near to his home.

He had walked on the street past the surveillance car, and each of the three men in the car, smoking behind the misted windows, had looked at him without expression.

Pyotr Rykov banged the door shut after him, and woke Irina. She said, sleepy in her bed, that the telephone did not work and would he have it fixed in the morning.

He stood by the window with the darkness of the living room behind him. His driver, his old friend who should have been at Moscow Military, had told him that he should be careful. He had said, his reply defiant, that the minister was the guarantee of his security.

Pyotr Rykov did not know that the brass plate bearing his name had been unscrewed from the door of the office next to the suite of the minister. He did not know that three video-cassettes had been watched in full in the Lubyanka, or that the number of his laminated ID card had been given to the guards at the four doors of the ministry with instructions that he be refused entry. He did not know the name of Olive Harris, or of her plan . . . He looked down onto the surveillance car . . . Pyotr Rykov did not recognize the moment he had not been careful and had made the mistake. He could not recall that moment.

Away up the channel the sea spray burst on the breakwater.

The rotating lamp, millions of units of candlepower, caught the spray and lost it. The light moved on, thrusting out over the whiteness of the seascape, before bouncing back from the mist of low cloud, turning again. A small boat was paddled up the calm water of the channel towards the thunder rumble at the breakwater and the moving lamp of the lighthouse. The boat had been taken from the inner harbour. Cold, trembling fingers had freed the boat from the iron ring on the quay wall.

It was a vicious night. Darkened houses and shops beyond the quay on the one side of the channel, darkened boats and stalls and the darkened fish-gutting shed on the other. Not a night, in the small bad hours, for man or beast to be out. Not a fisherman yet out of his bed, not a cat moving from the warmth

330

of a kitchen. The swell was with the small boat when it came level with the length of the breakwater. The lamp of the lighthouse found the small boat and discarded it. It lurched hard against the rocks of the breakwater's base, was lifted and fell.

A scrambled crawl over the wet grease on the rocks, and the mooring rope of the small boat was tied, the same trembling, cold, wet fingers, to a post on the breakwater's low rail.

Olive Harris slept.

She slept untroubled, and did not dream. The pill, taken with a half-glass of water, ensured that she slept free of troublesome images. She didn't see the faces of those who were, to her, irrelevant and a sideshow, nor did she see the face of the man she had described as a target of consequence.

It was important for her, in the small strange bed on the top floor of the embassy block, to sleep well because the morning would bring the start of a long day, unpredictable and dangerous but with the potential of high reward.

There was a clear printed sign in the police car. It forbade the smoking of cigarette, cigar or pipe tobacco.

Sometimes, on the night shift, when they were parked up and waiting for a call on the radio, if he was with a friend, the policeman could wind down the windows and smoke in the car. Not with her, not with the bitch fresh out of the training school at Dummerstorf-Waldeck. She sat in the driver's seat and pecked a plastic spoon into a carton of yoghurt, and he stood outside the car in the shadow beneath the block on Plater Strasse, and smoked a Dutch-made cigarillo. The wind brought the sleet shower off the Unterwarnow and across the Am Strande, funnelled it up the narrow road and gusted it into Plater Strasse. He cupped the cigarillo in his hand. He sheltered in the doorway of a shuttered restaurant. His arm was tugged. He had been watching her in the car, finishing the goddamn yoghurt, starting on the cholesterol-free sandwich filled with low-fat cheese and tomato. What she needed was a good smoke and a good drink and a good sausage and a good fuck. The recruits today were shit . . .

A street map was held in front of him. There was no light nearby. He shone his torch on the map and tried to hold it and his cigarillo and the map that blew in the wet wind. He strained to find the road he was asked for. The sleet came onto his spectacles. The knee came into his testicles. He gasped. The breath spurted from his throat. He was jack-knifed by the pain, head going down towards his knees, spectacles flying towards the paving. A hand chopped down on the back of his exposed neck; the hard heel of a hand. He was in the shadow behind the car, and the bitch ate her sandwich. He sagged to his knees and clutched at his stomach, fell. Hands tore at the pistol holster on his belt, ripped at the pouch for the handcuffs and their key. The sick pain squeezed his eyes shut. He heard the brush whisper of feet receding, running.

He crawled, gasping, heaving, towards the door of the police car where she ate her sandwich.

He had drunk the whisky, Scotch and Irish, from the room's cocktail cupboard and now he opened the bourbon miniature.

It was always a long night for Albert Perkins before an operation was launched the following day. After the Jack Daniel's there was gin, which he detested, and vodka, which he thought of as a woman's drink, but he would not take out the champagne quarter-bottle, not when the result of the mission was undecided.

He had rung home four times, first at ten o'clock and then again on each hour. She should have been back by midnight. Certainly, by one o'clock she should have been home to complain that she was asleep and that he had woken her. He had not rung again after one o'clock. The ice was finished. It was always in hotel bedrooms, with the ice finished and the whisky, that he spent the nights before an operation went to its end.

The missions that mattered were those in which men such as Albert Perkins were powerless to intervene in the last

332

crucial hours. They didn't accept that powerlessness, those back home, those who commanded from the bunkers of the old Century House or the new Vauxhall Bridge Cross; of course they did not accept limit on their omnipotence. Albert Perkins knew it. He had once before, unusually consumed by his own frailty, drunk himself to oblivion on the night before the crucial hours.

There was a hotel at Luchow, south east on Route 216 from Lüneburg, and across the minefields, fences and past the watch-towers was Salzwedel. It had taken eight months of Albert Perkins's life, and a quarter of a million DMs, to get to the point where he had drunk a hotel cabinet dry and waited for a man to come through the checkpoint on the Luchow to Salzwedel road. The summer of '85, the trees along the road pretty on both sides of the minefields and the fences, the fields yellow with ripe crops either side of the watch-towers. No power, no influence. In his binoculars he had seen the car stopped at their checkpoint. All so dreary and mute through the magnification of the binoculars, a man taken out of a car and escorted into a building and then driven away until the car that carried him was lost among the fields and trees behind the minefields, the fences, the watch-towers. Nothing he could have done to intervene on the side of the NationalVolksArmee officer bringing over the Soviet battle order, defensive strategy.

He let the miniature bottle, the Jack Daniel's, slip through his fingers and fall to the carpet. There was no tonic and no ice. He made a mix of orange juice and gin.

There were no minefields in Rostock, no death strips, no fences, no watch-towers and no dogs, but eating him was the same sensation of helplessness, of impotence, he had known too well. In three, four hours it would be dawn. With the dawn would come the start, the ticking clock, of the critical hours, and he would not be able to intervene. He reached, groped with a wavering hand, for the miniature of vodka, and he heard beyond the window the howl of police sirens in the night.

*   *   *

The great mouth of the hippopotamus crunched on the man, and he screamed. The scream filled his mind. He crabbed with his knees and the blankets would have slipped, and the cold would have settled on him. The scream . . . Josh woke.

He heard the scream of a siren going by the *pension*.

He shook, tried to scrape from his mind the intensity of the dream. Another siren was blasting further in the distance, and another coming closer. He glanced down at his watch, at the luminous markings, past three o'clock, and he looked across at her to see if she slept. He could see the shape of her in the bed, couldn't hear her breathing, could hear only the sirens, as though they were cats chorusing. He settled. He turned his back to the window and her bed, and pulled the blankets close around him.

He shivered.

The draught blew on his back. Josh, so slowly, so carefully, turned over again and saw that the curtain, beyond the silhou-ette shape of her in the bed, blustered out into the room. Behind the curtain was the grinding sound of the window being forced upwards.

He tensed. He was naked under the blankets.

The curtains parted. It was hard for him to see. The leg edged between the curtains. He strained to see better. The window was half a dozen feet from the bed. The second leg came through the curtains, and Josh saw the bulk of the body looming above the bed where she slept, still, silent. The body shape, big against the curtain, moved towards the bed.

He had no weapon. Of course they'd found the fucking place. They'd had enough bloody days to find it.

He coiled his strength.

He erupted off his mattress.

The blankets caught in his legs and he thrashed them clear. He went over the bed, over her, groped for the shape. Waiting for the blow with a cosh or the flash hammer of a shot. Scrab-bling to get his fingers into the bastard.

They were down.

334

They were beside the bed. Trying to get at the throat. He found the throat.

The gasped voice: 'For fuck's sake . . . Josh . . . leave it, leave it out . . .'

He was frozen rigid.

The coughing voice: 'Christ, Josh . . . pack it . . . daft bugger, get off me!'

He knelt above her. He sighed into his lungs great draughts of chill air. He loosed his hands and they shook: he could not control them. He could have wept. She came from under him, wriggled clear of him. She crawled towards the bed and reached for the light switch. He knelt in his nakedness. She slammed down the window and fastened it. He saw the shape in the bed, a bolster and a pillow. She was dressed for the cold of the night and she rubbed gloved hands on her throat. He felt a great and savage bitterness. He stood, naked, in front of her, and he trembled.

'You stupid bloody woman. I could have killed you. One punch, one kick, you were dead.'

There was a small gleam of wonderment on her face. Her face was bright flushed from the night wind, the sleet water sparked in her hair, and her eyes were wide in awe. 'You'd have killed for me, Josh? For me?'

'Where the hell have you been?'

'For me?'

The anger coursed through him. 'I make the decisions. I make the plans. When I work with an amateur, when my security is on the line, I take the responsibility.'

'You're quite funny when you're angry, Josh. I'm trying not to laugh, Josh, you're really funny.'

He turned away from her, to the mattress on the floor, scooped up a blanket and wrapped it around him. He felt shy, ridiculous.

She said, matter-of-fact, 'You didn't seem to have a plan.'

He said, empty, 'I would have done, just needed time.'

'Are you firearms trained?'

He spun. She was reaching into her pocket. She handed him the holster inside which the pistol was fastened. He heard the sirens out in the night, crossing the streets of the city. The policeman's name was stamped on the black leather of the holster, and there was an index number. The sirens came and went, growing in fury pitch and diminishing. It was a Walther PPK. He knew the weapon from far back. It was scarred, scratched, might have been twenty years old. It was probably used twice a year on a firing range. It would shoot with accuracy to thirty metres; a marksman would stop a man at thirty metres. He had not seen a Walther PPK for close to twenty years, when he had been at Osnabruck, when this weapon would have been new. He checked the safety catch. He slid the full magazine from the stock of the weapon. He did not expect that a bullet would be in the breech, but it was his training to check. There was the harsh metallic scrape in the room as he cocked it, aimed it down into his mattress and squeezed the trigger. He held the pistol loosely in his hand. He said, flat, 'Yes, I can handle firearms.'

She sat on her bed. 'I used to do guard duty, every twelve days, and we had firing practice. I was fine with automatic rifles, piece of cake. Pistols were different, bloody difficult. Did you ever shoot a man, Josh?'

He said, quiet, 'Once, shot at a kid, in Aden, not old enough to be a man.'

'Did you hit him, Josh?'

'I claimed a kill.'

He had thought that the handling of weapons was back in the dustbin time of his life thirty years ago. That day he was a young man and riding in a Saracen armoured personnel carrier from his billet to the Mansoura gaol where they did the interrogations. That day the Crown had put a firearm in his hand and given him licence to shoot to kill. He had seen the kid dart from the shadows of an alley, and he might have been about to throw an orange, or a stone, or an RG-4 grenade. Two machine guns hammering but their target was the sniper in the minaret of the mosque. He had seen the kid through the firing slit. He was crouched, sweating, in the cavern heat behind the armour plate. He had shot at the kid, twenty paces range, from the lumbering movement of the Saracen, and he had seen the kid go down. Might have ducked, might have been hit. He claimed the hit anyway. In the evening his warrant officer had bought him a can of lager, and the rest of the I Corps people had squirmed envy. Just another gollie kid dead and claimed, and they'd all got pissed up that night . . . And until she had put the pistol into his hand he had thought that shooting to kill was in his past.

'Did you feel bad about it?'

'I felt good.'

'When you shot at him, did you hate the kid?'

'It didn't seem important, didn't matter.'

She took off her coat and gave him the pouch with the handcuffs and the key. He was back down on his mattress and he pulled the blankets over him. She was throwing her clothes onto the floor. He put the pistol under his pillow. She stood beside his mattress, bare-skinned. She stood above him and he looked up at her thighs and her hair and the tuck of her waist and the hang of her breasts, lit and shadowed by the lamp bulb beside her bed.

Josh said, 'Afterwards begins when tomorrow is finished. Go to your own bed.'

She searched on the floor for her pyjamas. She switched off the light.

'Josh.'

'Yes.'

'I'll tell you the plan in the morning.'

'Do that,' he grunted.

'Josh . . .'

'Go to sleep.'

'Josh, do you hate him? Do you hate Dieter Krause?'

The hard shape of the pistol was sharp through the pillow and gouged at the flesh of his face.

He said, soft, 'The kid had bright eyes. I can see his eyes. He was only a target. It's what Dieter Krause is, only a target.'

The dawn came onto the old streets and old timbered buildings that the Hanseatic trading merchants had known half a millennium before, and onto the new streets and new concrete blocks that the Communists had planned a quarter of a century before, and onto the bright paintwork of the businesses of the newest gauleiter that sold Japanese cameras and cars and television sets. The dawn came to the city of Rostock.

It blew the mist and painted a grey pastel over the dock cranes that lined the Unterwarnow channel and the shipyards up the sea, way towards Warnemunde and the cold Baltic emptiness. The dustcarts roamed the streets, and those with work huddled in the carriages of the S-Bahn trains, drove iced-up cars and scurried on the bitter pavements.

The cold came across the flatlands from the Polish border and across the tossed sea from Finland and the Arctic waste. It was the same grey dawn that the city had known when the occupying armies had tramped through the old streets and through the new streets, that had followed the night raids of the bombers, that had come after the announcements of the closure of the shipyards and the docks.

The city was listless to suffering. The kids were pitched through their front doors to find their way to school. The city was indifferent to violence. The oldest went for comfort in prayer to the Marienkirche and the Nikolaikirche and the Petrikirche. The youngest went in search of work and hope. The newest culture of the city was self and survival. The people of the city, as the grey dawn came, lived lives dictated by the past. The past lived in Rostock.

On the radio, the announcer said that another low pressure trough approached fast from the north and the west, that after a dull dry morning there would be rain showers followed by sleet showers followed by persistent snow showers.

That day, unremarkable, ushered in by a chill grey dawn, the city and the flatlands around it, and the sand dunes and the

338

deep tossed waters of the Baltic, would again be a battlefield, and there would be few who would recognize the combat.

The radio announcer wished his listeners a happy and successful day.

18

He sat very still.

     He had drawn back the curtain and a dreary light seeped into the room. He sat on the hard chair and he held in his hands the Walther PPK pistol. He had stripped it and cleaned the working parts with the duster that he kept with his shoe-polish tins, and reassembled it. He held the pistol tight in his hands as if the feel of it would give him strength. He had taken each of the bullets from the magazine and then he had reloaded it because it was his experience that the breech mechanism of the Walther PPK could jam if the rounds were left too long in the magazine.

     He sat on the hard chair and looked down the length of her bed. He could see only the red autumn of her hair. She lay on her side and the bedclothes were close around her. Beside him was his grip bag and her rucksack, packed. It would be finished before tonight. After he had buffed his shoes, especial attention to the toe-caps, and after he had cleaned the working parts of the pistol and reassembled it, he had put the duster into the cloth sack, closed his grip bag and locked it. He had started, then, on her clothes. They had been scattered, haphazardly, on the rug and on the linoleum, and he had handled each item of her clothing with care as if it were precious. On the dressing table, neatly folded, were a sweater for her, a T-shirt with a Mickey Mouse motif, the bra she had worn the day before, the last of her clean knickers, the final pair of unused socks and the best of her jeans. He had left her wash-bag on top of her filled rucksack for when she woke, and her anorak. He had cleaned the room with his handkerchief, wiped each surface, sanitized the room. At the end of the morning, they would go, leave the room, and it would be as if they had never been there. His mattress and the pillow and blankets were already in the room next door, and the bed was made. He wore the good suit he had brought with him, a clean white shirt, the green tie and the polished black shoes. He had shaved with care so that he did not cut himself and had used a fresh blade. He had combed his hair and left an exact parting. It had seemed important to him. He sat and watched her and held the pistol. He did not understand how, at the dawn of the last day, she could sleep in such peace and calm . . . but he understood so little of her. He loved her, and knew nothing of her. The pistol was gripped in his hands, and the light of the last day settled on her hair.

'Aren't you going to shave today?'

He had come home late in the night. They had lain in the bed, separated. Sometimes, early in the morning, he went downstairs and brought her a cup of decaffeinated coffee, and sometimes a grapefruit juice, not that morning. He had dressed, he had shouted for Christina and told her it was time for her to be up. He was wearing the trousers he had used the day before, dirty and dried out from scrambling up the river's bank, and the same shirt.

He reached up and lifted down from the top of the wardrobe the suitcase, good leather, which they had bought him for his journey to England, and dumped it on the bed. He thought it necessary that he should pack it now. He did not know when the day would be finished, or how it would finish. She kicked her legs out of the bed.

She sneered, as she left the room, 'Are you going to take the appearance, on your last-chance day, of a refugee migrant?'

All the clothes that he packed in the suitcase were new, and the shoes. They had chosen everything that he packed, walked in the stores with him and told him what was suitable. Raub had cleared his old wardrobe and drawers, Goldstein had taken the old suits, shirts, ties and shoes to a charity shop on Doberaner Strasse. The schedule was in his mind – what he would wear when they came off the plane at Washington, what he would wear at the Pentagon and at the Agency and at the Rand Corporation. He packed the suitcase. He heard Christina's radio playing loud, and he heard her in the bathroom. Raub had shown him, with the superior grimace, how he should pack so that his new shirts were not creased in the case. He closed it and fastened the combination lock.

He took the Makarov pistol from the drawer beside the bed, put the spare magazine in his coat pocket, checked the safety, and armed the weapon so that the first bullet was in the breech. He carried his case down the stairs. He remembered, when he was in the hallway putting the case down by the street door, that he had not picked up the photograph of Eva and Christina in the silver-plate frame from beside the bed, but he did not go back up the stairs for it. He went into the living room.

The lightness of the robe and the sheer silk of the nightdress lay on her legs and on her breasts and on her hips. She had the old photograph album in her hands. There was little enough in the new house of their old life, but the album with the frayed and disintegrating cover was from the past. He walked behind her and rested his hands on her shoulders. She turned the pages of the album for him as if to taunt him ... Dieter Krause and the wife of Dieter Krause and Pyotr Rykov and the wife of Pyotr Rykov, in the kitchen of the commanding officer's house on the base with bottles on the table and the used plates, glasses raised. She turned the page. At the picnic site on the south side of the Malchiner See, the men in shorts and the women in swim costumes, and he did not have his arm around Irina Rykov and she had her arm around Pyotr Rykov, and they were laughing ... Another page. His fingers were hard on the bones of her shoulders ... Pyotr Rykov standing behind her, close, and she held the fishing rod, he guided her cast of the lure, and they were laughing ... His fingers ground at the bones of her shoulders, but she did not cry out ... Pyotr Rykov in his best dress uniform with his arm around Eva Krause, and they were laughing at the man who held the camera ... He held her so that he would hurt her. She looked up at him and she taunted him.

'He was your friend.'

He loosed his fingers from her shoulders. He scraped the photograph, Pyotr Rykov with his arm around Eva Krause, from the album, tore it into small pieces and dropped them on the new carpet.

'You boast that he was your best friend . . . and you betray him.'

He destroyed the photographs. He tore to tiny broken pieces the images of his wife and Pyotr Rykov as they laughed.

'You take him on the street. You are like a pimp with a whore. You sell him.'

What he had done was for her. Krause laid the album with the empty pages back on her lap. From the first day he had always told himself, he had gone to Cologne for her, and made his statement. He went to the wooden cabinet beside the television set for which he had the only key. He took the video-cassette, knelt and slotted it into the recorder. He switched on the recorder and the television. He would say to himself, and he would believe the lie, that everything he had done was for her.

He stood, again, behind her, his hands heavy on her shoulders, and watched, as the old clothes were ripped from her body, her kneeling in front of his friend, her loosening the belt and trousers of his best friend, her taking Pyotr Rykov in her mouth . . . She did not fight him. She did not turn away her head or close her eyes.

The week after he had shot dead Hans Becker in the small square near the church at Rerik, he had been called into the office of the *Generalleutnant* in the building on August-Bebel Strasse and he had been given the video-cassette. He left her watching the monochrome images of loving and laughter.

He told Christina that her mother was not well and should not be disturbed. He drove his daughter to school, and they talked in the car about the tennis match in the evening.

* * *

343

The station chief drove.

She had dressed herself that morning with particular consideration. Olive Harris had left in her bag, stowed in the locked boot of the station chief's car, her scarf and the hat that was a memento of her previous times in Moscow. They would have obscured her face and the profile of her head, would have hindered recognition of her features. It was her style to leave little to chance.

A light snow squall fell on the street. She peered between the wipers, recognizing what she had reconnoitred the night before. The shops were still shuttered but the first queues of the day had formed. The first market stalls were being set up and the vegetables laid out. She made the gesture for the station chief to slow. The shift duty of the watchers was changing. They should allow the new surveillance team time to settle and absorb. Two hundred metres down the straight street, blurred by the snow squall, was the old apartment block that she recognized where the target of consequence lived. They had not spoken that morning. He had been waiting in the hallway of the embassy for her. She had no need to speak to him. If the fool cared to sulk . . . They drove past the new surveillance car, three men, and the front passenger had a camera slung loose on a strap hanging from his neck. She pointed to where he should park ahead of the car, splitting the distance between the surveillance position and the street door of the apartment. The car would have a clear line of sight on them.

They waited. She had expected that a ministry car would be outside the street door. She had the photograph of him. He would be wearing uniform. She had no doubt that she would recognize him.

She checked again, for the third time, that her ticket and British Council diplomatic passport were in her bag. He gripped her arm, his face was cold and hostile, and he pointed. It annoyed Olive Harris that she had been looking in her bag and had needed to be alerted.

He was on the pavement. Quite small, but heavy in the Army greatcoat. His cap seemed to her too big for him and was low on his head. There was a woman with him, wrapped well against the cold: she carried two large shopping bags and a piece of paper. In between looking up and down the street for his driver, he checked the paper with her . . . God, how pathetic, a ranking colonel close to the greatest power in the Russian state was looking over his wife's shopping list, pitiful . . . He kissed her cheek, awkwardly because of the depth of the peak of his cap, and she walked away.

Olive Harris felt no emotion. She checked that her bag was fastened. She sensed, beside her, the contempt of the station chief, but when she was back in London she would bury him, deep, so he squealed. Colonel Pyotr Rykov was isolated, alone, on the pavement in front of the street door.

She walked from the car. When she crossed the road she made certain that she looked up the street towards the surveillance car. They should see her face clearly from it, and her greying hair that was gathered in a clip above the nape of her neck.

He looked once more at his watch. She was sufficiently close to him to see the annoyance on his face. It was always a precious moment, exciting to her, when the face of a target replaced a photograph's image.

She walked forward slowly, looked furtively behind her, then hurried towards him. He was trying to wave down a taxi but it swept past.

She reached him. Olive Harris stood in front of Colonel Pyotr Rykov. She spoke to him. She stood at the angle which guaranteed that the long lens in the surveillance car would have a sharp view of her face. She asked him about the weather and about the price of heating oil, and saw his bewilderment. She took his hand, and saw his confusion. For a moment she held his hand . . . She spun on her heel and did not look back at him. She was in full view of the long lens in the surveillance car. She dropped her head, and held her arm up and over her face, as if to shield it from any long lens. She swept open the door of the car.

The station chief sat stolid beside her and stared ahead. She slammed the door shut.

'Well, come on, get a move on. Don't hang about.'

He recited quietly, '*Nescio quis teneros oculus mihi fascinat agnos . . .*'

'What the hell's that?'

The station chief drove away. He said, 'I could see it in the mirror, the camera was up, they'd have banged off best part of a roll . . . It's Virgil, from his *Bucolics*, it's the evil eye that has the power to bewitch lambs. It's evil destroying innocence . . . The airport, Mrs Harris?'

She brushed the snow off her shoulders and off her hair. He had gone three blocks when he reached into his jacket pocket and took out a gummed-down envelope with no name and no address on it. He handed it to Olive Harris.

'It's my resignation letter. Please, be so good as to deliver it to the head man. Of course, I'll be expelled after this little charade, but I'd like my letter in first. I have to believe, Mrs Harris, that we're all answerable for our actions. One day. I hope, one day, you feel true shame. The airport, right?'

She put the envelope in her bag. She looked out at the streets of the Moscow morning. She wanted to see them, remember them, because she would never return.

He was unannounced.

A marine guard escorted him from the hall, up in the elevator, along the corridor, past another marine and through the bombproof door, to the rooms used by the Agency.

'What the hell's with you?'

'I've seen, Brad, what I call the evil eye. Sorry, it's not the time for riddles, sorry . . . I feel rather sick, and I'd quite like to hit someone. You have the resources, we do not, so I'm here with the begging bowl. The evil eye – sorry, again, sorry – has fallen on Rykov. We expect, don't ask me details, that Pyotr Rykov, in the next few hours, will be arrested.'

'You kidding? You know that? How the hell do you know that?'

'We'd like to know when it happens – your resources are so much better.'

'What's the charge?' the Agency man asked, distant. 'If Rykov is arrested, what's the charge?'

'Espionage.'

'Are you saying he's your man? Holy shit! That's not true. Not your man?'

'We'd like to be told, like your resources, to watch for it. I'll be out of here in a day or so, and we won't meet again. I don't wish to evade responsibility. Yes, we've done that.'

He could not look into the eye of the man who had been his colleague. He shuffled for the door. He would go home and he would tell his wife that the children's things should be packed, that they were going home, that the future was uncharted. He would tell his wife that he had not been able to look into the eye of an honourable man.

The marine, waiting outside the door, escorted him back to the embassy hallway.

'Where is he, Frau Krause?'

They had come to the house in the *Altstadt*. Raub had rung the bell beside the door. The house was luxury compared to the home he could afford in Cologne. Goldstein had banged with his fist on the door's panels. No answer, and they had gone to the window. She had been sitting in the chair facing the television. Raub had called through the window glass and Goldstein had rapped it, but she had not moved from the chair. The door had been unlocked. They had entered without invitation and gone into the living room.

'It is important, Frau Krause, that you tell us where is your husband.'

The light material of the robe had fallen away from her legs and sagged on her chest. She faced the television. Raub flushed. Goldstein stared at the clean shape of her legs under the silk smooth nightdress and the darkness at her groin and the hang of her breasts. She stared at the snowstorm television picture.

347

Goldstein thought a video had played on the television and reached its end.

Raub said, 'It is critical for your husband's future and your future, Frau Krause, that you tell us where we may find him.'

Her eyes were pale, without lustre. Her hands moved, clasping and unclasping. On the carpet was a photograph album with blank pages. She did not acknowledge the questions. Torn scraps of photographs were on the floor, ripped too small for Goldstein to recognize their content. She did not look at Raub. He went to the television and turned it off. She still stared at the screen.

Raub barked, 'It gives me no pleasure, Frau Krause . . . but, then, I have no pleasure in working with your husband. I despise your husband. I work with your husband because that is my duty . . . Now, Frau Krause, it gives me less pleasure to remind you that we own you. We own everything of you and your husband. Where is he?'

The blood ran in Raub's cheeks.

'You are nothing, Frau Krause, without us. You are back in the gutter with the other Stasi scum dirt without us. Without us he is driving taxis, sweeping streets, selling insurance on commission, guarding building sites at night. Where has he gone?'

With slow, deliberate movements she eased two rings from her fingers – Goldstein remembered paying for the rings that Krause had chosen – and they sparkled in the palm of her hand. She unhooked the clasp of the gold bracelet – Raub had paid for the bracelet when he had first come to debrief Krause in Rostock – and it folded into the palm of her hand. She fiddled with the fastening of the strap of her wristwatch – Raub and Goldstein had both been with her, on the orders of the senior official in Cologne, to buy the watch as a mark of his appreciation at the end of the first month of the debrief – and she let it fall into the palm of her hand.

'The last time, Frau Krause, or it goes badly for you, or your attitude is reported, or you go back where you belong in the gutter. Where is he?'

348

She threw the two rings and the bracelet and the wrist-watch with the gold strap on to the floor, near Raub's feet. She never looked at him. Goldstein knelt and pocketed them. He was close to the photograph scraps. He recognized the face. It would be magnified behind the jewel in Washington, as it had been behind the jewel at the barracks in England. He thought the life was gone from her eyes.

They went out into the street. Raub followed Goldstein. He left the street door wide open. They hurried against the wind towards the car.

'Heh, Ernst, if – hey, if – we get the shit bastard to America, what then?'

'Dumped.'

'Hey, Ernst, but he thinks he comes on the payroll, he thinks he's permanent.'

'Dumped, when he is no longer of use. Dumped.'

They had sat in the room all through the morning.

Earlier, when she had woken, the sound of the vacuum cleaner had seeped up the stairs, along their corridor and through their door.

She had gone to the bathroom, then dressed without shyness in front of him. She had talked, a long time back, through her plan and he had nodded his agreement. He was a man more comfortable when he was alone and he did not believe in talk that was not necessary. With their own silence, with their own thoughts, they killed the morning. They would talk afterwards, when it was finished. He had sat all morning with the pistol in his hand and she had sat on the bed and picked imagined dirt from under her fingernails.

Josh stood. He broke the silence.

'You ready?'

'Ready.'

He picked up his grip bag and reached for her rucksack. She shook her head. He carried his bag out of the room and she hitched her rucksack onto her shoulder. They went down the stairs. She murmured her anthem song. He thought she murmured its words to give herself strength. Afterwards, he would hug her. He would kiss her, if they were not on trolleys in the morgue . . .

The man who had the overcoat and the oil-slicked hair counted their money, note by note. He leered at them as he hung the two keys on the hooks behind him, and he wished them a good day.

They went out through the doors of the *pension* and the sleet storm hit them.

They hurried to the car.

Josh drove.

She was small, quiet, beside him and it was hard for him to believe in her strength. He felt a humility. Her strength was love. He had, as he drove, a sense of pride that she shared her love with him at the time when there was no going back. He would fight for that love, and shoot for it, and kill to deserve that love.

Peters smoked.

The smoke, acrid, from his cigarettes, carried on the wind gusts, was in Dieter Krause's nostrils.

The gutting shed was idle and the fleet, excepting WAR 79, was in the safe harbour. The storm winds came from the sea. The stalls were shuttered against the wind, which shook the plank sides and rattled the wood awnings. They could see the length of the quayside and there was one space for one boat. Peters looked for the young woman and the older man . . . Krause looked out to sea. The white sleet gathered on his coat, clung to his eyebrows and hung on the stubble bristle at the edges of his beard.

From behind, without warning, his shoulder was slapped, hard.

'Eh, Dieter, you look like you're dead.' Peters laughed. They were no longer the *Hauptman* and the *Feldwebel*. They were equals. They had shaken hands on a partnership. 'You look like you're fucking dead ... Wrong, Dieter, they should look, when they come, like they're fucking dead.'

Krause stared up the length of the quayside. He waited, the old Makarov pistol in his belt.

He had spoken to Mr Fleming.

Albert Perkins presented himself at the reception desk of police headquarters.

Fleming had told him, on Secure, tangled in the wires, sitting on his bed, of the Special Responsibility peg and the elevation to grade seven. He had walked, almost a jaunty step, from the hotel.

He was escorted to the control and communications area and saw them. They had been given a table to sit at across the area from the bank of screens and the radio input equipment.

'Morning, Doktor Raub, and good morning to you, Julius. A pleasure to see you again.'

Albert Perkins basked in a sense of mischief.

'Come to escort your vile man across the ocean, I see. But you are here and he is not, which tells me that you don't have control. Exasperating, yes, when control is lost?'

He walked towards them. He pulled up an additional chair and sat himself at their table.

'To us, you understand, this is a sideshow. Because you're way off the top table this is important to you – not to us. We already sit at the top table. Actually, I feel considerable sympathy for you, this being so important to you.'

The mischief gave Albert Perkins satisfaction.

He doubted that he would ever again in his professional life achieve such an opportunity for baiting. It would be his last throw for the recall of the good days, the old days, when the Service had stature over the BfV.

He sat comfortably in his chair and smiled kind warmth at the suppressed hostility of Raub and the undisguised dislike of Goldstein. The chance would not come again, and he milked it.

351

'Forgive me if I bore you but, because it is only a sideshow to us, I feel rather relaxed today. You don't seem to me, Doktor Raub, to be relaxed – nor you, Julius. You don't seem to be taking today in your stride. How many bodies is it now, scattered around the countryside? It's the messy old business of evidence, yes? If evidence is produced, if evidence of murder is laid before you, then there's no way out. Evidence, in open court, of your involvement with a murderer would be a nasty pill to swallow. So, we're just going to have to sit back and see what happens, what that young woman achieves, yes?'

It was, and Albert Perkins recognized and enjoyed it, a virtuoso performance in insult.

'I meant, sincerely, the sympathy. You are dogged by the past. You have made a great nation, a nation of engineers and technicians, musicians and artists, but it is never enough to turn away the past. You are never at ease because wretched little people like me will not allow you to forget the past. Always you are condemned to carry blame for the past. The past is the bad *Pfennig* in your pocket, Doktor Raub, and I expect young Julius doesn't spare you with blame for the past. So unfair . . . Right now, what I would really appreciate is a cup of coffee.'

The few fishermen had left their boats and gone to the shelter of the gutting shed. Peters tugged at his sleeve, pointed. The boats writhed at their moorings.

He looked across the channel, where Peters pointed.

He saw her first, and then Dieter Krause saw the man, who walked a half-dozen strides ahead of her. He saw the sharp flash of her hair.

They were on the far side of the haven channel and they went quickly, purposefully, heads tucked down, into the sleet and the snow. They walked away from the bridge that crossed the channel. He did not understand why they walked away from the bridge that would bring them to the fish quay, where the trawler would tie up. He was frozen cold in the wind on the quay, he could not think, he shivered. There was no fear in her.

She walked past the shops with their lights already bright, and past the houses with their summer balconies, and past the tourist boats that waited for the summer, towards the breakwater.

He stared. He did not understand. Peters kicked his shin and started to run. Dieter Krause followed him, past the gutting shed and the closed stalls and the moored trawlers and over the bridge that crossed the Alter Strom channel, but he did not understand . . .

The assistant deputy director met Olive Harris at the airport.

She came to him. With that passport she was the first of her flight through.

He thought, his first impression, that Olive Harris was quite radiant. He thought the triumph bathed her.

'Go well?'

'As I had planned it.'

'Just a bit of waiting, then.'

'They won't hang about. Should have it through tonight.'

'Well done, Olive. Not that it matters, but Albert's thing should be winding up this evening.'

'Not that it matters. Where's the car?'

They were by the lighthouse at the end of the breakwater. They were hunched down and the lighthouse gave a small protection from the weight of the wind gusts.

They could see out to the open sea to the east.

The big car ferry had come out, gaining speed as it cleared the Neuer Strom, from the channel at the back of the gutting shed and the fishing boats' quay. Its lowering shape had disappeared into the blur of the merged sleet and snow. The trawler would come, rolling and staggering, from the east and they peered into the grey-white of the mist and searched for it.

When they looked down the length of the breakwater, turned away from the watch on the open water, they could see the two men. There was more snow in the sleet and the light of the afternoon was slipping. Through the sleet and the snowflakes, they could see Krause with one man beside him. Krause and the man blocked the end of the breakwater, stood where it met the beach.

Around them the waves hit the rocks on which the lighthouse was built. Close to them was the rope, jerking and slackening, holding the small, open boat. Because the breakwater curved in a shallow arc, Krause and the man could not have seen it. A family had come onto the breakwater, and a small boy had shrieked excitement when the spray had deluged him, and a little girl had clung to her father's legs.

A bulk carrier had rolled out to sea from the Neuer Strom, and was gone.

Josh held the gun down between his legs and his hands were chilled and sea-soaked.

There was the rumble behind them, echoing in the steel-plated shaft of the lighthouse, of the automatic power. The light flashed. Its brilliance above them brought the night around them. The light rotated, spilled in a corridor, across the white wave heads, the grey-green sea, the tired, sheened concrete of the breakwater, the rocks . . . Josh saw it . . . The light caught the white and red paint of its hull. He saw the outline of the trawler. It seemed to be tossed up and then to wallow down. It came from the mist cloud that settled on the sea away to the east. The light, again, speared onto it, captured it, and discarded it. The trawler seemed to Josh so fragile, beating through the snow, the swell . . . The trawler was coming home, coming for the quayside . . .

The grotesque shadow of Tracy was thrown by the light-house beam over the water and the waves. She was down on the rocks, wrestling with the knot that tied the rope to the rail post. The trawler veered towards them. The rise of a wave obscured it, it rose again and the spray cloud fell above it. He saw the gulls. Incredible, in the wind the gulls held station with the trawler. He was mesmerized. When the trawler's bow was pitched up, Josh saw the black paint on white of the boat's identification. There was a man, stooped low behind the wheelhouse,

354

and he threw scraps into the air. The gulls broke station and dived for them. She had loosed the knot of the rope and took the strain of the boat. He felt such fear.

'Get in,' she hissed.

'Christ . . .' Josh went down the rocks and his feet slid from under him, his body scraping over the weed. He looked back. She hung onto the rope. 'Good luck.'

She shouted, 'A man told me you have to earn luck – start bloody earning it!'

His shoes had a grip. The water came over them but the rock was firm. He launched himself. He fell into the boat. It ducked down under the impact of his weight and water slopped on his face. He scrabbled up onto his knees. He saw her. She jumped. She was beside him. She had a paddle in her hand. She pushed the small open boat away from the rocks, and they were first lifted up and then thrown down. The lighthouse beam snatched, a moment, the colour of her hair. She paddled the boat out towards the trawler.

Krause and Peters, together, the same moment, understood. They sprinted forward . . . They had the length of the break-water to run . . . The little boat was bucking, weaving, in the waves, on course to intercept the trawler.

They ran, panted and heaved. Krause, frozen hands, buffeted by the wind, held the Makarov two-fisted, aimed, fired. He could not see the fall of the bullets, into the sea, among the wheeling gulls.

The drive of the snow was into his face, the force of the wind against his body. He fired until the magazine was exhausted, until the boat was lost against the hull of the trawler.

She threw the rope to the man who fed the gulls. The small open boat clattered against the wood planks of the trawler. Josh reached up and caught at the low rail. It took his weight and his feet kicked at air below him. He dragged himself over and fell onto the slithering mess of fish carcasses. She came after him.

The man who held the rope had an old, beaten face, and there was another face, as old and wizened, that peered from the door of the wheelhouse. At the wheel was a younger man. The gulls screamed above him. Josh stood, fell, stood again. He took the pistol from his belt.

He shouted, against the gull cries, against the engine drive, against the wind whistle in the wires.

'Which is Muller? Which is Willi Muller?'

A thin, aged arm, a gaunt, scarred finger, pointed to the wheelhouse.

'Willi Muller from Rerik?'

The head, lined, unshaven and weathered, nodded.

Josh yelled, 'He stays, you go.'

They went without argument, over the side of the trawler and down into the boat. They went as old men would who have known the authority of command, as old soldiers would have gone, too wise as survivors to confront a gun. They were cast off.

Josh was in the wheelhouse.

He was a tall young man with blond tangled hair and a lean face. He held the wheel easily. Josh had the pistol close to his head.

'Turn her round, bring her back out.'

The wheel was swung. Josh saw, through the water spray running down the wheelhouse window, their boat moving away from them. The two men had control of it and paddled it easily, and he saw Krause on the breakwater and the man with him. The young man stared straight ahead and the trawler pitched back towards the open sea. Tracy stood behind Josh.

'You are Willi Muller?'

'Yes.'

'You worked your father's boat in Rerik? And, in November of nineteen eighty-eight you took your father's boat out for the Stasi?'

'Yes.'

'You lifted a man from the Salzhaff? You saw him killed ashore?'

356

'Yes.'

'It was from your boat the body of the man was thrown back, weighted, into the Salzhaff?'

She beat the questions at him, savage, and his voice quavered the answers, afraid.

'Yes.'

'I want your evidence of murder. I'm taking you home.'

The shoulders of the young man shook. The colour of his face had gone. They went towards the west, beyond the small shelter of the breakwater, towards the last glimmer of the day's light.

They watched the trawler going. They watched it head for the reddening ribbon of the dusk.

'They are going to Rerik,' Peters said. 'They have been out four days, they will have little fuel left but they would have enough fuel to reach Rerik. We should meet them at Rerik.'

They walked back along the length of the breakwater.

19

'We are taking you home.'

The young man, Willi Muller, moved, dull-eyed, in the small space of the wheelhouse. She dominated him, was at his shoulder as he checked the fuel gauge where the needle was close to the red line.

'You have not dared to go home.'

She was close behind him when he squinted down at the compass, where the needle rocked with the pitch motion of the trawler, and when he took the wheel from Josh and set the course to the west.

'You let the fear, as a coward would, cripple you.'

She was above him when he lifted the hatch from the engine viewing box and peered with a torch down at the throbbed movement of the pistons.

'Without me, what I give you, you will always cringe, a kicked dog, with the fear.'

She was with him when he walked on the swaying stern deck, among the fish carcasses, to satisfy himself that the nets were stowed, the ropes coiled, and that the bilge pumps were operating.

'Don't think I apologize for coming into your life. You are a witness to murder. Fight me and you are an accessory to murder. But you are a coward, you won't fight me.'

She followed him, tracked him. Josh thought she overwhelmed him.

'The hiding time is over. You can't run any more. You have to have the guts now – about time – to stand. You are going home.'

He read her and he thought her vicious. He could not see in

her the woman who had come to his mattress, who had loved him, who had given and shared warmth, who had kissed his mouth so sweetly. She followed the young man because she did not care to give him room to think, she tracked him so that he was never free of her. There had been a savagery in her voice and she had set herself the task to obliterate the resistance of the young man. She surprised Josh, the professional: he had thought it would be him that played hard, and she would play soft. He had reckoned she would be close to the young man and seep a gentle voice into his ear and seduce the story from him. She would, he thought, have massaged the fear from him and coaxed out the story. He wished she had . . .

He held the wheel, he kept the compass course, and the engine droned in his ears. A small reflex action, but he took a hand from the wheel and straightened the tie knot at his collar, and then, again, both hands, he gripped the wheel. He thought back, a long time back, when he had bullied a man to his death. In the woodman's hut, in the heat, the mosquitoes at his face, his hands, his ankles, he had done it himself before he was his own man.

The sea swell cascaded onto the side of the trawler as they went west into the grey dark seascape beyond the window. The line of the land was a black ribbon and against the ribbon was the white of waves breaking on a sand beach. In the black ribbon, moving slowly and keeping pace with them, difficult to see but always present, were the car's lights.

Willi Muller said, 'I think the storm is blown out.'

'Don't give me shit about the storm.'

'I think we will have a good evening, very soon. When there is a bad time in the *Ostsee*, it is difficult but it does not last.'

'They will hunt you, without us, find you, without us, kill you, without us.'

'The storm will soon, very soon, be finished.'

'You have to chuck the fear, stop playing the coward, you have to go home.'

'I think the storm will be finished when we reach Rerik.'

He had, Josh thought, a fine, open young face. They had taken his life and tossed it, as if into the wind and the dark of the swell, hacked into a stranger's life.

Josh called behind him, aping her, the same bullying, cold voice, 'You take his statement, Tracy. You write it in German. You make him sign every page. Don't let him wriggle, Tracy, get it out of him.'

The car's lights were now bright pinpricks in the black ribbon of the land.

Krause was tight and silent, Peters was calm and talked.

'I could have gone – you know that, Dieter – I could have gone as Hoffmann went or as Siehl went, or Fischer. I had time to think when I was at Warnemunde, too much time, when I waited for him to return. Who would be interested in me, I thought, a simple *Feldwebel* who merely obeyed orders? I could have gone, but I stayed, because you made an advantage to me, you offered an opportunity. Don't believe, Dieter, that I stayed from affection or obligation. I stayed because, when I thought, you provided an opportunity. I stayed because, if I kept you out of the Moabit gaol, I made an advantage for myself.'

They were on the narrow coast road between Elmenhorst and Nienhagen, going west from Warnemunde and Rostock. Across the beach, and the darkness of the sea, were the fore and aft navigation lights of the trawler. They crawled, minimal speed, to track the trawler.

'I cannot save him. I know what he is to you and to the Army, but I cannot save him and you cannot.'

The photographs were scattered on the minister's desk in front of him, and in front of the GRU General who leaned his weight on the desk. They were the photographs taken that morning, in the street outside the apartment, and the photographs from the file of Mrs Olive Harris. They were, beyond dispute, photographs of the same woman. She talked in the street with Pyotr Rykov, she was listed in the file as deputy head,

Russia Desk. He looked from the photographs and into the face of the General.

The General murmured in the minister's ear, 'I have tried, I have tried with all the assets at my disposal, to protect him. I cannot counter this and I do not wish to, and nor should you. Without the photographs I would not have believed it, with the photographs I cannot argue against it. He has destroyed himself.'

The minister knew that Colonel Pyotr Rykov had been turned away from the doors of the ministry that morning and told that his ID was no longer valid. He knew that Colonel Pyotr Rykov had twice, that afternoon, telephoned the direct number in the outer office, and had been refused by the secretariat his shouted demand to speak with his minister. The Colonel of the intelligence service, who had couriered the photographs to Defence, stood, grave-faced, behind them, at the back of the room. The minister stacked them carefully, then closed the file on the British intelligence officer, Mrs Olive Harris.

'So be it.' He condemned his man.

They might take him on the street, throw him into a car. They might go to the apartment and knock down the door with sledgehammers and drag him away down the stairs. He would miss, desperately, the man on whom he leaned, but could not save him.

The minister handed the photographs and the file to the waiting Colonel.

The wind had slackened. Josh stood at the wheel. The trawler churned on, the bow dipped and rose, and spray broke across the glass of the windows.

They were on the floor of the wheelhouse. She sat with her back against the sink cupboard. He was crouched down across the wheelhouse from her.

Josh listened. Tracy wrote on her pad.

Willi Muller said, 'I was at the boat with my father. We were working on it in the evening because there was a problem with the transmission in the engine, and my father said it was necessary to make the repair then. We heard the shooting at the base across the water of the Salzhaff. It was just after the planes had flown over and then there were flares fired there. The base was a closed place to the people of Rerik, we had no contact with the Soviet military there. Because we had no contact we did not know, my father and I, at first, whether this was an exercise or something different. We continued to work at the engine. The shooting seemed to move across the base, from the *Ostsee* shore, through the middle of the base, through the buildings, and then to the shore of the Salzhaff. They were using the red tracers and the flares. I said to my father that I was frightened, that we should go home, but my father was definite that the repair to the engine must be finished. We worked on. We finished the repair. Two cars came. They were Stasi, from Rostock. The superior told my father that he needed the boat, it was an order. He had a beard, cut narrow on his cheeks and cut close on his chin. They said my father should take them out on the Salzhaff, but my father, and it was a lie, said that his back was hurt, that I would take them. I could have said what my father did not dare to, that the engine was not repaired, but I did not.'

She finished the page. She passed the notepad to him and he signed his name on the page, a fast, nervous scrawl.

He pushed himself up and he studied the course Josh held, took the wheel from him, and made an adjustment to the west. He went out of the wheelhouse door, stood on the open pitching deck, and looked towards the black ribbon of land.

They were on the road between Nienhagen and Heiligendamm. There were stretches of road that veered inland, where they had to strain to see the navigation lights on the sea. On those stretches, Krause drove faster, and when he came back to the sight of the sea and the slow progress of the lights he stopped and waited until the lights of the trawler were level with the car.

'We had, Dieter, a society that was disciplined. We did not have organizations, we did not have opportunities. We lived in the tedium of discipline, and the best we hoped for was a summer vacation at some stinking campsite in Bulgaria or Romania – it was the ultimate of our aspiration. You, I, could not buy advantage. The discipline suffocated us. The Wall came down, the *wessis* came to look at us as if we were some theme-park amusement, and they laughed at our discipline. Do I complain, Dieter? I can buy a tax inspector, I can buy an official in the department that issues import-export licences, I can buy a policeman, a politician, a priest. I can behave like a Sicilian, the discipline is gone. I can buy a former *Hauptman* and the purchase will bring me the protection of the Office for the Protection of the Constitution. You do not hear me complain, Dieter, do you?'

The old Makarov pistol lay on his lap as he drove. It was dulled from the years it had lain buried in the plastic bag inside the rubbish bin. He had checked the pistol and believed he would use it that night.

Tracy shouted at him, waved for him, through the door. He looked again at the lights on the shoreline and ducked back inside the wheelhouse.

'When we were out on the Salzhaff, the flares were fired over a part of the water that was half-way between the Wustrow shore and the Rerik shore. At first I could not see the target, but the man with the beard directed me to that place. There was a contact with the base on the radio and they told the base that the firing should finish. We had a small spotlight on the boat. They told me to switch it on, and then they directed it onto the water. It was when I saw him. He was trying to swim away from the light, but he could not swim strongly. They held the light on him. We went close to him and circled him. I was ordered to go very slowly. He went under, but he must have had the desire to live, because he came again to the surface. They pulled him onto the boat and I could see that he was hit.

363

There was a wound in his upper body and there was a second wound in his leg. He lay on the deck of the boat and he was very still except that he breathed hard. I remember that the men, there were five men from the Stasi, were all excited, and they kicked him on the deck and called him a spy and a saboteur, but I did not hear him say any words. He lay on the deck and he did not defend himself when they kicked him. I was fifteen years old, I was a patrol leader in the FDJ, I believed everything that I was taught at school about the hostile espionage units of the Americans and the British and the Fascist government in Bonn, and I hoped he would die. I hoped he would die, not because he was a spy or a saboteur, but so he would not feel any more the kicking. I brought the boat back to the pier at Rerik. The man with the beard held a pistol close against my face and he told me that I had seen nothing and that I knew nothing. They pulled him from the boat and onto the pier. He was very weak and it was difficult for him to walk and they dragged him along the pier towards where their cars were. I saw his face then, as they dragged him past me on the pier. He was tired, he was weak, he was in pain but, and I remember his face clearly, he did not drop his head. I remember that . . . They took him towards the cars . . .'

She passed the notepad to him. Its page was covered with her neat close-packed writing. He held her pen and his hand shook. Her eyes never left him. He signed.

Josh did not think, himself, he could have played so cruel cold with the young man. There was no sympathy, no charity, and he tried to hope that it was merely the strategy she had chosen. She took the page back, and the pen.

Josh held the wheel steady on the course. The swell had dropped. He thought him more frightened of the animal cruelty, the bullying, of Tracy, than of the car that tracked them along the shoreline. He could not fault the strategy.

The young man stood beside him and flicked his finger against the dial of the fuel gauge and always it bounced on the red line.

364

He went out onto the deck. A rope lashed a fuel can to the port side. He slipped among the fish carcasses. He united the rope, lifted the engine hatch and funnelled the remaining fuel down into the tank.

Josh thought the young man could have denied that he had the necessary fuel, and he thought his courage was supreme. Without the fuel they would not reach Rerik. She had given him, cruel and bullying, the courage to go home.

They were on the road between Heiligendamm and Kuhlungs-born. There was flat swamp ground between the road and the beach, few trees, the cloud had lifted and the wind had dropped. Away across the sea, the lights of the trawler were sharp, bright. The voice beside him dripped on.

'With the ending of the discipline, with the coming of the *wessis*, so many more opportunities have arrived. I am not talking, Dieter, about running cigarettes out of the East, as the Vietnamese do, and I am not talking about shipping a few cars into the East, as the Poles do, or the trading in immigration from Romania, or keeping whores on the streets, as the Turks do. I am talking, Dieter, about the big opportunities that can be taken from our partnership. Weapons, Dieter. The East floats on weapons. Not rifles, Dieter, not pistols. Weapons that can be bought cheap and sold expensive. Missiles, air-to-air and air-to-ground and ship-to-ship. Heavy mortars. Artillery pieces. Armoured vehicles. If you have dollars they will clear out an armoury for you, you can buy anything. You can go south, to Libya, Iraq, Syria, Somalia, Algeria. You can name your price. Chemical, nuclear, anything can be bought in the East and anything can be sold. But, Dieter, I do not want eyes watching me. I wish to be protected. I think we have a good partnership.'

Beside him, Peters belched.

The suitcase was at the front door of the house on the *Alt-markt*, packed. She was on the boat with the red and green navigation lights, and she had the power to tip the suitcase empty.

*   *   *

365

Across the seascape was the land, with the car's headlights, always with them. But ahead, on the closing horizon, was the concentration of lights.

She was taking him home to his past. His body shook.

She reached for him. She caught the waterproof coat he wore and rammed his body back against the planks of the wheelhouse, and again. He gasped.

Willi Muller said, 'He was near to the cars. I remember it very clearly because the clock was striking the hour. It was the moment after the last strike of the clock on the tower of the Sankt Johanniskirche that he broke from them. It was ten o'clock and he broke from them and ran from them. They did not know Rerik. Perhaps, if he had not been wounded, in the darkness he might have escaped from them, perhaps . . . I followed then as they searched. He tried to get into the house of Doktor Brandt, the school-teacher, and into the home of Doktor Gerber, the refuse administrator at the *Rathaus*. He was going towards the church. He tried the last time at the house of Doktor Schwarz, the engineer of the railway, he threw a stone at the window, and Doktor Schwarz came to his bedroom window and looked out at him, but did not open his door to him. Could you not have found one of them, all educated men, and taken a good statement? Why did you come for me? I thought – I remember what I thought – how was it that a spy or a saboteur had come so far from our frontier without support? Did he have no colleagues with him? He reached a small square between apartments near to the church. I cannot say whether he was attempting to reach the church. I came behind, I saw him in the square. He was pulling with his fingers on the ground as if to drag himself away, but the strength had gone from him. I watched. They ran forward with their torches and their guns to where the one who had come the fastest stood over him. I saw it . . .'

Josh held the wheel. The page was passed and signed. It was as if he had been there, as she had been there before she had run. The young man stood beside him and took an old piece of

366

bread from the cupboard under the sink, and chewed on it, and stared out at the lights where his home would be, and the lights of the car that were always with them.

A tractor passed them, pulling a trailerload of beet and turnip. He saw, in the tractor's lights, that Peters' head was back against his seat, that his eyes were closed, that he was at peace. The tractor went by them. They were close to the sea, and he saw the change in the course of the trawler, swinging to the south west and coming for Rerik.

'You do understand – of course, you understand, Dieter – the limitations of partnership. There are partners in any commercial organization, but there is a senior partner and a junior partner. It is the same as before. There was the rank of *Hauptman* and there was the rank of *Feldwebel*. That is not difficult to understand. I reckon a seventy–thirty split, only of course when I have the need of protection, no split when I do not need the protection, but you will do well. Seventy–thirty is good for you. I think it will work satisfactorily.'

Krause stopped the car and walked to the beach. The sand was soft under his feet and the grass fronds blew against his legs. He could see, when he squinted and strained, the shape of the man in the wheelhouse. He wondered if Eva had helped Christina pack her bag, or whether Eva was in the kitchen, ironing the short white dress that Christina would wear. He felt love for them and the sand blew from the beach onto his face, into his eyes, and the tears flowed on his cheeks. He held the Makarov in his hand. He did not try to wipe the tears and the sand from his beard and from the stubble growth. He looked out beyond the beach, beyond the fall of the waves on the tideline, towards the trawler. He turned quickly and walked back to the car.

He opened Peters' door.

Peters' eyes were closed. He smiled. 'Did you need to piss, Dieter? Are you frightened? Myself, I killed an Armenian and a businessman from Stuttgart, and, I tell you in truth, I did not feel the need to piss.'

367

He placed the barrel tip of the Makarov pistol under Peters' chin, caught the shoulder of his coat and jerked him out of the seat. He took him, fast, across the road and onto the beach. He could not see the shock spread on Peters' face, or the wide eyes. He heard the babble voice.

'Eh, fuck, what's the game? Eh, cunt, what you doing? Eh, doesn't have to be seventy-thirty. Can talk. Try sixty–forty. You're shit, Krause. Can't wipe your arse on your own. Eh, Dieter, you misunderstood. Dieter, we can deal. Dieter, Dieter, please. We can go fifty–fifty, no problem . . . I stayed with you, no other fucker did. Dieter, please . . .'

He dragged Peters across the soft loose sand and across the hard wet sand to the sea. The chill of the water was at his waist and in his groin. Peters did not fight when he tripped him. He held Peters' head under the flow of the waves and felt his legs thrash against his own and he did not weaken his grip.

The body floated face down. The tide had turned. Dieter Krause stood on the beach and squeezed the water from his trousers, emptied the water from his shoes. The body drifted on the tide away from the beach. He went back to the car. The last business was ahead of him. Afterwards, Dieter Krause would go to America and he would stand in front of the audiences at the Pentagon and Langley and the Rand Corporation, and hear the sweet song of their applause, and behind him, huge, would be the magnified photograph of his best friend.

He was not believed.

The photographs were held in front of Pyotr Rykov's face, and the light shone, fierce, into his eyes. The small blood stream dribbled from his mouth. His tie was taken and his belt of polished leather and the laces of his shoes.

He tried to ward away the panic.

'I have never seen her before. I have never met her before, never heard her name before. She came to me on the street, said something about the weather, something idiotic, and was gone. I have never had contact, in any form, with foreign espionage

368

agents. I am a patriot, I am a true son of the great Mother Russia. I could not countenance the betrayal of my country. I do not know why she approached me.'

The panic, cold sweat on his back and in the folds of his stomach, was because he knew he was not believed.

'I fucked the Krause woman, yes, but that does not make me a spy. She was a good fuck, and her husband was an arsehole, and I gave her what he did not give her, but that does not make me a traitor.'

They did not believe him.

They took him from the interrogation room to the top of the flight of stairs that led down to the cell block. He was pushed and fell, bouncing on the cold concrete of the steps. Stunned, frightened, he did not know why the plot had been made against him. The cell door slammed shut.

Josh felt so old, so tired, so flattened. It was what they had come to hear, it was why he had made his commitment. He listened.

'He was turned over from his stomach to his back. The one who I think had caught him turned him over with his boot. The one with the beard stood over, stood above his feet. I watched it and I cannot forget it. They shone the torches into his face and they laughed. The superior one, the others called him by the title of *Hauptman*, looked down on him as if he were something to be played with. I was fifteen years old. All I knew of death at that time was what we did to the fish on the deck of my father's boat. There was no warning of it, he kicked up into the balls of the man with the beard, and the man screamed out. Not fear, but pain. I saw it. He was doubled up, swearing. He aimed his gun down at the young man. I wanted to look away and I could not. One of them put his shoe on the throat of the young man. There was one shot. A jeep came and the lights found me where I stood. A gun was aimed at me and I had lost the chance to run. There was a Soviet officer in the jeep, and there was a big argument. The Soviet officer said they should not have shot him, should have kept him for interrogation. They threw his body

369

into the back of the jeep, and they made me hang on the tail of it. We went back to the pier. Three lobster pots, with heavy stones, were tied to the body and I took the trawler back out into the middle of the Salzhaff and the body was put over the side. When we came back to the pier they made me show them where I lived. My father and my mother and my sister were in my house. The superior one, the bearded one, the *Hauptman*, said that my father would lose his boat if I ever spoke of what I had seen and what I had known. My father told him that he would send me away. My father did not fight for me, nor my mother, nor my sister. I was sent away to be with a man my father called a friend. I was sent out. I have never lost the shame.'

It was the statement of murder. He signed the evidence statement of murder in cold blood. She had the notepad. She pulled open her coat and she hitched up her sweater and T-shirt. He saw the pale skin of her stomach as she slid the notepad under the waist of her jeans, against her skin. The triumph blazed on her face.

Josh pointed up to the radio that was nailed above the cooking stove. He said, softly, 'Who hears the radio, Willi?'

The mumbled answer. 'Rescue, they hear it, the marine police, Customs.'

'Can you hook into Rostock police?'

'For a year we have been able to – they ask us to radio them if we have suspicion of narcotics' smuggling from the sea. We can reach the police at Rostock.'

'Do it, please – and, Willi, thank you.'

The young man stood. He moved as if the life were beaten from him. He went to the radio, switched it on and turned the frequency dial. There was the howl and the crackle and the static. Just old, just tired, just flattened, Mantle took the microphone.

'For Police Control at Rostock – this is Warnemunde-based trawler, identification call sign whisky alpha roger, figures zero seven nine. Are you hearing me, Police Control at Rostock? This is Warnemunde-based trawler, whisky alpha roger zero seven nine . . . Are you receiving?'

* * *

Albert Perkins leaned far back in his chair.

'You people, you won't mind me saying it, you try too hard ... All this business about getting to top table, sitting down with us and the Agency, you're trying to run before you've learned to walk. Don't take offence, nothing personal.'

His feet were on the table and the soles of his shoes faced Ernst Raub. In short bursts he had, through the late afternoon and the early evening, maintained the mischief. A technician at the control desk, sharp movement, hunched forward and pressed the headphones closer to his skull.

'Really, you'd have been better advised – and I speak in friendship – to give this sort of business to the professionals. I mean, passing over all the Iranian stuff for the Saarbrucker Strasse address was ridiculous. We benefited hugely, but where did the trading get you? You're out of your depth, and it shows.'

The technician, hand above his head, waved for his supervisor and passed him a second pair of headphones.

Raub broke. 'Yesterday, for twenty years, because it was necessary, we obeyed your patronizing instructions. Today, for twenty years, because it is advantageous, we tolerate your arrogant postures. Tomorrow, the future, we will ignore your—'

The supervisor threw a switch on the console. The voice boomed out, from the loudspeakers, across the control room.

'I am Joshua Mantle, British national. I am with Tracy Barnes, British national, and Willi Muller, German national. I am bringing the trawler, call sign whisky alpha roger zero seven nine, to Rerik harbour. Arrival at Rerik is estimated at twenty-one thirty hours. I require police assistance at that location for the arrest of Dieter Krause – kilo roger alpha uniform sugar echo -- former *Hauptman* in the Rostock offices of the Staatssicherheitsdienst, for the murder on the twenty-first of November nineteen eighty-eight of Hans Becker, formerly resident at Saarbrucker Strasse, Berlin.'

'Oh dear.' Albert Perkins swung his feet off the table. 'A shame, seems tomorrow may be too late.'

The voice, distorted, had faded but came again.

'The charge against Dieter Krause will be supported by the written and signed statement of Willi Muller, trawler deck-hand, a witness to the murder. Over. Out.'

The voice died, was gone. The static screamed through the control room until the supervisor flicked the switch and killed it.

'Bad luck, an open transmission, so many people would have heard that. How embarrassing. Can't shove that under the carpet, can't ignore evidence . . .' Albert Perkins stood. He smiled abject sympathy. 'I'd much appreciate accompanying you, hitching a ride down there.'

He drove on the road between Kagsdorf and Rerik. He could no longer see the trawler. There were high trees beside the road. It did not seem important to Dieter Krause that he could not see the lights of the trawler. He knew its destination.

'Where is he?'

'If he were able to be here, he would be.'

'Stupid selfish bastard. He knows I never play at my best when he doesn't watch me – where is he?'

Eva Krause hit her daughter across the face. She picked up the bag and the tennis racquets and threw them out onto the pavement. She dragged her daughter into the street and locked the door behind her. She wore the old clothes, taken from the one suitcase she had kept. The skirt was long and plain. The shoes were imitation leather and would let in water if it rained. The blouse was a size too small and buttoned modestly to the neck, the coat was thin and dull. She was the FDGB organizer, the woman who sat in the meetings at the Neptun shipyard and dreamed of the apartment in the Toitenwinkel district, the wife of the *Hauptman* who worked from the second floor of the building on August-Bebel Strasse. She tossed the bag and the racquets onto the back seat of her car, and pushed her daughter down into the front seat. The skirt, the shoes, the blouse, the coat had been the best clothes she had owned. She had seen them that day. She always wore her best clothes when she went to the apartment in the Toitenwinkel district. She had seen them on the video, scattered on the floor, that day, beside the bed.

She drove. Her daughter was sullen quiet beside her.

Josh gave the wheel to Willi Muller. He felt faint. The wind had gone and the sea had calmed. He thought he might be sick and went out onto the deck. They were coming past the peninsula that masked the lights of Rerik. The stink of the fish carcasses was around him. He reached for the spotlight, aimed it at the peninsula shore, and called to Willi to give him the power. The beam burst out across the water and onto the shoreline of the peninsula. The light found the beach where the boy would have landed, and came to the squat concrete bunker where the radar had been housed, which had been his target. The trawler edged along the coast. Near to the end, where it was little more than a spit of sand and dune grass, the beam of the spotlight settled on a low tree, broken and dead, and a big bird flapped mutely away beyond the range of the cone of light. Tracy was beside him, and put her hand on his arm.

Josh said bleakly, 'You're never free of ghosts, Tracy, they cling to you and they suck you dry. You should never walk with ghosts.'

She laughed. 'That's right bullshit, Josh.'

They rounded the headland. The lights of Rerik were ahead of them, across the Salzhaff. He called out to Willi Muller that he should switch off the lights on the trawler, all the lights, and the night darkness fell on them . . . He thought the boy had died for nothing.

'We did it, Josh, we did it together. God, I've been a proper little bitch to you, don't think I deserved you. You've been fantastic, wonderful.' She lifted her head, she kissed his cheek. He stared out towards the lights and the piers of Rerik. 'You all right, Josh?'

He pushed her hand off his arm.

He took the Walther pistol from his pocket, checked it, armed it.

373

He called through the wheelhouse door: 'Willi – the officer, the *Hauptman*, will be on the pier. He will kill to preserve your silence. I am in the front. She is behind me, you are behind her. We stand in front of you, Willi.'

They came in fast towards the piers.

He stood where the longest one rose from the shingle and weed of the beach. Josh saw him. There was a light close to the road, behind him, that outlined Dieter Krause. Josh saw that he stood motionless at the far end of the longest pier.

There was no fear, no elation.

Josh, by the wheelhouse door, said, 'Bring her in gently, Willi. Bring her home like you would have brought in your father's boat.'

Josh went forward and took the rope from the deck. They were close to the pier. Smaller fishing boats groaned and swayed in the dropping wind at the shorter, narrower piers.

Perkins saw him. He was the idiot who had gone into man-trap country. Perkins felt, a short moment, the sense of wonderment that was always there – every field officer said it – when an agent, an idiot, came through, stepped out from the man-trap country. Always that stark short moment of almost disbelief when an idiot came out of the darkness of danger, emerged from behind the fences and walls and minefields and wire.

The trawler boat nudged the pier.

Josh jumped and lashed the rope to a post. Krause stood so still and Josh saw that he held the pistol at the seam of his trouser-leg. The engine cut. There was a silence, then the clatter on the planks of the pier as Tracy came behind him and then the young man. They faced each other. Josh looked down the length of the pier.

'You should know, Doktor Krause, that we came to find evidence and we have found it. We came for an eye-witness to murder and we have found him. You may have thought, Doktor Krause, that time washes away guilt. It does not.'

He started down the pier, towards the beach, the road and the lights in the windows of the houses, towards Dieter Krause. He went steadily, his own pace, slow steps. Krause clasped the pistol in his fist and slowly raised it. Josh walked forward.

The aim of the pistol locked.

'Don't, Doktor Krause, because it is over. For you, it is finished.'

Josh was a dozen paces from Krause. It was the moment he realized that Krause would shoot. Krause would have seen the slow, sad smile pass on Josh's face, as if he didn't care, as if he was too wearied and beaten to care. The finger, Josh saw it, moved on the trigger, tightened . . .

The light burst from behind Dieter Krause.

The big spotlamp beam trapped Krause, threw his shadow forward to Josh's feet, blinded Josh. The brilliant white light was in Josh's face. He could see nothing. He heard the clatter as the Makarov pistol landed on the planks of the pier.

The shadow forms moved warily forward, huge and grotesque, and Dieter Krause raised his hands high above his head.

Raub hissed, 'Run, Krause, run for the darkness.'

He heard, ahead of them, his head half turned.

Goldstein said, 'If he runs, Raub, he runs over my dead body.'

Raub spat, 'It was history. Too long ago. The past, the past is gone.'

Goldstein said, 'There is no honoured history without justice. Tell a Jew that the past is gone, tell a German Jew that the past can be forgotten. He will go over my dead body.'

Krause held his hands above his head.

Perkins chuckled, 'Well said, Julius, sensibly spoken.'

Josh stumbled, so tired and drained. He asked Tracy for the statement, and she took the notepad from under her coat, her sweater and her T-shirt. It was warm from her skin. The senior policeman held Krause's arm and the handcuffs twisted his wrists into the small of his back. Josh led Willi Muller to the senior policeman and he identified the witness, and he gave him the notepad and showed him the written pages and the signature on each page.

'You will go to your home, Willi?'

The young man shrugged.

'You should go to your home.'

'For the night, perhaps. My boat is my home.'

'Because you did not run from the principle of justice, Willi, I am proud to have known you.'

The voice blared, nasal, behind him. 'Mantle, come here, Mantle.'

At the edge of the light Perkins was with Tracy, holding her hand as an uncle would have done. Perkins grinned. 'I was just telling Miss Barnes . . . Hey, come on, Mantle, don't look so damned miserable . . . Just telling Miss Barnes what a quite fantastic young woman she was. If a quarter of the snot-nosed pillock recruits coming into Vauxhall Bridge Cross had her resourcefulness our Service would be the envy of all. With a bit of help from you, you old hack, and I'm being generous, she has achieved our policy aims, bagged, packaged, wrapped . . . An asset is destroyed, a public trial beckons, recriminations commence. Poor old Dr Raub, my German colleague, still walks in the time warp, thought they could slide the guilt out of sight, the modern equivalent of putting him on a boat to Paraguay. No chance. Mantle, she is fantastic. All for love. Marvellous thing, love, so they tell me. My suggestion, get back to Rostock and buy our Tracy an impressively expensive dinner. Hey, Mantle, your old pencil hold any lead still?'

Tracy took his arm. Perkins walked away and his laughter rang in the night. The cars were revving. Josh saw Krause pushed down, awkward, into the back of a car. He loosed her hand. He walked back down the pier.

The trawler rolled gently beside him. He took the Walther pistol from his waist and threw it high, far, into the water of the

Salzhaff. The cars pulled away, made a convoy. He stared at the distant treeline on the shore of the base, the home of ghosts. He stood on the pier along which the boy, wounded, had been dragged. She called again. There was one car left in the road and she ran to it. It was all history, it was all gone. It was the past, it was finished. It was all for love.

He fed the message.

Status: SECRET.
Information flash – ex Moscow staffer to Russia Room.
Status of info. unconfirmed, but from 'reliable source'.

RYKOV, Pyotr Nikolai, army rank Col., current position P/A to Min. of Def., arrested 18.00 local by Fed. Int. Service, and held on espionage/treason charge. Believed SIS involvement – requested we onpass to VBX, London. It's dirty, I have a bad smell on this one.

Understand RYKOV subject of German junket at Pentagon, Langley, Rand Corp. – suggest you cancel and leave bottles corked and keep *sauerkraut* in the refrigerator.

My assessment: If RYKOV arrested by FIS, then he is dead in the water, irrelevant.

Bestest, Brad.
End.

The message was sent.

She had taken her bag and rummaged in it. She had changed in the lavatories. While she had changed, Josh had picked from his suit trouser legs, meticulously, the last of the fish scales.

She came through the swinging door into the hotel's lobby. She wore her cleanest T-shirt, from the Peenemunde day, and the least crumpled of her old jeans. There was dark lipstick at her mouth and shadow colouring at her eyes, and the copper-gold of her hair was spiked up. She took his hand. She was the woman a man could love for the rest of his life, all of his life. She

377

squeezed his hand, laughed. 'Come on, Josh, a bloody great meal and a bloody great bottle, it's what we're owed.'

She led him towards the restaurant door, behind which the band played.

20

Josh took out his wallet. She looked at him and a vague, confused frown came to her forehead.

He put the wallet on the table, picked up the menu card. He checked what she had had, what he had had, and what the wine cost. He made the calculations.

There was nothing chic, nothing smart about the restaurant. There were a few couples and a few lone men, and tables had been put together by the far windows for a bus party of affluent pensioners. He had toyed with his food and barely touched the plate of vegetables. She had eaten everything put before her. He had sipped at the wine, she had drunk most of the bottle. A three-piece band played, tired and without enthusiasm, and in front of them was a deserted polished-wood dance floor square.

Josh stood. He was looking for the head waiter.

'Will you settle up?'

'Why?'

'I'm going.'

'Going where?'

'I'm going to sort the car.'

'What's the matter with the car?'

The police had brought them back, taken them on through Rostock to Warnemunde. They had sat in the back seat and not spoken to the two gloomy-faced, silent men. She had held his hand, he had allowed her to and she had snuggled close to him in the darkness. They had been dropped without comment beside their car, but they had felt the hostility. The police had driven away and Tracy had given their tail-lights a finger. The hire car was now in the hotel forecourt, next to the tourist coach from Bremen, and his grip bag and her rucksack were on the back seat.

'What needs doing to the car?'

'Will you settle up, please? I'll be about half an hour.'

'What the hell, Josh? What needs doing with the car?'

He peeled banknotes from his wallet, counted them, dropped them in front of her.

'I'll come back for you.'

The confusion had passed, replaced by annoyance. 'I want to dance.'

'Then dance.'

'Dance with you.'

'You'll have to dance on your own,' Josh said.

He walked towards the restaurant's push doors. He heard the scrape of her chair behind him. He felt old, he was so tired. He turned at the door and looked back. His banknotes were abandoned on the table beside the bucket with the upturned bottle. She stood, the urchin waif, in the centre of the dance floor, alone. Quiet conversations, from the tables, murmured around her. Her head bobbed with the rhythm of the band's music. She used her hands, gestured, for the tempo of the music to be stepped. She danced. He saw the grace and the gentle movement of her.

Josh went out of the hotel.

It was a crisp, chilled night. There was a small moon and many stars. He went past the tourist coach and the hire car, towards the taxi rank down Lange Strasse. He walked slowly and without spirit. He felt a bleak sadness. He had no hatred. If he had hated it would have been easier. He walked to the head of the taxi queue and dropped down onto the back seat of the lead taxi.

'Could you take me, please, to the middle of the *Sudstadt*? Thank you.'

The driver turned, nodded, started the taxi. Josh remembered him, had seen him on the breakwater. He rode in a yellow Mercedes taxi with a white flash down the length of it, and he remembered the vehicle coming bumping on the track from the farm at Starkow. There had been light on his face from the street lamp when the driver had turned. Ahead were the dull-lit tower blocks of the *Sudstadt*. The driver spoke, a faraway voice, and his head never twisted from the road ahead. 'Did you win?'

Josh said, 'I don't know if anybody won.'

'Did you take Doktor Krause?'

'He is arrested, he is accused of murder.'

'You found evidence?'

'We took the statement of Willi Muller. He was the boy who sailed the trawler out onto the Salzhaff. He was an eye-witness to murder.'

'Then you won?'

Josh said, 'I have to believe there's something worth winning. I don't know if I've won, will win.'

'You came from England. You turned over the ground and exposed what was buried. The past was buried, a long time ago was covered. Why was it important to turn over the ground?'

Josh said, heavy, 'It was a matter of principle. I have to believe it is always worth winning on a matter of principle.'

'I don't understand you.'

'I don't ask you to.'

The taxi stopped. The tower blocks climbed gaunt above them. Josh paid the driver. He walked away from the taxi and into the shadows of the buildings. He stood among the lines of cars parked under the height of the buildings.

The point was lost.

Her daughter looked up, into the stand, at the empty seat.

Eva Krause wore the old clothes that could not be taken from her. She wore no jewellery, because they could take the necklaces and bracelets and rings from her.

She felt the finger on her back. She turned. Two policemen were standing in the row of seats behind her. The one who had

381

touched her back beckoned for her to follow. She lifted up her old coat and her old bag. Their faces were unforgiving. She edged along the row, away from the empty seats. She knew that her husband had been taken from her.

She climbed the aisle steps to where the policemen waited for her. She turned to look a last time at the floodlit court below. The opponent waited to serve. Christina was staring up at the empty seats. Her gaze raked the stand. Her eyes found her mother at the top of the aisle steps, and the policemen. Quite deliberately, she put her foot on the face of the racquet, ripped away the strings and walked towards the chair and her bag.

Eva Krause followed the policemen. She did not know of anything more that could be taken from her.

He heard her voice, singing.

He stood outside the restaurant's curtained glass door. The band played and she sang. He heard the soft beauty of her voice.

He pushed open the door and went inside. All of them, from the coach party and the couples and the lone businessmen, were rising to their feet and pushing back their chairs, standing, applauding. It was her moment. She seemed so small and so young, and she curtsied low to her audience. A man, out of the coach party from Bremen, snatched a red carnation bloom from the vase on his table and hurried to her. The clapping boomed around Josh. She kissed the man's cheek. She shook the hands of each of the members of the band, she had captivated them, she waved to the stamping, cheering audience. She skipped towards Josh, between the tables, the child with happiness found. He held the door for her. A last time, she waved. It closed behind her. The applause rippled, muffled, through the door. She reached for his hand but he walked ahead of her.

He walked into the night, into the cold.

She hung back. She would have gone to the coach, to where the hire car was parked. He called her. He went on and into the deep darkness at the extremity of the forecourt. She ran to him.

'What the hell's this?'

She would have seen the shadow outline of the Trabant, two-door, small and angled, the little car from the past.

Josh said, 'Always wanted to drive one – won't have the chance again.'

Astonished. 'You nicked it?'

'Borrowed it – let's keep some politeness. I went down to the *Sudstadt*, thought I'd find one there.'

'You actually stole it – you, Josh, honest and upright Josh! Bloody hell!'

'Took a loan of it.'

She giggled. 'It'll shake your bum off.'

Josh said, 'It's what you drove back to Berlin that night, after . . . you drove back Hans Becker's parents' Trabant, after . . . It seemed right. It seemed right for the end.'

He didn't think she heard him. Her giggle tinkled close to him. She took his hand, kissed his fingers. The applause would still be in her ears. She put the stem of the carnation bloom in her mouth and dragged open the passenger door. His grip bag and her rucksack were behind her. He reached forward, fiddled the wiring and the engine coughed to life. The smell of the fuel engulfed them.

She patted his arm. Her head was back. The laughter shrieked. 'Josh, for God's sake, good old Josh, car thief, joyrider! Josh, where did you learn to wire up a car? Christ, where *did* you learn how to get into a bloody locked car?'

'Has to be an upside from working with toe-rags, have to learn something from them . . .'

'I don't believe it.'

'I work with kids who have honours degrees in borrowing cars, something has to rub off. Just sit back, enjoy the ride.'

It was the pride of the past. The seat was harder than any he had known, the engine noisier. The body of the Trabant shook. He looked at his watch, four minutes before midnight. He drove away from the hotel. It was easiest to go on August-Bebel Strasse. The great building was dark. From August-Bebel Strasse it was a straight run to the *Rostock Sud* intersection for the autobahn. He

383

had filled the tank. It would be a good drive to Berlin, he told her, smooth, and she grinned and tossed her carnation bloom behind her.

He had permitted young Rogers to make the ciphered communication with Vauxhall Bridge Cross and told him his story. He had also rummaged in his case and his wallet for a mess of receipts and bills, and requested, told, the ancient history graduate, first class, to knock his expenses into shape.

Albert Perkins sat in the Savignyplatz café, a half-bottle of champagne in front of him. A rare pleasure gripped him. Any of the others, his rank, at Vauxhall Bridge Cross would have been fighting to get on the secure telephone to make a personalized report on the outcome of a successful mission. He thought that the report going back second hand set him on a pedestal of achievement. He sipped the champagne. Even Helen had seemed pleased – rarer than August snow – that he was awarded a new peg, no detail over the phone, and more pleased at the new annual increment. He would be home in the morning, for the weekend, to fiddle about in the garden and in time for the game at Craven Cottage and the pint with Basil. His world, he believed, was set in an aurora of success.

Past midnight. The café was full. At the bar, haggard, disputing, laughing, no champagne but beer drunk from the neck, were four of the foreign press corps. They had an office block in Savignyplatz. He had used the café, in the old days, to be close to the foreign journalists, assuming the identity of a businessman too stupid to understand the secret life pulse of divided Berlin. He had enjoyed their amused banter when he had met them in the old days – they knew nothing. When he had finished the champagne, he would insinuate himself into the group of journalists and they would boast to the ignorant stranger of their contacts and their knowledge – they would still know nothing.

She was, in his opinion, a quite remarkable young woman. She would have achieved her objective, his opinion, without the trailing Mantle. Too good, his opinion, to disappear. When he was back in Vauxhall Bridge Cross, after the weekend, he would sing her praises. There would be a place for her, should be a place for her, in the Service. Such raw courage, such focused ability, a crime to lose it . . . Albert Perkins sat in the café and mused on the brilliance of Tracy Barnes, and was at contented peace.

'Double whammy,' Violet shrieked from the door.

The cassette player – and the Rolling Stones tape – was loaned from Mid-east Desk. The party gang were from German Desk and Russia Desk. The drink – gin, vodka, Scotch, wine, beer – was out of the ADD's store cupboard. They had all stayed on, bugger the outside commitments, bugger the husbands and wives and children, bugger the last trains out of Waterloo and Victoria and the last tubes to Fulham and Hampstead and the last buses. The party rolled on, wild . . . always a party when the Service triumphed. Sweating girls and panting men, yelling and howling, dancing and cavorting, celebrating . . .

Violet shrieked from the door and waved the sheet of paper. 'For Christ's sake – it's a double whammy!'

Fleming went to her, and Olive Harris. The ADD and the Russia Desk chief and the girl clerks, and the new men and the old men, all gazed at Violet. They had enough cause, already, to celebrate. They had Pyotr Rykov, destroyed. They had the signal from Langley, the lecture on Rykov was cancelled. Fleming read the paper Violet held, and she yelled into his ear.

Fleming clapped his hands. 'What Violet says, it's a double whammy. Old Albert's come up rose-scented . . . Albert's done his end . . . Rykov's in the chokey, and Krause is in the chokey . . . double win bloody whammy . . . Poor old Hun chaps, lost their pride and glory, put back in their bloody place. Evidence against Krause that'll go to open court, embarrassment by the wheel-barrow load for the Cologne chaps, we're weeping for them. Whammy, whammy, whammy.'

The music thrashed on, out through the open windows of Fleming's room, out across the deep flowing water of the

Thames. In the high room in the monolith building, the dancing resumed, frantic, flailing arms and swinging hips. Fleming had the sheet of paper that Violet had brought and folded shapes with it. Mrs Olive Harris pirouetted, shoes kicked off and the upper buttons of her blouse unfastened, in front of a librarian from Archive. The ADD clutched the new girl on Russia Desk, and the chief of Russia Desk kissed, lip to lip, the new married lady from Violet's pool, and the Scotch was poured like it was beer, and the beer was drunk like it was water, and the older woman from Russia Desk massaged the groin, as they danced, of the new-appointed graduate on German Desk . . . The party rolled on, and to hell with the morning, and to hell with who woke in whose bed, and to hell with it all.

North of the Neuruppin intersection, the lights and the sirens had come past them. She had been asleep, and he had not woken her. Three cars with lights and sirens . . . He had seen Krause, in the back of the middle car, flanked by two others. The lights and the sirens had swept past them.

South of the Neuruppin intersection, he had eased off the maximum speed of the Trabant, dropped down from the hundred kilometres per hour that the old car could reach, eased down on the dial. He had made the calculation on the time he could reach Berlin, how long it would take on an autobahn empty of traffic at night. With the calculation made he had no more need to push the Trabant to its limit. She slept well. Remarkable that she could sleep inside the shuddering noise of the car. He slowed, cruised in the inside lane. He reached into his pocket.

'Tracy . . .'

She stirred.

'I've something for you, Tracy. Don't wake.'

She smiled. Her eyes were closed. The heater blew foul hot air over her.

'A present, Tracy . . . Just something . . .'

She murmured, 'Gone soft, old Josh gone sentimental?'

386

'Don't open your eyes . . . Your wrist, Tracy.'

Languid, half awake and half asleep, beside him, she raised her arm and her other hand pulled up the arm of her coat. Her wrist was bare. Her eyes were closed.

'Don't bloody crash – you're a proper old sweetheart, Josh, you're a soft old bugger.'

The smile was at her mouth . . . With a sudden, brutal movement, he snapped the handcuff ring shut on her wrist, jerked down the link chain and closed the second ring on the iron support bar of her seat.

The anger exploded. 'What the fuck . . .'

Josh said, simple, sad, 'You lied.'

'Get the fucking thing off.'

She tried to kick him and, with her free hand, to reach him and claw at his face. He drove on. He took the kicks on his legs. He held the wheel hard. He tried to save his face from her nail slashes.

'You lied to me, and in the lies was your mistake.'

She was convulsed. Her fingers went for his eyes, and he held her off him, and he knew that the anger storm would subside. She was twisted in the seat but her shoulder was pulled down by the handcuff on her wrist, locked tight to the metal bar under the seat.

'You live a lie and you will always make a mistake. The mistake may come from stress, may be from conceit, but the mistake always catches out the lie.'

She aimed a last kick at him, pure venom, and she would have wrenched her shoulder, in pain.

'Right, you clever bloody bastard, what was the lie?'

The face that had been lovely to him was ugly and twisted in anger.

'You said, Tracy, your story, that you saw Hans Becker brought ashore and break free and run. You were too frightened to intervene but there wasn't anything, anyway, you could have done. You said that you ran out of time, that the clock killed you, you had to break away . . . I thought, believing the lie, it was the most tragic moment, for you, that I could imagine. You left him, hunted and wounded and alone, because you had to be back in Berlin to get through the checkpoint by midnight. The day visa pass ended at midnight. You went through before midnight, you say. On the trawler, Willi Muller said the clock at the Rerik church was striking ten o'clock as Hans Becker was brought onto the pier. Your lie, Tracy, you drove a Trabant to Berlin, dropped it, went through the checkpoint before midnight . . . Tracy, it can't be done . . .'

She flopped in her seat. She stared ahead.

'You left at ten, truth. You drove to Berlin, truth. You went through the checkpoint before midnight, lie. I think you came to the checkpoint in the Wall late. I think you pleaded with the guards to let you through. You were distraught, weeping. The guards would have called for an officer . . . You should not have been in Rerik, you were in direct contravention of Colonel Kirby's orders, you stood to be drummed out of I Corps, which was your life, you were traumatized by what you had seen. Of course the officer was not going to let you through. Of course the officer would have wondered why a student was hysterical at being late for the checkpoint. A strip search, Tracy? You would have carried ID. Where was the ID? In your bra, in your pants, in a condom inside you? Doesn't matter where. They found your ID, or you gave it them. The East Germans had a procedure. The procedure was the call to the Soviet Military Mission . . .'

He drove slowly, spoke slowly. She sat, so still, so small, beside him.

'You are isolated. You are beyond help. In a holding cell. You are very young and very frightened. The East Germans may have roughed you, may have shouted at you, threatened you, but not the Soviet military intelligence officer. He would have been GRU, highly sophisticated, and very kind. Sophisticated enough to see that you were literally desperate to get through the checkpoint before dawn, and kind enough to let you get through the checkpoint . . .'

388

Each time he paused, Josh waited for the denial. She said nothing.

'They would have filmed you and taped you. They had evidence of you. They would have driven, Tracy, nails through the palms of your hands and into the wood. You belonged to them, Tracy. Before dawn, the intelligence officer would have put the stamp on your visa, and he would have told you that you should not be frightened of the future, and you would have wept your gratitude to him, but the nails had been hammered through your hands, Tracy . . . The last best chance you had was that morning. When Colonel Kirby came to work, nine o'clock, you could have told him then, there, what had happened, made the confessional. You did not. And each day afterwards it would have been harder. Each month afterwards, it would have been worse. Each year afterwards, it would have been impossible . . . You opted, chose, to live the lie . . .'

They were past the Wittstock intersection. The signs were for Berlin *Mitte*. Nothing was denied. She seemed not to hear him, seemed not to care to listen to him.

'The moment the chance died, would have been buried, was two years, three, four years afterwards. The intelligence officer would have been a patient man, and the people to whom he passed the file. A new world order had come. I doubt you thought the nails were out of your hands. The GRU continued to exist, continued to probe. Did you believe, Tracy, in the new world order, that you were free of them? A phone call, a letter, a chance meeting that wasn't chance, after two or three or four years . . . Of course, little Corporal Barnes doesn't seek promotion, doesn't seek a transfer. She stays at Templer Barracks. She is an asset, she is a talent spotter, she goes to her office each morning an hour before her officers come and for that hour she can read any file she wants to. At first she is coerced but that ends. Later she is overwhelmed by the arrogance of her superiority. The arrogance is the secret that she holds. The last instruction was for the hacking down of Dieter Krause . . . I, stupid and infatuated, was a used bonus. That's what hurts,

Tracy, wounds me, that I was just used. You did very well. The only mistake was the clock at Rerik church, and that, for you, was bad luck ... It was a lie. The lie that I believed was that it was all for love.'

He drove on. They were coming towards Berlin from the north. The first lorries of the day were on the road. Nothing denied and nothing explained.

'You were Knautschke. You were the hippopotamus in the mud. I thought, Tracy – I thought, Knautschke – that you came from the mud in your own time. They called you, Tracy – the keepers called for Knautschke. You came from the mud, Knautschke, when they called for you. They were, they are, your keepers ...'

The lights of the oncoming traffic sparkled indistinct in his eyes. The tears welled.

Tracy turned to him. 'What choice, Josh, do you think I had?'

'It starts with a small lie, but the lie has a life of its own. The small lie grows, overwhelms. They all say they had no choice, all the traitors.'

'That's a speech, Josh. What'll they do to me?'

'Hate you for embarrassing them, lock you up, throw the key away.'

'What good will that do?'

'About as much good as locking up Dieter Krause.'

'We had a life.'

'We have no life, the lie killed the life.'

'Don't believe you, don't believe old Josh. Josh loved Knautschke. Josh wants to cuddle and fuck with Knautschke. Josh wants to make babies. Josh is old, wants to be cared for, Josh doesn't want to be old alone. Old Josh wants love. The love, Josh, wasn't a lie.'

'The love, Tracy, is dead.'

'You are such a daft, bloody innocent.'

She reached, difficult for her, behind him. She took the carnation bloom. She put the stem in her mouth. She picked the petals from the flower and they fell on her lap.

* * *

390

Dieter Krause sat on the bed in the cell. The Moabit gaol, around him, was waking. He had not slept. They had told him, before they had locked the door on him, that in the morning a lawyer would be appointed to represent him that day.

They had taken him all the way to the cell door, and Raub had grimly shaken his hand, and Goldstein had grinned and said he should claim he was merely obeying orders. Dieter Krause, as the gaol woke around him, waited for the coming of a lawyer.

He saw the face of the boy on the frozen dirt of the ground.

He stood above the boy and held the pistol loosely.

He was kicked by the boy, doubled up, in pain.

He fired the pistol, involuntary, in the shock of the pain.

He had the rank of *Hauptman*, he had little experience of firearms. It was several years since he had practised with a fire-arm. Firearms, of course, were issued to officers of that seniority but they had no call to use them.

He had not realized that the safety was off on the pistol.

He had shot the boy in a regrettable accident. If he had not kicked, made the sudden pain, the boy would not have been shot.

He agonized over the tragedy of the death of the boy. He was, himself, a parent. There were witnesses who could be approached, persuaded, to tell the truth of that night: Klaus Hoffmann, a respected dealer in property. It was an accident: Josef Siehl, a trusted security guard. He carried no guilt: Ulf Fischer, a much praised orator at funerals . . . It was a tragic accident of history, the past.

Dieter Krause, with the noise of the waking Moabit gaol with him, planned what he would say when the lawyer came.

The policeman on the pavement of the Unter den Linden gazed in astonishment.

A Trabant car parked at the kerb, driven by a man in a good suit who had the bearing of a military officer, and produced from it was a young woman in handcuffs . . .

Josh led her by the arm through the door, ignored the late protest shout that parking in front of the embassy was forbidden. The doors swung shut behind him, behind her.

It was dawn. The first glimpse of the sun would be up behind the television tower on Alexanderplatz, and behind the hill of Prenzlauer Allee. God alone knew where they found them, the older men, stout, comfortable, who were the night-duty security officers in the service of the embassies . . . No sunshine, at the beginning or the middle or the end of the day, reached the fortress cubbyhole of strengthened plate glass in which the security man sat. He had a mug of steaming tea in front of him and a plate of thin-cut toast, and he was listening to the radio music that came from Britain on the satellite.

She looked at Josh, as if to test him.

The security man, crumbs at his mouth, studied him. Then he looked past Josh and saw the young woman, the handcuffs, and the frown spread on his forehead. He drank from the mug and wiped away the crumbs.

Josh said, 'My name is Joshua Mantle, I am a solicitor's clerk from Slough in the United Kingdom. I have brought with me a prisoner, Miss Tracy Barnes, of the Army's Intelligence Corps. The charge against her is espionage – Section 1 of the Official Secrets Act. There's a man called Perkins, Albert Perkins, in Berlin. You should find him. He'll be flying out today, but you should reach him before he leaves. From this moment, Miss Barnes is in your custody, you are responsible . . . Oh, please, I'd like some paper to write my arrest statement. Thank you.'

He was given the paper and a hard chair at a low table, and he started to write. He wrote the story of a killing at Rerik in the night darkness, and the chiming of a clock high on a church tower.

The security man was on the phone, and she leaned forward on the wood shelf in front of him. The security man smiled back at her grinning face and she lifted her handcuffed wrists and took a slice of his toast, as a squirrel would have stolen from a bird table.

A young man came through the inner security door, earnest-faced, shirt-sleeved, with his collar open and his tie loosened and the tiredness in his eyes, and asked why he had been called.

The security man talked in a low voice into the ear of the young man. The head was shaken in disbelief. She finished the toast on the security man's plate and she took his mug and drank his tea, and she smiled sweetly at the young man.

He wrote the story of Hans Becker who had died alone, in courage, for nothing. He folded the paper. He put the pen back in his pocket, and felt for the knot of his tie.

He walked to the desk, uncertain, weak in the legs.

'My name's Rogers, I work with Mr Perkins. What in heaven's name is all this about?'

Josh gave him the folded sheets of paper.

She had the light of the mischief in her eyes that he had seen and known and loved. She challenged.

'You can tear it up, Josh, tear it into small pieces. If you don't tear it up, Josh, there is no afterwards. If you don't tear it up into small pieces you'll live to be old and alone . . .'

Josh rocked.

'. . . old and alone, Josh. You can't sleep with principles, can't love with them, can't find happiness. With your principles, you'll be old and alone.'

Rogers, young face curled in anger, snapped, 'What good does this do? It's out of history, it's cobwebbed. No-one will want to know.'

Josh said, stark, 'It is evidence. Just because it is not convenient, evidence cannot be ignored. Because it is embarrassing, evidence cannot be shelved. I promise you, and pass my promise to Mr Perkins, that if I see the signs of compromise I will bring down on his head the accusation of cover-up. The whole circus will land on his head. Someone once said to me, "They can't buck the process of law, they can't block evidence," and I believed it. My regards to Mr Perkins . . .'

He looked at her, into the small, enigmatic, masked face. He did not know her. He reached into his pocket and gave the handcuffs' key to the young man.

He walked out of the embassy and onto the Unter den Linden.

Four policemen were gathered round the Trabant and they were laughing at it and poking with their shoes at the bodywork. Josh took his grip bag from the back seat. He was told he could not leave the car parked there.

He said, 'It belongs to the young lady. She always drives a Trabant. That was her mistake. Better ask her to move it.'

He carried his grip bag away and the spring sunshine was warm on his back.

'Yes, of course you were right to call me immediately. I'll be with you in half an hour, a call to make and a shower and a shit and a shave. Thank you, Rogers . . . What time is it? Must have been tired, don't usually sleep in. I'll see you . . .'

Albert Perkins put down the telephone.

He rubbed the deep sleep from his eyes. He shook, stretched.

He crawled from his bed and pulled back the curtains. Sunshine spilled into the room. He sat among the confusion of the sheets, pillows and blankets. Her face was in his mind. He saw every line on it, and the thrust of her chin, the brightness of her eyes and the colour of her hair. He sat, long moments, with his head in his hands.

He snapped upright. No requirement to go secure and unravel the bloody wires. He dialled.

It was more than the cleaning lady's life was worth, to pick up a ringing telephone.

She should have been out of there thirty-five minutes before the telephone started to ring in Mr Fleming's room. She had most of the drink stains off the carpet, but the red-wine spatter on the wall behind Mr Fleming's desk was her headache. The phone rang insistently. It did not surprise the cleaning lady that Mr Fleming was not yet at his desk, an erratic gentleman, but it astonished her that Violet was late. Her plastic bin bag, on the marked carpet beside the desk, was half filled with the plastic cups and the emptied bottles. She had scrubbed the wall with kitchen tissue, might have to be repainted, and the carpet might have to be replaced. She gathered up her mop, her bucket and dragged her vacuum cleaner to the door.

She left the telephone ringing, and locked the door after her.

It was a great city in the heartbeat centre of Europe.

With his grip bag, Josh Mantle was a snail in the path of a caterpillar track.

The cranes and the bulldozers and the earth movers were fitted with the caterpillar tracks that broke the shell of the snail and buried the past and destroyed the history.

He was alone on the street. He was the pygmy figure among the racing, hurrying thousands, who made the pace of the new city. He walked with the ghosts, the few, who were rejected by the thousands. The ghosts held him tight below the towering cranes, beside the bulldozers and the earth movers that wiped out the faces of the ghosts. The short length of the Wall, preserved for tourists, so fragile where there had been permanence and death, mocked him. If he had stood, if he had put down his grip bag, if he had held out his arms, if he had snatched at the thousands who hurried past him and went about their business and lived their new lives, if he had shouted his truth, would any have cared for the forgotten past and the forgotten history? It was the conceit of Josh Mantle that he, alone, knew the debt value of the past and the history.

He was at the checkpoint.

The new buildings and the new cranes obscured the warmth of the sun from the street. The block where the holding cell had been, where the interrogating officer had come, where she had begged and wept for her freedom, was eradicated. A watchtower was still standing. They would have followed her, with their binoculars, when the bar had been raised, when she had crossed the no man's killing zone, would have focused on her from the squat little watch-tower when she had gone into the shadow dawn with the lie and the deal. The dust of the building site choked in his throat. A freedom belonged to him . . .

The car came from behind him, blasted its horn.

Perkins's face poked through the open window.

'If I'd known you'd be here, I'd have bloody wiped you off the road. Never could keep out of business that wasn't yours, could you, Mantle? Always had to interfere, hadn't you? You think we wanted her – wanted her paraded in open court? But the little man, little shit-faced man, has to bleed his bloody principles over us. I hope you're proud. I hope you rot.'

He shouted, 'I was, I am, it's precious to me, my own man.'

The window surged up.

She was alone in the back of the car. Afterwards, for ever, he would swear to himself that she smiled at him.

The car pulled away, went fast through the old checkpoint where there was no barrier, no guns, no past that survived, and he watched the car until he could see no longer the copper-gold of her hair above the seat, until she was gone from the mud pool and the rippled water was still.

'The best practitioner currently working in the UK . . . quite simply the most intelligent and accomplished'
Independent

'In a class of his own'
The Times

'One of the modern masters of the craft'
Daily Mail

'A master of the thriller set on the murky edges of modern war'

i

'A stylish writer'
Observer

'One of the most venerable names of the thriller genre'
Independent

'Richly imagined novels that bristle with authenticity'
Washington Post

'The dabbest hand in the industry . . . a master'
City AM

'The pace leaves you breathless . . . he is the master of the thriller genre'
Edinburgh Evening News

Turn the page to find out more about the thrillers that have earned Gerald Seymour the title of 'best thriller writer in the world today' (*Telegraph*) . . .

THE OUTSIDERS

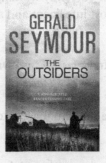

'Once again demonstrating his ability to probe the moral murki-
ness of the spy trade and create an absorbingly diverse ensemble,
Seymour crafts a sophisticated, reader-teasing tale.'
The Sunday Times

MI5 officer Winnie Monks has never forgotten the death of a young
agent on her team at the hands of a former Russian Army Major-
turned-gangster. Ten years later, she hears the Major is travelling to a
Spanish villa and she asks permission to send in a surveillance unit.

There is an empty property next door, perfect to spy from –
and as a base for Winnie's darker, less official plans.

But this villa isn't deserted: the owners have invited a young
British couple to 'house sit' while they are away.

Jonno and Posie think they are embarking on a carefree holiday in the sun.
But, when the Secret Service arrives in paradise, *everything* changes.

'Those [Seymour] sends off into dangerous territory are, in fact,
his readers. With each book, we enter a dangerous universe, and
are totally involved with utterly plausible characters, faced with
moral choices that are rarely straightforward.'
Independent

HODDER

A DENIABLE DEATH

AN EPIC NOVEL OF HIGH COURAGE AND LOW CUNNING, OF LIFE AND DEATH IN THE MORAL MAZE OF THE POST-9/11 WORLD.

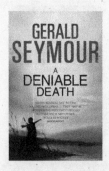

'Gerald Seymour is the grand-master of the contemporary
thriller and A DENIABLE DEATH is his greatest work yet.
Gripping, revealing and meticulously researched, this is a page-
turning masterpiece that will literally leave you breathless.'
Major Chris Hunter, bestselling author of *Extreme Risk*

YOU WATCH. YOU WAIT. THE HOURS SLIDE SLOWLY PAST.

A WHOLE DAY. THEN TWO.

YOU LIE UNDER A MERCILESS SUN IN A
MOSQUITO-INFESTED MARSH.

YOU CAN'T MOVE, LEAVE, OR RELAX.

YOUR MUSCLES ACHE FROM CLENCHING TIGHT FOR SO LONG.

IF YOU ARE DISCOVERED, YOU WILL BE TORTURED THEN KILLED.

AND HER MAJESTY'S GOVERNMENT WILL
DENY ALL KNOWLEDGE OF YOU.

'Great storytelling . . . you just have to read this novel . . . absolutely gripping'
Eurocrime

HODDER

THE DEALER AND THE DEAD

THE ARMS DEALER BETRAYED THEM.
THE SURVIVORS WANT REVENGE.

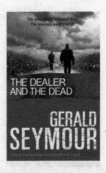

'*The Dealer and the Dead* is Seymour firing on all cylinders
and his rivals need, once again, to look to their laurels'
Independent

In a moonlit field near the Serbian border, Croatian villagers waited for an arms shipment that would never come. They
will never forget that night, or the slaughter that followed.

Eighteen years later, a body is discovered in a field, and with it the identity of
the arms dealer who betrayed them. Now the villagers can plot their revenge.

For Harvey Gillott, it was all a long time ago. But now the
hand of the past is reaching out across Europe, to Harvey's house in leafy England. And it's holding a gun . . .

'The final scenes are brilliantly orchestrated . . . Without doubt, *The Dealer
and the Dead* is one of the finest thrillers to be published so far this year'
Yorkshire Evening Post

HODDER

THE COLLABORATOR

CORRUPTION. BETRAYAL. REVENGE.

'A dense, intensely satisfying thriller from one of the modern masters of the craft, Seymour's latest novel will remind the world just how phenomenally accomplished a thriller writer he is.'
Daily Mail

Eddie Deacon has a new girlfriend. She's beautiful, clever and Italian.

And then she disappears.

What Eddie doesn't know is that Immacolata Borelli is the daughter of a merciless Naples gangster. She can no longer live with her conscience and has decided to collaborate with the police to bring down her own family.

But the Borellis will not lose their empire without a fight. They will use or destroy anything and anyone to prevent her from talking.

Including Eddie.

'Tight writing and meticulous research . . . Seymour paints the streets of Naples and their dark denizens with an artist's brush that lingers equally on the grime, the glitter and the blood'
The Times

HODDER

In the best books, the ending often comes as a shock.
Not just because of that one last twist in the tale,
but because you have been so absorbed in their world,
that coming back to the harsh light of reality is a jolt.

If that describes you now, then perhaps you should track down
some new leads, and find new suspense in other worlds.

Join us at www.hodder.co.uk, or follow us on
Twitter @hodderbooks, and you can tap in to a
community of fellow thrill-seekers.

Whether you want to find out more about this book,
or a particular author, watch trailers and interviews, have
the chance to win early limited editions, or simply browse
our expert readers' selection of the very best books,
we think you'll find what you're looking for.

And if you don't, that's the place to tell us what's missing.

We love what we do, and we'd love you to be part of it.

www.hodder.co.uk

@hodderbooks
HodderBooks
HodderBooks